# CAN YOU MEND IT?

## Part 1 - REUNION

'An interrupted love story' Series

## by Billy Wood-Smith

**Thank You,**
**Sheila, Carolina, Elke, Billie and Greg**
for being my first (unexpectedly enthusiastic) readers,
for your typo-detection, your very helpful feedback and for your
confirmation that the story works...

The city of **Deens**, where a good part of the story takes place, is a
**purely fictional location**. But if it existed, it would probably be
somewhere in **Western Europe**...

For **more on this book** (such as Who's Who; some more info on the
characters; a timeline etc.) check out the official website
www.billywoodsmith.com

# Table of Contents

# Leaving

"Good morning, Honey," she tweeted as she strolled into the kitchen.

Joe glanced up from the paper that he had spread out on the table in front of him and set the coffee mug down. Stone faced he watched her walk across the kitchen – her long blond hair damp from the shower, her short pink silk kimono loosely tied around her waist.

As she approached the table, she tilted her head. "Are you still not talking to me?" she sounded like a pouting little girl, her left hand playfully whirling one end of her belt around.

He watched her come closer, his jaws tightly locked.

She stepped up to the right side of his chair and laid her hand on his shoulder. "Come on…" she purred as she bent down a little and ran her hand over to his other shoulder. Her arm draped around his shoulders now, she blew a kiss onto his right temple. "Don't be like that," she whispered and leaned her forehead against the side of his head.

With the way she was positioned, and with her kimono not being really tight around her body, her bending down like this revealed an unobstructed view. Joe took that in for a short moment and then glanced up at her. Did she really think that still worked?

Apparently she did! He could feel her breathing close to his ear while she slowly let her fingertips dance from his shoulder along the collar of his shirt, her thumb teasingly running up to the back of his neck and her other fingers extending towards his left cheek, obviously attempting to make him turn his head her way.

"Just cut it out, Liz," he snapped and jerked his head away from her face and from her hand. "Just leave me alone!"

"Honey, come on!" She let out a silly, nervous giggle and perched against the table. "This is *so* silly! It's Saturday, you've been angry long enough!" She reached out to touch his face.

"Stop that," Joe scoffed as he turned away. Then, with a quick movement, he pushed back the chair and got up. "I assume you're done in the bathroom and the bedroom for right now?" Without waiting for an answer, he walked out of the kitchen, across the hallway into the bedroom.

He pulled the curtains open with a lot more force than necessary and opened the windows. It still smelled like alcohol and smoke. She had definitely been drunk when she had gotten home sometime around two in the morning. He had pretended to be sound asleep on the sofa, but he had heard her stumble around, and the air in here spoke for itself. The tiny cocktail dress she must have been wearing lay crumpled on his side of the bed. That's probably where all the smoke-smell was coming from. With a disgusted growl he snatched it off the bed and flung it onto the floor on her side.

He walked over to the closet, almost tripping over one of her high heel sandals. He gave it a kick that took it flying under the bed.

He pulled the small trolley he used for business trips down from the top shelf of his closet and set it on the bed. From the corner of his eye he could see Liz appear in the doorway. He shot her an irritated look. The sweet smile and pouting-girl expression from earlier had been replaced by a furious grimace.

"How much longer are you going to act like this?" she hissed.

Ignoring her, Joe opened the suitcase and started filling it with clothes – three dress shirts, a pair of nicer shoes, one pair of sneakers, three ties, a pair of jeans, two polo shirts, socks and underwear for four days. His suit and another pair of slacks were already in a suit-bag that was hanging behind the door.

"So you *really, really* have to pack right now, don't you?" she snarled.

"Leave me alone," he mumbled, keeping his eyes on the suitcase.

"You aren't leaving until tomorrow anyway," she said. "So why do you–?"

"The flight leaves today at two," he told her coldly.

He heard her gasp.

"Since when?" she snapped.

"Does it matter?" he shot back.

"Did you change it? Are you seriously going to leave with things being messed up like…?"

He cut her off. "Just let me pack, okay!"

"You're such an asshole!" she screamed.

"Sure," he scoffed.

For a moment he expected her to throw herself at him, with raised fists, but instead she just violently stomped her foot on the floor, pulled the kimono tighter around herself and grabbed each end of her belt with one hand, pulling so hard on both ends that the knot that had been loose at first, turned into one tiny tight lump. Joe suspected she would have to cut it off, if she ever wanted to get out of that kimono again.

"This was the *last* peace offer you'll get from me," she hissed.

*"Oh, no!"* he mocked as he zipped up the suitcase and set it next to the bed on the carpet. He went back to the closet and squatted. From the very back of the bottom shelf he pulled out his big duffle bag. He laid it onto the bed and opened it up. He could feel her watching him.

Pretending that she wasn't there, he took a few folded T-shirts, short-sleeve shirts and two cotton sweaters from his top drawer and put them in the bag. He pulled open another drawer and got out a pile of socks and underwear – enough to last for about ten days – and placed them in his bag.

"What the hell do you need all *that* for?" Her voice suddenly sounded a bit shrill. "It's just a three day business trip!"

Joe turned around and looked straight at her. *"So?"*

There was a short silence in which she stared at him, while he had already turned around again. He took two pairs of shorts out of another drawer, folded them in half and laid them into the bag.

"What is this supposed to be?" she barked and took a step into the bedroom.

Trying hard to tune her out and stay calm, Joe rolled up a belt and slid it into his bag between the socks. He could feel his hands get slightly shaky.

"Joe!?" she yelled. "Answer me!"

"It's not all *that* hard to figure out, Liz," he said brusquely.

"Ah, I see," she snarled. "You're going for real drama here, aren't you?"

*"Me???"* He shot her a short, puzzled look, but then he just shook his head. *"Do me a favor Liz, go and have breakfast or whatever. Just leave me alone!"

Looking at the now half-filled bag, he tried to decide what else to bring. Another pair of jeans and maybe nicer slacks, his rain jacket, sweat pants maybe, some stuff from the bathroom, one or two more pairs of shoes and his jacket.

While he walked around the room collecting and packing some more clothes, Liz was yelling something about how much she hated him and how he was just the worst thing that had ever come her way. He abstained from returning the compliment, even though it would have hit the nail right on the head. He carried on with his packing.

"You're crazy!" she hissed with a shake of her head as if she still couldn't believe it. "You can't just *go*!"

Looking up at her, Joe let out a bitter laugh. "Watch me!"

He could see her jaw drop. He kind of liked that effect.

"This is just ridiculous!" she yelled.

"I've had it, Liz," he told her sharply. "That's it! You need to get help and I need to get out of here!"

"There's nothing wrong with *me*!" she screamed. "*You're* the one that... Oh, just go then!" She threw her hands in the air. "I don't need you!"

"Good!" Joe flattened the contents of the bag with his left hand and checked how much space he had left. Not a whole lot.

He had just turned to his dresser again, when she suddenly came flying at him from behind. He saw it too late, even though he should have expected that this would be the next stage. Her hands like claws in front of her face, she lurched forward and had already grabbed his shoulder by the time he realized what was happening.

"You're such an ass...!" She dug her fingernails into his left shoulder so deeply that it hurt. "You told me this was just another business trip! And now..."

He jerked his shoulder out of her grip by turning around abruptly. She grabbed his right arm.

"Well, that's what it is − just another business trip," he growled through clenched teeth. "I just won't be coming back here afterwards. But since you just told me how much you hate me, I'm confident you'll be relieved to see me go!" He had managed to pull her hands off his arm an, unexpectedly, she had taken a step back, seeming momentarily confused.

"By the way," Joe said in a fake-friendly tone, "you might be interested to know that Eric is not coming with me. I mean, just in case you need someone to warm your bed..."

Before she could stage another attack, he turned around and walked into the bathroom to get some stuff from there.

She followed him, hissing obscenities now.

After half a minute of this it must have finally dawned on her that he wasn't even listening. So she changed her strategy: she started sobbing.

Joe had to keep himself from parroting this theatrical performance.

"If this is about Eric…" she croaked, shaken by another sob.

Joe sharply cut her off. "I couldn't care less what you do with Eric or Bob or *What's-his-name* from upstairs…"

There was a short silence.

"Well, and that–" Almost choking on the words, she nodded towards his right hand. "I didn't do that on purpose."

"Right," he coughed and continued filling his toiletry case with things he took out of the mirror cabinet.

"Well, think what you want, you asshole!" Liz screamed and clutched one of her hands around the wood on the doorframe, where she scraped her fingernails against the paint so hard that Joe couldn't help glancing at the floor to see if any of those false things had been ripped off yet. Amazingly they had all stayed put. The doorframe had a few pink lines now, though, from where the nail polish had rubbed off.

He shrugged and zipped up his toiletry case and, after a quick look around the bathroom, grabbed two plastic bottles from the shower. Then he pushed his way past her, back into the bedroom.

He stuffed the toiletry case and the shampoo bottles into the side pocket of his bag and zipped that part up. Liz had dropped into the chair next to the bathroom door and gone back to sobbing mode, her face buried in her hands.

Joe acted like he didn't hear it. Maybe two years ago it would have still had the desired effect and he would have found it heart-wrenching. But at this point in their relationship he had seen it all (or at least more than enough for his taste), and he knew that every tear had a well-calculated manipulative element to it. The sobbing didn't get to him anymore. And it definitely didn't make him soft. It hadn't for a long time. For a while it had actually made him furious. Almost as furious as her ranting and screaming could make him. Before he had met Liz he had actually not even known he could get so angry. Sometimes it had taken all his self-discipline to keep that anger under enough control, so he wouldn't just lash out at her and physically harm her – for that would have started an entirely different kind of disaster.

By now he rarely ever got really angry anymore – no matter what insanities or provocations she delivered. He liked to tell himself that the reason was a protective coat he had developed over the years. A protective coat all the venom just bounced off from. He told himself that this was a good thing. But sometimes his own calmness and indifference shocked and scared him. It scared him more than the anger and the struggle to control it ever had. The anger had been normal, given the circumstances, the numbness wasn't. And lately, that numbness seemed to be spreading to other areas in his body and his life.

"I know *exactly* why you're in such a hurry to get to Amsterdam!" Liz interrupted his contemplations. "There's some bitch you can't wait to..."

"Now look who's talking!" Joe let out a little breathy laugh. "Just shut up, Liz, okay? The only thing I really can't wait for in Amsterdam is peace and quiet!"

When Liz countered this with another round of hissing obscenities and verbal attacks that were way below the belt line, interrupted by well-delivered sobs, he realized that staying halfway calm and focused here – at least on the surface – was getting harder by the minute. It was only a matter of time before his protective coat, as good as it may be, would get porous. He knew the signs. He was already starting to feel worn out, his hands weren't quite steady anymore and he was finding it hard to focus. He definitely needed to finish packing and get out of here before she managed to drive him crazy – before the protective coat lost its ability to keep him sane! It was like with a rain jacket and too much rain.

The drama had dragged on for days now and Liz's malice had been delivered in dosages that were way above average, even for her standards. They had been at war ever since he had returned from a business trip exactly two weeks ago. Three days later, on a Tuesday night, things had gotten totally out of hand... Once he had returned from the emergency room that night, his mind had been made up: he was pulling the plug. Finally. It had been long overdue.

Since then he had made sure he had as little contact and interaction with her as he possibly could. He had slept on the sofa, he had left for work while she was still asleep and he had come home late at night. She had made a few attempts to sweet-talk and make up with him, but he had just totally shut her out. At work he had tied up the loose ends, he had rescheduled the flight to Amsterdam and he had had a long talk with Steve.

Joe looked at the duffle bag in front of him and then went to get his trekking sandals from the closet, laying them into the main compartment of the bag, soles up.

That's when the sobbing and hissing behind him suddenly stopped. It was amazing how she was able to just turn it on and off like that.

On high alert, Joe focused his attention on what he could only see from the corner of his eye: Liz had risen from the chair and was now leaning in the doorway to the bathroom.

"You'll have to come back anyway," she told him – her voice surprisingly calm now.

"No, I don't," he retorted keeping his eyes on the bag.

"Well, what about the company?" she insisted triumphantly. "Are you going to run away from that as well?"

Pretending to ignore her, he took out the sandals again, put another sweater underneath and then put the sandals back in.

Liz let out a nasty little laugh. "Or are you going to move into your office now?" She laughed again. "Kind of pathetic for a co-owner, but why not, huh?"

Joe turned around and shot her a cold look. "Nooo, I'm not moving into the office. Besides, Steve can run the company by himself for a while. I don't need to be there."

Liz looked puzzled. She had obviously thought she had it all figured out, his plan that for sure was never going to work. And now it turned out that the plan might be entirely different after all.

There was a trace of panic in her eyes suddenly. Joe couldn't help enjoying that for the moment it lasted.

"I'm taking a time-out," he told her matter-of-factly. "Your brother has already given me his blessing."

"Oh, you've already discussed everything with Steve," she screamed.

"The business side of it? Yes!" Joe said. "*This* mess? No!"

Suddenly she took two quick steps towards him and reached over from the side, got hold of the bag and tried to pull it off the bed.

"You can't just leave!" she yelled at him, her face red with fury.

"God, stop that!" Joe grabbed the strap of the bag with his left hand and jerked it back to where it had been, giving her a dark look. But Liz was still holding on to the flap of the outside pocket with one of her hands. Pushing back a strand of hair with her other hand now, she grinned at him. "Get it if you want it…"

Joe shook his head, reached over and grabbed her hand on the bag with his left hand. He knew he better keep his right hand out of the struggle here. Somehow he managed to keep her from getting the second hand on the bag by blocking her with his right arm. With his left hand he struggled to pry her fingers off the bag one by one.

"Let go of my hand," she whined and tried to pull it out of the tight grip he had on it. His eyes locked with hers, he gave her fingers a well-measured squeeze as a warning. He could crush them right here. And he was barely keeping himself from doing just that.

Finally he let go of her hand. And then quickly turned around, stepped behind her and slung his arms around her. "Let's go!" he growled and, while she kicked and screamed, he half carried, half shoved her out of the bedroom into the hallway. And before she could spin around and try to catch up with him, he had slipped back into the bedroom, slammed the door shut and locked it.

Drawing in a deep breath, he took a few shaky steps to the bed and sank down on it. Burying his face in his hands for a moment, he tried to calm down and steady himself. From the kitchen he heard something shatter. His coffee mug maybe? Another bang. Maybe the juice glass?

Then he heard her shuffle around the kitchen. A minute later she came back towards the bedroom again.

There was a short silence.

Suddenly there was a metallic noise and the key Joe had just locked the bedroom door with, fell from the keyhole onto the bedroom carpet. Shit, had Liz found another key? After a few seconds of the other key clunking around inside the lock – Liz obviously trying to unlock the door from outside – Joe heard something metallic hit the tile floor in the hallway. Liz must have thrown or dropped the other key in frustration because it hadn't fit.

Joe rubbed his forehead and got up from the bed. He'd better finish and get out of here.

Outside the door Liz was swearing. Then she started banging and kicking against the door, calling him all kinds of names. He zipped up the bag and grabbed his jacket from the hook behind the door. While he slid it on, he bent down, snatched the key from the floor and stuck it back into the keyhole. And it surprisingly stayed there despite another hard kick Liz had just given the door from the outside.

Joe checked the pockets of his jacket for his wallet and his car keys. It occurred to him that he still had another spare car key in one of the drawers in the living room. Trying to retrieve it now didn't seem like a good idea, though. Besides, he still had one in the office at work as well.

Suddenly he thought of something else. He went back to the bathroom, opened the drawer of the mirror cabinet and took out the package of painkillers. He pulled out one of the two sheets of blister-packed pills and the leaflet and then stuffed the box back into the drawer.

Back in the bedroom he slid the pills and the leaflet into the side pocket of his bag and paused for a moment, once again going through his mental list of all the things he shouldn't forget to take with him. He couldn't think of anything else he needed. The laptop and the iPod were in the car where he had started to keep them since Liz had smashed his mobile phone during one of her tantrums three weeks ago. He touched the back pocket of his jeans to make sure the new phone was there.

He reached for the duffle bag and slung the strap over his shoulder. Then he grabbed the trolley from the bedside, took the clothes bag from the hook behind the door and sucked in a deep breath. Okay! He was all set. Time to go!

As he set the trolley down to unlock the door, he realized that it had become suspiciously quiet outside. He listened for a moment, but then he just turned the key.

Bracing himself for any kind of attack that he decided to fend off with the suitcase, he opened the door. To his surprise Liz was sitting on one of the chairs in the kitchen across the hallway and was not, as he expected, standing right next to the door, ready to fling herself at him or stab him with a knife or something of that sort.

Not losing any time, he headed for the front door that led into the common stairway. He had almost reached it, when he heard Liz get up, the chair scraping against the tile floor in the kitchen.

"Joe, I–" she had changed to a less aggressive tone for the moment.

He didn't even look over his shoulder, just extended his right hand and reached for the door handle. He had just pushed it down, when Liz got hold of his hand and tried to hold him back, keep him from walking out.

He jerked his hand away from her, consequently feeling an instantaneous, sharp pain flashing up from the broken fingers all the way up to the top of his head. For a moment there he was literally seeing stars. Momentarily slowed down like this, he stared at her. And she stared back at him and tried to push between him and the door to block his way.

"My God, Liz, just get out of my way!" he growled and shoved by her and out the door.

As he left the flat with her following in her pink kimono and barefoot, he hoped – for the sake of the neighbors – that she wouldn't continue screaming out here where everyone would hear her. But if he was honest, he didn't really care anymore what she did.

He kept walking towards the stairway, with Liz currently hissing some incomprehensible stuff right behind him. Then, suddenly, in a perfectly calm and clear voice, she said. "Oh, *now* I get it!"

Joe kept moving, not about to show any interest in what she thought she had just figured out.

"You're going to *Deens*, staying with your sister... – *Sarah*. Aren't you?" She was just probing.

Joe ignored her.

"Oh, I'm sure Sarah is just thrilled!" Liz snarled.

Joe gave an irritated shake of his head and kept walking.

"Oh... and *what's* her name?" Liz gloated. "*Danielle.*" She dragged out the name. "Right? Danielle. I bet she'll be *really* happy to see you, too. Who knows, maybe she'll even take you back!"

Joe stopped and jerked around, the duffle bag swinging around his hip, the bottom of the suitcase dangerously close to hitting her legs. Unprepared for his sudden change of course, Liz almost bumped into him. Baffled and momentarily in danger of losing her balance, she quickly grabbed the railing of the staircase to catch herself. A nasty grin appeared on her face as she tilted her head now and looked straight into his eyes. Provocation at its finest.

Joe swallowed. His initial impulse had actually been to turn around and hit her with the bag or the suitcase. But he knew better. Besides, who cared what she said anymore. He shook his head at her, a hard look on his face, turned around and started walking down the stairs. Two floors to the underground garage. There was no way he was taking the elevator today, as that would have meant being locked up in a very small space with a very crazy girl for at least ten endless seconds.

Finally he reached the door to the garage. He pushed it open and headed for his Volvo.

She followed close behind, screaming again. "Oh, and won't it be nice for you to see Jack again? Now Jack and you can compare notes about me..."

"Oh just shut up!" Joe hissed. "Do you really think that's something I want to share with anyone?" He threw the bags in through the driver's door, afraid that, if he took the time to put them into the trunk, she might pull them out again or come up with some other kind of stunt before he could even get the car started.

He shoved the stuff over to the passenger side and slipped into the driver's seat, quickly pulling the door shut and locking the car from the inside. Maybe he was overreacting but he didn't really think so. Better safe than sorry…

Liz was standing a few feet away from the car, an incredulous expression on her face. Like she was only now coming to the conclusion that he hadn't been bluffing.

He started the engine. Still kind of expecting her to throw herself at the car as he backed it up, he tried to decide what to do in such a case. Surprisingly, though, she just kept staring at him from where she was standing. And as he pulled out of the parking spot, she turned around and stormed off towards the door to the stairways.

Driving out of the garage, Joe realized that he was shaking. His hands were really trembling and he had a hard time changing gears. Of course the brace around his right hand, and the fact that he seemed to be unable to give that hand the rest it desperately needed, didn't help at all. He felt a throbbing pain all the way up to his elbow now. Well, he would have to ignore it for the moment.

He drove for fifteen minutes to get some distance between him and Liz. Then he pulled into the parking lot of some grocery store and parked the car – far away from everyone else.

Leaning back in his seat, he took a few deep breaths. Okay, he had finally done it. It was over! With his left hand he pinched the bridge of his nose and closed his eyes. He couldn't believe how drained he felt.

Opening his eyes again, he gazed into the distance where people with shopping carts were moving around, some on their way into the store, some on their way back to their car. People in business outfits, young mothers with little children, an older lady with a cane, a guy and a girl in a close embrace, stopping a few times to kiss. Joe looked away.

The extreme tension that had had a grip on him for the last few days was very slowly starting to ease a bit. Still, he felt like someone had literally sucked the life out of him. That had, of course, happened gradually over the past two and a half years. He could hardly expect it to go back to normal (whatever that meant) from one day to the other. He imagined it was like being exposed to some toxin for an extended period of time. The effects don't stop right when the exposure stops. Some damage might even be irreversible. It would take a while to see. Maybe the numbness and the cynicism he had developed over time would just be part of him from now on. He surely hoped not, but who knew, really. Liz had definitely brought out the worst in him.

He got out of the car and moved his luggage from the passenger seat to the trunk. His right hand was really hurting now. He held it up and had a closer look. The two broken fingers that were fixed to the molded plastic brace by a padded black Velcro strap seemed more swollen than they had been this morning, the color almost purplish. Even the other fingers seemed kind of swollen. He loosened the strap around the broken fingers a little, and also the one around his wrist, as everything just seemed too tight right now. Then he let the arm sink to his side, as staring at the damage surely didn't help him block out the pain. He glanced at his bag in the trunk. Maybe he should actually try the painkillers they had prescribed at the hospital. Might help… So far he hadn't really needed them because the stuff they had fed him right after it had happened had been potent enough to get him through the first few days. After that the pain seemed to have settled a bit. And it would have probably stayed that way if he hadn't gotten his hand banged up again last night when making his bed on the sofa. And then once more just now in his row with Liz.

With his left hand he reached into the side pocket of his bag and pulled out the sheet of pills and the leaflet. Chewing on his lower lip, he unfolded the leaflet and scanned through it. The side effects, of course, ranged from drowsiness to vomiting to hallucinations all the way to heart failure. He just hated taking medication!

As he turned the page around, he saw the warning in bold letters never to drive a car or operate any heavy machinery within two hours of taking the pills. Great! He could forget about throwing one in right now then. Unless he wanted to just risk it. Which he definitely didn't! After all, he still had a forty minute drive to the airport ahead of him.

With a frustrated growl, he stuffed the pills and the leaflet into the front pocket of his trolley. He would just have to stand the pain until he was in the hotel in Amsterdam.

# Pictures and Memories

D was pulled out of her sleep by the barking of the neighbor's little dog. She drowsily reached for the alarm clock on the bedside table and squinted at it. Ten o'clock already? She rubbed her eyes. She hardly ever slept past nine. But then, of course, she had watched TV until 1:30 in the morning last night which was somewhat untypical too.

Rising from her bed, she stretched and went to pull back the curtains. The bright sunlight made her blink until her eyes adjusted. It was going to be another beautiful August day. Yeah, and there was Tiffany, the neighbor's little spoilt Yorkshire terrier hopping around in the back yard, obviously already having had her walk. Like always, Tiffany was wearing a ribbon on her forehead and a matching scarf. Yellow today. Had it been raining, the dog would have been dressed in a shiny yellow rain cape. Just as Tiffany was pulling on her leash, eager to get moving, Mrs. Terrance glanced up and spotted D in the window. She smiled and nodded. And, smiling back, D gave her a little wave.

D stepped away from the window and shot herself a quick look in the mirror doors of the wardrobe. She ran her fingers through her hair and tried to decide if she should have a shower and wash her hair right away. Or should she have breakfast first? She didn't have to be anywhere anytime soon. She would have to leave around 3:30 in the afternoon to drive to her parents' house for Mom's birthday party, but that was about it. Robert was cooking.

Thinking about food in general and her brother Robert's creations in particular, D felt her stomach growl. A clear sign that she should have breakfast first.

She picked up her sweat pants from the chair next to the window and pulled them on. For a moment her eyes rested on the pile of clothes on that chair – the ironing pile. Sometime when the weather was bad, she should really iron that stuff and put it back into the closet.

The ironing pile wasn't the only pile of clothes in her bedroom at the moment. In fact, ever since she had started the project of cleaning out her wardrobe and drawers, her bedroom looked like a bomb had exploded and splattered stuff all across the room. There were piles of things everywhere. The initial plan had been to very swiftly go through the entire contents –

all her clothes, shoes, bedding, sheets, extra towels, table clothes and whatever else might surface – and generously get rid of stuff she wasn't using anymore.

The sudden urge for that project had overcome her two weeks ago. And immediately she had pulled out everything and started going through it all. At the beginning with still a lot of enthusiasm and energy, as she had expected a liberating experience at the end. Unfortunately, the project had slowed down last week and was now kind of stalled – at least for the moment. Work had been crazy the past few days, and in the evenings she had just not been in the mood to deal with the mess in her bedroom. Instead she had tried to do something relaxing and fun outside while the weather was still so nice. She had biked to the lake and gone for a swim on Monday, she had met Sarah at a café for dinner on Tuesday, and she had gone to the lake again on Wednesday.

The bedroom situation wasn't hopeless, though. Thursday evening she had at least finished the screening process and consequently divided all her stuff into things she wanted to keep and things she was most likely going to get rid of (after another short period of reflection). And last night – before her extended TV session – she had put most of the keepers neatly back into their respective places in the closet or drawers. Only the things in the ironing pile and some towels that she had washed but not folded yet, still needed to be stored away.

The things she wanted to part with lay in three big piles on and around the bed. Two of these piles were covering almost the entire half of the bed she didn't sleep on; the third one was on the floor between the bed and the wall that had Robert's giant blue painting on it. The three *get-rid-of* piles were made up of all kinds of clothes she had outgrown, her curtains from the dorm that still looked nice but were too short for the windows in this flat, a few mustard-colored towels that had belonged to her grandma and that had unfortunately come with the flat. There was also the cocktail dress that Pete had bought her and that revealed just way too much cleavage. And then there was the wildly flowered table cloth with eight matching napkins that Aunt Sauvie had given her for her twentieth birthday. After almost seven years of keeping them in the darkest corners of her closets, she had decided to get rid of them, even if it made her feel guilty.

Leaving the mess behind her, D headed out of the bedroom, through the sun-flooded living room towards the kitchen that was separated from the living room only by two waist-high cabinets and the bar counter.

D started the coffee machine and put two pieces of bread into the toaster. Then she opened the fridge and took out the butter dish, a glass of jam, two eggs and some cheese.

Ten minutes later she was sitting on the big sofa in the living room, a plate of toast, scrambled eggs and a few slices of cheese on her lap and the coffee mug on the table in front of her. She pressed a few buttons on both the TV remote and the DVD control and continued watching the show she had been watching the previous night. It was a sixty-episode comedy-romance show that had first aired on TV twelve years ago. She had been addicted to it then, like almost everyone else around her. Over the years she had almost forgotten about the show until a few months ago, when Robert had given her the complete DVD set for her birthday. Now she was working her way through the episodes, watching one or two (or four like last night) when she had time. It was fun and relaxing. And it reminded her of old times. Only that she – or her view on some things – seemed to have drastically changed over the years. Maybe that was a sign of growing up? She noticed it most with the somewhat chaotic relationship two of the main characters had during the first season and that fell apart in the season finale. As a teenager she had been devastated and furious when that had happened. And she had been hoping desperately that they would make up in the next season, which they hadn't done. Today, probably as a result of some more life experience, she was perfectly fine with the girl refusing to ever talk to that jerk again. He clearly deserved it!

She had just finished eating her egg and was chuckling over a funny scene, when her phone beeped from the coffee table. Sucking in a quick breath she lifted the plate and leaned forward, bracing herself for a text message from Pete. But then it turned out to be a message from Sarah instead:

> *Hi D,*
>
> *Are you up yet? Don't forget to look if you have any good photos for next weekend. I could pick them up early this afternoon. I'll see Jack tomorrow.*
>
> *Sarah*

D stared at the message. Somehow she had hoped she would be able to escape this task that had been looming over her head for more than two months now. She had dreaded it ever since Rick and Jack had come up with the idea of assembling a show of photos and films for the get-together next weekend. Everyone was supposed to contribute their best or funniest photographic material.

Chewing on her lower lip, D considered what to do. Obviously Jack and Sarah weren't going to let her get away with not delivering anything. So, maybe she should just finally bite into the sour apple and get it over with. Tapping her finger on the phone a few times, she sent a message back to Sarah:

*Okay. D*

Then she directed her attention back to what was happening on TV. She didn't get to enjoy it very long, though. After not even two minutes the phone beeped again. Another text message. From Robert:

*Danielle, do you have any birthday candles that you could bring for the cake?*
*Thanks,*
*Rob*

She typed in a quick response saying,

*I'll bring some. D*

She resumed watching TV, the food on her plate almost gone now. She had just picked up her coffee cup to take a sip when the phone came to life again – ringing with a call coming in. This time the display showed Pete's picture – the one she had taken in London. D glared at it for a moment. She absolutely didn't want to talk to him right now! And she should probably finally delete that picture, because all it did anymore was trigger a bunch of very uncomfortable emotions.

With a slight, irritated shake of her head, she turned off the TV and the DVD player and got up from the sofa. The phone rang a few more times and then fell silent.

Over in the kitchen D put the dishes into the dishwasher. Then she opened a few drawers, looking for the birthday candles. She knew she still had some. Finally she found them in the back of the drawer with the plastic bags and the foil. There were seven left. Well, that would have to do. She set the small package with the candles next to her purse on the bar counter so she wouldn't forget it when she left this afternoon.

She checked the clock in the kitchen. It was 10:55 am. Scratching her head, she tried to make up her mind if she should have her shower first or… No, if she needed to do the picture thing, she better do it now!

She went over to the closed door of the room she generally referred to as the extra room. When her grandma had still been living here, this had been the sewing and guest room. D remembered Robert and herself bouncing up and down on the guest bed as kids, almost making it collapse a few times.

After Grandma had passed away Dad had inherited the flat and rented it out for a few years. When she had graduated from university a little over two years ago and had found a job in Deens, the flat had luckily just been abandoned by some crazy, messy tenants that had almost driven her parents nuts. With the flat being free and her needing a place in Deens, it had been clear that she would move in. It had been the perfect arrangement. The place had needed some repair and remodeling first, of course, and her parents, Robert and herself had put in a lot of time and effort into fixing it up. Jack, Tony and Sarah had helped quite a bit as well. Only Pete hadn't been around much for that fun and messy project, not even during the weekends.

D opened the door to the extra room and stepped inside. Along the wall to her left there were still a few unopened moving boxes with stuff from the dorm and her room at home. Boxes that contained things like school books, old CDs and videos, childhood photo albums, stuffed animals... There was a plastic container with Christmas decoration and a paper bag with wrapping paper and ribbons.

In the back of the room was all her camping stuff: tent, air mattress, electric cooler, camping table... She hadn't touched it in over three years. Going camping had never been an option with Pete. Whenever they had gone anywhere together, it had had to at least be a four star hotel.

D turned to her right where the desk with the old PC and the monitor sat against the wall under the window. She hardly ever used this computer anymore since she had the laptop. But today she needed it. All the pictures of the time period her friends were interested in were saved on this PC.

As she walked over to the desk, she could feel the anxiety creep up on her. She shook her head, angry at herself. This was just pathetic! She drew in a deep breath and huffed it out through her nose. She was going to do this and it would be fine!

She sat down on the squeaky desk chair and turned on the computer. It immediately started humming.

While she was waiting for the old machine to boot up, D's glance fell on the stack of paperwork next to the mouse pad. Letters, receipts, bank statements, insurance information and other things like that. She accumulated it here and filed it away every three or four months once the pile had reached a certain height.

She squinted as the corner of something blue sticking out underneath the top few pages caught her eye. Was that the London folder? She pulled it out. On the cover there were pictures of Big Ben, the London Eye, Tower Bridge and, in the left bottom corner, the swan logo of the company she worked for. She had been looking for this folder during the last few days all over the living room, the bedroom and the kitchen – without any success. Obviously she had accidently brought it in here, maybe with the last credit card statement.

With the folder in hand she got up and walked out into kitchen where she placed the folder on the bar counter. She would have to finally browse through that folder this weekend, because on Monday at work June would for sure ask her again what she thought about it.

Back in the other room the PC was finally ready. Slouching on her chair, D clicked her way through until she reached the *My pictures* folder on the C drive.

The fact that she had never taken the time to organize her photos properly but had just downloaded them from her camera every two to four months and saved them in untitled folders would make this task all the more fun...

On the screen she saw at least 23 nameless folders to choose from – the first one dating back to when she had gotten her digital camera nine years ago. She would have to guess what each folder might contain just by looking at the date of its creation. Great!

Chewing on her lower lip, she tried to decide which folder to start with. She had come to Deens almost seven years ago in September to attend the university here. Counting back the years in her head, she steered the cursor to a folder that had been created two months after she had moved into the dorm.

She had just double clicked to open that folder and the computer was doing its thing at an annoyingly slow pace, when she heard her phone ringing again from the living room. Briefly closing her eyes and grinding her teeth, she exhaled. She just knew that it was Pete again, and she felt this very strong urge to crush the mouse in her hand.

On the screen the folder had opened up and an overview of all included pictures in miniature format had appeared. D clicked on the first photo and it popped up: her parents' car in the crowded dorm parking lot, the trunk stuffed to the limit. Clicking on the arrow below the image, D clicked through the photos. There were Robert and Dad carrying parts of her shelf in from the car; Mom in the dorm entrance hall, smiling; dorm room 415 in its initial bare state; her parents in a café in Deens; Robert perched on the desk in her dorm, eating an ice cream cone, boxes, bags and other moving stuff all around him.

The following picture must have been taken a few days later and showed her dorm room again, now looking a lot more inviting. The rug that she had brought was spread out on the floor, the ugly brown dorm curtains had been replaced by her own yellow and white striped ones, her bookshelf was up between the bed and the desk, the TV was sitting on the top shelf, the new plates and cups were stacked in the shelves underneath, and, leaning against the side of the bed, was the framed print with the thunderstorm clouds that she still had hanging in her entry way today.

Looking at these old dorm photos, D suddenly remembered how her state of mind over these first few days had constantly and rapidly switched between excitement and anxiety and happiness and loneliness and contentment and frustration… It had been an emotional roller-coaster ride. She had never lived away from home before, she had been unfamiliar with the new city and she had had no friends in Deens. Figuring out the somewhat complicated university system had been a struggle, and dorm life had still been a bit overwhelming with so many new people…

She had quickly gotten used to it, though. Most people in the dorm or at least on her floor had turned out to be nice, and the common kitchen had soon become the place to go when it got too lonely or boring in her own room all by herself.

D speed-clicked through the rest of the dorm pictures as they would be of no interest to her friends and finally reached the end of the folder. She closed it and opened a new one.

The first photo that came on showed Sarah rolling her eyes at Jack. Good! Contently D straightened up in her chair. Here we go!

She had met Sarah in an extracurricular intermediate-level Italian language course they had both signed up for. During one of the first lessons the professor had wanted everyone to team up with the person sitting next to them and work out and perform a doctor-patient dialogue. D's desk neighbor had been Sarah. And even though they had never talked before and didn't really know each other, they had had an absolute blast creating and reciting their dialog. Sarah had impersonated a flirty elderly male doctor and D a whiny hypochondriac female patient.

And even though Sarah was a year and a half older than D and was studying chemistry, while D was in economics, they had clicked right away and quickly become good friends. They had the same kind of humor, same taste in music and films, similar views on the big issues of the world, and they both had a brother to complain about (only that Sarah's was studying far away and was a year younger, while Robert was over two years older than D.)

Sarah had grown up in Deens. She lived with her parents in a house not too far from the university and had a circle of friends, most of whom she had known since kindergarten.

D clicked through the pictures a little further. There was a good photo of Carrey and Rick, sitting on the sofa in Jack's parents' house, smiling into the camera.

D remembered how Sarah had dragged her along to this party of Jack's and introduced her to her friends.

Tapping her finger on the mouse, D worked her way through the pictures. There was Jack hugging a giant bowl of chips; Tony, Anja and Sun sitting on the carpet laughing; Sarah and Carrey chatting in the hallway...

After Jack's party it didn't take long for D to become part of that group of friends. A group that at the time had consisted of Jack, Anja, Carrey, Tony, Sun, Rick and Sarah. They had always had something going on: hikes, bike rides, parties, watching films together, going to one of the lakes or on little trips by train or car. It had been a lot of fun!

On the computer D created a new folder that she named 'For Sarah' and copied the three best pictures from the party over.

With a quick swipe of the mouse and a click on the next folder, a new miniature picture overview came on. D opened the first photo and found herself looking at Sarah, who was leaning against a stack of wood, a water bottle in her hand, a backpack on the ground in front of her. Then there was a shot of some trees, a stream and some snow-covered mountains in a distance; then Jack with a big stick pretending to herd some sheep; Rick and Carrey, smiling, surrounded by sheep; Carrey, still surrounded by sheep, looking into the camera a little uncomfortably, her arms crossed.

As far as D remembered, these sheep had been impossible to get rid of. The herd had followed them all around, and finally even on the way

25

down the mountain. It had been funny at first, but when it had started to rain and the grass had gotten slippery, and the sheep had come stomping down a sloped pasture right behind them, it had really freaked them all out. They had eventually made it over a fence before anyone could slip and get trampled, but they had all been pale and shaky by the time they had reached safety.

The next folder she opened started with some shots from another hike she had taken with Sarah and her friends. Must have been in late October. There were Jack and Rick, standing on a muddy path looking a bit unhappy; a close-up of what looked like one frog mounting another; an unfocused shot of Rick and Sun posing arm in arm, typical photo-smiles on their faces; Carrey and herself sitting on a bench, munching on sandwiches…

D marked the best three of the hiking pictures and copied them into the Sarah folder. Then she scribbled a quick note on a piece of paper to help her remember which folders she had already looked at and moved on to the next folder.

As expected, there were a few photos of the friends in Deens just before Christmas: Jack feeding Sarah a Christmas cookie; Sun and Anja wearing Santa hats; mulled wine party at the dorm with Richard, the craziest dorm mate ever, passed out on the table. The next pictures were of her family at Christmas: her Mom modelling the new coat she had gotten as a gift; Dad presenting a new tool; Robert hugging a massive cook book…

The shots with the Santa hats and the one of Jack and Sarah with the cookie found their way into the collection for Sarah.

D decided to skip the following folder as it was sure to contain mainly pictures of Christmas and New Years with her family and of Robert's 22nd birthday – no material Jack would want for his picture show.

She moved the cursor down a bit and opened a folder that had been created the following spring.

And there was Venice! Great! Just what she had been looking for! There was Sarah in front of a bunch of gondolas, grinning. D smiled to herself at the memory of this fun trip they had taken with the Italian course sometime in early March. She clicked to the next photos: Sarah and someone else waving from the Rialto Bridge; herself leaning against a graffiti-covered house wall, eating a slice of pizza; Sarah and herself with wet hair and looking drenched in a restaurant, huge plates of steaming pasta in front of them. They had gotten into a downpour on their way to the hotel and fled into this little over-priced trattoria. Very good picture. Very tempting looking pasta, too. D was glad that she had just eaten breakfast or she may have felt the urge to go and cook herself some pasta right this minute.

The next photo showed herself getting in line for the elevator up to the top of the Campanile on St. Marc's square. She was rolling her eyes at the camera about the stressed-out Japanese couple behind her that they had run into at least three times that day.

D clicked on further. There was a shot of Sarah posing in front of the huge bell on the Campanile. Only seconds later that thing had started to swing... They had quickly jumped on the next elevator down, before the bell could really get started and blow their eardrums out.

The last picture was of herself, trying to fend off some extremely insistent street vendor.

D picked five images from the Venice trip and added them to the Sarah folder.

After making a quick note on her piece of paper, she tried to make up her mind which of the 23 folder-icons she should click on next. She decided to just go with the following one.

It started out with a grinning Robert next to his new car in front of their parents' house. Must have been right after he had gotten the car.

She clicked further. There were a few photos of some people in the dorm kitchen looking a bit drunk. Then Jack came on, standing on a wooden porch, a wine glass in his hand. D realized that his must have been in Sarah's parents' backyard. The following photos showed Carrey talking to Sarah; then a nicely set garden table with a cake on it and finally a close-up of the birthday cake. *Happy 21st Birthday.*

D felt her throat go dry. This was Sarah's 21st birthday party...

Glaring at the screen, she paused for a moment. She was definitely entering more uncomfortable territory now! Drawing in a long breath, she resisted the urge to jump to some other, more harmless folder. Her expression tense, she clicked to view the next photos. There was one of some birthday guests she didn't know; a great shot of Sarah's parents; one of Rick, Carrey and Sun holding up their glasses; Sarah's Grandma Reilley sitting on a chair, looking exhausted...

Another click and Grandma disappeared. And on came a picture of the entire Reilley family under their cherry tree. D swallowed, her hand on the mouse trembling. There was a smiling Sarah with her Mom and Dad and Grandma – and Joe.

D's first impulse was to quickly find the X on the right hand corner of the screen and close this folder. But then she stopped herself. Because it was just silly! This picture was almost six years old. She didn't seriously still have a problem with that?!? Or did she? She kept her gaze on the family as a whole for a moment. Then, her heart beating up to her throat, she forced her eyes to focus on Sarah's brother.

Up until that birthday party she had never met Joe. She had only heard of him when Sarah, her parents or one of the friends talked about him. He had been studying somewhere a few hours away from Deens at the time and not come home except for Christmas.

This first encounter with him at Sarah's birthday party had, by no means, been a life-changing experience. They had said *Hi* and that had been it.

D let her eyes trail towards the window for a moment and tilted her head from side to side to loosen up. Then she shifted her gaze back to the screen where the Reilleys were still smiling.

When she had sat down in front of this PC fifteen minutes ago, she hadn't been sure which emotional impact looking at these photos would have. It came as an immense relief now to find that it actually was okay. Sitting eye to eye with his picture here, she was still doing fine! She had obviously reached a state where this was nothing but a bunch of old photographs anymore!

She clicked through the rest of the birthday shots feeling content and somewhat elated – almost like after passing a dreaded exam.

Before she closed out of this folder, she copied a few pictures of the birthday girl and friends (not brother, though!) into the Sarah collection and scribbled down some notes. Then she stretched and yawned, telling herself that she could probably stop now. She had enough pictures for Sarah to prove that she had made an effort. That's all that mattered. There was no need to look at any more!

On the other hand, why not look at some more? Now that she had realized that she was okay with it…

So she opened the next folder and found herself looking at Sarah and Anja next to their bikes, some beautifully blooming trees behind them; then a shot of herself and Sarah soaking in the spring sun on a bench. D remembered that during this bike ride Sarah had told them that her brother was going to be transferring to the university in Deens the beginning of April, and therefore he would be moving back home. Sarah hadn't seemed to really know the reason for Joe's sudden transfer, but she had had her theories – which she happily shared: she had this vision of a furious professor that had caught his daughter in some kind of compromising position with Joe... Almost a year later D had found out that Sarah's vision couldn't have been further from the truth.

As she absent-mindedly clicked through the next photos, some images of herself and Robert in Stockholm flashed by. She and her brother had taken this trip together during the Easter holidays to visit a friend of Robert's who had been studying there for a year. The many shots of them in the Swedish capital were followed by photos of a dorm party. One picture showed some idiots, including Richard, smoking cigars in the dorm kitchen and grinning into the camera stupidly and probably drunkenly. D swiftly moved through those shots. When she reached a picture that showed Carrey and Anja painting a wall bright orange, she slowed down again. This photo had been taken in the little flat Anja had rented after moving out from home in May of that year.

As D kept going, more photos of the painting crew came on: Jack and Rick taping off the windows so the paint wouldn't be all over the frames; Sarah showing her paint-splattered hands; Anja and herself with big paint rollers...

Glaring at the screen, D paused for a moment. Joe must have been back in Deens by that time. He wasn't in any of the pictures, though. Probably because he had kept to himself in the first few months after his return. One reason had been that he had his hands full trying to adapt to the slightly different courses and requirements at Deens University before the end of the term and the final exams. The other reason, and this was one that Sarah just couldn't help nagging about, was that he just didn't seem to have much interest in hanging around with his sister and her friends, most of whom had been his friends in the past as well. He did go out with Jack every once in a while, but that was about it. It used to really upset Sarah. She had initially been thrilled to have him back in Deens and had expected him to be around more. When that hadn't turned out to be the case, it had totally pissed her off. D still remembered Sarah's regular little fits when, instead of a nice bike ride to the lake or a hike with them, her brother had decided he preferred to risk his life on that dangerous motorcycle or/and mess around with one of his bimbos (as Sarah used to call the girls she suspected him of picking up left and right.)

D scratched her head, trying to concentrate on the photos rather than the memories that were trickling into her mind here. She picked out a few pictures from their painting project and copied them to the compilation for Sarah. Then she moved on to the next folder.

It started with a shot of Jack in front of the Reilleys' house, showing off his newest remodeled car; then Sarah in the driver's seat, a skeptical look on her face; Jack and Joe in front of the car, the motorcycle parked on the side.

It had happened gradually. Her falling in love with Sarah's brother.

She had been over at the Reilleys' a lot that summer. Sometimes just to pick up Sarah to do something together, sometimes to work on arrangements for the fundraising event for the Italian earthquake survivors that Sarah and she had volunteered to help with.

With all these visits to the Reilleys' home and the regular invitations by Mrs. Reilley to just stay around for dinner, it had been unavoidable to run into Joe every now and then. Or sit across from him over dinner for that matter. Their exchanges had, however, not gone beyond *Hi* and *Bye* and the occasional *Could you pass me the butter, please?*.

And then, one Saturday in late July, things had started to change. She had biked over there to pick up Sarah. They had wanted to ride their bikes to the river, meet with Robert and Maria there, watch some water skiing event and have a picnic. Unexpectedly Joe had decided to come along for that. And since his bicycle had recently been stolen, the three of them had ended up driving Mrs. Reilley's car.

Remembering that day now, D was starting to feel hot. Her hand on the mouse was starting to get sticky. So she took it off the mouse and ran it over the fabric of her sweats a few times.

They had hardly arrived at the river and found Robert and Maria, when she had started feeling sick. Totally sick. Strong headache and nausea – symptoms that pointed to stomach flu... Joe had ended up driving her back to the dorm. And somehow something had been triggered that day. Even though she had been in a haze and frantically trying to keep from throwing up, and all he had done was take her home and make her some chamomile tea...

Blocking out any deeper thoughts about this, D continued going through the photos. There was Sarah on Joe's motorcycle with a look on her face that showed how much she detested that thing; Joe and his Dad, both smiling, the tension tangible despite the friendly faces. It had taken D a while to figure out that this particular smile of Joe's was just a cover-up of some major unresolved issues.

The next few pictures showed Joe and Jack pruning a tree in the Reilleys' backyard. Must have been in early August while Mr. and Mrs. Reilley had still been on vacation. Joe and Jack had started out with clippers and ended up using a chain-saw, making a real mess of the tree. Mr. Reilley had *not* been pleased with the result. D caught herself smiling at the memory – a smile she immediately wiped off her face as soon as she became consciously aware of it.

She clicked further. There were pictures from up at the mountain opposite Deens. She felt her hand on the mouse get a bit unsteady again but continued nevertheless. It had been snowing in the mountains a few days before, but this Saturday morning had been clear and sunny. They had decided to take the cable car up the mountain, so Sarah's cousin from California, who was visiting at the time, could see some real snow. The first few shots showed some fabulous views taken from the cable car: white sun-lit mountaintops all around, fog in the valley; then a picture of Rick and Sarah in front of the cable car station, putting on their gloves and knitted hats; Jack, Rick and Joe building a snowman.

D swallowed, her eyes fixed to the screen. Joe had come along for this. It had been the first time he had actually participated in any group activity like that.

On the next photo the snowman was finished, wearing someone's knitted hat, Jack's scarf and some of Carrey's cookies as buttons; then there was Tony pretending to strangle the snowman with the scarf; Joe attempting to protect the snowman by threatening Tony with a broken ski pole he had found nearby; Rick walking away with the snowman's head under his arm; Anja observing the scene with a fake shocked expression on her face, Sarah cracking up behind her. The next picture showed all of them standing in two rows around the headless snowman, Sarah in the front next to her, cradling the snowman's head, while Jack seemed to be patting it from behind her.

D paused for a moment and took in that picture. Struggling to keep the memory at arm's length, she exhaled. Joe had (probably by pure coincidence) been standing right behind her when that shot had been taken. Not close enough to touch, but way too close to ignore. And it had

31

been the first time in recorded history that she had wished for him to stand just a little bit closer.

Stubbornly ignoring the pang that photo had just sent through her stomach, D marked it and made sure it found its way into the Sarah folder. It was a good picture and there was absolutely no reason not to include it!

She clicked out of the folder and drew in a long, somewhat shaky breath. Leaning back in her chair she stretched her arms above her head and glanced at the list of folders on the screen. Maybe it was time to stop now. What she had seen so far had affected her less than expected, and that was very alleviating. There was no need to push it, though. And something told her that the material in the next folders *would* be pushing it. They were sure to contain clear evidence of her relationship with Sarah's brother. And she really didn't need to see that.

Or did she?

Twisting a strand of hair around her finger, she dropped her eyes to the keyboard. To stop or not to stop?

She glanced back up at the screen. Whatever the motives, some crazy part of her was itching to see more. Maybe just to check it out, maybe to test herself? She wasn't quite sure. She just knew that she did need to look at some more. But not all of it…

Hesitantly she steered the cursor towards the next folder. She opened the folder with a double click and then, as soon as the overview of miniature pictures came on, she changed the view to *list*. The screen immediately changed and instead of the 40 mini pictures, there was now a list of 40 file names, each made up of a *P* followed by a 7-digit number. There was no way of telling now which picture was behind which file number.

Gnawing on the inside of her cheek, D suddenly had an idea: She was going to play this like Russian roulette – blindly steer the cursor to anywhere on the screen and double-click on whichever file it landed on. She was going to open exactly four randomly-picked pictures this way. From this folder and the following two. Then she was going to call it quits and have her shower.

For a moment she let the cursor hover over the list. Then, pressing her lips together, she double-clicked on a file: there she was, standing next to her bike, shooting an undecided look into the camera. Had this been on that bike ride with Joe? (When he had borrowed Sarah's baby-blue bike?) He must have just grabbed her camera and taken the shot.

She didn't give herself time to think about it. Quickly she closed the photo and picked another one: Joe on her dorm bed, holding a coffee mug. She could feel her mouth go dry at this. That had been after the accident. In fact, there, in the right hand corner she could kind of see the bottom half of his crutches leaning against her desk.

She went back to the list and drew in a deep breath. She was still doing fine, right? Yeah, no problem!

She placed the cursor on another file name and double-clicked. Her parents' Christmas tree with a lot of nicely wrapped packages arranged underneath. Her jaws pressed together tightly, D tried to block the thought of how she had left Deens to spend the Christmas days with her family. She had caught a cold and landed in bed with a fever on the 26th, with no chance to travel back to Deens for her friends' New Year's celebration. Joe had showed up at her parents' house on the 28th and ended up staying over New Year's...

Releasing a shaky breath, she left this folder and opened the next one. Looking at the list of numbers before her, she tensely steered the mouse almost all the way down, then opened a photo. On the screen Jack appeared, leaning against a tree and eating a banana, Tony and Kim hugging in the background. Probably one of the first times Tony had brought his girlfriend Kim along.

D moved to the next photo. It showed herself, sitting on a bench with a big sandwich, Joe and Jack standing behind her, Joe pretending to be clawing for her sandwich, an evil grin on his face.

The next photo she picked showed the totally messy kitchen of her dorm after the cleaning service hadn't showed up for four days in a row. She had e-mailed this to the carrier that ran the dorm.

Next picture: Robert, Joe and herself in her parents' living room, Joe's arms wrapped around her while she was trying to get away because he was tickling her. Dad had taken that picture...

Before she could get sucked into memories here, she closed the picture and the folder and then just sat there and stared at the screen for a moment. Did she really want to see more?

Not quite sure what was driving her, she spontaneously decided to change her Russian roulette rules and, instead of opening the following folder, she chose the one after that.

First picture: a small wooden cabin at a lake, trees around it, Joe's car parked next to it. They had spent a few days up there, in his aunt's cabin.

Running her fingers through her hair, D told herself that she should click out of that picture and view something further down the list next. But her hand had already clicked on the arrow below the picture, skipping to the consecutive shot: Joe standing in the lake, the water up to his waist, hair dripping wet. In the background there was the cabin. She swallowed. It really couldn't get much worse than this. The only thing with more hurt-potential would be a picture of the mattress they had dragged down from the loft and placed right in front of the fireplace that night. Fortunately such a picture didn't exist. She gave the guy on the screen another glance and then made him disappear. Okay. Deep breath… Seen that, survived it!

Last two pictures. Her hand annoyingly unsteady now, she clicked on whatever the cursor landed on: Joe grilling something, holding a dangerous-looking fork in the direction of the camera, a big smile on his face.

D exhaled. Okay. That was clearly enough! She opened her eyes again, clicked out of the picture and scrolled all the way down, opening the very last photo. It was taken in a Chinese restaurant, lots of bowls with lovely looking Chinese food in the center of the table. Sarah was smiling at the camera from across the table. To her left, Rick was holding up his chopsticks, grinning. And to Sarah's right, there was Jack, with Liz cuddling up to him. At the sight of this, D pressed her jaws together so tightly that it almost hurt. She closed the picture, closed the folder and then she closed her eyes for a moment. She reached back and curled her hand around the back of her neck, massaging it. Wow! That had been a bit much! She opened her eyes again and huffed out a breath. She was okay. Yeah, definitely okay!

She straightened up and placed her hand back on the mouse. She opened the collection of pictures she had put together for Sarah. It was a presentable amount. Sarah couldn't complain!

With a few quick movements D took a CD out of a drawer, placed it in the tray of the computer and burned the contents of the Sarah folder onto the CD.

# Grocery Shopping

Sarah pushed the shopping cart into the aisle with the noodles. It was 11:30 and the store was crowded. She hated grocery shopping on Saturdays. The plan had been to do this early in the morning. But first the alarm hadn't gone off because she had forgotten to set it. Then, during breakfast, she had gotten caught up on the phone with her Mom, who was currently in Spain with Aunt Tess. Mom had wanted to catch up with her and ask if she had heard anything from Joe, which Sarah had not. After the phone call she had spent some time putting together a shopping list and she had sent a quick text message to D, pushing her about the photos again…

Looking at her grocery list, Sarah tried to concentrate. She wanted to get the shopping done today, so she could prepare the sauce for the lasagna during the weekend. There wasn't any time for it on Monday as she was working all day, and on Tuesday she wasn't getting home until three in the afternoon which would give her just enough time to quickly make the béchamel sauce, layer the lasagna and push it into the oven before Joe arrived.

She glanced from her shopping list into her cart. She already had two packages of lasagna noodles and a head of lettuce. Beside her a young mother was trying to reason with a screaming toddler who wanted to return to the sweets section.

Eager to get away from the screaming, Sarah steered her cart around the corner into the next aisle and towards the canned food section. She had just passed the pineapples when her phone started to ring. She pulled open her big purse and started digging through the contents in order to find the phone before the call could go into voice mail. She was too slow. When she finally managed to locate the phone and pull it out, it had already fallen silent again. The call had been from Joe.

She was about to call him back, when the phone rang again. It was Joe again. She picked up.

"Hello… I was too slow."

She heard him laugh on the other end. "Do we maybe have a little too much stuff in our purse?"

"Nothing I don't need," Sarah retorted.

"Of course! You limit yourself to the absolute essentials, right?" He was definitely making fun of her.

"Yeah, yeah, just make fun of me!" she said. "Where are you?"

"I'm on my way to the airport."

Sarah was confused. "I though you weren't going to Amsterdam until tomorrow."

"Well, the initial plan has changed a little," Joe said evasively. "I'm going today. And I'll probably have the phone turned off most of the time. There's just going to be so many meetings and stuff... But I'll check my messages every once in a while."

"You're still coming back Tuesday though, right?"

"Yeah, that hasn't changed. I land around four-thirty. So, I should be at your place around six. I'll give you a call from the airport, though, once I get in."

"Okay, sounds good," Sarah said and took four cans of tomatoes from the shelf in front of her. She also grabbed some tomato paste and then pushed the cart on towards the cooling section.

"I'm just buying stuff for making lasagna Tuesday night," she told him. "I'm going to try Mom's recipe. So, make sure you're hungry!"

"Sounds great!" Joe sounded thrilled. "Don't worry, I'll be hungry. Makes me drool already."

"Good!" The phone tucked between her head and her shoulder, Sarah leaned down and reached for a carton of milk, almost dropping the phone in the process. She caught it in mid-air and straightened up putting the phone back against her ear and the milk into her cart.

"I still can't believe you're actually really coming," she said.

"Yeah, I know..." he laughed but it sounded a bit forced. He said something else, but the connection was starting to go bad. "Can... still hear me?" he asked, but he was breaking up.

Sarah frowned. "The connection is pretty bad," she said, not sure how much of it he would even understand. The last thing she heard of him sounded like "...call you Tuesday..." Then he was gone.

Snorting, Sarah ended the call and was about to put the phone back into her purse, when she heard a text message coming in. It was from D:

*Photos ready. You can come for coffee and pick them up any time before 3.*
*D*

Sarah raised her eyebrows at this pleasant surprise. Who would have thought? She checked her watch and then quickly wrote back.

*Great. I'll come by around one.*

After she had packed away the phone, she worked off the rest of her shopping list. She was already on her way to the checkout when she changed her mind, turned around again and went to get ladyfingers, mascarpone and an additional carton of eggs for making tiramisu – her favorite dessert and, as far as she remembered, her brother's as well.

# At the Airport

Joe reached the airport after a forty-minute drive. He took his trolley, the suit bag and the laptop out of the trunk and headed for the terminal.

It was only noon. Still two hours to kill. He bought a sandwich and something to drink at one of the snack stands and sat down in the waiting area of a gate that didn't have any flights scheduled anytime soon and was therefore deserted. He would eventually move to his designated gate but for right now he was just going to sit here, eat his sandwich and watch the crowds hurrying by. It was somehow relaxing.

If things had gone as planned, he wouldn't only be flying out tomorrow instead of today, but he would also be travelling in the company of Eric, Steve's geeky assistant. But things had absolutely not gone as planned.

Eric had been supposed to become his backup regarding SCANY, the Dutch company Joe was about to visit. SCANY wasn't only their most important customer/business partner but had also been the very first... He would never forget how, at a time when the Homepage of their new software company had still been running a little bumpily, the company name – which they had decided would be Reilley&Davis – hadn't yet been properly registered and the e-mail account was barely set up, they had suddenly received an inquiry from the Netherlands. It had been from a Jan van de Velde who wrote that he had just come across their website and was wondering if they might be able to come up with a tailor-made solution for a filing and documentation software that he needed for his company by the name of SCANY. Steve had gotten in touch with Jan and asked for SCANY's specific requirements, which Jan had consequently sent them summarized on six pages.

Joe remembered Steve and himself spending the next two days and parts of the nights in the small office they had been renting at the time, feverishly trying to figure out if – and how – they could do it. They had been so excited. And they had finally come up with a draft solution. And Jan had been just enthusiastic about it. It sounded like Jan had talked to several other companies previously – with very little luck regarding both, the programming itself and his requirement that someone at SCANY's IT department would be trained in the new program well enough to do the basic troubleshooting and support in-house. To Steve and Joe that requirement hadn't been a problem but rather a great relief as, at the time, R&D had consisted only of the two of them and a part-time assistant. Therefore, not having to do all the support for SCANY themselves had seemed like a blessing. They had eventually closed the deal with SCANY – making more money on it than Steve and he had thought realistic. Still, the price seemed to have been considerably less than what Jan had anticipated. SCANY had consequently played a big part in R&D's taking off as quickly and well as it did, simply because Jan knew a lot of people that he recommended R&D to. Through Jan R&D had gotten in touch with other potential customers, many of which had actually stuck.

Today R&D had a pretty good customer base and had grown from three people in a tiny office to 10 people occupying the entire first floor of a new office building that Steve's Dad had built.

Eighteen months ago R&D and SCANY had entered into a cooperation that would let SCANY represent R&D's products and even do some of the servicing, mainly in the Benelux states and Scandinavian countries. Clearly a win-win situation. Only that six months later that whole nice arrangement had almost fallen apart because of some stupid misunderstanding between Jan and Steve about a commission payment. Joe, who normally was Jan's primary contact, had been out of the office for his Dad's funeral and had, upon his return, found the whole SCANY cooperation in jeopardy. Jan's and Steve's accounts of what had happened contradicted each other drastically, almost like with two pouting kids who now blamed each other for starting the fight. Knowing both Steve and Jan, Joe guessed that they had both had a bad day before the disastrous telephone conversation and, since they both did have a bit of a temper when under a lot of stress, one thing had probably led to another and they had ended up yelling at each other on the phone (that's where their reports matched). The call had ended with Jan announcing that he was going to quit every contract he had ever had with R&D. Then he had hung up.

When Joe had finally come back and heard about the clash, he had called Jan – with little hope of still being able to save anything. To his surprise, Jan had not just been willing to take the call but had also calmed down to the point where he wasn't raging anymore, just nagging a bit. They had had an unexpectedly productive conversation at the end of which Joe felt positive that they had successfully straightened things out. With the funds having been transferred as well, there hadn't been any talk about Jan not wanting to work with R&D anymore. He had, however, insisted that he didn't want to deal directly with Steve ever again. This had been a condition that Joe had felt they simply had to accept, even though it was highly inconvenient as Steve had always been his backup for everything, including SCANY.

In the following months Joe had handled all phone calls and visits to SCANY exclusively while Steve had stayed involved but only in the background. It had been clear, though, that sooner or later there needed to be someone new who could cover for Joe when it came to SCANY. The man of choice had been Eric, who had already been Steve's right hand for a while and who knew the program SCANY was using by heart. Eric had never met Jan or any of the other SCANY people yet or even talked to them on the phone. Therefore, it had seemed like a good idea for Joe to take Eric along for this trip, introduce him to the key people, get him acquainted with the SCANY facility... That had been the plan. Until Joe had realized three weeks ago that he absolutely couldn't travel with Eric.

He had first noticed that Eric was acting kind of weird around him over two months ago. He hadn't given it much thought, however. Then, one evening about three weeks ago, he had been in the office later than normal, and suddenly Eric had dropped in. He had looked pale and unusually nervous and had asked if they could talk. A little surprised Joe had offered him the chair across the desk from him, and Eric sat down, reeling off some strange introduction about how he just needed to get this off his chest, even if he was probably going to be fired as a consequence. Joe's imagination of possible offenses at that point ranged from Eric embezzling money to Eric selling company secrets. And while he was still considering how he would react to any of that, Joe suddenly found himself listening to Eric describing his recent visit to an art gallery – to the opening night of an exhibition featuring Eric's favorite contemporary sculptor, to be precise. Avoiding eye contact, Eric went on to report running into Liz right when he had arrived. That's when Joe made the connection that they were obviously talking about the gallery Liz was working for. Liz's job there was actually a day-time office job that involved arranging for paintings or sculptures and whatever else was called art nowadays to be booked, properly wrapped, shipped, insured and later unwrapped and set up in the gallery as impressively as possible. Sometimes she also planned the evening receptions, arranged for the invitations to be sent to the VIP guests and booked the caterer. Personally attending those

40

evening things wasn't part of Liz's job description. But she still wouldn't miss it for the world! It was probably the part of her job she liked the most...

Eric had immediately recognized her, of course. She had shown up in the office often enough – to see Joe or her brother. And she had probably never given Eric as much as a nod at R&D. But now, at the art gallery, she had (according to Eric) been treating him like a good old friend. And Joe could just picture it, too. Low-cut dress, dangerously high heels, lots of make-up, some alcohol, sweetest voice...

Sitting before him in the dimly lit office, Eric continued his account of that evening: Liz had been so nice as to introduce him to the artist in person. A real uplifting experience, of course, because that guy (Joe had forgotten the name as soon as it had been mentioned) was *the* name amongst contemporary sculptors working with bronze.

Joe was about ready to tell Eric to speed it up, for God's sake, and get to the point instead of being so annoyingly specific on all the boring art details. He didn't know the artist and didn't give a shit either. Especially since it was crystal-clear to him by now that the whole art-crap was only unimportant information on the side. From the moment Eric had first dropped Liz's name, Joe had had the distinct feeling that he could predict where this was going, even if just roughly.

Still, Eric kept on babbling about some of the magnificent pieces the gallery had had on display that night. And that in the course of the evening he had had a bit much of the complimentary sparkling wine. Finally Eric started talking about it getting late and his picking up his coat to go home. And that's when – surprise! – he ran into Liz again. She was about to leave as well and (according to Eric) suggested that they share a taxi. Because she supposedly was a bit scared all alone as a woman at that time of night. And after all, they only lived a few blocks apart. Eric had been surprised and, so Joe suspected, flattered that she even knew where he lived. And that she apparently viewed him as prime protector material.

Joe had to keep himself from moaning and rolling his eyes at so much naiveté. But who could blame Eric? He just lacked the extensive experience Joe had gathered with Liz over the last few years. Experience that made it possible for him to imagine very clearly even the many things Eric hadn't mentioned yet or was for sure going to be leaving out. Liz all tipsy and giggly from the drinks she had undoubtedly had, merely stumbling into the taxi, her pushed-up breasts barely contained in the low-cut dress, freshly painted lips smiling at Eric as he slid in next to her, Liz huddling against him during the drive, telling him some anecdotes from the art gallery, her persuading him to get out at her place and come upstairs just for a quick drink – just to make sure there were no predators looming in the stairways. Then, in the flat the strap of her dress slipping as she served the drinks; her telling Eric that she was lonely and unhappy; her applying one of those highly seductive kisses that were lethal to the untrained victim... And while Joe was already wracking his brain if geeky Eric had actually had the guts to sleep with her and if so, where and how, Eric was still lagging way behind with his report, babbling about the taxi ride and how she had leaned closer than he had felt comfortable with, but well, he didn't want to offend her. And then... – ahem... she had kind of persuaded him to come upstairs with her... His voice suddenly cracking and his eyes firmly on the desktop between them, Eric insisted that he didn't know how it had happened, but that he had had way too much to drink obviously, which hardly ever happened, and that she must have gotten him in a really weak moment because otherwise he would have never... Well, but then she had been kissing him and – yeah...– well...– you know... Shit! – I'm really sorry...

Digging his fingers into the armrests of his chair, Joe tried to keep a straight face when at the same time he was torn apart between getting up and breaking Eric's nose and just bursting out in a crazy laughter. Not because it was funny. It really wasn't. It was anything *but* funny. But he knew that kind of kiss, didn't he? A kiss that literally wiped your mind clear of any good judgment. A kiss that assured you that she was fine with anything you could possibly dream up. It had worked on him, hadn't it? Three years ago? Not at the very first attempt, but eventually it had worked just fine even on him.

Across the desk Eric had fallen silent. Obviously unable or unwilling now to put the rest of his story into clear words or full sentences. He was sitting there, hanging his head and probably waiting for Joe to explode, fire him, kick him out of the office and end his misery. But Joe, not even sure himself what was driving him, felt this sick need to hear more. Make absolutely sure he had understood correctly and he wasn't misinterpreting anything or assuming things that really hadn't happened.

He cleared his throat and looked right at Eric. "Okay, Eric..." Even to himself he sounded ghastly unemotional, almost a little bored. "If I'm reading this right, you're trying to tell me that you screwed my girlfriend, right?"

Eric's eyes darted up and then quickly away again. Face beet red, he was scrambling for words. Obviously he would have preferred being fired and kicked out to having Joe phrase his offense so accurately.

"So, where exactly did this happen?" Joe inquired sharply. "In our bed?"

Eric's eyes widened at the question. Then he gave a short shake of his head, which could either mean a negative response or just a sign of disbelief at the question itself. Joe wasn't sure.

"*Where?*" Joe pressed, leaning forward on the desk a little. "In our bed? On the kitchen table? The washing machine? The sofa? So many possibilities…"

Eric stared back at him like he doubted Joe's mental sanity. Then he shook his head again and looked away.

Furious at the cowardice, Joe slammed his hands onto the desk and then pushed himself away from it on the rolling chair, almost running into the file cabinet behind him in the process. "I asked you a question – even multiple choice…" he barked, "and I want you to fucking answer me! *Where?*" Finally he was finding words and a tone that seemed to fit the situation…

Eric had closed his eyes for an instant and shaken his head some more. But then he cleared his throat and choked out an answer: "Sofa."

Drawing in a deep breath, Joe glared at him for a moment. Then he exhaled sharply. Okay. Now he knew… Maybe, if Liz hadn't a few months prior to this, revealed to him with a lot of satisfaction that she had slept with Bob, her boss's husband, Eric's account would have shocked him. But it didn't. Not really. Not anymore. After all, he was almost sure that there hadn't just been Bob – and now Eric. He had reason to believe that she also had had or was still having something going on with the dorky neighbor upstairs and some body-builder delivery guy from the gallery. Maybe even with some of the artists, who knew? From the way it looked, she didn't seem to be real picky… And of course she justified it to herself as being just a pay-back for all the affairs she suspected him of having.

Joe scratched his head trying to decide how to proceed with Eric here. He had absolutely no idea what was customary in this kind of situation. Whatever it was, it surely didn't involve asking for more detailed information. But as sick as it was, he would have just loved to continue his cross examination, find out the exact position maybe. He was just burning to know if Liz had chosen the more conservative or the really wild ride with this particular victim. One look at Eric made it seem unlikely, though, that he was going to give that kind of information unless physically tortured. And in a way Joe wasn't entirely sure if he himself was really withdrawn enough to be able to handle an honest answer.

"Did you stay overnight?" he had asked instead.

Staring at him wide-eyed, Eric looked like he was in pain. (Even without actual torture!)

"I mean, it's a comfortable sofa…" Joe pushed.

"I was drunk," Eric said evasively.

"Right. So, you fell asleep right afterwards and stayed…"

Eric nodded. He seemed to have shrunk over the last ten minutes. It made Joe realize that Eric probably felt like the mouse that was being teased by the evil cat. Which was ironic, because if there was an evil cat in this game, it was definitely Liz, wasn't it? Only that, if Liz was the cat and Eric was the mouse, Joe wasn't quite sure what that made *him*. He absolutely refused to see himself as just another mouse. Maybe he could be the dog that chased the cat and the mice…

"I'm *really* sorry," Eric mumbled, his gaze down on his lap. "I know I totally screwed up… And believe me, it's really been haunting me. And I didn't want you to find out from anyone else."

"Yeah, well, thanks for that," Joe said dryly, unable to see great advantages of finding out this way.

"I normally don't do this kind of thing," Eric insisted. "One night stands are absolutely not my thing. Let alone with…" he sucked in a quick breath instead of finishing the sentence. "Anyway, it happened. And I understand if you want to fire me. You can tell Steve tomorrow…"

Joe scratched his head. "Like, *Oh, good morning Steve! By the way, I fired your assistant because he screwed your sister…* Like that?"

Chewing on his lip, his expression frozen, Eric shrugged.

Joe watched him for a moment, trying to concentrate. This was just the weirdest situation.

"Okay Eric," he finally said through clenched teeth. "As sick as I may find this, I don't see much benefit in firing you. You're good at what you do, *workwise* I mean…" He had to keep his thoughts from wandering off and imagining Liz and Eric without any clothes, entangled in some twisted Kamasutra position and Eric being good at that. "You're Steve's assistant, not mine. And as far as I'm concerned, Steve doesn't really need to be informed about this."

Eric gave him an almost incredulous look.

"Don't get me wrong," Joe growled, "I *do* find this disgusting. But you're not exactly Liz's first – how shall I say?- *adventure*… It might come as a disappointment to you, but it's not that you're so extremely irresistible, Eric, but just that she's so… never mind!"

While Eric stared back at him blankly, he continued: "But even though I want you to stay on, I personally don't want to have anything to do with you in the near future. So, try to stay out of my way, okay? And come up with some excuse why you can't fly to Amsterdam with me."

"Okay…" Eric had nodded, his expression reflecting both confusion and relief about this arrangement. "Thanks…" A little shakily he had gotten up and left.

Joe hadn't gone home that evening but spent the night on his office-sofa. The next morning he had sent Liz a text message.

*Just in case you're wondering. Didn't feel like leaving the*
*office after Eric dropped by last night and told me about*
*you f\*\*\* him. Your brother's assistant of all people!?!*

She had called him back right away but he hadn't picked up.

Then he had received a test message.

*Jealous, Honey? Well, I guess I was lonely that night.*
*Blame yourself! Eric's pretty good, by the way…*

And he had sent her back,

*You're just sick…!*


The loudspeaker calling some passengers for the final boarding of a flight to Oslo jerked Joe out of his unpleasant memories. He looked at his watch and realized that the boarding of his own flight was about to start. He grabbed his stuff and made his way to the crowded gate for Amsterdam. It would be a short flight.

# Guess Who's Coming

Sarah drove home and put away the groceries. Then she warmed up some leftover soup in the microwave and ate it leaning against the fridge.

She still couldn't quite believe that Joe was really coming. And even less that he was coming alone – without Liz.

He had only been back in Deens twice over the last three years.

The first time had been for his last two exams, just three months after he had left. He didn't even stay at home for that. He had asked Jack for asylum; supposedly to avoid his Dad. But Sarah suspected that Joe had also wanted to avoid his sister ... She hadn't really cared to see him either. She had still been so mad at him for being what she considered unbelievably stupid.

Mom had gone and met with him, of course, on the second evening of his stay. To celebrate that he had passed his two exams just fine. Sarah had refused to come along. Just to make a point.

Looking back now, she could hardly believe she had ever been so childishly stubborn. She would have probably even let him leave and stayed mad at him forever (or at least for a few more months or years). But then he had called her on the last evening. Because Jack had made him call her. They had grumbled at each other on the phone a bit and then just fallen into this frozen silence. That's when Jack had snatched the phone away from Joe and given her a piece of his mind. He had said something like, "Okay, Sarah, either you come over here right now, and you and Joe stop behaving like silly little brats and try to work things out, or I'm not going to talk to either of you ever again!"

Somehow that had maybe been the push she had needed. She had gone over there. And at first Joe and she had grumbled at each other some more in Jack's small living room, while Jack had been sitting in his TV-chair, keeping a close eye on them like a referee. Finally they had given up the grumbling and talked like normal people. And they had admitted that they actually *did* miss each other. They hadn't talked about Liz, though. Or D. Because there was this mutual understanding that they would never find any common ground on these issues. Instead Joe had told her that he was trying to start a software company with Liz's brother, and how living somewhere away from home was just something he felt he had to do. And she had said she understood, even though she had wanted to scream at him why in the world his *moving-out-from-home* experiments had to involve Liz…

She had left Jack's place a few hours later feeling halfway relieved and as if she and Joe had just successfully averted the danger of losing each other.

They had stayed in touch after that. Not as much as they should have probably, but they had exchanged e-mails every other week and talked on the phone at special occasions like birthdays and for Christmas.

All this time she could never tell for sure how he was really doing. He claimed to be fine on a regular basis, but she didn't quite buy it.

Then, thirteen months ago, their Dad had died. Totally unexpectedly. In his office. From a heart attack. While working late. His assistant had found him and called the ambulance, but there had been nothing that could be done.

Joe had arrived two days before the funeral – with Liz. It had been crazy with all of them functioning in a haze, shocked from the loss, overwhelmed first by the hurried preparations for the funeral and finally by the bleak fact of the funeral itself.

Sarah had hoped she and Joe would get a chance to talk sometime during the four days he was in Deens – just the two of them. But then Liz had seemed to be glued to him at all times. And with her around Sarah just didn't feel like having conversations of any depth with him.

Then, on the morning of the day Joe and Liz were supposed to leave again, Sarah had gotten up early to go to work. Unexpectedly she had found her brother sitting in the living room all by himself, sipping coffee. Maybe it had been a coincidence, maybe he had gotten up early to get her alone – Sarah wasn't sure even today.

She had gone and sat with him for a few minutes.

"You probably think I don't care, right?" he had said, his head leaning against the back of the sofa.

"No, I don't," Sarah had responded. "I know you *do* care. And even if it's just about Mom and me and Gran."

"I *do* worry about Mom," he had said and chewed on his lip.

"Yeah, it's real hard on her…" Sarah remembered saying, "but she'll be okay after a while." She had put all her conviction into that, even though she had been equally concerned at the time. "I'm worried about *you*, though?"

"Me? Why?"

"You and Dad never made peace. That must be hard…"

"Yeah I guess," Joe had mumbled evasively, and she had assumed he just didn't want to talk about it. So, determined not to pressure him about his feelings regarding Dad any more, she had asked how he was doing – in general. And he had insisted that things were going great. Or had he just said 'Okay'? She couldn't remember now. Still, she had told him that if he ever needed a vacation (from work or anything else…) he could come back and use his old room anytime. And he had laughed, leaned over and given her a spontaneous hug.

They had been in closer contact after the funeral. More calls, regular e-mails. And, even though he kept telling her things were fine, she had this nagging feeling that they were not.

Of course, part of it might have been wishful thinking because even after the over two years that he had been with Liz by then, Sarah couldn't imagine how he could possibly be happy with Liz.

When the idea of doing the reunion get-together had started to take shape, she had forwarded Joe the invitation. And so had Jack. Not in their wildest dreams had they expected a positive response. And then, one morning three weeks ago, there had suddenly been this e-mail from him, titled 'Coming'.

It had just been this very short message:

*Hi Sarah,*

*just decided I'd like to come for this. Could I stay with you?*

*Joe*

She had reread it twice to make sure she didn't get it wrong and then sent it on to Jack, who had been equally thrilled. She had responded:

*Hi Joe,*

*Wow! I'm still trying to recover from the surprise! Sure you can stay with me! I've got a whole house here… The longer the better! Jack says Hi. Wants to know if you want to share a room with him at the hotel? We'll make the reservations.*

*Sarah*

Joe had answered:

*Hi,*

*Sharing a room with Jack sounds great. Tell him Hi. I might actually really stay a little longer. Would that be okay?*

*Joe*

48

And she had texted back:

*Hi Joe,*
*Yes. Would definitely be okay. Would be great, in fact!*
*Sarah*

Sarah put her empty soup cup into the dishwasher and refilled her water glass. Somehow, until Joe's call this morning, she had still feared he might cancel the whole thing. From the way it looked, that could be ruled out now. He was going to be here for their get-together! And with that being clear now, it was high time for her to tackle a problem she had tried to avoid worrying about so far: She needed to finally tell D!

~~~

"Hi, Sarah!" With a big smile D let her in. "We can have coffee outside, if you want..." She nodded towards the deck outside the big living room window behind the sofa. "The sun is shining, the birds are singing and surprisingly no one has started a lawn mower yet." D made a swirling gesture with her hand.

"Sounds good!" Sarah smiled and followed her friend through the small entryway into the living room and over to the kitchen.

"Here are the pictures," D held up the CD case that had been lying on the bar counter. "I burned them onto a CD. But you can check them out on the old computer while I make coffee."

"Oh, okay. Sure... Thanks." Sarah placed her purse on one of the bar stools and relocated to the other room where the big PC was humming. She sat down in front of it, her eyes fixed on the screen. She felt tense. Her mind was buzzing with possible ways of breaking the news to her friend out there, that Joe was coming. Unfortunately she hadn't been able to come up with anything really promising so far. She actually had *no* idea how to deliver this gingerly.

Lost in these kinds of thoughts, Sarah clicked on the folder with her name on it. It was kind of encouraging that D, after obviously having spent part of the morning going through her pictures here, still seemed to be in a much sunnier mood than Sarah had expected. But maybe D had just very selectively looked through the right kind of pictures...

Sarah flipped through the photos. They were actually really good. The picture of D in front of the Campanile in Venice made her laugh out loud. She clicked further. And laughed some more. Man, had she and D really had haircuts like that?

"What was that?" D called over from the kitchen, apparently wondering which of her pictures had made Sarah laugh.

"Our hair," Sarah chuckled, "in the Venice pictures. And boy, the ones with the sheep – Jack was so skinny and tall…"

"Well, he's still tall," D laughed. "Just not quite as skinny. Looks better now if you ask me."

Sarah nodded to herself and clicked further.

D must have actually really made an effort here. There were shots from various events and years. It didn't look like she had limited her search to pre-Joe pictures. Sarah moved through the photos more quickly now, knowing that once Jack had incorporated those in his big slide show, she would get to see them on the big screen in the hotel anyway.

Suddenly she stopped. Squinted at the photo before her. Leaned towards the screen a bit to have a closer look. There was everyone gathered around the big snow man. Everyone including Joe…

Sarah clicked her tongue in surprise. That was an unexpected shot to find in this collection! Maybe a good sign? Maybe D wouldn't find the news so bad after all? One could always hope…

Sarah sped through the rest of the folder contents looking for more encouragement of this kind, but in the end, the snowman photo remained the only one that *did* have her brother's face on it.

She closed the folder and returned to the kitchen.

"Some really good shots!" she beamed. "Thanks for digging them out!"

She stepped up to the bar counter and took the coffee mug that D had set there for her. Suddenly the blue folder with the Tower Bridge picture caught her eye. "What's that?" she asked with a nod at it.

"Oh, nothing," D said a little too quickly.

Sarah raised her eyebrows.

Countering that look, D shrugged. "Well, you can look through it. It's not *that* exciting."

"Are you sure?" Sarah meant it. She didn't want to poke around things that D didn't want to share.

"Yeah, just look at it…" D nodded.

Sarah pulled the folder towards herself and started flipping through the first few pages.

"I didn't know your company had an office in London," she said with a surprised glance across the counter at D.

"They've had it for two years or so," D told her while putting some cookies from a package onto a plate.

"They're looking for people to go over there, huh?" Sarah had gotten to the pages with the job descriptions.

D nodded. "Yeah, there are three jobs they are trying to fill."

Sarah closed the folder and shot a cautious look at D. "Are you thinking about it?"

D shook her head. "Not really. I haven't even properly looked through the folder yet." She paused for a moment, picked up her coffee cup and the cookie plate. "June is probably going, though," she said, "and she's been bugging me to at least read the folder before I reject it."

"June is going? Really?" Sarah knew that June was D's favorite colleague and the one she shared the office with.

"Yeah, she kind of jumped on it as soon as the opportunity came up. Wants to get away. She's really excited about it. And I get to hear every new detail she finds out about it, whether I want to or not."

Sarah got up from her chair, her eyes still on the folder cover.

"And they want you to go as well?"

"More or less."

"Wow. That's kind of exciting, though," Sarah said. "You're not even tempted?"

"Like I said, I haven't even really looked into it," D responded a little impatiently.

"I thought you liked London during the two exchange semesters," Sarah pushed.

"Yeah, sure…" D shrugged. "I liked it. Still… moving there for work, well, I don't know… So far I haven't given it much thought. Really. I'll look at it, though. Even if just to satisfy June. And if then I suddenly decide to apply after all, you'll be the first to know!"

"Thank you!" Sarah smiled.

"You're welcome."

Her mug in one hand and the cookie plate in the other, D stepped out of the kitchen area into the living room. "Let's go outside." She headed towards the door to the deck and Sarah followed her, shooting a quick look towards D's half-open bedroom door.

"Still cleaning out your closets, huh?" Sarah asked.

D sighed. "Yeah, but I'm almost done. Even if it doesn't look like it. Just need to go to the container sometime."

Sarah had come to a halt in the living room. And from where she was standing, she was glancing towards the piles of stuff on D's bed.

"Do I see Pete's favorite dress in that pile?" she asked.

"Yep," D laughed. "What good eyes you have. You can have it, if you like. Still fits, so it should fit you. I'll even throw in some deadly sandals to go with it."

Sarah quickly shook her head. "No thanks! But if that's the curtains from the dorm under that horrible table cloth, I'll take those before you get rid of them."

"Sure. I can't really use them here. And I *do* need to get rid of some stuff. So, if you want them. I think there are two small pillow cases somewhere as well..."

"Yeah, maybe. If you could save this stuff, that would be great. I'll pick it up next time I'm here."

"Sure." D stepped out onto the deck, put the plate and her mug down on the round wooden table and opened the umbrella that was attached to the railing. Then she came back to the table and sat down across from Sarah. "Have you found a way to take Wednesday evening off, yet?" she asked reaching for a cookie.

"No, there's no way." Sarah shook her head and took a quick sip from her coffee. "I tried, but now, on top of everything else, one colleague, the one that is having a baby, has called in sick. So now we're one person short even." She paused. "I'll have Friday and the whole weekend off, though. That's cast in stone – Thank God!"

"Well, that's at least something," D agreed, trying to sound positive. "Too bad about the grill party, but the main thing is that you'll be there for the weekend, of course!"

"Yeah..." Sarah nodded with a weak smile. Her job at the hospital had some irregular hours, some very early shifts and some late shifts that were compensated with time off during the day, when people like D had to work. Sometimes getting time off was a real pain, though. But since she loved the job and the people she worked with, she had stuck with it so far.

Glancing at D, who was sitting comfortably leaned back in her chair, legs crossed, both hands wrapped around her coffee mug in her lap, Sarah wished she was feeling nearly as relaxed as D looked. The unfinished business of delivering the Joe-related news was starting to weigh heavily on her.

She let her gaze wander around; to the different plants D had arranged on and around the deck, most of them blooming nicely – with the exception of one potted tree that looked dead.

On the stairs that led from the wooden deck into the small garden below, there were planters with tomatoes. Even though the tomatoes were still green, they did look promising.

With an uneasy feeling in her stomach Sarah forced herself to look back at her friend.

"What?" D asked, tilting her head. "What's with the silence and the strange look?"

Sarah swallowed. Was it that obvious? Well, it was now or never! As much as she hated to destroy D's good mood, she really couldn't put it off any longer. She would have to drop the bomb sometime.

"Well…" Sarah drew in a deep breath, her eyes trailing off towards the tomato bushes again. "There's actually something I need to tell you…"

From the corner of her eye she could see D set down the coffee and shoot her a quizzical look. "What kind of an introduction is that?" There was a trace of amusement in her voice. "Has someone died?" Of course she knew that no one had died.

With a forced little laugh Sarah shook her head. "No, no one has died, " she said while thinking to herself that it was more like someone rising from the dead. But she could hardly say that out loud.

"It's probably not even a real big deal…" she said trying for a light and cheerful tone despite the sudden dryness in her mouth. The way D looked back at her proved that she wasn't buying it. Instead she seemed to already be feverishly trying to figure out what this could possibly be about.

So, before D could come to any conclusion, Sarah just said it.

"Joe's coming for the reunion."

Plop! There it was. Bomb dropped. Waiting for it to explode…

It took a few seconds for the message to sink in. Sarah could see it in D's face. First she blinked a few times. Then, for just a fraction of a second, she had this *deer-in-the-headlights* look that was almost immediately replaced by a controlled, unreadable mask.

"Oh is he?" she scoffed, her gaze dropping to the cookie plate. "What a great surprise!" With her thumb she brushed over the rim of the plate. "Absolutely makes my day…" The tone was pure sarcasm.

Sarah watched her cautiously. She couldn't even remember when she had last mentioned her brother's name with D around. She had avoided it whenever she could. But today she didn't really have a choice. Joe was coming and D had to know!

"He's coming Tuesday afternoon," Sarah said – the underlying message being that, while she wasn't going to be there for the grill party on Wednesday, one member of the Reilley family would.

D nodded, her eyes never leaving the plate. She sucked in an audible breath and took a cookie.

Sarah was scrambling for something to say. "D, I know…"

"It's fine!" The cookie still in her hand, D looked up at Sarah. A hard look. "It's perfectly fine… It's a surprise, of course – and not exactly a good one, if you allow me to say so. But if he wants to come…" Instead of finishing her sentence she shrugged and stuffed the cookie into her mouth.

Sarah drank some of her coffee, feeling guilty. Even though she couldn't exactly have said of what.

"I should have probably told you earlier," she finally said. "I mean, I've kind of known for two weeks that he *might* come. But until this morning I was still expecting him to cancel. I didn't want to upset you unless I was perfectly sure…"

D's eyes seemed to narrow a bit. "I'm not upset at all!" she insisted, picking up her mug. "Why would I be *upset?* He can do what he wants. *I* don't care!"

"Right," Sarah said dryly. "Good for you."

The sarcastic edge to Sarah's tone wasn't lost to D, of course. She gave Sarah a brief sour look, then quickly raised the cup to her lips and drank a few sips. Then she set it back down on the table, cupping it in both hands. A seemingly endless minute passed without either of them saying a word or allowing eye contact.

Finally D let go of the cup, leaned forward a bit, her elbows resting on the table and started stacking the remaining cookies into a little tower.

"Is *she* coming too?" she inquired, her eyes firmly on the cookie construction.

Sarah shook her head. "No, just Joe."

Gazing at her cookie tower, D was trying to pull herself together. God, she just hated how this threw her off. This kind of thing really shouldn't have such an impact! What was her problem anyway? There had always been the possibility that he'd come, hadn't there? After all, the underlying goal of a reunion was to get everyone together. Only that, after he had so totally dropped out of all of their lives (except for maybe Sarah's), it had appeared safe to not even seriously consider that he might show up for this thing. It had seemed so unlikely, that she had just ruled it out. Her mistake! He was coming after all! Voila! Boom! Crap! She better get her act together here very quickly!

She peered across the table at Sarah, who was pretending to be fascinated by the appearance of the limp-looking apple tree in the neighbor's garden.

This was a real crappy situation for Sarah as well. D was aware of that. Sarah was probably totally torn apart between her brother, who she was doubtlessly looking forward to seeing, and her best friend, who would rather not be reminded that this brother even existed. It sure couldn't be fun.

D tried to imagine the same constellation with her own brother and Sarah. It made her cringe. It would be close to impossible to constantly filter out everything she might have on her mind regarding Robert... And something told her that Sarah probably had quite a few things on her mind regarding *her* brother. Realizing that, D straightened up. She owed it to Sarah to behave like an adult here and not make this extra hard on her.

"It really isn't a big deal," she claimed with a light shrug and a smile. She was impressed how calm and reasonable her voice sounded. "It's good to know, though." She leaned back in her chair and tried to relax a little. "I'll prepare myself for that encounter and it'll be okay. Not a big deal! Really!"

Sarah looked back at her, not entirely convinced yet but appearing a little less tense. "Well, I'm glad to hear that," she said, sounding relieved. "I mean, it's not like I could have done anything about it anyway, but still..." She took a cookie from the pile.

"The main thing is that I don't have to see *her*," D said. "Everything else I can easily handle – especially if it's in a group setting."

Sarah smiled and nodded. "Yeah, that's kind of what I was thinking. It shouldn't be too hard for you guys to stay out of each other's way with a whole bunch of other people to talk to and hang around with." She paused and took a sip of coffee. As she sat down her mug on the table, a somewhat conspiring smile appeared on her face. "To be honest, I'm actually absolutely thrilled myself that Madame isn't planning on coming," she said. "I'm almost hoping I'll never have to see her again, but that's probably asking way too much!" She let the bit of coffee she still had left in her cup swish around a bit. "I'm not sure what's really going on with them at the moment. But I guess I'll find out…"

With a little shrug she looked up at D.

D bit her lip, struggling to keep her expression neutral. She couldn't blame Sarah for maybe wanting to talk about this with a friend. She just knew that in this special case it absolutely couldn't be her. Because there was just no acceptable and civilized response that came to her mind. *They can both rot in hell as far as I'm concerned!* would hardly qualify as a constructive comment in the eyes of his sister. So, instead of any response, she took her own coffee cup and poured down what had been left inside. When she glanced across the table again, she found Sarah looking back at her with an apologetic half-smile.

"Sorry," Sarah said. "I know you probably don't want to hear my contemplations on this."

Mirroring Sarah's expression, D shrugged. "It's okay," she muttered. "I just don't know what to say. Can't really think of anything nice…"

The way she said it, made Sarah laugh. And at the end, they were both laughing, relieved that this tricky talk had gone relatively well, and both of them determined not to worry just yet what kind of strain Joe's being here might put on their friendship.

"I should get going," Sarah announced with a quick look at her watch. Time to make a cut before this whole situation returned to being uncomfortable.

They picked up their cups and the almost empty cookie plate and headed inside.

Just as they stepped into the living room, D's phone started to ring on the sofa.

"Go ahead, get it," Sarah said, "I'm almost out of here anyway…"

"No, that's okay," D kept heading for the kitchen. "I can always call back later." She felt Sarah's eyes on her as she opened the dishwasher and put the dishes in.

"Is that Pete then?" Sarah asked darkly.

Nodding, D closed the dishwasher and turned around to Sarah. "Most likely."

Sarah frowned. "Has he *still* not given up?"

Shaking her head, D leaned against the counter next to the sink. "At this point I'm not sure he will ever give up!" she said.

"Oh, God, that stupid…Grrr…" Sarah growled.

"He just drives me insane…" D said with an air of resignation. "And I just hate, hate, *hate* how guilty he makes me feel!" She lifted her hand and rubbed her left temple.

"Don't feel guilty then!" Sarah retorted. "Nothing to feel guilty about! You *do* need to stop talking to him, though! Really! It doesn't help him and it sure isn't good for you!"

D exhaled sharply. "I *know* that," she said with audible exasperation, "but unfortunately it's a *lot* easier said than done, believe me." She ran her hands along the countertop behind her. "I mean… I'm not picking up right now, am I? And this is probably already his fourth call today that I haven't picked up…"

Sarah threw her arms up in frustration.

D let out a bitter little laugh and shrugged. Sometimes it was comforting to see that Sarah found it equally frustrating. It was good that, when it came to Pete, there was no need to censor what they said to each other. None of the inhibitions that came with the Joe-topic applied to their talks about Pete.

"All I can tell you from my latest experiments with picking up and not picking up," D told Sarah, "is that *not* picking up doesn't help at all. He just keeps calling. He's persistent. And then, when I actually *do* pick up, we spend the first ten minutes discussing why he can't reach me and how that makes him feel and *blah blah blah.* Under normal circumstances he calls me at least every third day and every call I don't pick up seems to make the ones I actually do take three times as bad. It's like a snake that grows more heads each time you cut one off." With her hands she made some movement that was supposed to indicate the many snake-heads floating around.

"Well, what the hell does he still want?" Sarah burst out. "Can't he just accept…?"

D shook her head, her jawline hard. "He wants to see if we can meet or if he can come by and we can go out together, he wants to hear me defend for the hundredth time why I thought I wasn't been happy with him, he questions if I even *know* what would make me happy, he insists that we need to give it another chance, he tells me that we could still go on vacation together since we're both alone now, he bitches about his work…"

Sarah rolled her eyes and huffed out an angry breath.

"Well, and the newest thing..." D said before Sarah could articulate her doubtlessly many thoughts on the bleak summary. "The newest thing is... It's all about us being *friends*."

She managed to pronounce *friends* like a bad word, and the quotation marks she indicated with her fingers, added an additionally suspicious touch. "So, that's where we are right now."

Sarah raised her eyebrows. "*Friends*, huh?"

"Yeah, all he wants is to stay *friends* now," D said with acidic sweetness. "But man, I'm even a disappointment in that department! Really! How in the world can I be so cold and cruel to refuse him even this modest little wish?"

Sarah hit her forehead with her flat hand. "Oh God, that idiot! He doesn't just want to be *friends*. That's total bullshit and it never works."

"I know that and you know that," D agreed sounding increasingly frustrated. "But it's kind of hard to flat-out tell him I don't even really want to be friends with him at this point. Especially since that was one of my great lines when I broke up – that I value him as a person and I would like to keep him as a friend..." She let out a bitter laugh. "See, how these things come back to haunt you?!?"

Sarah pursed her lips. "Well, yeah. But you didn't mean it like that!"

"No, not as the life-long obligation to stay in close contact that he turns it into..."

"Oh, I can just see it," Sarah grumbled. "It probably goes like this: *Oh, Danielle, all I want is your friendship, and as friends we need to talk on the phone three times a week, meet regularly, share all our secrets...*"

"Yeah something like that..." D said and, staring at the floor, pushed herself away from the counter a little only to let herself fall right back again.

"And he seriously still wants to go on vacation with you?" Sarah asked.

"He did until last week. He still hadn't cancelled the trip to Spain."

"You're kidding!"

"I wish! No, I'm *not* kidding. I wasn't aware of it until he mentioned it last week. Told him to cancel it finally. So, maybe, by now..."

"How does he even think that would work?" Sarah blasted. "You two happily sharing a hotel bed? The next thing he'll probably come up with..." Sarah paused for a moment before she actually finished her sentence. "...is that since you're lonely and he's lonely and since you're such good friends, it's really no big deal to sleep together..."

D's head jerked up, her expression angry. "Thanks a lot, Sarah, for this very valuable contribution!" she snapped.

"Sorry!" Sarah mumbled, taken aback by that unusually harsh reaction. "Maybe that was taking it a little too far." She just hoped that's what it was, and not that she had just accidently hit the nail right on the head. Because knowing Pete, her vision wasn't all that far-fetched.

"I just really think he's manipulating you, though." Sarah said just to say something less controversial.

"Yeah, he probably is," D agreed darkly. "And trust me, I do my best not to be manipulated. But sometimes I just can't be so cruel." She paused for a moment, as if to gather her thoughts. "I mean, I don't understand why he's doing it. Because what he'll really achieve in the end is that I hate him *and* myself..."

She rubbed her temple again. "Okay. And now, let's stop talking about him because it just absolutely wears me out! Unless you have some ingenious new approach..."

Sarah had picked up the CD case from the counter and set it on one of its corners while holding the opposite corner by pressing her index finger on it. She gave the CD a little push and made it spin a few times. The Pete subject was so tricky. She wished D would just recklessly pull it through and cut Pete off once and for all. This really seemed to be turning into an endless and painful split-up. And D wasn't normally weak or easily manipulated or undecided. It was more that Pete seemed absolutely unwilling to let go. And he obviously knew exactly which buttons to push to drag this on and on and on.

Sarah cleared her throat. Something had suddenly crossed her mind.

"It's kind of hard to come up with some new ideas here," she admitted, "but thinking about it now, maybe you should just tell him that you've suddenly fallen madly in love with someone else and that that makes a friendship with him totally impossible." It was just a sudden inspiration. "Of course it's cruel. But at this point almost anything is. And it might just be worth a try. It would at least signal that you're *not* lonely or bored and that there might be some big, strong guy having a jealous eye on you..."

D couldn't help laughing. "Yeah right..." Suddenly her gaze fell on the blue folder on the bar counter. "Or maybe I'll just have to leave the country. That might solve it too!" She made it sound like a joke. But Sarah wasn't quite sure it really was one.

# Reaching Amsterdam

Amsterdam was rainy. Joe took the train from the airport into town and then a taxi to the hotel, which was close to the Van Gogh museum.

It was early afternoon when he closed the door to his room, put the suitcase into a corner and flung himself onto the big bed. Peace and quiet! He had two hours before he was supposed to meet Peer and Christine for dinner. Peer had been an exchange student at the university where Joe had first started, and they had stayed in touch even after Peer had returned to the Netherlands two years later.

Joe always enjoyed seeing Peer and Christine when he was in town. They were a nice, fun and obviously happy couple, and they didn't seem to mind his not being very talkative during their latest get-togethers. Sometimes he simply didn't know what to say. The things he seemed to be spending most of his time with anymore – fighting with Liz, going to work and taking off on as many business trips as he could – didn't make for great dinner conversation. Thankfully Peer and Christine usually had enough to talk about. And their stories (and sometimes worries) took his mind off his own problems at least temporarily.

Stretched out on the hotel bed, Joe crossed his legs at the ankles and draped his left arm behind his head. His braced hand was resting on his belly, the pain almost gone now. He wouldn't need to try the pills after all.

Staring up at the unusual light fixture on the ceiling, he let his mind wander. It was such a weird feeling to know that he wouldn't return to the flat he had lived in with Liz. It had been long overdue, of course. And it sure was a relief! But it was still strange.

Over the last year and a half, or even earlier than that, things with Liz seemed to have slowly spun totally out of control. It had gone from bad to worse. Now that he thought about it, he wasn't sure when it had ever been really good...

The downward spiral had started with Liz taking that job at the art gallery and getting more and more involved in the evening program even though that wasn't her job. She would spend hours getting ready for those events. Sometimes it had literally made his jaw drop when, on her way out, she had blown him a kiss, dressed and made up almost like a wannabe Hollywood star heading for the red carpet.

She had dragged him to two of these happenings right after she had started working there. She had really wanted him to come along. To experience what she thought was just sooo great and exciting.

He had joined her, not knowing what he was stumbling into. God, it was a world of its own! The art that he had a hard time identifying as such, all the people pretending to know just *what* the artist had meant to express with the distorted piece of metal or the smeared mess of paint on the canvas, and finally the artists themselves, *oh, my*... It had been somewhat fascinating to watch, though, from one of these stylish and surprisingly comfortable chairs in the back corner.

After the first such evening he had refused to go again. Because it just didn't do anything for him. But then Liz had tormented him until he agreed to try it just one more time. Because this time was going to be different, and because she really wanted to finally introduce him to her boss.

So he had agreed... He had headed there right after work, running a little late, feeling hungry and stressed out. And he had found himself surrounded by the same crazy theatrical crowd as the previous time, with Liz fitting in just perfectly. He still remembered her coming towards him in that extremely tight glittering dress, on her high heels that made her almost taller than him. She had given him a kiss on the cheek and stopped a passing waiter to get a glass of wine for herself and one for him. Then she had lead him across the room through all the people and presented him to Linda, her boss. Linda had turned out to be a nice and – considering the environment – relatively normal woman in her early forties. Her husband, Bob, had been there as well. He seemed a bit older, maybe forty-five, thinning hair, very tall, rough features, piercing light-green eyes, but a friendly smile. Joe had shaken his hand (a *big* hand!) and made some small talk. Little did he know that ten months later those hands would be all over Liz.

Joe remembered searching for food after meeting Linda and Bob. His stomach was growling and he had lost Liz in the crowd to someone she absolutely needed to talk to. He had found the buffet and retreated to his favorite fancy chair in the second exhibition room with a bunch of hors d'oeuvres on a plate. Munching on the tiny culinary creations, he had let his gaze wander across the room over all the strange people and the weird art. Finally his eyes had come to rest on the life-size bronze mermaid that was hovering right next to his chair. She had some truly mesmerizing, perfectly shaped breasts...

At some point he must have nodded off. He remembered being woken up by Liz kicking his leg with her pointy shoe, hissing something unfriendly. He had quickly straightened up and lifted his head from the mermaid's chest that it had tipped against during his little nap. Liz had been fuming at him for his obvious lack of interest in art and his horrible manners. And he had groggily gazed back at her, rubbing the right side of his face and distracted by his seriously aching cheekbone that had obviously been resting against the mermaid's prominent bronze nipple a little too long. He had never been invited to the art gallery again.

Liz went every time, though. And a lot of times she had way too much to drink there. She had always been somewhat irrational, short-tempered or plain bitchy, but the alcohol magnified that to an unbearable extent. He had tried to talk to her a few times, but it had each time just lead to her screaming at him and totally freaking out.

He had started being gone a lot. On business trips. Intentionally. Because he simply couldn't stand being around her. But at the same time he hadn't been at all ready yet to just call it quits. Not because he had been so attached to Liz, but because breaking up had seemed like such a logistical mess, with their living together and his owning a company with Steve. Plus, he had still been extremely reluctant at the time to admit to the world (and especially Sarah) that he should have never gotten involved with Liz in the first place.

Then, about a year ago, he had found the pills. It had been after an especially crazy night. She had come home drunk, they had had a fight, he had made his bed on the sofa and at three in the morning she had suddenly appeared in the living room and snuck under his blanket, pushing all possible buttons and begging him to be good again. They had ended up having some very ill-advised sex. He had gotten up in the morning, mad at himself. And while Liz had still been asleep, he had followed a sudden intuition, gone through her stuff in the bathroom and found the three different packages of pills, tucked under a shower cap she never used. The first package contained painkillers, the second sleeping pills and the third some stuff that could keep you awake for days. He had tried to talk to her about it – probably the last time he had ever attempted to have a reasonable conversation with her. But it had just turned into another gruesome scene.

There was no doubt in his mind that she had an addiction problem. Alcohol, pills – and the sex thing was possibly another facet of it. Sometimes he wondered how much his being gone so much had to do with all this. It really was a chicken-egg problem: Was the mess caused by his being gone so much or was he gone so much because it was unbearable to be around Liz. He liked to think it was the latter. In fact, he was convinced it was the latter.

He would never forget when half a year ago, during another fight, she had suddenly triumphantly revealed to him that during his last business trip she had slept with Bob, Linda's husband. Despite his already progressed emotional detachment at the time, the news had still felt like a kick to the stomach. Part of it had probably been male pride, but there had also been utter shock that, to Liz, it didn't even seem to matter that she wasn't only hurting him but also Linda.

Hurting him was intended, of course. And she had justified it the same way she justified the thing with Eric a few months later: A pay-back. A pay-back for all the affairs he was surely having during all his business trips.

The funny thing was, of course, that during all the time he had been with her – three years in total – he had really only had one little fling on the side. There had been this girl in Stockholm. Annika. And that had been *after* Liz had served the Bob-affair to him. He had liked Annika. And she had definitely been crazy about him. But somehow, with the Liz problem still unsolved and Stockholm being a plane-ride away, he hadn't let it progress very far. He had cut it off before it could turn into anything serious. He had just felt like he couldn't keep it up. Or maybe he had been scared. Because after how that thing with Liz had turned out... That, in fact, might be a deterrent to get into a serious relationship again anytime soon!

He had almost nodded off when his mobile phone started to ring.

It was Christine. He looked at his watch as he groggily sat up. It was almost five.

"Hi, Christine!"

"Hi... How are you?" she sounded weird.

"I'm fine," he said. "Are you okay?"

She didn't answer right away. "Not really...," she finally admitted. "Listen... ahm... I know we were supposed to meet this evening," she paused for a moment and cleared her throat. "There's been a change of plans – or circumstances..." She seemed to be trying to find the right words. "It would only be you and me... Peer is... He's gone. We split up."

"*What?* When?" Joe was scrambling for something to say.

"A week ago." Christine sounded like she was on the verge of tears. "It's a longer story."

Joe scratched his head. "I guess it always is."

"Do you still want to meet... – even if it's only me?" Christine asked.

"Sure. If you feel like going out."

"I think I actually need to get out," she said with a nervous laugh. "Otherwise I'll go crazy here."

"Alright," Joe said, trying to sound encouraging. "Then, we should definitely go out! Where do you wanna go?" He was pretty sure she would want to avoid the restaurant the three of them had been planning to meet at. But then that was exactly the one she picked.

After he had hung up, Joe let himself fall back onto the bed, the phone still in his hand. He had actually been looking forward to a fun evening with a couple that worked and not more proof of how relationships never seemed to last.

# Doing Dishes

After Sarah had left, D felt like a steamroller had flattened her.

She had really had enough on her plate already with Pete clinging to her like an octopus. That by itself was enough to keep her awake at night. Having Joe thrown in there now as well, was a bit much. And no matter what she had told Sarah, the news had come as a real blow. She was only starting to feel the effect now. It just made her dizzy to think that there was absolutely no way to avoid seeing him. Unless, of course, she was willing to stay away from both the grill party and the weekend at the hotel – both things she had been looking forward to for a long time. Until half an hour ago. It made her so mad that now he would come and ruin it all! She didn't want to see him! Plain and simple!

Like in a haze she walked out onto the deck. She closed and covered the umbrella and checked the moisture on the tomatoes. Then she went back inside and packed a few things in a small travel bag. She was going to stay with her parents overnight.

Once on the road she called Robert to tell him that she was on her way. And the second she hung up, her mind darted right back to what she actually didn't want to think about: Joe.

Over the last three years she had seen him exactly once. A little over a year ago at his father's funeral.

"I'm so sorry for your loss." She had already said the same thing three times – to his Mom, Sarah and his Grandma – so it came out easily even when she was standing in front of him now. She had held out her hand and forced herself to look up at him. It was shocking how much he had changed. He looked nothing like she remembered. Hair cropped real short, and it seemed as if he was growing some kind of beard... In a way she was relieved that he looked like a stranger.

There had been a short, awkward handshake. His eyes briefly meeting hers. He still had the same grey-green eyes.

And the same voice. "Thanks, Danny."

Hearing him say it – familiar voice, calm tone and his still calling her *Danny* – made her feel like someone had knocked the air out of her.

It had taken her a few days to fully digest this encounter. Her mind had gone through the few seconds over and over again and, for a few crazy moments, she had even regretted that there hadn't been a chance to talk. But that feeling had passed, and she been glad that seeing him again had been so quick and relatively painless.

She arrived at her parents' house around 5:15 pm.

"Danielle, *finally*…" Robert seemed a bit stressed as he opened the door for her. "If we wait any longer the roast will be dry and everything else overcooked or cold!"

"Yeah, I'm sorry but there was a lot more traffic than I thought. Everyone else here already?"

"Yes, they're all in the dining room. I made them sit down, but I'm not sure how long I can keep them that way…" A grin appeared on his face. "Aunt Sauvie was getting on my nerves in the kitchen and Dad and Sven were getting out the cigars, so… I think it's high time we feed them."

"Okay, getting fed sounds very good! I'll just say *Hi* and *Happy Birthday*, and then I'll help you serve the food, okay?" D headed towards the dining room from where she could hear happy chatter of familiar voices.

It was Mom's 58<sup>th</sup> birthday, and Robert and his girlfriend, Ann, had arranged a little party for her with some of her friends and relatives. Robert loved to prepare big fancy meals from his many recipe books. So, any birthday or anniversary was a good test field for him. And his test results always got a lot of applause.

This dinner turned out to be no exception. Everyone was completely satisfied and well-fed after the main course, a roast with so many side dishes that the plates had been barely big enough to hold everything. It had been delicious. Not even Robert had found anything wrong with his work this time.

As D folded her napkin, she realized that she had eaten way too much. Feeling tired and paralyzed, she tried to follow one of the many conversations that were going on around her, which was making her even more tired. Aunt Sauvie was talking about her son's new car, Mom's friends were explaining to Dad how to best prune some exotic-sounding plant, and Mom was assuring the neighbors that feeding their birds during their trip to Costa Rica was no problem at all.

D's eyes met Robert's and she hoped he would get the hint. He did.

"I think we'll clear off some dishes," he said in a tone that wouldn't allow any contradiction. "Need to run the dishwasher more than once, anyway. So we'll get the first round started! And then we'll be back with dessert."

"Right," Ann got up next to him and began to collect some of the plates.

"I'll help you!" D proclaimed, rising from her chair as well.

In the kitchen Robert opened the dishwasher and positioned himself right in front of it as if he was defending the goal in a soccer match.

"I'll load it," he informed them.

D and Ann looked at each other with a shrug and a conspiring smile.

"Sure. After all, you're the only one who knows how to do it..." D teased. "But there are worse things than a guy, who insists on doing kitchen work!" She took the garbage can out from under the sink and started wiping the plates one by one with the napkins that were lying on them. The dirty napkins she dumped into the garbage can, the wiped plates she stacked on the kitchen table next to her for Robert to take.

Ann was at the sink, filling it with soapy water to wash some of the dishes that were either too big or too delicate to go into the machine.

"We're going to grill some steaks with Mom and Dad and her parents at our place next weekend," Robert said as he took one of the plates right from D's hand. "I finally want to test the new barbecue... Do you want to come? We'll probably do it Sunday. The weather is supposed to be nice."

Keeping her gaze on the plate in her hand, D shook her head. "Sounds nice, but I've got that reunion-get-together thing. Remember?"

"Yeah, right!" Robert said, obviously remembering now. "I totally forgot about that!"

D nodded a little absent-mindedly. "Yeah, that's this weekend..." Unintentionally it had come out so strikingly non-enthusiastic that it made Robert pause in the middle of putting some plates into the dishwasher. He looked up at her with a frown. "What's wrong?" he asked. "I thought you were looking forward to that."

D swallowed. Robert sometimes seemed to have this seventh sense that detected traces of things she was actually trying to hide.

"Danielle?" Her hesitation, of course, just confirmed that he was onto something.

D was fighting with herself. It wasn't too late to insist that nothing was wrong and quickly change the topic. Robert would get the hint and let it go. But maybe she actually did want to talk to someone? And in this particular case it couldn't be Sarah, who normally was her preferred confidant for personal matters of this kind. Sarah was just too closely related to her problem!

"I was really looking forward to it," she finally said, weighing her words. "Only that things look a little less enjoyable now…"

Robert gave her a puzzled look. "Meaning?"

Pursing her lips she shrugged. "Meaning that Sarah revealed a wonderful surprise to me today." She paused and gazed at the glasses on the table next to her before she looked back up at Robert. "She said that… ahm…" Crap, she couldn't even say his name, could she? She cleared her throat. "Sarah said that her brother is going to bless us with his presence. So…Yippee! We'll all be happily reunited without any exceptions! What more could we possibly wish for?"

Robert raised his eyebrows. "Uh oh!" He sounded as if he had just watched someone step into dog poop.

"Right. *Uh oh…*" D repeated dryly while she started moving the glasses around on the table until they were positioned in a perfect three by three square. She could feel Robert watching her.

"Well, you know," his hands behind his back Robert leaned against the countertop across from her, obviously deeming this topic important enough to interrupt his activities at the dishwasher for a moment. "I was actually kind of wondering if there wasn't at least a chance he'd show up for that. But since you didn't say anything I figured he's either not coming or you're okay with it. I didn't really dare to ask you…"

D shot him a sour look. "Oh, come on Rob, aren't you a poor intimidated creature!"

Robert shrugged. "Well, you've told me often enough to keep out of this very, very touchy subject, so…"

"Well, there was no hint of him coming until today," D insisted testily, ignoring Robert's last comment. She shifted the glasses into a new pattern – an almost perfect circle. "And… I mean… he can do what he wants, of course! I don't care! But can't he just come back some other time, when I don't have to see him? I was actually looking forward to a nice and relaxing weekend with friends…"

"And now it won't be quite as relaxing," Robert concluded with a trace of amusement.

"No, not relaxing!" D agreed, a bit irritated at his cheerfulness.

"What's this with Sarah's brother?" Ann asked from the sink, where she was trying to get the burnt-on sauce off the roast pan. "I didn't even know she had one."

"Well, she *has* one," Robert assured her flatly. "But we kind of have this *oath of silence* when it comes to him because he happens to be her ex…" He nodded towards D.

"That sounds like a crappy constellation!" Ann concluded while she kept scrubbing the pan.

"You can say that out loud!" D agreed darkly.

"Is he bringing *her* too?" Robert asked, eyeing his sister cautiously. "I mean, *Liz*…"

At the mention of the name, D swallowed. Then she shook her head. "Doesn't sound like it."

"Well, that's at least something!" Robert said. "Are they even still together?"

"I guess so," D said with an especially indifferent shrug. "But Sarah doesn't say much, fortunately, and I don't ask because I really, really don't care! I'm just glad I don't get to deal with the double-package! That's all that matters to me!"

Robert nodded, not looking very convinced. "Is it a real big deal then, if he comes?" he asked. "I mean… it might not be real relaxing with him around, but is it a serious problem? You've seen him at the funeral, haven't you? And that was okay…" He turned back to the dishwasher.

Chewing on her lip, D stared at her brother's back. "Sure, that was okay," she said gloomily. "But that's not saying much, as that was a five second kind of thing where the required communication didn't go beyond me saying 'I'm sorry' and his saying 'Thanks.' That's a whole lot different than an entire weekend with various *Oh-how-happy-we-all-are-together* activities and a grill party on Wednesday to start it all off…"

Chuckling at that summary, Robert put away the last plate and started on the glasses. "Yeah, I guess that's a little different than a funeral," he agreed with a little twitch around his mouth. "Especially since the people around you won't be there for a silent mourning but to have some fun."

"Exactly…"

"Yeah, well… what can I tell you?" Robert paused for a moment, obviously really trying to come up with something constructive here. "You need to avoid an open display of the feud between Joe and you, that's for sure. That would just be really uncomfortable for everyone."

"I know that!" D snapped. "I'm not planning to do that. Do you think I'm stupid? Besides, there's absolutely no feud!"

"No, of course not," Robert shot back, parroting her tone. "It's real comforting and reassuring to hear you say that. Especially your tone… You shouldn't have *any* problem at all being civilized around him."

"Oh, I'll be civilized, alright!" she said with acidic sweetness, "I'll be oh sooo civilized and friendly! Even though I would just love to—"

"What?" Robert challenged. "Scratch out his eyes, punch his nose?"

She shrugged. "Yeah, something like that."

Robert turned around again and gave her a serious look. "*Danielle*," Robert said in a more somber tone. "It's been what? Three years? It's a little late now, don't you think? I told you then, when there was a justification and a chance, to kick his ass, yell at him, do whatever else you've got to do in order to get it out of your system…" He paused and watched her glance to the side, a stubborn expression on her face. "He wanted to talk to you, remember?" Robert didn't let her out of his sight. "He even called *me* that one time, right after you had moved out of the dorm. But you told me to stop meddling and left for London!"

Shooting him a furious look, D sucked in some air as if she was going to give him some snappy answer. But then she didn't say anything after all. Just shook her head and rubbed her forehead.

"I'll be fine, okay?" she finally said, trying for a calm and grown-up tone. "It's just been a little surprising, that's all. And admit that I would have been just *perfectly* happy if I *never* had to see him again. But since I pretty much have to now, I'll just try to ignore him as much as I can, and if I can't, I'll be gracefully indifferently friendly like I am with every random stranger on the street."

Robert nodded with a smile. "Good girl! Good plan!" He reached out and patted her on the shoulder encouragingly. "You'll be fine. Just make sure your sarcasm doesn't get the upper hand, okay? And don't take everything he says as an offense that you have to retaliate with nuclear missiles!" He paused when he saw her face. "Yeah, well, don't look at me like that! We both know that's what you do! I personally doubt that he'll want to have a lot to do with you anyway. With some luck he'll avoid you and you'll avoid him and things will be fine."

D thought about that for a moment. "Yeah, you're probably right." She grabbed a towel and joined Ann at the sink. There were two pots already washed and upside down waiting to be dried.

Ann looked over at her. "What happened with that guy? Or should I not ask?"

"His name is Joe, by the way," Robert threw in.

D had to keep herself from turning around and knocking her brother upside the head with the pan in her hand. Did he enjoy this? Was there really any need to say the name out loud?

"He replaced me with a tramp and ran off with her." It was a blunt and cold summary.

"And she really was a tramp," Robert suddenly jumped in. D glanced over her shoulder, checking for any sign of mockery. There was none.

"Wow. So you agree, huh?" she huffed with exaggerated surprise.

"Sure, I agree," Robert said. "No doubt about that." He closed the dishwasher. "I never told you this," he said turning around again, "but she actually came on to me once."

"Liz?" D didn't believe her ears. "*Liz* came on to *you?*" A pot that she was just drying still in one hand and the dish towel in the other she turned around and gave him an incredulous look.

Robert laughed. "Which part of it is so hard to believe now, huh? The *Liz*-part or the *me*-part?"

"Nothing…" D hurried to say with a quick shake of her head. "Either part sounds perfectly believable! It does sound, though, as if – unlike Sarah's brother – *my* brother didn't land in bed with her. Or did you?"

Robert shook his head. "Nope. I didn't. Probably could have, though…"

"I don't doubt that for one second," D let out a dry laugh. "Guess that proves that *my* brother has more brains than Sarah's…"

Robert shrugged. "One way to look at it."

"When was that?" D pushed. "What happened?"

"That birthday party Sarah threw you… for your twenty-third I think," he squinted as he tried to remember the details. "I didn't even really know her… I mean Liz… except for what you had told me about her and Jack. Jack had brought her along to the party, but then he left earlier for some reason and she must have stuck around."

"Okay… and?" D sounded impatient.

And Ann suddenly seemed quite interested was well. "Right, Rob… *And?*"

"Well, there's not *that* much to tell, really," Robert tried to tone down their expectations. "I was just standing alone in a corner sipping a drink and actually ready to call it a night, when she strolled towards me and struck up some conversation. I don't even remember what it was about… something totally irrelevant, I think. I do clearly remember her dress, though – or the lack of it… Anyway, after a few minutes, totally out of the blue, I suddenly had her hand running up my arm. And she proposed that we take a drive to the river because the party was way too crowded and boring." Robert paused for a moment. "And really, the way she phrased it and the body language was unmistakable even for me, and I'm not exactly the fastest when it comes to…"

"No, you're not!" Ann teased.

"Thanks, Annie," he said and gave her a fake pouting look. "Well, anyway… despite the very generous and tempting offer, I politely skipped the chance and drove home to my own bed all by myself."

"How come?" D frowned at him.

He frowned back. "What do mean? Why did I not go for it?"

She gave him a shrug-nod.

He considered his answer for a moment. "Well, she was Jack's girlfriend for all I knew, right? And even without that, quite honestly, she seemed a bit gaga to me. That kind of really turned me off." He let out a little laugh. "So, I suppose, you could say I was too scared."

"How come you never told me about this?" D wanted to know.

"I'm awfully sorry, but at the time I really didn't see any reason to inform *you* of all people, if that's what you mean. The only one that probably *would* have had a certain interest and even a right to know, was Jack. And I didn't really think it would come across so well if I told him. Like, *By the way, Jack… Might have earned me a bloody nose.*"

"Yeah…" D mumbled, lost in thought. "But still…"

"But still *what?*" Robert challenged. "Did you want me to tell you *after* Joe–" He paused for a moment. "Like, *By the way, Danielle, sorry about your boyfriend, but she's already tried the same thing with me too. Only that I didn't let it get to the point where I could have discovered her possibly irresistible talents…?*"

"It would still have been kind of interesting to know," D insisted, unwilling to let it go.

"Well, you know it now," Robert retorted and, with an encouraging smile, he took the pot from her that she had just dried.

# Dinner in Amsterdam

The weather in Amsterdam had cleared up and the ten minute walk to the restaurant felt good. Joe had just turned into the street where the restaurant was, when he heard a bike bell right behind him. It was Christine.

"I thought that was you!" she said a bit out of breath as she stopped and jumped off the bike. "I wasn't sure, though."

She let him kiss her on the cheek. "You gave up the real short haircut, huh?" she said as she looked at him. "Last time I saw you, it was this short..." Between her thumb and index finger she indicated a few millimeters. "And didn't you have a beard as well?"

Joe laughed. "Yeah, that look was just a lost bet kind of thing. I didn't end up liking it very much." The truth was that he had done both the haircut and the beard only to piss off Liz.

They walked the rest of the way together, with her pushing her bike. Joe was relieved to see that she was in an unexpectedly cheerful, not a suicidal mood. He had braced himself for an evening of comforting a sobbing girl, so this was a pleasant surprise.

He watched Christine lock her bike and then followed her into the restaurant. She had called ahead and reserved a table for two. They were seated in a secluded dimly-lit area with a candle on the table.

"I guess we're giving the wrong impression here," Christine joked once the waitress had disappeared.

"Seems like it..." he said with a weary glance at the two neighboring tables were couples were holding hands and looking at each other dreamy-eyed. Naïve idealists...

"Hey, what happened to your hand?" Christine frowned, her gaze on the brace around his right hand.

"Stupid accident," Joe said with a dismissive shrug. "Broke some fingers..."

"Ouch... that must have hurt!" Christine cringed at the mere thought. "But no, don't tell me the details, thank you..."

"Oh, why not?" Joe couldn't help laughing at her horrified face.

"Because it would spoil my appetite," she retorted. "Because it might make me faint, because it could make me throw up..."

"Oops, we don't want that!" he assured her with a grin.

"Sucks that it's the *right* hand..." she said.

"Yeah, that's the worst part actually. And I'm not all that great with my left hand *yet*. I'm learning, though. But the fractures supposedly are uncomplicated, so they should heal pretty well. And since I can at least still use the thumb and the index finger..." For demonstration he raised his hand and tipped the fingertips of the two intact fingers together right in front of her nose. "And the small finger, of course..." He stuck it out and made a stuck-up face with it. Christine laughed and opened her menu.

When the waitress came back, Joe ordered steak and fries, and Christine a soup and something French that he didn't know.

"You have to have some beer, too," she told him. "You never drink our beer when you're here, but you should. We're in Holland!"

"Okay, I'll have a beer this time."

As he watched the waitress stroll off, he tried to remember when he had last had any alcohol. He had kind of stayed away from it since things with Liz had started to get so crazy, and it had seemed crucial that at least one of them keep a clear head and some sort of control. But since that was over now, he may as well have a beer or two. He didn't even have to drive afterwards.

Christine's soup came right away.

"This is the first time in more than a week that I'm actually a bit hungry," she admitted as she dipped her spoon in. "Might be your influence."

"Oh, sure!" he laughed. "I'm famous for my appetite-enhancing effect on other people."

Chuckling, Christine dropped her gaze to her soup. She looked paler and skinnier than he remembered her. Her eyes were a bit swollen, probably from crying. But she definitely had an appetite and wasn't drowning in tears and grief at the moment. He was really glad about that because he wasn't sure how well he would have dealt with her having a breakdown here. He would have managed, of course, because she was a friend, but it would have been exhausting.

"Okay, we've talked about my broken fingers now," he said and took a quick swig from his beer. "What about your broken heart though? Or did you break his?"

She blinked at the unusual introduction but seemed okay with it.

"No..." she slowly said while stirring around in her soup. "He broke mine." She ate a spoonful, before she continued. "It's a bit complicated. Because actually–" Suddenly her voice failed her and she turned away, blinking frantically to chase away tears.

"Sorry!" She wiped the corner of her eye with her bent index finger and took a deep breath that she blew back out immediately, obviously trying her best to regain her composure. "Sometimes it still just... Well, it kind of comes in waves." She turned to look at him again, and a faint apologetic smile appeared on her face. "Sorry about that!"

"No problem!" Joe smiled. "We don't even have to talk about it if it..."

"No, it's fine. We can talk about it!" She paused for a moment, then she said, "He's in love with someone else."

Joe was still trying to come up with an appropriate reaction to what he had just heard, when Christine added: "And it's a guy from his work..."

Joe's eyes widened.

Christine must have known she would get this kind of reaction. "Yeah, it's not a tall blonde with big boobs!" she laughed, only to then fall silent abruptly as it hit her that this description, that she had just spontaneously made up, perfectly fit Liz.

Joe only realized it when he saw her embarrassed expression now.

"Sorry," she muttered, gritting her teeth. "I'm such an idiot! I really didn't mean to..."

Joe couldn't help laughing. "Don't worry about it! Doesn't sound like anyone *I* know..."

There was a moment of silence and a weak somewhat grateful smile before Christine returned to the initial subject. "He's been spending a lot of time with this guy," she explained. "At work and also afterwards. If it had been a woman, I would have probably been suspicious after a while, but this way..." She paused for a moment. "I was just kind of annoyed that he was gone so much, even during weekends, supposedly finishing work projects." There was a bitter little laugh before she continued, "Not in my wildest dreams would I have thought of that, though!"

She had finished her soup and put the spoon aside.

"I didn't like that guy at all," she told Joe. "Right from the start. I've met him a few times. And I normally don't have strong feelings about Peer's male workmates. But this one... Grrr... I didn't like him one bit and he didn't like me. He was good-looking but..." She exhaled audibly.

"Well, to make it short," she finally said, "it seems like this guy is Peer's love of his life now, so…" She shrugged. "I better deal with it." She choked up at this last comment and there were tears in her eyes again. She was struggling to hold them back.

"Crap," Joe huffed with a concerned look at her. "I'm so sorry!" He paused for a moment, not quite sure what to say. "I guess it doesn't matter if it's a tall blonde girl or a short bald guy, huh?" he said with a little wink. "Hurts either way…"

"Yeah…" With a weak smile she nodded. "Hurts either way."

The waitress came with the main course and took the soup bowl away.

Surprisingly Christine hadn't lost her appetite over the unhappy conversation. Joe was amazed at how she was digging into the mashed potatoes and the duck she had ordered. He glanced at his own steak and the French fries and realized that he didn't feel like eating much himself. That wasn't like him at all but given the circumstances it could be explained.

"The fact that it's a guy just makes it harder to understand, I think," Christine contemplated, her eyes on her food. "I try to tell myself, though, that if he's really into men, I couldn't have made it right, no matter what. And even if I miraculously happened to turn into a man overnight, I might not be his type…"

Joe nodded with a smile. "Yeah, there's always that risk, isn't there?"

"But you know what really bothers me most?" Christine shot a quick look up at him. "I keep asking myself… and actually some of my friends have asked me this too: did I never notice anything? During all that time… Did I never even suspect that he was gay?"

Joe decided not to comment on that. Picking up one of the French fries with his fingers, he thought of the time when he had first met Peer. Had he ever noticed anything? He actually had. At the very beginning. There had been a few things that Peer had done or said that had at least made him wonder. But then Peer had always been surrounded by plenty of girls. He had constantly had a girlfriend, sometimes even more than one. And then, half a year after his return to the Netherlands Peer must have met Christine. And they had lived happily ever after until obviously a week ago… Joe realized that he had completely forgotten about having any doubts regarding Peer's sexual orientation.

"I did–" Christine interrupted his thoughts. "I *did* notice some things, but I really didn't think about them much. Only in the light of what I know now, those things *do* kind of stick out." She shot Joe a quick glance. "Don't worry," she hurried to say, "I'm not planning to go into any more detail here! I'm just saying..." Her voice was failing again. "Man, I was such an–" She was fighting tears again. "Sorry!"

Joe gave her an encouraging smile. "Don't be sorry! A few *waves* like this are perfectly justified!"

"I can't help it anyway," she said with a helpless shrug. "It's just hard to realize that I spent almost five years and invested all these feelings in something that was probably wrong right from the start."

"Maybe it wasn't," Joe said. "It's hard to imagine that he could have just been pretending all that time."

"Well, maybe not," she admitted. "He says he didn't know it himself until a few months ago." She paused and put down her knife and fork, her food almost finished. "I'm not sure if he's being honest or just lying to make me feel better, but I guess it doesn't make a difference anymore. It's what it is and I can't change it."

Joe nodded at the wise approach, not sure what he could possibly add to that.

"I don't want to be friends with him, though," she said firmly. "I couldn't take that. It would just hurt. Because, as crazy as it may sound, I still miss him. Or maybe I just miss the routines we had..." She managed a weak smile. "I'm making progress, though. It's getting better... Especially since it dawned on me that maybe I haven't been all that happy with him anyway. I thought I was, but now I think I may have just been *content* and not *happy*."

Joe gave her a surprised look. "I guess there's a difference, huh?" he said more to himself than to her while trying to determine where exactly the line was between being content and being happy.

"I would have never thought of leaving Peer," she told him. "Contentment that we mix up with happiness is still a lot better than the unknown, I suppose." She bit her lip and looked at him, obviously not sure how he would deal with so much personal information.

"That sounds pretty poetic," he said and smiled.

She looked a little embarrassed now. "I wouldn't call it poetic, but thanks! Like I said, I'm making progress..."

"Yeah, you've got to give it some time," Joe said with a nod. The thought of patting her hand crossed his mind, but he resisted.

"Are you still in the flat?" he asked instead.

"I thought about moving out," she told him. "Mainly because everyone around me seems to think I need to. But two days ago I realized that I don't want to move. Not just because it's so much work but also because I like the place. And he doesn't want it. Sure, I'll change some things, and he still has to pick up his stuff – I'm not looking forward to that, by the way. But I decided that I'm going to stay there." She nodded as if she needed to confirm to herself that this was the right decision.

Suddenly her eyes fell on Joe's unfinished plate. "What's wrong with *your* appetite?" she asked. "I don't think I've ever seen *you* poke around in your food like that. Did I spoil your appetite with my stories?"

He shook his head. "No, it's not your fault!" he assured her. "I just wasn't really hungry."

Christine squinted at him. "Is that really all it is, or is something wrong?"

Joe looked back at her undecidedly. He really didn't feel ready to discuss with anyone just yet what was up with his own *horror love story*.

"There's something wrong, isn't there?" Christine diagnosed, not letting him out of her sight.

His eyes trailing off to the side now, he rubbed his cheek with his good hand, debating if he should just deny that there was anything wrong.

"Joe...?" Christine had leaned forward a bit.

Joe scratched his head. Now, did he really want to get into this?

"I left Liz," he finally said flatly without looking at her.

"Oh..." Christine was scrambling for words. "When was that???"

"This morning."

"Wow," Christine let herself fall back in her chair. "And you just sit here and let me talk..."

He gave her a little apologetic shrug. "Not my favorite topic, I guess."

"So, you don't want to talk about it then?" Christine asked.

He dropped his gaze. "I don't know," he said, playing with his fork. "Even if I wanted to talk about it, I wouldn't even know where to start."

Christine took a sip from her glass. "Start with...– Well, was it *you* breaking *her* heart or the other way around?"

Joe let out a little laugh. "Good question," he said. "Let's see... Regarding my heart I'm pretty sure it's not broken. If anything it's been dissolved in too much acid. And hers... – I'm not entirely sure she's got one."

"Wow," Christine sighed. "That's quite an assessment!"

"Well, maybe that wasn't totally fair," he admitted.

"How long have you been together?" Christine asked, ignoring the fairness issue.

"Too long," he said dryly. "Since you were talking about wasted years earlier..." He let out a bitter little laugh. "Three years down the drain here..."

"What happened?" she asked.

"Oh, I don't know," he shook his head, his eyes trailing off to the couple that was sharing a plate of chocolate mousse. "Nothing in particular," he said, "or everything, depending on the point of view." He bit down on his lower lip, trying to come up with something to say that would actually make any sense. "It's kind of hard to describe when you don't know her."

"Yeah, that's probably true," Christine nodded, apparently ready to drop the subject if he wanted to.

But then he didn't want to. Because it suddenly occurred to him that it wasn't true that Christine didn't know Liz. They had met once.

"What did *you* think about her the one time you've met her?" he asked.

Christine suddenly looked a bit uncomfortable. She shrugged, avoiding his gaze. "I don't know," she muttered. "It was just for one dinner... And it's kind of hard to judge someone after spending just a few hours with them. She's probably a lot different when you're alone."

Joe grinned. Not a happy grin. "Not a whole lot."

"Okay... Well, if you really want to know... I can't say I liked her very much. And I *did* kind of wonder why you two were together."

He gave her a questioning look. "Why was that?"

"Well... – how should I put this?" Christine seemed hesitant to spell out her thoughts. "You just didn't seem happy or... ahem... you didn't even really seem like yourself. Of course I didn't know you all that well then, but you'd always seemed like a pretty nice, laid back person. But that night you were... you seemed irritated, frustrated, tense, impatient..."

"Well, she brings out the best in me," he said with obvious sarcasm, "and maybe also the other way around."

Remembering that dinner two years ago still made him cringe. It had been horrible. Liz had initially said she wasn't coming. To punish him for something, or just out of spite. When she had realized that he was perfectly okay with going out by himself, she had suddenly decided she'd join him after all. Because who knew if he was really just meeting friends!?!

81

They had been late, of course, because it had taken her forever to get ready. She had ended up strutting into that restaurant looking like Glamour Barbie. And she had behaved like a stuck-up bitch.

"So, have you met someone else?" Christine interrupted his thoughts.

He shook his head. "No, there's no one else. At least not on my side. On her side, yeah, there's a whole bunch of guys." He shrugged. "But that's only a side-topic, really. There were so many other problems…" He paused for a moment. "I don't even know where to begin. Take what you've seen of her and add alcohol, pills and a possible mental problem to it – borderline or whatever they call it…" He sucked in a quick breath that he released while rubbing his forehead. "Or maybe it's not even all her fault. Who knows? Maybe it's *me* that causes her to be like that, I don't know. I simply don't know. Maybe I'm even going crazy myself…"

"Well, you seem pretty sane and stable to me," Christine said, "but if you're already having doubts about that, it's probably a good thing that you left."

His eyes trailing to the side again, he nodded. "Yeah, I guess."

"You haven't really moved out yet, though, or have you?" Christine asked.

"No, I just packed a few things and left. And after this trip I'm going to visit my sister. That should give me some time to figure out what I wanna do. And regarding my stuff, I packed what I really need, and if it comes down to it, she can keep the rest."

He picked up his glass and took a sip of his beer. It was warm by now and tasted pretty disgusting.

Christine's face had brightened up. "That's good!" she said cheerfully. "Get away, be with family… and you still have friends there too, right?"

"I guess." He nodded. "I haven't been in touch much lately but yes, there are some friends. In fact, they're having a get-together next weekend. Maybe that's what inspired me to go…"

"Sounds like perfect timing to me!" Christine laughed and patted his hand.

# Such a Nice Guy!

"So, Danielle, why didn't you bring your friend tonight? What's his name?"

It was almost nine, the birthday cake had been diminished to only a quarter of its size, and everyone seemed tired and slightly paralyzed from all the food. Only Aunt Sauvie had just come back to life. She was a night person, and she was a friendly but slightly nosy woman. Being their late grandmother's sister, and their Mom's godmother, she was a regular guest at most family gatherings.

"Was it *Peter*?" Aunt Sauvie squinted trying to recall that nice guy's name.

D managed a forced smile. "No, Aunt Sauvie, I didn't bring him today," she said through gritted teeth. "And his name is Pete."

"Ah yes, Pete..." Aunt Sauvie beamed. "He's such a pleasant and smart young man."

"Oh, I know," D said, having a hard time masking her irritation with a friendly smile.

"And he's got a good job, too," Aunt Sauvie remembered.

"Yeah, he does," D said, the smile slowly hurting her face because it was such a struggle to keep it up. "But I've got a good job myself!"

"Yes, young women are so independent nowadays," Aunt Sauvie contemplated, "and I guess that's good. But still, once you have children, it's important that the man..."

"Aunt Sauvie," Robert interrupted in a joking tone, trying to come to his sister's rescue. "You *do* need to stop because you're scaring Danielle..." He laughed and so did Ann.

"Well, at some point you *do* want to get married and have children, though?" Aunt Sauvie looked from D to Robert to Ann and then back to D, while the three of them were shooting each other concerned looks and shrugged.

"Maybe. At some point..." Ann and D answered almost simultaneously; then they looked at each other and burst out laughing, which kind of cut the tension.

When Robert asked Aunt Sauvie now how the apricots and figs in her garden were coming along, and she started describing in most enthusiastic terms the almost completed ripening progress, and how Robert and Ann and whoever else wanted, should soon come by to harvest some of the fruit, the topic had successfully been changed.

Around nine-thirty the party ended. Everyone was getting ready to leave and D's Dad slipped into his shoes to drive Aunt Sauvie home.

With all the guests gone, D, Robert, their Mom and Ann cleared the last dishes from the dining table.

"I'll walk with you a little ways," D said, pulling on her jacket as Robert and Ann were ready to walk home. "I need some air after all that food. You wanna come too, Mom?"

Her Mom, looking tired but happy, shook her head and dropped onto the sofa, flapping her arms to her sides. "No, I think I'll just sit here for a moment and enjoy the quiet house."

Robert and Ann lived just a fifteen minute walk away. It was good to get out and take a few steps. The air was still warm and it was a clear night. Walking next to her brother and his girlfriend, D realized that for the first time in ages, she was walking next to this couple, not being part of a couple herself. For a long time it had always been her and Pete. Strangely enough, though, what she felt at this moment was a delightful sense of freedom.

"Why didn't you just tell the old crow that she'll never see Pete again?" Robert suddenly asked as if he could read her mind.

She shrugged.

"Or has that changed?"

"No, that hasn't changed," D said with quick shake of her head. "I just wasn't in the mood to discuss it over coffee and then deal with her shock at this horrible misjudgment of mine. *How could you? He was so perfect...*" She made an almost perfect imitation of Aunt Sauvie's voice.

Robert and Ann both laughed.

"Yeah." Robert chuckled. "You can't deny that Pete's a real big hit with aunts and grandparents!"

"Definitely," D said dryly.

"It's his gentlemanly manner, my dear," Robert said, doing his own Aunt-Sauvie-impersonation. "And his good job and his great *I've-gotta-compensate-for-something* car..." he carried it further. It earned him a scolding look from Ann.

"Anything you want to tell me here?" D challenged.

84

"No, no!" Robert reached out and patted her shoulder reassuringly. "You know I'm actually so glad you didn't think he was material to…" and now he fell back into Aunt Sauvie tone, *"get married to and have children with."*

D nodded, lost in thought.

"What's wrong?" Robert suddenly noticed her grave face.

She shook her head. "Nothing."

"When you say *nothing* like that–"

With an exasperated sigh, D shrugged. "No, it's *not* nothing," she admitted grudgingly. "The thing is that I'm still kind of struggling to get him to accept it."

Robert smacked his tongue. "You're kidding, right!? I thought he took it so well."

"Initially it seemed like it, yeah. But that was only because he thought – and I quote here," she tried to mimic Pete, "that I'm *just confused and in a bad mood, and I will take it all back very soon.*"

"Which you didn't," Robert concluded in a hopeful voice.

"No." She shook her head. "And he doesn't understand. And he doesn't want to understand and …well, *how can I not see how perfect we were together?* Blah blah blah… Anyway, I'm actually too tired right now to discuss this. It just makes me mad. Can we talk about it some other time?"

"Sure," Robert said, biting down on his lower lip, as if he was having a hard time postponing everything he had to contribute to this topic to a time that was more convenient for his sister.

"I actually think I'll say good night here," D suddenly said and came to a halt. Robert and Ann stopped beside her.

"Okay. Good night", Robert took his arm off Ann and gave D a hug. "Sleep well in your old room. We'll see you tomorrow."

# Morning Sun Sneezes

Joe stretched and looked over at Christine. She was still asleep. But now that he had moved, she seemed to be entering the waking-up phase as well.

"What time is it?" she mumbled without opening her eyes.

"Eight-thirty," he said.

Pulling the sheet up to her neck, she turned his way and opened her eyes, blinking rapidly. "Where am I? Who are you? How did I get here?" She delivered these questions with a fake clueless look.

Joe grinned as he propped himself up on his elbow and brushed a strand of hair from her forehead with his other hand. "It won't help you at all if you pretend you had nothing to do with this…"

When they had left the restaurant it had still been warm outside. Joe had truly enjoyed the evening. Amazingly, telling someone about leaving Liz had improved his mood immensely. He had felt liberated and strangely revived. Also Christine's mood seemed to be excellent now. And since there was a clear and present danger that, once she got on her bike and went home and once he returned to his hotel room, they might both fall back into the black hole they had just crawled out of, it seemed stupid to let the evening end just yet.

After a moment of undecidedly standing outside the restaurant with Christine pulling the key for her bike lock out of her purse, they decided to take a stroll towards the square in front of his hotel together and get an ice cream cone there.

They ended up sitting in the square, eating their ice cream and chatting. And once the ice cream was gone, they just stayed on their bench, talking about all kinds of things, laughing, watching the square and all the people in it. They hardly noticed it getting cooler and the square starting to be less busy. Finally it was almost midnight and Joe realized that – as much as they might like to – they couldn't stay on that bench forever. Even if they both seemed to dread leaving. Of course there was an alternative to saying goodbye. And it wasn't staying glued to that bench and freezing their butts off. After all, he had a big hotel room just across that square… The idea had crossed his mind more than once over the last two hours. And it was tempting in more than just one way. But God, he couldn't seriously be considering making a move on Christine, who had just lost her boyfriend to another guy and who was, after all, a friend... It was ludicrous! Especially since it had been barely twelve hours since he had broken up with Liz. If Christine had any idea what he was thinking, she would probably never even talk to him again.

"Okay..." Christine finally said with a sigh, pulling him out of his thoughts. "You look like you're about to nod off. I guess I better leave and let you go to bed."

Instead of getting up, though, she glanced over at him, her eyes locking with his.

"I wasn't really nodding off," he assured her, dropping his gaze, "just thinking..."

"About what?"

"Oh, just... nothing important," he lied, desperately hoping that she couldn't read his mind.

There was a moment of silence in which he stared at the ground and she played with the clasp of her purse.

"What if I didn't feel like going home now?" she asked quietly.

His eyes shot up at her, his mind briefly blank.

"I haven't felt that good in a long time," she said with a little shrug. "And I'm pretty sure that won't last once I go home."

His gaze trailing back towards the square, Joe exhaled. Finally he nodded. "I know..." he said and turned to look at her again.

"Would you take me with you?" Her voice was a little shaky, but she held his gaze.

"Would I take you with me?" Joe repeated slowly, his eyes trailing off again as that made it easier to think. What now? Wasn't that exactly what he had wanted? What was he waiting for? Something held him back.

"I usually don't do this kind of thing," Christine assured him, almost sounding embarrassed. "Actually no, I've *never* done this kind of thing before. But tonight... Well, really ... what would be wrong with it?"

Joe let out a nervous little laugh. "Okay, let's see–" He cleared his throat. "I can't deny that the thought *has* crossed my mind as well. It's tempting. Really, no doubt about it!" He gave her a firm look. "But... is this really – I mean, it doesn't seem like such a great idea amongst friends, does it?"

Christine shrugged. "Probably not. But if I had the choice between you and some stranger, I'd definitely pick you."

Joe was still fighting with himself, without really knowing why. Ten minutes ago he had wanted exactly that, hadn't he?

"There's no strings attached, I promise," Christine told him, "I'm not looking for a new relationship and neither are you."

"Not really," Joe mumbled suddenly feeling a big weight being lifted. That had been the key, hadn't it? No strings attached. That's what he needed. No strings attached and no expectations deriving from whatever they decided to do in his hotel room.

"And we wouldn't be hurting anyone," Christine pointed out. "So, what would be wrong with it?"

Joe decided right then that there would be *absolutely* nothing wrong with it.

"Sure, I would like to take you with me," he said truthfully. "Who wouldn't?"

With a smile, he got up from the bench and offered her his hand. She let him pull her up.

"As far as I know I'm paying for a parking spot in the hotel garage," he said, taking her bike, "so, if you're looking for a place for this…"

They walked across the square in silence with him pushing her bike. They parked the bike in the garage and took the elevator up to his room.

Without turning on the light they stood in the semi-dark entryway for a moment.

"You *sure* about this?" Joe had asked as he had gently put his hands on her hips. Instead of an answer she had placed her hands around his face and kissed him. If he had still needed a spark, that kiss and her pressing her body against him had been it. No holding back after that. They landed in bed together without any further considerations within less than three minutes.

Pulling the sheet over her eyes now, Christine sneezed. "The morning sun…" she mumbled.

"Oh, is *that* what it is?" Joe chuckled. He slipped into his underwear and got up to open the curtains enough to actually let a bit of the morning sun in. "Go ahead," he told Christine as a few rays of sun illuminated the bed. "N*ow* you can sneeze…"

She pretended two more little sneezes and sat up, holding the sheet up to her neckline. She took a deep breath and looked at him with a weary smile. "It's probably totally inappropriate to say this," she said. "But thanks for not sending me home last night. It was… great!"

"Well, same here!" Joe laughed.

"Wow, I've never done this kind of thing before!" She shook her head at herself. "Maybe I *did* actually miss out on something."

Perched at the desk, Joe decided not to reveal to her that after a one-nightstand, being able to still look at each other, let alone have a normal conversation, wasn't exactly the norm. And that the only reason why they still seemed to be okay in that regard was probably that they had neither been drunk last night, nor strangers, nor stumbling into this expecting it to be the start of a long and happy relationship.

"I would say we can do this again," she said fishing for her bra, her underwear and her T-shirt that were lying on the floor next to the bed, "but I'm afraid we might endanger the *no-strings-attached* motto if we did."

Joe slowly nodded, amazed at her honestly. "Yep, there'd be a risk, I'm afraid…"

She laughed. Holding the sheet up to her chin, she put on the bra and her panties and finally slipped into her T-shirt. Then she pulled back the sheets and swung her legs out of the bed.

Joe watched her, feeling a wave of confusion hit him. For a short moment there he had been scared to death that she might declare the *no-strings-attached* rule void. In that case he would have welcomed it if she left right away. Now that she had actually confirmed that it still applied, he suddenly felt like spending some more time with her… Oh boy, he was all screwed up!

"So, what are you going to do today?" he asked as he handed her her pants that had been lying to his feet.

She shrugged. "I don't know. No special plans. And you?"

He watched her pull on her pants and put her hair up in a ponytail.

"I don't really have to be anywhere until five thirty for a business party," he said slowly. "So… I mean… you really don't have to leave right away."

"Oh, okay…" Christine gave him an undecided look. "Do you want to…– I don't know – …do something together still?"

"Sure. If you feel like it." He smiled. "You could always stay for breakfast and we could do something afterwards…"

Christine thought about it for a moment. Then she smiled back at him and nodded. "I guess we could. But if we do that, I better take a quick shower here."

# D's Sunday Afternoon

It was almost two in the afternoon when D drove home from her parents.

They had all gone out for breakfast to a nice countryside café that her Mom had wanted to try for a long time. The food had been excellent and the area really pretty, so they had stayed around and gone for a walk there afterwards.

All in all, she had had a great time with her family. They were always easy to be with. And it was good to see her Mom and Dad enjoying themselves again so much after the tough last year they had had with her Dad going through chemo and the scare the cancer had caused for everyone.

When she got home it was still warm and sunny outside. She had kind of planned to get something done in her bedroom, but as she stepped into the flat now, she dropped that idea. It was far too nice to spend the rest of the afternoon inside. She could always do the bedroom the next time it rained. As long as she still had enough space in the bed for herself, that was sufficient.

She got something to drink out of the fridge and sat on one of her bar stools, turning it to where she could look out the window behind the bar counter. Outside she could see her neighbor taking Tiffany for a walk – scarf and hair clip in blue today.

D's gaze fell on the blue London folder on the dining table next to the window, where she had put it before leaving for the birthday party. She should look at it finally. June was for sure going to ask her about it on Monday.

She was just slipping off her chair to get the folder when she heard her mobile phone ring from her purse on the coffee table. She clicked her jaws together and drew in an angry breath. Without any doubt that was Pete again. Even though she really didn't want to deal with him now she went over to the sofa and fished the phone out. By the time she held it in her hand, it had already stopped ringing. And she realized that the call had actually not been from Pete but from Jack.

Her first impulse was to call him right back. But then she stopped herself as it had suddenly occurred to her that Jack might be calling to see how she had digested the news of Sarah's brother's looming visit. Jack knew as well as Sarah that she absolutely didn't want to see Joe. And with some bad luck Jack would (just like Sarah and Robert) want to give her some good advice how to best handle it.

She was still weighing if to call Jack back or not when the phone in her hand vibrated from a message coming in.

> *Do U want to drive with me Wed night. I'd pick u and Sun up. Just want to make sure u are still coming...*
>
> *Jack*

Smiling to herself, she responded,

> *Why would you think I might not be coming anymore??? ;) Driving together sounds good.*
>
> *D*

She put the phone down and shot a look out through the window towards the deck and the backyard. Maybe she should just try not to think about Joe until it was absolutely unavoidable – which would be on Wednesday just before she left for the grill party. Yes, that would be early enough to worry about it. For right now a little work-out might be advisable, such as a bike ride to the lake and a quick swim before the sun went down. She could bring the London folder and look at it there.

She quickly changed into her bikini and a dress, grabbed a bag, stuffed her big towel into it, placed the London folder on top, slid her wallet and the phone into an outside pocket and took off.

The fifteen minute bike ride to the lake led through some fields, up a little hill and then through a forest.

There were only a few people still at the lake when she arrived, and some of them were just in the process of packing up their stuff to leave. She spread out her towel on the ground and slipped out of her dress. Sometime she came here after work when most people had already gone home and enjoyed the evening sun and the quiet.

Barefoot she walked the few meters down to the lake, went out on the pier and then took a step off it and let herself drop into the dark green water. Once she re-surfaced, she swam to the wooden float anchored in the middle of the lake, took a short break and then swam back.

Out of breath she returned to her towel, dried herself off and laid the towel out again. She grabbed the London folder and stretched out on the towel, lying on her stomach and propping herself up on her elbows. Okay. Time to look through that folder… Harry had handed it out six weeks ago during his presentation on the London project. They were finally determined to get the London branch of their company going. The folder contained information on the location of the new offices, on the layout, on the team that was already there – headed by Harry's brother David – and details regarding the three available jobs. Harry hadn't made a big secret out of the fact that, for the company, the ideal arrangement would be if D and June transferred there for two years or so. June had jumped aboard right away. D had been flattered but had rejected the idea, citing her relationship with Pete and her flat as main reasons. Harry had accepted that and said that they were going to put an ad in the paper to fill the remaining two jobs.

It was June who had still not given up trying to persuade D, especially since she had gotten wind of the split-up with Pete.

Going through the folder now, D found that it didn't contain anything she didn't already know. The new offices were located close to Liverpool station – just a few blocks from where Pete had been staying during their time as exchange students. The job description of the positions in London matched exactly what June and she were currently doing in Swan&Co's headquarters in Deens, only for a different market. The company offered to help with the apartment search in London. In fact, as far as D knew, June had already received a few interesting–looking links from David's assistant. Travels home for Christmas and Easter would be paid for, plus three additional flights home over the course of the year; twice a week they appeared to have lunch catered to the office and on Friday they quit work around two… All in all, it sounded like a nice arrangement.

Lost in *what-if* considerations regarding London, D was glancing towards the lake, when the phone started ringing again in her bag. She closed the folder and sat up. Once she pulled the phone out, she could see Pete smiling from the display. Great. She better just deal with it! She picked it up.

"Hi Pete…" she said as friendly and cheerfully as she could.

"Danielle? Hi." He sounded surprised to actually hear her voice instead of the mailbox.

"Hi, Pete," she repeated patiently.

"Are you ignoring me now or what?"

"I'm not ignoring you," she said trying to stick to her plan to stay calm and friendly and not get caught up in a discussion with him. "I've just been kind of busy every time you called. One time I missed it because I was in the shower, then Sarah was here and last night was my Mom's birthday party. I stayed there overnight, just got home."

"Right – your Mom's birthday," Pete muttered, "everyone alright?"

"Yeah, everyone's fine," D said, knowing that he wasn't really interested in the answer. "Robert cooked. It was great."

"Well, great," he said in a non-committal tone as if to quickly be done with this subject. "You could have called me back, though..."

Obviously. She could have called him back. She hadn't.

"You could have sent me a message or left a voice mail," she countered, knowing that this was, of course, a bit lame.

There was silence on the other end.

"So, you're back from your trip..." D said, trying to divert the attention to a different topic, although she didn't even remember where he had been and for which purpose. She just knew it had been some kind of business trip. "How was it?"

"It was okay," he said curtly, "nothing spectacular..." There was a short pause before he added: "I've been trying to reach you since I got back Friday night." He wasn't ready to let this go, of course.

"Yeah, I know." She allowed for a trace of guilt. "What's so important then?"

"Well, if it had really been important I'd be screwed by now anyway," he responded snappily. "It doesn't always have to be something important, does it?"

"No, guess not," she said, wondering if she had overreacted or this was his manipulating her into thinking so.

"Anyway, now that I've finally got you on the line, there are two things I'd like to talk to you about..."

Just from his tone she sensed that she probably wouldn't like what was coming. "Okay..." she said questioningly.

"Well..." he started, "I've actually been trying to reach you because I thought I might be able to come by your place sometime this weekend and get my stuff. But since I could never reach you..."

"Oh... Okay." D didn't quite know what to say as the first thing that came to mind was, *Thank God it's too late for that now!*

"I guess I could still come by now," she heard him contemplate on the other end, "but of course, it's already kind of late, and if I left now, and then afterwards I'd still have to drive home..."

D straightened up, suddenly on high alert. Sarah's words were ringing in her ears. But no, he couldn't seriously be trying to invite himself to stay overnight, could he?

With her free hand she grabbed the next-best rock from the ground beside her towel and threw it into the lake.

"What do you think?" Pete asked innocently.

"Tonight isn't really good for me," she said slowly.

"Why? What are you doing?" There was an accusing edge to the question.

D sucked in a quick breath. She felt the anger start to burn in her stomach. It was none of his business what she was doing. Why couldn't he finally start playing by the new rules? Not being together anymore should change the rules, shouldn't it?

"Are you going out?" he pushed.

"No, I'm not going out," she said a bit snappily.

"Hot new guy coming by, huh?" He made it sound like a joke, but D wasn't quite sure that it was one.

"What makes you think there's just one?" she replied copying his tone.

"Well, what's the problem then, if I quickly swing by?" he wanted to know.

Biting down on her lower lip, D tried to keep herself from losing her composure and slipping into hissing or yelling. This was hardly the place for it. Had she been in her home with the windows closed she may have let it out, and it would undoubtedly have opened up a whole new can of worms... *Why are you so mad at me? You're so angry sometimes...*

She was angry, yes. Because she had wanted him to pick up his stuff (clothes, toiletry things and other knickknacks he still had at her place) for the past months and a half. Ever since they had broken up. And she had also asked him more than once to please bring along *her* things from *his* flat – a pair of slacks, a blouse, pajamas and some makeup stuff. He had come by twice and then always *forgotten* to take his stuff with him. And he had never even mentioned hers let alone brought it. So, she was very, very angry. But she was going to control herself!

"Do you need your stuff so badly suddenly that it's worth driving all this way to just quickly pick it up?" she asked as calmly as she could.

95

"Well, I thought I could pick up my stuff and maybe spend a little time with you. We could go out to eat if you haven't eaten. Or do something else. What's wrong with that? I mean – I thought we were still friends…"

So, there it was. Of course there was no 'quickly coming by'. Picking up his stuff was just an excuse to be able to pay her a visit that he would try to drag out as long as he could – maybe (and this was Sarah speaking now) even overnight.

Letting out a controlled breath through her nose, while ramming a pointed rock into the soft soil next to her towel, D tried to decide how to handle this.

"But as a friend it should be possible for me to tell you that tonight really doesn't work for me," she pointed out.

"Fine," he growled, "even though I quite honestly don't understand why you can't make some time for me if you're not going out and no one else is coming by…"

"I want to finish something for work tonight, okay? I'm kind of in the middle of it now."

"Sounds like you're outside somewhere," he countered.

D drew in an audible, irritated breath. "Yes," she said sharply, "I'm at the lake – alone, by the way – looking through a folder from work and then I will go home and work on this some more."

"What is it?"

"Company secrets! If I tell you they'll hunt us both down and kill us…"

He didn't laugh. "Pretty bad if they now even make you work on weekends!" he said testily. "I told you, you should have taken that job at my Uncle's company. It would have been perfect…"

"I happen to like my job," she said through clenched teeth, barely keeping herself from yelling. "And no, *they* don't make me work on Sundays. I just want to finish this because it's interesting for me…"

Silence.

"Pete, you already said yourself that even for *you* tonight isn't ideal because you'd still have to drive back home." This was her way of telling him that he shouldn't even think about maybe being able to stay overnight. She was just hoping she had been clear enough. She would hate to have to be any clearer…

"Okay, whatever!" he snapped, "I get it!"

The silence that followed was hard to take.

It was like a stand-off. D realized that her first impulse was to take a step back now. Do something that would make her feel less guilty and make him feel better. Like offer him to come sometime next week, in the evening, not just to pick up his stuff but also for dinner, she could cook… Not because she thought she'd enjoy it, but because she felt like she needed to make it up to him, compensate him for being so bitchy. The only thing that stopped her was the looming problem of him then possibly wanting to stay overnight.

"What about next weekend," Pete inquired sourly. "May I get an appointment then or is one week notice still not enough?"

D bit her lip and swallowed a scathing remark. "I've got my thing with Sarah and Jack and them next weekend," she said instead. "I'm pretty sure I told you about that…"

"Ah yes, *that*," he said condescendingly. "That doesn't last all weekend, though, right?"

"Pretty much," D retorted. "It lasts from Friday afternoon till Sunday night, and there's a grill party on Wednesday night."

"Great!" Pete huffed angrily. "Where is that thing anyway? In Deens?"

"No, it's at the resort at that lake where your parents went for their anniversary two years ago."

"Oh, really? That's a pretty spendy place," he said it almost like he couldn't believe she was so wasteful with her money.

"Rick got us a good deal," she informed him. "Knows the owner or something."

"I see," Pete said, obviously already pondering something else. "Well, maybe you can drive there with someone else and I could pick you up early on Sunday and we could do something together then."

D was squirming on her towel. Couldn't that thing be on the moon and his space ship temporarily broken?

"I really don't want to leave early. I'm sorry." She wasn't sorry at all.

"I'd just like to see you, I guess," Pete admitted with a big portion of hurt in his voice.

"I know," she said, trying for a softer tone, "but is us spending time together really such a good idea at this point? I mean– Really?"

"I don't see why not?" he said like that was a no-brainer. "If we're still friends…"

She didn't agree. And neither would anyone in their right minds.

"And if there's no one else, I don't see any reason at all why we can't spend time together," he pushed, sounding like a pouting little kid. "But then again, I still don't see the reason why we can't *be* together! We were a great team, we had a lot of fun and then you go and throw it all away…"

Great. Here we go again, D thought. This just seemed to go in circles. All the time. Always the same. But today she was determined to avoid getting sucked into the discussion about her motives for ending their relationship and the validity of those motives. She bit her lip and forced herself to keep quiet.

"Anyway," Pete finally said darkly, "I actually also wanted to ask you a favor." He paused. "But I can probably save myself the effort, because you'll say no anyway."

D sucked in a quick breath. "God, stop being so… Just say what it is, would you?"

There was a short pause in which Pete obviously weighed if he would rather pout some more or pursue whatever favor he had wanted to ask.

"Our firm's summer party is coming up again. It's also the 25-year anniversary," he finally grumbled.

Her jaws tightly locked, D closed her eyes. She unfortunately knew *exactly* where this was going…

"Well," he sounded very uncomfortable now, like he wasn't even sure if he dared to continue. D wasn't sure if it was authentic or fake hesitation, though.

"I was kind of hoping we could go together," he told her, "like the last few years… I'd just hate to go there alone. And everybody's bringing someone."

"I don't know," D said half-heartedly.

"It's just–" Pete was sounding helpless now. "It would be just as friends, I promise. And it would definitely be the last time I'd ever ask you that kind of thing, don't worry!"

D concluded that no one at his work had any idea that they had split up. Not that it really was any of their business. And maybe guys didn't discuss personal matters at work like she and June did.

In the back of her head she could hear Sarah whispering "Manipulation, manipulation…" Still, she wasn't sure she could live with herself if she told him no.

"When is it?" she finally asked, "and where?"

A few minutes later she hung up, slightly disillusioned with herself.

Her gaze fell onto the blue folder again. And suddenly she saw with total clarity that she should apply for the job in London. She would be an absolute idiot not to. It was heaven-sent, at exactly the right time. She needed a change in her life! Get away for two years, possibly more. She had always liked London as a city. And it wasn't going to hurt career-wise either. Above all it, would solve the problem of having to keep Pete at arm's length and feeling crappy about it. Once in London she would be far enough away so he couldn't just drop by…

Motivated by her decision, she got up from the towel and walked back down to the lake and out to the end of the pier. And even though the sun had gone down already, she flung herself into the water, diving in head-first, arms stretched over her, pushing deep into the green lake. For a moment there, she just let herself fall, be cradled by the water all around her, feeling weightless. Then, as she was running out of air, she swam to the surface. Once her head was above water again, she turned onto her back. Paddling a bit with her hands and legs, she kept herself afloat while her eyes just zoned out towards the weirdly-shaped clouds in the sky. Her mind was made up. She was going to get her application for London prepared as soon as she got home this evening. With her having so far rejected the idea of being sent over there, HR had run the job-ad in the paper once already and would do so again over the next few weeks. So, the sooner she let Harry know that she had changed her mind and was interested, the less danger there was that someone else might snatch the job away from her.

# Party and Pills

Joe took another appetizer from the tray that the nicely dressed lady from the catering firm was holding out to him. It was SCANY's annual summer party where everyone – including all the business partners – seemed to be invited. He wouldn't have come to Amsterdam just for that, but since he was in town and Jan knew it, he pretty much had to attend.

He had arrived at the party a little late. Christine had persuaded him to take the train to the coast to Zandvoort. It had been fun. Windy, sunny and relaxed. Only getting back had been quite stressful as the train had had a mechanical problem. They had arrived in Amsterdam almost half an hour later than planned, and they still had to get back to the hotel for Christine to pick up her bike and for him to get changed.

In the hurry he had slipped into his shirt in such a clumsy way that he had gotten his broken fingers caught in the sleeve somehow. It had hurt like hell and he had had to sit down for a moment until the pain had subsided enough so he could finish getting dressed and call a taxi.

Joe had been at the party for an hour and a half now. After a quick chat with Jan and his wife, he had exchanged a few words with the few SCANY employees he knew better, then he had gotten a second glass of wine and stumbled into a somewhat comical conversation about Dutch beer with one of Jan's Italian customers, Luigi, and Anders, one of SCANY's IT people. It had ben fascinating to see Luigi, who didn't speak much English, get his point across perfectly by using gestures, facial expressions and some nice-sounding Italian. After the beer talk, Joe had wandered around some more and finally come to lean against a concrete column that was somewhat hidden behind a big plant. His hand was starting to really bother him. It had hurt ever since he had left his hotel room and, unlike on the previous afternoon, it didn't seem to be getting any better by itself tonight. It actually seemed to be getting worse.

Sipping his wine, he wondered if leaving right now would be very rude. He had no desire to immerse himself in any more small talk. A quick look around convinced him that no one would miss him if he left. So he downed the last sip of wine and was just pushing himself away from the column, ready to take off, when a young woman came up to him and commented on how he seemed to be hiding behind the plant. He laughed politely and said that he had indeed been hiding.

"Well, I guess you weren't hiding well enough," she said. And then she started a conversation about the weather in Amsterdam being almost as bad as it was in Edinburgh where she was from. Even though Joe didn't contribute much more than one-syllable responses, she merrily kept on talking and finally confided in him how she seemed to somehow always wake up hung over after Jan's parties. That's when Joe decided it was time to go. Because somehow he couldn't help detecting a slightly flirtatious note that seemed to have snuck into her tone (maybe he was just imagining it, though) and he wasn't really in the mood to have a flirt right now. Not when the pain in his hand was starting to drive him crazy.

The way he excused himself surely didn't make the young woman's day, but so be it.

When he climbed out of the taxi in front of his hotel half an hour later, all he could think of anymore was the painkillers.

In his room he took off his suit jacket and ripped off the tie. He peeled out of his shirt, being extra careful with his hand and stripped down to his underwear.

In the bathroom he dug the sheet of sealed pills out from his toiletry case. He looked at them for a moment. The doctor had said he could take two, but after reading the leaflet yesterday, maybe he should only try one at first. Especially since he had just had two glasses of wine at the party.

He pressed a pill out of the blister pack and washed it down with half a glass of water. Then he brushed his teeth and returned to the bedroom.

Sitting on the bed, he turned on the TV and flipped through the channels. There was going to be a good movie on TV in half an hour.

He reached for his laptop that had been sitting on the bedside table and turned it on. He could as well check his e-mails and read the online news while waiting for the movie to start.

He had hardly gotten onto the hotel's Wireless when he started feeling slightly drowsy. He had a hard time keeping his eyes open and an even harder time remembering the password to his e-mail account. He rubbed his eyes and struggled to focus. His hand was starting to feel better, which was nice, but at the same time it was almost impossible to think a clear thought or come up with the energy to move. Everything seemed to be happening in slow motion.

With some effort he lifted the laptop back to the bedside table and slid down on the bed, his head sinking into the pillow. He would just lie down for a while...

# Monday at Work

From the moment D turned on her computer at work, it was clear that this was going to be a crazy Monday morning. It started with the computer system being down for reasons that even to the IT department seemed to be in the dark. And while the experts were frantically trying to fix it, everyone else was feeling lost with neither e-mail nor access to any of their documents on the server.

D had had a clear plan for this morning or at least for the first half an hour that she usually had the office to herself before June arrived around eight-thirty. The plan had been to send the London application off to Harry. She had prepared it the evening before. She had revised her resume and composed a short e-mail/cover letter and then forwarded everything to her work e-mail address so she could read through it again in the morning before sending it off.

With the system being down, her application e-mail was still stuck somewhere and the plans had to be changed. It really bothered her because she just knew that, once the computer system worked again, she would be swamped with incoming e-mails and other things and there wouldn't be any time to deal with the application. She could always send it off on Tuesday morning instead, of course. It wasn't a big deal. Still, it made her nervous. Because she was afraid that she might still change her mind…

June blew in around nine, totally stressed out and babbling something about how Jim had turned off her alarm clock and how that's why she had overslept.

The mention of Jim immediately made D frown. "Which Jim?" she asked skeptically. "Not *that* Jim!?!"

June nodded, confirming that *that* Jim had obviously gotten close enough to her bed again to turn off the alarm clock.

"Man, June… Not *that* Jim again!" D shuddered. It must have been almost three months now since June had sat in that exact same chair, her eyes brimming with tears, ranting about how Jim had suddenly felt that he should return to his ex-ex-ex-girlfriend, the one he had a kid with. It hadn't been the first time that Jim had suddenly taken off. It had been the first time, though, that he had done so not to chase after a new girl but out of some sense of responsibility for anyone or anything. And that, for some silly reason, had made D believe that she might have finally heard the last of Jim. She had gotten used to his disappearing and reappearing from June's life over the two years June and she had been sharing the office but, somehow, this time it had seemed like Jim might be gone for good. Obviously she had been wrong! Jim was back – again!

D had long given up trying to understand the motives June had for getting back together with him again and again. It seemed to be some sort of game – on both sides...

"Just happened," June said lightly. "I ran into him in the pub on Main Street Saturday night. And he's single again and so am I. So, why not?"

"Yeah right, why not?" D said with a hint of sarcasm that June completely missed.

"I don't object to a nice time with an old friend," June said with a meaningful smile. "Life is short!" She shrugged. "And the sex is always great... Maybe we'll even go and spend the coming weekend at his parents get-away. The one with the pool and the sauna."

D cringed at the casual way the words *friends* and *sex* had just been linked together. "Just don't get too attached to Jim again, okay," she recommended, "because we know that he's like a bird..." She made some fluttering movement with her hands. "Or a bee..."

June laughed. "Yeah, I know. Just want to have a bit of fun. Nothing serious. I'll be leaving for London in six or eight months, so... Still, why not have some fun with good old Jim."

D decided to abstain from commenting. June was grown-up. "Speaking of London," she said instead. "I think I might apply after all."

"Really?" June clapped her hands together. "You are? Oh that's great news!"

D felt almost a little embarrassed by June's enthusiasm. "Yeah, I had another look at the folder over the weekend," she said, "and... well, it *does* look kind of tempting."

"Yeah, doesn't it?" June was all thrilled. "I told you! And even if you're not a hundred percent sure yet, just apply at least. Nothing's going to be cast in stone. In two weeks we're going to London for that conference anyway and then we can check it all out, talk to David and stuff. I think if you apply, you'll probably get to stay an extra day after the conference as well. Normally we'd go back on Wednesday but yesterday Tara said she changed my return flight so I can use Wednesday to clarify things regarding the job, spend some time with David and the others, see the place, ask questions if I've got any. I thought that was kind of nice..."

D nodded. "Yeah, that sounds like a good arrangement," she said. "It would help a lot to be on-site and meet the people we'd be working with... And then you're flying back Thursday right?"

"Yeah, Thursday around noon," June confirmed.

"Okay." D thought about that.

"When are you going to tell Harry?" June wanted to know.

"I was going to send him my application today but the system is down and I think we'll be swamped once it's back up again. I'll do it tomorrow morning then."

"Yeah, do it tomorrow. Don't wait any longer, though. Because Susan from HR told me that they've already gotten some applications to their ad in the paper. And we definitely don't want some guy from the street to snatch the job away from *you* – not that I expect that could even happen, but still..."

"I know, I know!"

June nodded, a broad delighted grin on her face. "Wow! That would be so great if we could go together!"

"Yeah, that would be great!"

Around ten-thirty the news spread that the server was up and running again and that everybody needed to reboot their computers.

When D opened her e-mail account ten minutes later, she forgot all about London. There were 25 e-mails, some of them marked urgent. She managed to read three of them before she had to leave for a meeting with Mike from the accounting department, an older guy who always appeared as if he was on tranquilizers. Meetings with him were usually a test of her patience...

~~~

Joe had spent the morning in SCANY's claustrophobic little server room together with Anders, Jan's IT whiz, trying to solve some problems. They had been trying different things for hours until it had finally dawned on them that they were actually dealing with a hardware rather than a software problem. They needed to replace an electronic part. Anders had called a few places and located a store close by where he could pick up the part right after lunch.

Since they couldn't do anything until they had that part, they decided to take an early lunch break.

While Anders went to the company's cafeteria to have something to eat and bike over to the electronics store afterwards, Joe decided to go for a walk, catch some fresh air and maybe find a place to eat. He knew he had about an hour to kill.

~~~

D got back from the meeting feeling irritated and on edge. Meetings with Mike always did this to her. It usually helped to let off some steam by vividly describing to June the highlights of the meeting. But June wasn't in the office. D dropped onto her chair and immersed herself in her load of unopened e-mails. She started with one that she knew was urgent. It had several attachments with a few pages each. She decided to print everything out. There was no way she could read all this from the screen. She was on her way out the door to retrieve her printouts from the printer down the hallway when her office phone rang and she returned to the desk to take the call.

After she had hung up she remembered her printouts and hurried to the printer, but it was already too late. Already from a distance she could see that there was nothing lying on the machine itself anymore. Someone had taken all the pages, hers and whoever else's, and tossed them on the shelf under the window next to the printer. D could just feel her blood start to boil. How she hated that! She grabbed the messed-up pile of paper and glared at it. It actually looked like everything had been mixed and shuffled. It took her a while to pick the 40 pages that belonged to her out of the mess.

With the papers in hand she returned to the office. June was back at her desk now and looked up as D marched in.

"The mysterious printer villain has struck again!" D announced. "I'm going to write to Harry that I want a surveillance camera out there so I can actually find out, who does that!"

June laughed sympathetically. "Yeah, that would be interesting for all of us!"

"And…" D growled while going back and forth between the e-mail on her screen and the printouts on her desk, trying to get them in the right order again. "I want a button on my desk that lets me give that person an electric shock when I spot them through the camera doing their evil thing."

June giggled at the thought. "Sounds great! Harry might actually go for that..."

"Mhmmm, he better..." D muttered darkly and tacked her pages together with a bit more force than necessary. That's when her mobile phone suddenly vibrated on her desk. It was Robert. A quick look at her watch confirmed that it was already 11:55 am. She was supposed to meet Robert for lunch ten minutes ago.

"Hi, Rob," she said as she quickly picked up. "I'm coming! Sorry!!! Five minutes..."

"Uh oh!" June gave her an understanding smile. "Crazy day, huh? You better go and eat before you smash something."

"Oh, what makes you think I would do that?" D grabbed her purse. "I'll be back in forty minutes or so, okay?"

"Take your time," June said and motioned for her to get out quickly.

D hurried down the hallway towards the stairways. She would have probably spent her lunch break in the office today if she hadn't told Robert that they could meet. He was in Deens every other Monday for a class he was taking, and they tried to meet in the small Chinese restaurant opposite her work for lunch on those days. It was a good opportunity to catch up and have a private brother-sister chat.

~~~

Joe took a stroll along a canal, turned into a small street for a while, then followed another canal. It was a little cloudy today but still warm enough so he was fine without a jacket.

After a ten-minute walk he found a nice-looking bistro with an appealing menu and stopped there to have lunch.

His hand was fine today, but he was still a little freaked out by the overwhelming effect the painkillers had had the previous night. That stuff had surely helped fast, not just to make the pain go away but also to paralyze his brain and the rest of him. Amazing! He had woken up at six in the morning from the next door neighbor dropping something in the shower. The open laptop on the bedside table had gone into sleep mode sometime during the night, but the TV was still running on low volume just as he had left it. He had missed the movie he had wanted to watch...

~~~

Robert was sitting at a table close to the window when D arrived at the Chinese restaurant. She was out of breath, stressed and really hungry. "Sorry, I'm late..." she huffed.

"No problem," he said as she sat down. "I just called because I wasn't sure…"

She stared into her menu for a while. But when the little Chinese lady came to take their order, she ordered the same as always.

Once the food came and she had had a few bites, she felt better. Robert was telling her something about a few improvements he had made to the new website for his catering business. He had just started it ten months ago, but it seemed to be running very well. And he just loved it. It was great to see him so enthusiastic about something.

"Maybe I'll send you the test link and you can look through it when you have time," he said. "See what you think and check if you find any more typos."

D nodded. "Sure, just send it to me." She watched him dish up some more rice and eight treasures onto his plate.

"I've got to tell you something, by the way…" she said.

He looked up expectantly.

"It's maybe a little crazy…" D predicted.

Robert raised his eyebrows. "Don't tell me you're not going to your weekend thing after all, because really…"

D she shook her head. "No, it's got nothing to do with that, and I don't want to hear that right now either. It's something totally different: I'm thinking about applying for a two-year job my company has in London."

There it was.

"Really?" Robert seemed pleasantly surprised. "That's definitely the good kind of crazy," he said. "Wow, I mean… It would suck not to have you around, of course, but I kind of think it would be good for you. And we'd come and visit." He grinned.

"I've been thinking about it for a while," D told him, feeling incredibly relieved at his positive reaction. "Not real seriously, but, well… June is going to transfer for sure. And she kind of got me infected. It would just be for two years or so. It sounds pretty interesting and maybe I need a change of scenery anyway…"

"Yeah, I think you might," Robert said in a tone that showed D that she was not the only one who had Pete in mind here. "And you *did* like London and you like working with June, so that sounds perfect. And there's going to be some solution for the flat and your car while you're gone."

"Yeah, I'm a bit worried about that, but... well... Don't tell Mom and Dad about this yet, though, okay?"

"I won't," Robert assured her. "But I really think you should go for it. You need to do these things while you can! And the flat belongs to Dad anyway, so it can just stay the way it is until you come back. We might use it during the weekends a few times and check if everything's alright, so..."

D nodded gratefully. "That would be great."

"When will you know?" Robert asked. "And when would it start?"

"Sounds like they would want us to start in six or eight months. I don't know how fast they'll decide. I haven't even sent my application yet. I've got it all ready, just haven't pushed the button yet. But I'm pretty sure that I've got a very good chance, once I tell them I *do* want it."

Robert laughed. "Sure, you do! Send it off! I think it would be good for you!"

~~~

It was around 1:30 pm when Joe returned to the server room. Anders wasn't back yet, so he got himself a coffee from the machine and drank it while standing at the window in the hallway looking out at the canal he had walked along earlier.

He contemplated if he should call Christine. To see if she wanted to do something together after work... The idea had occurred to him already in the early morning, but he had pushed it aside. Well, it kept popping up. They could always go to a movie or something, or not? There would be nothing wrong with it! They just had to make sure, and this seemed like a crucial thing here, that they stuck to their good resolution not to sleep together again. Not that he didn't want to. The night with her had been great. No doubt about it. And in a way it had even been a comforting reassurance and a relief, as it had shown that normal sex with a normal person was actually still great. He hadn't been entirely sure about that beforehand. In the very back of his mind he had been terrified that the crazy stuff he'd gotten into with Liz might have somehow screwed him up. Thank God that didn't seem to be the case.

He should probably feel bad for analyzing the night with Christine like it was some sort of experiment, but something told him that, intentionally or not, it had been some kind of test run for Christine as well. Something to compare her nights with Peer to. Joe realized that it was kind of ironic that Christine might now view him as the standard example for what a normal straight guy was like in bed when at the same time he himself was struggling with the question of how normal he still was.

The dingdong of the elevator arriving pulled Joe out of his complicated considerations. It was Anders with the part that they needed to continue their work.

~~~

When D got back to the office after lunch, she had five new e-mails, still a lot to catch up on from the morning and a meeting scheduled in an hour with Dennis from the IT department – about adaptations to a program June and her were using. She decided postpone sending off her London application until the next morning. There just wasn't any time to tinker around with an e-mail to Harry today…

~~~

When Joe got ready to leave SCANY that evening, it was already seven. Anders and he had been so immersed in their work that he hadn't called Christine after all.

Looking at his watch on his way down in the elevator now, he considered for a moment if he should still call her. It seemed too late, though, and he did feel kind of worn out and tired.

As he left the building, he ran into Jan and another guy who were standing outside chatting and waiting for someone else. They said that they were on their way to have a beer and something to eat in a new pub around the corner.

After a little persuasion Joe decided to just join them. He was starving anyway.

It turned out to be a fun two hours and a half at the pub, with good food, beer and some interesting conversations.

When Joe was finally walking back to the hotel around 11:00 pm, he felt a little drunk but unexpectedly upbeat. He was somewhat regretting that now it was really too late to call Christine. Because after the beers and a few hours with three guys that didn't take life too seriously, his reservations about possibly spending another night with Christine suddenly seemed totally unnecessary, very narrow-minded and absolutely negotiable… Something told him though, that he might see things a bit differently come tomorrow morning, and that waking up in his bed alone might be a good thing!

# Leaving Schiphol Airport

As he finally took off from Schiphol Airport, Joe leaned back in his seat. There had been a delay of almost 90 minutes due to some technical problems with the plane. He had ended up getting rebooked on a flight operated by a different airline.

The guy in the seat next to Joe was nervously flipping through what looked like a printout of a PowerPoint presentation. He was shuffling the papers and scribbling notes on them.

Joe closed his eyes trying to tune him out. He really couldn't wait to get to Sarah's. Now that he only had a few more hours left to go, it was finally starting to seem real – the thought of being in Deens, staying in the house he had grown up in, seeing Sarah and his friends, meeting with Mom, sleeping in his old room, his bed – without Liz stirring next to him… It had something immensely comforting. In a way it felt like an opportunity to slow down to a walking pace after an uncontrollably crazy, fast ride that had left him exhausted and disoriented. He had considered pulling the brake before. Not just on his relationship with Liz but also on immersing himself way too much in his work. Returning to Deens had been on his mind for a while, but it just hadn't been an option as long as his Dad had been alive. He simply couldn't have dealt with being around that man.

He had never had a very good relationship with his father. Ever since he could remember there had been tensions. Dad had always been extremely critical of him. Maybe because he had been the only son. Dad hadn't been like that with Sarah. But in him, Dad had always had these sky-high expectations that he had just never been able to meet – even at times when he had still tried to. He had just always lagged behind. As a seven-year old, when he had competed in the elementary school's science project and only coming in third; as a twelve-year old when Dad had taken him along to go fishing with two professor colleagues and their stupid stuck-up sons. Joe remembered punching the one kid's nose bloody for laughing about the book he had brought to read. (*You're still reading children's books?!?*)

At fifteen he had already sort of given up trying to score points with Dad and therefore insisted on taking guitar lessons on Tuesday afternoons even though Dad had really wanted him to sign up for some extracurricular biology class instead.

And the greatest disappointment for Dad had doubtlessly been when his only son had informed him of his plans to study computer science at a university four hours away from Deens rather than following in his renowned scientist-professor-father's footsteps in the field of genetics.

Dad and he. It had always been a bit of a struggle. He couldn't remember ever having enjoyed being around that man. And then, after that thing had happened five years ago, being around his father had become literally unbearable.

Joe remembered having had some unusually late class and then getting held up chatting with some people. His knee, not quite back to normal after the motorcycle accident a few months earlier, had been bothering him all afternoon. He left the building to head for the bus stop and spotted his Dad's car still parked in the university staff parking lot. And even though he normally preferred the bus to a tense car ride with his father, the pain in his knee that day convinced him to walk over to the building his Dad's office was in and just catch a ride home.

The hallway in the genetics wing was deserted and dark except for the emergency lights and some light coming through the glass door of the last office which happened to be his Dad's. He walked into the front room where Dad's assistant, Patricia, had her desk. The light was on, Patricia's desk chair was empty and the door to his Dad's office was closed.

Joe figured that the assistant must have already gone home. Just because his Dad seemed to have turned into a workaholic lately, didn't mean Patricia had to work night shifts.

Joe was heading for the closed door to knock when something made him stop in his tracks. Something seemed off. And it wasn't just that he had suddenly spotted Patricia's coat draped over one of the armrests of her chair. There were some noises – muffled voices from behind the closed office door. Muffled voices – and giggling… Patricia's giggling. It wasn't just the usual kind of cheerful giggle but this special kind of hoarse giggle that, in this setting, immediately sent a shiver down Joe's spine.

Part of him knew right away what this was. Even before he heard that giggle turn into soft moaning mixed with muffled grunting. Trembling he stepped up to the door and gently pressed down the handle – convinced that the door would be locked anyway. But the door wasn't locked. It opened easily, giving him a clear view of his Dad's desk and the visitor's sofa right next to it.

The naked girl was kneeling on the carpet, her upper body resting against the seat cushion of the sofa, her body partially blocked from his view by his father's big frame. His father kneeling behind the girl, his pants and underwear around his knees...

Paralyzed, Joe watched them for a few seconds. As his Dad pushed and shoved, the girl moving with him, her hands pressed against the back of the sofa now, some engagement ring sparkling from her right hand, the grunting and moaning growing louder, more intense. Watching the aging half-naked guy who was his father and the naked girl who was hardly any older than Sarah, Joe realized that it was almost comical in a sick kind of way. Like in a very bad and tasteless movie.

He didn't know for how long he had been standing there, but when he had seen enough and they were still at it, totally oblivious to his presence, Joe intuitively reached into the fruit bowl on the shelf next to him and grabbed the next best thing to throw. (Appropriately enough, it turned out to be an apple.) He flung it full force, and it happened to hit his Dad against the back of the head.

"*Fuck,* Dad!" Joe yelled. His Dad whisked around, clutching his hand against the spot of impact on his head, his lower body still connected to the girl. There was disbelief, embarrassment and utter shock in the face of the man that claimed to be the exemplary perfect father, husband and scientist...

Drawing in a deep breath, the airplane's engines humming soothingly, Joe opened his eyes and glanced at the flight attendant coming down the aisle with the beverage cart. He couldn't believe how this memory of Dad and Patricia was still so vivid! It still made him feel almost nauseous.

This incident had turned an already strained relationship into an impossible one. Right after it had happened, his Dad had, of course, tried to smooth things out, talk to him, explain, assure him that it had been a one-time thing, that he had no idea how it had even happened (*but, well, you know, Patricia's sometimes so...*) and that it would never ever happen again.

Joe had blocked all attempts to talk it over by just walking away or slamming doors shut between them. It had been a real dilemma, though. On one hand he had almost enjoyed seeing his father so scared for maybe the first time in his entire life, scared that the whole thing would come out, blow up right in his face and end his marriage and possibly his career. On the other hand Joe really loved his Mom, and he had made up his mind early-on that he couldn't tell her – or Sarah. Because he simply hadn't had any idea how to.

So, for a while there, he had just kept it to himself. And where family life had previously been annoying at times, it was now, at least from his perspective, absolutely unbearable. Because he knew his Dad's dirty little secret. And his Mom didn't. And Sarah didn't. And they would all still sit around the dinner table and pretend to be a happy family. It made him feel like an even bigger liar than his Dad.

Joe remembered how seeing Dad act like the caring, faithful husband, and his totally oblivious Mom responding accordingly just used to make him sick – and frustrated, grouchy and irritable. Not just with his Dad but also with everyone else – Mom, Sarah… and even Danny. The thought of her sent an uncomfortable tingle through his stomach and he quickly steered away from there.

His father's sudden death had been a shock. Heart attack. Just like that. No warning or anything and his Dad had been gone. Forever. And it had made the rift between them irreversible, with absolutely no chance of reconciliation. Not that he was sure he would have wanted one.

He had gone back to Deens for the funeral. Liz had insisted on coming along. As support. He would have preferred to just go by himself, have some time to digest everything, come to terms with it, be with his Mom, Sarah and Grandma for a few days. But, of course, Liz had had to be there. And instead of having some much-needed quiet time with what was left of his family, he had had to deal with Liz and her ever changing moods, her being too cold, too warm, nagging about how Sarah had said something she didn't like, or how there had been some bacon in the potato soup his Grandma had made (obviously unaware that Liz was currently on a vegetarian trip.) And oh my, what should she wear for the funeral?

Yeah, Liz had a way of distracting him from the really important things in life…

They had buried his father and he had been just amazed and shocked at how little it affected him. Standing there at the grave-site, he had forced himself to think it through: that his Dad was gone forever and all that kind of stuff. He had tried to focus on it and feel something. But there had been nothing. As if he didn't really care. Which had been both scary and a relief.

He had been worried about his Mom, though. And Sarah and his Grandma. And he wished he had been living closer and able to give them more support. But first of all he had had his hands full with Liz, and secondly, he had been afraid that he might, in a misguided attempt to comfort his Mom, spill the beans about what he had seen in his Dad's office.

For Mom, Dad's sudden death had been a real shock. Fortunately she had had Sarah and Aunt Tess to lean on. Especially Aunt Tess had been great! Up until then Joe had always found her a bit too flamboyant and high maintenance but since his father's death he saw her as sort of a crazy fairy who had saved Mom from drowning in grief and inspired her to completely change her life instead.

In the time since Dad had passed away, Mom had evolved from a dedicated housewife who had given up her job when Sarah was born and who had always been striving to be the perfect mother, wife, cook and homemaker, into someone who, from the looks of it, was just rediscovering the fun side of life.

Eight months ago Mom had surprised them with the decision to move out of the family home and move in with Aunt Tess. The sisters, both having recently lost their husbands, were now living together again like in their college years…

Aunt Tess hadn't lost her husband through death. He was very much alive. Only that he had been a notorious cheater and, after several years of heartache and forgiving him one affair after the other, Aunt Tess had finally filed for divorce. And since the husband had been super-rich, she had gotten the house just outside Deens, the cabin at the small lake and the beach house in Spain, along with a monthly alimony that enabled a worry-free lifestyle.

Joe had felt a little funny when Mom had first hesitantly talked about her plans to move in with her sister. But it had turned out to be the perfect arrangement. Mom seemed to really enjoy living with her sister, going to the movies and to the theatre together, taking little excursions around the area or trips to Spain or other places.

It had taken Sarah a while to get used to living in the house all by herself. For a while selling it had been discussed, but then Mom, Sarah and he had agreed that unless Sarah wanted to move to some smaller place, they'd just keep it. Then Sarah had met Andy and – to Joe's unpleasant surprise – that guy had moved into the house with Sarah not even a month later. Joe had only met Andy once. He hadn't liked him. And then Andy suddenly had vanished again and Sarah had been strangely evasive as to what had happened exactly. She had just said that there had been some things going on in Andy's life (including drugs) that she couldn't accept. So she had kicked him out. And as far as Joe knew, Jack had been assisting in that, one way or the other. Joe had never heard the details, though, and he had decided not to push for them either.

"I've got lots of space now," Sarah had been telling him on the phone every once in a while since Andy's disappearance. "So, if you want to move in with me...," she had joked, "still got your room under the roof..." He had always laughed. Even though there had been times when he hadn't felt like laughing at all. In contrast, sometimes returning to that house and hiding in his old room had seemed so incredibly tempting that it had almost hurt. But he couldn't tell Sarah that. Not then. Not when he was still struggling to keep up appearances that he was ever so happy with Liz and that he had made the right choice.

Well, things had changed. He was on his way to stay with Sarah now.

# Tuesday Evening

D returned home after work and a quick stop at the supermarket, feeling almost a little lightheaded.

Harry had called her around noon, saying that he had just gotten out of a meeting and seen her e-mail application for the job in London. He had told her that she really wouldn't have had to send him such a formal application, but that it was good to have it, so he could just forward it to his brother David.

Harry hadn't left any doubt that, if she wanted to transfer to London, he wouldn't just fully support it, but that he still thought June and her over there would be the perfect solution for the company. And D had thanked him, thinking to herself that it probably wasn't just the perfect solution for Swan&Co but also for her…

Her mind still whirling with this telephone conversation and the upcoming trip to London, she put away the groceries that she had gotten on the way home. As another bout of London-related thoughts flashed through her head, she pulled her phone out of her purse, feeling a spontaneous urge to call Sarah. Call her and tell her the news. She had already singled out Sarah's name from her list of phone contacts and was about to press the call button when she stopped herself. *When* had Sarah said her brother was coming in exactly? Tuesday afternoon or Tuesday night? She wasn't sure anymore. Maybe Sarah hadn't even been so specific about the time. It couldn't be ruled out, though, that he was already there…

D felt her throat go dry and her mood drop a few degrees at the thought. Strangely irritated at herself for that, she drew in a deep breath. If just imagining him in the same town had that effect, what would it be like tomorrow, when she had to actually see him in person? She better get her act together. And no, she wouldn't call Sarah right now.

She considered calling Robert instead but then decided against it because he might try to give her some more valuable advice for the grill party tomorrow…

~~~

It was almost seven when Joe finally lifted the trolley into the car. Once he was sitting in the driver's seat, he placed the headset in his ear and turned the phone on to let Sarah know he was on his way. He had sent her only two short messages earlier: one about the delay and then another one when he had boarded the plane. She had sent him a text message back, asking him to let her know once he got to his car so she could put the lasagna into the oven.

The phone dialed Sarah's number.

"Joe…" she picked it up after two rings.

"Hi, I'm finally on the road," he told her, "I should be there in fifty minutes or so."

"Great! Hope you're still hungry."

"Don't worry! I'm starving…" There was a short pause, then he hissed, "Crap!"

"What?"

"Grrr! I just got on the highway and everything's jammed up. Shit… This could take a while… I'm sorry! I'll call you when I know more, okay?"

"Okay. I'll turn on the oven in the meantime…"

Trapped in a sea of red brake lights, Joe turned on the radio to see if there was any traffic news. Not even two minutes later he saw the ambulance approach from behind him, blue lights flashing, police car and a fire truck flying by as well.

Since traffic was still creeping along, even if only at the speed of a snail, Joe changed into the lane that would eventually allow him to exit the mess and take a detour. He had almost made it to the next exit when the traffic news came on. From what they said he realized that the accident still lay at least seven snail-speed kilometers ahead and it would still take at least half an hour to be cleared. Joe took the next exit and headed for Deens on the slow roads that were crowded now too.

He tried to call Sarah but only got the answering machine. She was probably caught up in some cooking activity she wasn't able to just drop. He left a message on the voice mail telling her that it would take him at least another hour.

When his phone rang only 30 seconds later, he picked it up, assuming it was Sarah calling him back.

"Hello?"

"Hi…" there was a hint of shyness. It was Liz.

Joe cursed himself for picking up. "Hi," he said without any trace of warmth.

"So, you finally got your phone turned on again..." there was an accusing edge in her voice.

"You just got lucky, that's all."

"Wow, aren't you Mr. Charming!"

"What do you want, Liz?"

"What do I want?" It sounded like he had asked a question that should answer itself. "I wanted to see if you've actually come to your senses again!"

"I wasn't aware I'd ever *lost* my senses," he retorted, trying to stay calm.

"Oh, come on. That scene you made last Saturday..." She let out a hysterical little giggle. "Even you must see by now..."

Joe felt the heat creep up his neck. "See what?" he asked darkly.

"Well, sorry, but you can't be serious!" She sounded a bit shrill now. "You just pack your stuff and take off? And that's it?"

His left hand cramped around the steering wheel, he could feel a ball of anger building up in the pit of his stomach. Was she seriously still pretending to herself that it was all just some silly bluff on his side?

"I know you were mad," she said generously. "The thing with your hand and – yeah, I know I started that fight on Tuesday, but... I mean, you can't just *leave!*" She let out a breathy laugh to underscore how crazy she found it.

Chewing on his lower lip, Joe was trying to keep the anger from boiling over.

"You have to come back here!" she told him with a trace of panic, "We need to work this out!"

"There's nothing *left* to work out, Liz!" he said flatly. "I'm out of it. That's it!"

"Honey, please..."

He cringed at hearing her call him *Honey*. She must have guessed it.

"Joe... *Please*, come back!" she sounded close to tears now, and Joe concluded that they must be entering the sobbing phase now. He could only hope his protective shield would hold or he would just have to hang up. Thinking about it, hanging up might be a good idea in any event. But then he would just have to deal with it all some other time, of course.

"Listen, Liz…" He was struggling to keep his voice from trembling. "I'm on my way to Sarah's, I'm tired, I'm hungry and I'm *really* not in the mood to argue about this again. You know *exactly* why I left. This is not just about my hand!"

"We can start over…" she said frantically. "You forgive me, I forgive you and we'll be alright! Just come back home, okay? I promise…"

Joe swallowed. Why on earth hadn't he checked the phone before he had taken this call?

"We both screwed up," she insisted. And then there was the first big sob.

Joe drew in a sharp breath. "Where did I screw up exactly?" he inquired through clenched teeth. "Tell me, please! I just need to know this! I mean, yeah, you can hold against me that I wasn't around much lately, but you know perfectly well that there were a few good reasons for that."

"Yeah, yeah, you got your reasons!" she blasted, her voice choked with tears.

He didn't say anything. He simply didn't know what to say.

"Well, guess what!?!" she screamed between sobs. "I had my reasons too!"

"I don't doubt that one second," he said dryly.

"They made me feel great," she hissed. "Fantastic! I'm glad I did it! And Bob was the best I've ever had…!"

"Good for you!" he cheered. "Really! And what a great choice, too! I just hope for you that Linda never finds out that you're messing around with her husband. You could probably kiss your job goodbye if she did."

"Are you threatening me?" she snarled.

"You mean would I tell her?" He couldn't help laughing. "No, don't worry! I *do* think it's kind of funny, though. I mean… you were *so* eager to tell me all about this and now you're scared I might share your secret with his wife? It is a bit ironic, don't you think?" He let out another little giggle just to tick her off. Somehow the sarcasm sometimes helped him over the worst and made him seem cool when he really wasn't. He wasn't cool about this and he wouldn't be in a hundred years.

"Well, sorry," she blasted. "I happen to have my needs too, and since you were gone all the time and even when you were home–"

"Oh, no, don't apologize!" Joe mocked, trying hard not to let this conversation distract him from what was going on on the road. "I totally understand. Of course you have your needs."

"Oh, come on," she yelled. "Don't tell me that on all your little trips *you* didn't fuck around yourself."

Joe couldn't help letting out a coughing, bitter laugh. "Here we go again! Just because you keep repeating a lie won't make it true, Liz. But believe what you want, I don't give a shit anymore."

"It can't be that you didn't even once..." she insisted, a trace of doubt in her voice now.

"Not while we were together, no!" he said sharply. "I had plenty of drama in my life with just you, and adding another woman to that would have just been a bit more than I thought I could handle. It did get pretty close once, yeah, but I didn't do it. Sorry! I know it's against everything you believe. But if it helps, Liz, I actually *did* sleep with someone this time – in Amsterdam." He said it and wondered at the same time why he was even telling her about this. Just to hurt her? How low had he sunk?

"Well, *good* for you!" Liz hissed furiously. "I hear Amsterdam is just full of little sluts... I just hope it didn't cost too much and you didn't catch anything!"

Joe scoffed. "Thanks *so much* for your concern! But you *really* don't have to worry! I *do* know how to use protection, remember? And as for the girl, I've actually known her as a friend for quite a while. She's real nice! Great personality, smart and... *great* body! Yeah and the sex – what was the word you used earlier?... Fantastic!"

"Go to hell!" Liz yelled.

"I've already been there!" Joe shot back.

"You asshole!"

He laughed.

"Well, you know what I will do?" she snarled.

"No, please tell me," he whispered with fake suspense.

"Well, since I'm so free now and there's a party at the gallery tonight..."

"Oh no, let me guess," Joe interrupted her in a scathing whisper. "You'll go there, get drunk and take the artist home, or Bob if he can get away from his wife... Are you and Bob still – you know – since he's *so* good?"

There was total silence on the other end now. He expected her to hang up or yell some obscenities. But then all he heard was a soft sobbing.

He swallowed. It wasn't like he wasn't used to the abrupt changes in direction and mood by now, but somehow it still threw him off.

He tried to concentrate on the road. It was still busy and there was an extremely unpredictable driver right in front of him, changing speeds like Liz changed moods.

"But I don't want the artist!" Liz screamed sounding like a little child whose favorite doll had just been snatched away by an evil aunt. "I want *you*! I *love* you. You can't just dump me like this."

"Liz, please…" he tried for a softer tone. "I didn't *dump* you. We just don't work, okay? And now… you need to calm down! Really!"

"I can change, *Honey*, please… – I *need* you!"

Joe bit his lip, exhaling sharply through his nose. He was trying hard not to lose it here.

"Liz, now listen…" Surprisingly his voice still sounded halfway steady. "I know you don't want to hear it, but you really need to do something. Get help. Go and see a doctor or whatever. About the mood swings and the fits and all the other issues, because not even a fantastic guy like Bob would be willing to put up with that."

"I'm not a lunatic!" she yelled.

"I didn't say that," he said, "but you need to get it under control! Not for me but for yourself! Do you hear me?"

"Oh, aren't you so…"

"And you need to stop drinking…" he interrupted her. "And for God's sake, stop playing with those pills!"

He heard her inhale, probably getting ready to scream or sob or whatever. But he just didn't think he could take another round. So he hung up and turned off the phone. He also turned off the radio and opened the window a little to let some cool air in.

He drew in a deep breath and exhaled slowly, biting down on his lower lip. He felt drained, absolutely drained after this telephone conversation. It was plain scary how she still managed to push all his buttons. It was a special talent she seemed to have – a talent to make him feel really bad. He had only experienced such overpowering bad feelings with one other person ever – and that had been his Dad.

He had planned to tell Sarah about the breakup with Liz tonight (over dinner or for dessert). But somehow that determination had faded over the last few hours of being delayed at the airport, being starved and tired and especially after just having had this delightful talk with Liz.

He suddenly wasn't even so sure anymore that this whole Liz-drama was even over yet. He had a bad feeling that it wasn't, and that telling Sarah about it might be jinxing it.

Besides, he really didn't want to think, let alone talk about Liz anymore tonight. Maybe tomorrow. Because talking to Sarah about stuff like this required the willingness to go into detail, answer questions, let her analyze... And he didn't think he had the patience for that tonight.

# Lasagna Dinner

Sarah glanced up from her plate. Across the table Joe had just finished a huge piece of lasagna in no time at all and was leaning back in his chair smiling at her.

"That was really good!" he said, rubbing his stomach with his left hand. "I was starving."

Sarah couldn't help laughing. "Obviously! Do you want another piece?"

He thought about it for a moment and then nodded. "I think I will!" He pushed back his chair.

Sarah watched him walked over to the stove, the plate in his left and the braced hand hanging to his side. That hand… She had first noticed the brace when he had given her a hug and it had felt weird against her back.

"What's wrong with your hand?" she had asked as soon as he had released her.

He had shrugged and looked at the brace with a crooked smile. "Broke a few fingers."

"When was that?" She had held the door open for him and he had come in and set the bag and the suitcase down.

"A few days before I left for Amsterdam," he had responded lightly. And then he had walked straight into the kitchen where he had inhaled and smiled and said how good it smelled. (And they had dropped the hand-topic.)

Sarah was happy how the lasagna had turned out. It didn't look exactly pretty after it had been in the oven a bit longer than planned, but it surely tasted good.

She finished her own piece and put down the fork.

"I still can't believe you're actually really here!" she said leaning back and crossing her arms.

"Neither can I," Joe said. He had returned with another big piece of lasagna. "Took long enough anyway. Crazy trip today…" He smiled. "But it's really good to be here!"

"Yeah… Now I just have to get used to having you here all to myself," Sarah said in a half-hearted attempt to maybe steer the conversation into the direction of why he was here by himself. "The last time was probably when we were both still studying and Mom and Dad were gone on vacation."

"Probably," Joe nodded his gaze back on his plate.

Watching him, Sarah realized that he looked exhausted. But at least he had obviously given up that ultra-short-haircut-plus-beard look he had shocked them with at the funeral. He was back to looking like himself. Only exhausted... He definitely didn't look like he was still in the mood to talk about anything of magnitude tonight, though. And if she was honest, she was tired too.

Joe looked up again. "When's Mom coming back?"

"Next Tuesday," Sarah said. "If she had known earlier that you'd be coming, she probably wouldn't have gone to Spain at all, but since they'd already booked that trip and since you said you'd stay longer than the reunion..."

He nodded. "Yeah, maybe I'll try to go over there next Wednesday then."

"How long can you stay, do you think?" Sarah asked.

Joe met her eyes. "How long can you take it, do you think?" he asked back.

"That depends on how you behave," Sarah said, trying for a joking tone.

"Oh, I think I'm a relatively uncomplicated house guest." he retorted.

"Then you can stay as long as you want..."

The silence that followed made them both only too aware of all the unanswered questions and elephants in the room.

"*What?*" Joe finally asked with a little frown. "Are you trying to read my mind and diagnose all the things that are wrong with me now?"

"Why would you say *that?*" Sarah retorted, feeling slightly irritated that he seemed to see straight through her.

"I know that look," Joe laughed. "You definitely got that from Mom. But on you it looks even more investigative..."

"Well..." For a moment there Sarah was scrambling for words. "It's just... You look tired," she said in an effort to pick the most harmless description.

He nodded. "I *am* tired."

"Just from Amsterdam?" Sarah asked, eying him cautiously.

Drawing in a long breath, he slowly shook his head. "Nope," he slowly said and ran his left hand over his face. "But I'm too tired right now to tell you all the reasons *why* I'm tired."

"Okay. I'll have mercy on you tonight then," Sarah smiled.

"Good. So we can do the interrogation some other time?" he asked jokingly.

"I'm not *that* bad!" she grumbled, hardly suppressing a grin, "and seems like you're not denying that there *are* reasons for interrogation."

"No, I'm not denying that. Just not now, okay?"

"Understood. You can't escape me, though! Since we'll be living under the same roof for a while..." She gave him a triumphant look.

With a weak chuckle he nodded. "Yeah, I was afraid you'd say that!"


They took the dishes to the kitchen and Joe put them into the dishwasher while Sarah dished up some tiramisu.

They moved to the living room, dimmed the light and stretched out on the L-shaped sofa, both leaning against one of the armrests, their legs stretched into the corner, their toes almost touching.

"So, what's going on with you?" Joe asked without looking up from the plate in his lap.

"Oh, not that much since I got rid of Andy. Just work and hanging out with friends."

His eyes flickered up at her for a moment but then quickly dropped back to the tiramisu.

"Can't wait to see Jack," he said without looking up. "Was organizing this get-together his idea then?"

"Yeah. Jack's and Rick's. It just seemed like the right time, and then it just sort of fell into place. With the location and everyone having time that weekend, even you..."

He nodded, looking a bit absent-minded. "So, what's everybody been up to?" he asked just a tad too lightly. "Anything I need to know before I throw myself in there tomorrow?"

Sarah gave him a quick look. "I don't know. Well, I guess you're a bit out of the loop..."

So she started bringing him up to date.

About Tony and his girlfriend and their four month old baby.

About how they had almost split up over the pregnancy but now seemed happy.

About Rick, who was probably soon going to take over his Dad's doctor's practice.

About Jack, who had recently moved to a new flat.

About Carrey, who had gotten a divorce after just two years.

About, Sun, who was still the same carefree party girl.

About Anja, who had gotten married a year ago.

"The grill party tomorrow night will be at Anja and Gerry's house," Sarah said. "They've been remodeling it – must have belonged to his aunt or something. Cool house. You'll see it tomorrow. And you'll meet Gerry…"

Joe nodded. "Yeah, that'll be nice…" he said, balancing his fork on the rim of his empty plate. "So, tomorrow night… everybody is coming, huh?"

"Except for *me*, yes."

"Ah, right…" He glanced up looking a bit embarrassed that he had forgotten about that. "You really can't? No way at all?"

Sarah shook her head. "No…"

"That really sucks!"

"Yeah, but what can I do?" She shrugged. "At least I've got the weekend off… And the hotel looks really nice!"

Joe nodded. "Yeah, I saw that. Checked it out on the internet."

"Belongs to Rick's cousin or some other relative," Sarah said. "That's why the price is so reasonable. Pretty spendy normally. Conference rooms, spa area, right on the lake…" Sarah caught herself before she could babble on about how D had been quite excited about the lake-part. She wasn't really sure what effect her mentioning D in this conversation would have on her brother. It was hard to tell. She probably didn't have to be half as careful with him as she had to be with D. After all, he had caused the whole mess in the first place. He couldn't be so touchy. And, looking at him, he probably wasn't. But somehow she didn't really feel like trying that out right now.

"So, Jack and I are sharing a room, right?" Joe asked.

Sarah nodded. "Yep. Like in old times…" That wasn't entirely correct, of course, because the times when he had shared rooms with Jack on trips had ended at the point where he had started sharing rooms with D.

"That's great," Joe said almost a bit too cheerfully. "And you?"

Sarah raised her eyebrows. Okay, now what? There was no way to avoid mentioning D now, was there? Or was this maybe his way of asking

127

about D? He must know that she was sharing her room with D… Sarah pursed her lips and checked his expression for a clue of how to handle this.

"Me?" she finally said slowly. "Now, what do you think? Who would I be sharing a room with?"

He blinked a little more than necessary but otherwise held her gaze, obviously realizing now that she wouldn't make this easy for him.

"Well, what do you think?" Sarah repeated, giving him a challenging look.

With a little irritated shake of his head Joe exhaled, his gaze wandering off to the side.

Sarah decided that she would just skip the answer.

For a moment no one said anything.

"How *is* she?" he asked in a by-the-way manner and pushed the fork to the middle of his empty plate on his lap.

"Good," Sarah said with shrug. "She's good."

There was another short pause with both of them avoiding eye contact.

"I'm glad that you're still friends…" Joe mumbled, still staring at his plate. "At least I didn't wreck that…"

Sarah didn't quite know how to respond to this. But then again, he probably wasn't really waiting for a response anyway.

Silence again.

"Is she–" Joe paused and cleared his throat. "Is she going to be at the grill party then?"

Sarah looked up and was surprised to find him looking back at her.

"Why?" she asked, suddenly finding this slightly amusing "Are you scared now?"

Joe gave her an exasperated shake of his head. "Ha…Ha…Ha!" he mocked.

"Well, sorry!" Sarah said defensively. "Yeah, she's probably going to be there… Unless she's changed her mind after hearing that *you* will be coming."

"Okay," Joe said flatly. "Does she still hate me then, I gather?"

Sarah raised her eyebrows. Was this a serious question?

"I don't know if she still hates you," she said with slight irritation. "Probably. I would definitely hate you!"

With a shake of his head and a breathy humorless laugh he dropped his gaze.

"Anyway... " Sarah scrambled to end the topic for the sake of them both. "I don't know for sure if or how much she hates you. D and I usually don't talk about you." She paused for a moment. "I told her that you're coming. Pretty much had to. But that's it. It's just not very becoming of our friendship to talk about you, if you know what I mean."

"Yeah, I get it..." Joe said with some exasperation. He slid his legs over the side of the sofa, ready to get up. "Is... *what's-his-face* coming too?"

Sarah squinted in confusion. "Who?"

"*Pete...*" Joe growled, shooting her an irritated look as if he suspected her of playing dumb on purpose. "Is *Peeeete* going to be at the party as well?"

Sarah shook her head. "No," she said and then paused for a moment. "I think we can rule that out. They kind of broke up..."

Joe gave her a puzzled look. But then he didn't say anything else or even ask what *kind of* was supposed to mean in this context. Sarah was glad he didn't because she was feeling increasingly uncomfortable having this conversation with him. It did suddenly occur to her, though, that not being able to attend the party tomorrow night had one significant upside: she would miss the doubtlessly very, very awkward moments when her best friend and her brother would have to somehow figure out how to best deal with each other or ignore each other for the coming days. She could only imagine how that would go. There was, surely, still going to be plenty of weird moments at the hotel, but hopefully the worst would be over by then. She had no desire whatsoever to get caught in the middle!

She saw Joe glance at his watch. He was really looking worn out now.

"You should go to bed," she said, giving him an encouraging smile, "and I think I should, too."

With a little nod he got up from the sofa and stretched.

"The food was great. Really!" He seemed to be suppressing a yawn. "And thanks for the update." He reached out and gave her shoulder a little rub. "And for letting me come." He paused. "It's so nice to be h– here."

Sarah squinted. Had he just almost said *home*? She reached for his hand that was still lying on her shoulder and gave it a gentle squeeze. "I'm still in awe that you really came!" she said with a little smile. "Good night..."

"Good night!"

## Potato Salad Preparations

D got off work around 2:50 pm. With Thursday being August 15th and therefore a holiday and Friday being off as well, almost everyone had been leaving early. June had already left around 2:00 to go and have another dose of Jim. Around 2:30 pm Harry had dropped in on his way to the elevator, wishing her a nice, long weekend. That's when she had decided it was time to flee the scene as well.

On her way home she went by the bakery in her neighborhood and got two loaves of white bread she was supposed to bring for the party.

It was shortly after three when she got home. Jack was going to pick her and Sun up around five. She had plenty of time to get ready.

She decided to quickly prepare the potato salad so that would be out of the way. She had already boiled the potatoes and the eggs the previous night. All she still had to do was slice them, add a few diced pickles, make a mayonnaise dressing and mix everything.

While she was slicing the boiled potatoes, her thoughts wandered off to what lay ahead. She had avoided thinking about it until now. But with only ninety minutes left to go she better start bracing herself. There was no use denying that the prospect of an entire evening with Joe around was making her extremely uneasy. She could only hope that she would manage to get through it without any weird scenes or embarrassments. The master plan was to ignore him when she could and be indifferently friendly when she couldn't ignore him. She better not mishandle this. Because, as Robert had pointed out, it would be a crappy situation for everyone.

She tasted the potato salad, added a little more salt and then tried it again. Finally declaring it finished, she covered it with foil and put it into the fridge. It was 3:45 pm.

The next 45 minutes she spent slightly touching up her make-up and getting dressed for the party, which involved slipping in and out of several different outfits until she ended up with something she felt good about: navy-colored linen pants, a white blouse-type shirt and sandals. She grabbed a blue sweater and draped it around her shoulders for when it got cooler in the evening and shot a final look into the mirror door of her armoire. She looked fine. Without giving the impression that she had spent hours getting ready or that she was out to impress someone. Somehow, that seemed important for tonight.

Five minutes before Jack was supposed to pick her up, he called to say that he was running half an hour late because he had had problems getting his car to start.

A little frustrated D sat down on her sofa. She hated waiting around like this, when there was something unpleasant waiting at the end. Hugging a cushion, her feet on the coffee table, she tried to think about things such as the London application, or work, or her parents – anything to distract her. But her mind kept returning to the party. Something had just occurred to: there was probably going to be a lot of hugging and cheek-kissing going on. She usually didn't have any problem with that, but tonight there was going to be exactly one person that she absolutely didn't want to have any form of physical contact with! She wasn't quite sure, however, how to avoid it without causing a scene. But who knew, maybe he wouldn't show up after all.

# Grill Party

Jack pulled up almost half an hour later than planned.

Sun was already in the car, sitting in the front passenger seat and babbling cheerily. To D that came as a relief. She had been a bit worried about being all alone in the car with Jack on the way to Sun's place, with both of them trying not to mention the elephant in the room (or the car for that matter.) There was no doubt in her mind that Jack had a pretty good idea of how she felt. He knew her well enough and he'd seen enough. So, he definitely knew. But she didn't want it spelled out to her ten minutes before the party, and she was really hoping Jack's concerned look wouldn't be following her around all evening.

She glanced at Sun, who was bubbling with energy, going on about something funny her cat had done this morning. She was talking with hands and feet and giggling a lot. It made Jack laugh. And D couldn't help laughing herself.

Sun was unique. She looked like a shrunken film star: red flowing hair, amazing curves, slightly more make-up than necessary (but not enough to cover her funny freckles), low-cut summer dress, flat golden sandals and a toothpaste-commercial smile. And she seemed to almost always be in a sunny mood that nothing could destroy.

When Jack turned into the street that Anja and Gerry lived on, D could feel her heart pick up speed. With a quick glance out the window she scanned the street. There were a lot of cars parked along the sidewalk. Some were probably the neighbors', some were her friends'. She spotted Carrey's small Ford ahead on the left side, Tony's blue Kia and Rick's VW SUV across the street from it.

Right behind Rick's car there was a sand-colored Volvo Cross Country. D let out a slow gust of air as she felt her stomach knot. She couldn't say why, but she just knew that this was Joe's car. So, if she had hoped he wouldn't show up at all, she could kiss that dream goodbye now. He was already here!

Jack parked the car a little ways behind the Volvo.

Holding her salad bowl cradled in one arm and trying to keep the strap of her purse from sliding off her shoulder, D snatched the bread bag with her free hand and got out of the car. She was in no hurry at all to walk up to that front door!

So, while Sun was already bouncing up the paved path to ring the bell, D stuck around the car and watched Jack lift the big cooler out of the trunk. Whenever there was a grill party, Jack brought the meat. His uncle happened to have a meat store and Jack seemed to always be able to convince that uncle to supply him with great steaks and sausages.

Straightening up, Jack shot her an encouraging smile over his shoulder. "You ready for this?" he asked.

D let out a dry little laugh. "Guess I don't have much choice... – but yeah, it's fine! No problem."

Nodding, Jack slammed the trunk shut.

"How about if you try to sit far away from me, though?" he suggested, "and I'll make sure I get Joe to sit with me."

"Sounds good," D said with a crooked smile. "Thanks, Jack!"

At the door Sun was hugging Anja.

"Hi!" Anja waved at them as Sun released her. "We were already kind of afraid the meat would never arrive!"

"Well, here it is!" Jack held up the cooler with a proud grin. "And we've got lots of it! – I hope I didn't just get invited because I bring the meat, though!?!"

"Well, without that, who would want to put up with you?" D teased.

"I've got a *lot* of other qualities!" Jack insisted with a fake pouting look.

"Oh, we know, we know!" Anja said laughing as he gave her a kiss on the cheek. "You can take the meat outside right away. Gerry and the guys have the grill all fired up."

As Jack headed down the hallway, D gave Anja a short hug. "Where do you want the salads?" she asked.

"We have a buffet table set up outside for all the side dishes," Anja said. "I think you can probably put yours out there already. The barbecuing shouldn't take them forever. Hopefully."

D laughed. "You don't trust them, do you?"

"Well, I sure don't trust Gerry," Anja chuckled, "or Jack..."

"Yeah, that's definitely *not* one of Jack's *many* qualities," D nodded with a suppressed grin. Then she held the bag with the bread out to Anja. "Here. Can you take that to the kitchen? I'll come back in a minute and cut it."

As Anja headed back towards the kitchen with the bread, D took a few steps down the hallway towards the living room from where she could hear voices and laughter. She reminded herself once again to stay calm and composed here – at least on the outside. She absolutely needed to pull this off! Drawing in a deep breath, she took the step into the living room. Here we go!

Hugging her salad bowl, she walked over to where Sun was talking to Tony and Carrey, who were both sitting on the living room sofa munching nuts from a little red bowl.

"Hi, D!" Tony called out to her as she came in.

"Hi, how are you!" D managed to sound a lot more cheerful than she felt. Especially after having just caught a glimpse through the window front that gave a good view of the entire backyard. Under the big oak tree in the far right corner Jack was just setting the cooler down beside the grill and the three guys who seemed to be monitoring it: there was Gerry, Rick and – with his back to the house – Joe.

She would probably still recognize him anywhere. In a crowd, at any distance, in any light, with his back to her… Some things just seemed to stay burned into one's mind.

Giving Tony and Carrey a smile that didn't exactly come easy, D tried to pull herself together. Had she really thought she was prepared for this and it wouldn't affect her? The way she could feel her pulse thudding against her temples now seemed to prove her wrong!

With some effort she focused on what Carrey was telling Sun about having received an e-mail from someone the two of them had gone to school with. D didn't know the person they were talking about.

"Kim not here?" she asked Tony.

He shook his head. "Na, we couldn't find a baby-sitter for tonight. She'll come with me on Friday, though."

"That's good," D said. "You two probably can really use a weekend alone–" She paused, then grinned. "Well, not that you'll actually *be* alone this weekend of course, but…"

Tony laughed. "No, I know what you mean." He chuckled. "We actually can't wait!"

"I haven't seen Kim in a long time," D said. "Last time must have been a month or so before the baby was born."

Beside her, Sun had just proclaimed that she was going to drop off her salad outside and say Hello to the others. D stayed behind with Tony and Carrey.

"What did you bring?" Tony nodded towards the salad bowl in her arms. "Hopefully potato salad?"

Laughing at his expression, which indicated drooling, D nodded. "I'd probably get kicked out if I brought anything else."

With both Carrey and Tony assuring her that that wasn't so, D finally turned to the patio door and was about ready to head outside when Rick came storming in and almost ran into her.

"Oh, sorry!" He stopped. "Hi, D!" He gave her a big hug despite the salad bowl and then walked off towards the hallway to get something the grill masters needed.

D stepped outside. Gerry and Anja had a nice big backyard. On the brick patio right outside the house everything was already set up for the feast. To the left of the patio door D spotted the 'buffet' table Anja had been talking about. It already had several salad bowls and a stack of dinner plates on it. Next to the table on the ground sat a cooler that held drinks.

To the right of the patio door there were two joined, colorfully set tables, ready for dinner, with seven chairs around them.

D approached the buffet table and set her salad bowl between the others. From the corner of her eye she could see Sun joining the little group at the grill, giggling and hugging everyone.

Rick had returned with a big serving plate and a special fork he put on the side table of the grill, and Sun was just hugging Joe.

D took off the aluminum foil that she had covered her salad bowl with and crumbled it into a little ball. How exactly was she planning to handle the greeting ceremony?

"What happened to your hand?" she heard Jack ask from over at the grill. D glanced up and realized that the question had been directed at Joe. She saw Sun releasing Joe from an extended embrace and reach for one of his hands, a concerned look on her face as if he was actually missing at least an arm.

"Yeah, what happened?" Sun sighed.

From where she was standing D didn't have the best view of the hand in question but it almost looked like there was some kind of a brace around it.

"That looks so painful," Sun moaned.

135

With a dismissive shake of his head Joe pulled the hand out of Sun's.

"Stupid accident," he said with a little laugh. "Hopefully I'll survive it."

D wasn't prepared for it when his eyes suddenly flickered over to her.

"Hi, Danny," he said with a short nod.

"Hi," she felt her throat go dry as she found herself caught in his gaze, even if just over this distance. Unlike at the funeral, he didn't look like a stranger today. Which was unfortunate! He looked way too much like in the pictures she had looked through a few days ago: his haircut was close to what it used to be and he had a healthy tan and no trace of a beard. He did look a bit worn out, though. And, just like her, he seemed to have rehearsed a neutral friendly face.

With some effort she shifted her gaze over to Gerry.

"Hi Gerry," she said, trying for a light and cheerful tone. "The table looks really nice."

Gerry nodded. "Yeah, Anja did almost all of that. She had the day off. All *I* did was starting the grill."

Beside Gerry, Rick burst out laughing. "I thought I saw Joe start the grill..."

"No, no," Gerry said with mock indignation. "He was just assisting..."

D managed a half-hearted chuckle. "Hopefully, with so many assistants the food will turn out alright," she teased.

"You sound like you don't trust us!" Jack gasped, acting as if he were truly hurt by that.

As an answer D just looked back at him with her eyebrows raised. "Oh, *no*," she said and batted her eye lids. "Why would *that* be, Jack?"

Over everyone's laughter, D caught Jack's nod towards where his jacket was draped over the chair at the far end of the table. That was Jack reminding her of their little seating arrangement conspiracy.

"I've got to go inside and cut my bread," D announced and turned towards the house. On her way inside she made sure to hang her purse over a chair that was located far enough away from the one that had Jack's jacket on it.

In the kitchen Anja was standing at the island in the center cutting some cucumbers for a salad.

"Ah, right, your bread," she said when D came in. She put her knife aside and got out a wooden cutting board and a knife for D to cut the bread with.

136

"We're really lucky with the weather," she said. "We did kind of have a Plan B to eat inside in case of rain, and it would have probably worked, but it would have been a little tight in the living room…"

"We would have made it work," D said with a smile as she put the first loaf of bread on the cutting board. "Inside, outside… I think it's just great that you let us do the party here! It's a lot of work for you."

"Not at all," Anja assured her, "and we love to have parties!" She brought over a bread basket and placed it next to D's cutting board. "So, that's no sacrifice at all!"

With about half of the bread loaf cut, D realized she was making a real mess. There were crumbs everywhere. She tried to scrape the ones that had landed around the cutting board together. Some had already fallen on the floor, though.

"Don't worry about it," Anja said. "Gerry has just gotten us a new vacuum cleaner and he needs to test it anyway."

"Well good, then I'll give him something to enjoy!" D laughed and continued slicing with even more crumbs flying around.

She had just arranged the slices into the bread basket and was about to start cutting the second loaf, when the kitchen door behind her flew open.

"Hi there…"

D almost dropped the knife when she recognized Joe's voice.

"I've been appointed to grill the steaks!" he informed them as he stepped into view and leaned against the kitchen island next to Anja.

"Thank God!" Anja said. "I'm sure glad you're doing it, because Gerry keeps burning my steaks. And Jack…" Instead of finishing her sentence she just rolled her eyes.

Joe laughed. "I just met your husband," he said, "so I can't say anything about his grilling abilities. But as for Jack, I tend to agree. Experience has shown that whatever great meat he gets from his uncle, he destroys it…"

He placed a small piece of paper on the counter and held it down with his left hand.

"So, how would you like your steaks?" he asked while scribbling something with a pencil he was somehow holding in his braced right hand. On the paper a crooked $A$ and a shaky $D$ appeared.

"I'd like mine done, but not too done," Anja said.

"Okay." Joe drew a *d* next to the *A* and added a little wavy line (that turned out more like a zigzag) to remind him not to get the steak too done.

D shifted her eyes from Joe's little paper note back to her hand on the bread and was incredibly annoyed by how uncomfortably hot she was starting to feel.

"And you?"

Even though D had her eyes glued to the bread, she sensed that he had just turned to her.

"Danny?"

As he said that name again, her eyes darted up at him. She had it on her tongue to tell him to stop calling her that. But then she stopped herself.

"Medium, right?" he asked, with a hint of a smile, his eyes meeting hers. It was just a normal harmless question, friendly even. Nothing wrong with it! She should have just said *yes*. He had often enough grilled for her, so what was the point? He would have gone and grilled, and no harm would have been done.

But it irritated her to no end how he behaved like they were good old friends and he knew exactly what she wanted. And then that smile on top of it…

"I don't want a steak, thanks," she heard herself say. It had come out a bit snappy.

The smile vanishing from his face, Joe straightened up and raised his eyebrows at her. "You don't want a steak?" he made it sound like she had just requested the heart of the cow served on a bed of chocolate chips.

She looked back at him trying for a halfway neutral face. "No, thanks," she confirmed with frozen politeness, her heart pounding against her ribs violently.

There was a moment of silence in which Joe's expression went from bewilderment to something like sober enlightenment.

"Would it make a difference…" he asked with a bit of sneer, "if Jack grilled it?"

D struggled to hold his gaze and abstain from blinking.

"I'm sure Jack would do that for you, Danny," Joe said with an acidic undertone, "but I *do* think you're much better off if *I* grill your steak, even if…" Instead of finishing his sentence, he scoffed and looked up at the ceiling for a moment.

"I don't want a steak, thank you very much!" she insisted, giving him a cold look.

"That's just stupid and you know it!" Joe snapped. He opened his mouth to add something else, but then he just shook his head and walked out of the kitchen, leaving the door open behind him. It had probably been either that or slamming it.

With the sounds of his footsteps fading, it became very quiet in the kitchen. Anja had stopped cutting her cucumber.

D repositioned her hand on the bread and picked up the knife again, but there was no way she should handle a sharp object now. Not when her hands weren't steady. She felt Anja looking at her.

"Don't say anything Anja, please," she said without looking up. "I know this was childish…"

Anja laughed – a friendly, sympathetic laugh.

"Maybe a little," she said and went to close the kitchen door. "If I was in your place I probably wouldn't want a steak from him either. I might want him *on* the grill…"

That made D laugh in spite of herself.

~~~

When Anja and D joined the others outside a few minutes later, Jack, Gerry and Joe were at the barbecue, while everybody else was standing in little groups spread around the backyard, chatting.

"The sausages are ready and the steaks are almost done," Joe called over from the grill, waving the grill tongs like a conductor. "You may want to get your salad and sit down…"

Everyone started moving to the salad table.

"Do you want me to get you some salad too," Anja waved an empty plate at Gerry.

"Yeah, sure… no noodle salad, though. No offense, Tony!"

D shot a look towards the grill at Jack, who was holding the big serving plate so Joe could load the grilled sausages onto it.

"Jack, can I get you some salad as well?" she called over to him.

"That would be great, yeah," Jack responded with a look over his shoulder, "a little of each, please."

"Joe, do you want me to prepare a salad plate for you?" That was Sun at her sweetest.

"No, thanks." Briefly turning around halfway, Joe shook his head. "I'd rather do it myself later. I'm pretty picky…"

D wandered back to the table, two salad plates in her hand. She delivered Jack's to his spot at the head of the table and then returned to her own chair. She was sitting with her back to the garden and the grill, with Tony to her right at the head of the table and Carrey and Rick to her left. Anja and Gerry were right across from her with their backs to the house wall. Next to Gerry, Sun was just taking her seat now, the empty chair she or Jack had assigned to Joe right beside her.

"Ta Da!" Jack set the sausage plate down in the center of the two tables.

"All done," Joe announced from the grill.

With the smell from the sausages reaching her nose, D suddenly realized how hungry she was. She hadn't had much for lunch and only some chocolate in the afternoon. The sausages looked good, but now she almost wished she hadn't acted like a stubborn little child earlier and actually ordered a steak like everybody else. But of course she would rather die than admit that.

Dedicating herself to evenly and perfectly spreading butter on a piece of white bread, D heard the lid of the grill being closed and Joe's steps approaching on the gravel path across the backyard. And then he stopped right behind her chair. She didn't like that at all! To distract herself, she quickly reached for another piece of bread from the basket and started buttering that as well.

"Let's see," she heard Joe say behind her. "Tony – one *rare* for you…"

From the corner of her eye D could see his arm with the fork reaching over and sliding a really nice-looking steak (even if a little too bloody for her taste) onto the plate Tony was holding up.

Still hovering right behind her, Joe continued delivering steaks to Rick and Carrey and then – to D's great relief – wandered away towards where Jack was sitting.

Once Jack and Sun had their steaks and Joe had placed one on his own plate as well, he relocated to his spot behind D's chair.

Only too aware of his return, D felt herself tense up. She couldn't see him and he wasn't close enough to touch of course, but just sensing him behind her was making her edgy. And that absolutely annoyed her.

"Anja," she heard him say, "done, but not too done…"

Across the table Anja held up her plate. "You know how to do this now?" she asked her husband.

"I hope so!" Gerry laughed and held up his own plate to receive his steak.

D was starting to relax a bit. With the last steak just having been delivered and Joe's own starting to get cold over there, he would hopefully soon disappear from behind her.

"And another medium..." Joe announced, his voice shockingly close to her ear. And before she could even make sense of it, his arm appeared over her right shoulder and the steak landed on her plate. She almost dropped her wonderfully buttered piece of bread into her salad. She gasped for air. Her first impulse was to take that plate with the steak and fling the whole thing right back at him. Alternatively she considered pushing her elbow back into whichever body part of his happened to be right behind her at that moment. But Joe, maybe anticipating a reaction just like that, had already walked over to the salad bar.

Still a little dumbfounded, D glanced up and across the table, and found Anja shooting her a wink and a smile. Giving a little shrug, D couldn't avoid a wary smile herself. Yeah right, she had gotten a steak after all. There were definitely worse things that could happen. She should just eat it. After all, it did look really good, and he had probably gotten it just right.

She tried to keep her eyes glued to her plate, while at the same time, from the corner of her eye she was aware of Joe piling some salads onto a plate and finally walking behind them to his chair.

He had just sat down when Jack burst out in laughter. "Oh, my Joe... – You *really* don't like the potato salad, huh?"

Stabbing some cucumbers on her plate, D bit her lower lip. Of course he liked potato salad, but since he knew she had brought it, he probably had made a point of not touching it – as a payback for the steak.

"Well, there's still some left," she heard him say in a saintly tone. And as she took a quick glance over at his plate, she saw the exorbitant amount of potato salad he had piled up there, next to a little spoon of Sun's tomato salad and some noodle salad. Maybe some things never changed...

While they ate and conversations popped up around the table, D tried hard to focus on and participate in what was going on right around her, like Tony now talking about his little baby boy.

For some annoying reason however, she had Joe on her radar constantly, with absolutely no way to stop it. And it wasn't as if he were talking especially loud or behaving in any way that would particularly stick out. No, it was just that some stupid, confused, defective sensor in her brain was tuned to him. She noticed him get up and get something to drink. She heard him laugh out loud about something Jack must have said, and she caught a glimpse of his face when he told Sun in a nice enough way that she should maybe not have any more wine.

D tried to steer her attention back to *her* end of the table. Tony was just handing his mobile phone over to Anja, so she could look at a few pictures of the baby. As far as D knew, the boy was about eight months old now. It was good to see Tony so enthusiastic and proud, because it was no secret that his girlfriend's getting pregnant had been a real test of their relationship. Tony had almost taken a job abroad to flee the scene because he had been so freaked out. It was mostly thanks to Jack's and Sarah's interventions, that Kim and Tony had at least kept talking. And then, right before the baby had been born, and at a time when everybody had more or less given up hope, they were suddenly back together. Looking at Tony now, one couldn't tell that he might have ever had any second thoughts. He seemed really happy.

"Kim looks good!" Anja said as she scrolled through the pictures.

"Yeah, she's doing well," Tony smiled. "It's too bad her parents didn't have time to baby-sit tonight, but I'll bring her for the weekend."

"Well, sounds like you're happy!" Gerry said from across the table.

Tony nodded, looking a little embarrassed. "Yeah, after getting over the initial shock and after behaving like a jerk… I'm really happy! It's exhausting, but at the same time it's so exciting and rewarding. I can actually recommend it now. Believe it or not! Just in case you're considering it for yourself."

Anja blinked with a glance at Gerry. "Um, not right now, thank you…" she said. "Maybe in a few years."

Gerry laughed. He reached out and rubbed Anja's back. "There's no rush, don't worry…"

Once Anja was done looking through the photos, she handed Tony's phone over to D, who quickly scrolled through as well. The kid was really cute. Kim looked happy too. The next few photos showed what must have been the baptism with lots of family gathered around.

As she gave the phone back to Tony, D couldn't help overhearing Rick two seats to her left talking about a concert he had been to recently. He went on to tell that his cousin had apparently founded a band with some friends and they were playing some small unplugged sessions at clubs, doing cover versions of classics and some stuff they had written themselves.

"You should go and hear them sometime," he said with a look in Jack's direction. "They're at the Irish Pub every other Friday. They're pretty good."

"Do you still play, Joe?" It was Sun that asked the obvious. "I still sometimes remember that time when we were at that place up at the mountain for Rick's birthday and you had the guitar with you. That was so cool..."

D felt her stomach cramp as the memory hit her. Joe had done that one song... Before she could stop herself, her eyes had flickered over to him. He was looking at Sun – baffled and clearly uncomfortable. But then his expression quickly returned to an uncommitted smile and he shook his head. "Nope. I haven't played forever," he said. There seemed to be some regret in his voice, but D couldn't have said if it was real or fake.

"The guitar is still in Sarah's house, though" Joe said, his eyes on Sun, "but... well, with this hand I can't play anyway!" He raised his braced hand off the table and shrugged. "You're actually lucky I can still grill..." With this last remark his gaze suddenly shifted, and D couldn't look away fast enough before his eyes met hers across the table.

"I hope the steaks were alright!" he said saintly, his mouth twitching as if he was barely suppressing a grin. D clicked her jaws and looked away while everyone around her assured him that, of course, the steaks had been perfect.

As she reached for her glass to have a sip, D realized that he had successfully steered away from the touchy guitar subject. She had to give him that.

"What's going on with you, Carrey?" D heard Anja ask from across the table.

"Oh, I'm okay," Carrey hurried to say. "Now that the divorce is through and everything. It was pretty hard for a while, but now–" She paused for a moment, lost in thought, her eyes on the glass she was playing with. "Of course, we should have never gotten married in the first place. But when you're young and stubborn and your Dad tells you that you absolutely can't, then, I guess, you just have to." She looked up and across the table at Anja. "At least we didn't have a kid. That would have been a real disaster."

"Yeah, sometimes it's like you don't know a person until your everyday life with them starts," Tony said from the head of the table. D found herself nodding in synchrony with Anja and Carrey and she was just about to add something to the conversation, when Sun's giggling from the other end of the table distracted her. A glance over there revealed that Sun now had her hand on Joe's shoulder and was giggling uncontrollably, briefly even snuggling up to his arm while he played with his glass, looking a little skeptical.

D pulled her gaze away from them and glanced at the silverware on her plate instead. She rearranged it until the fork and the knife were perfectly aligned.

Then Sun giggled again and Joe muttered something that D didn't understand. She was starting to feel hot and kind of sick, though. Because she could pretend all she wanted, it all came down to the fact that she just couldn't tune him out. It was nerve-wrecking! And trying to cover it up was starting to really wear her out. When she saw Anja get up across from her now, she saw a ray of hope.

"Can I help you take in some dishes?" she asked, already rising from her chair.

"Oh, I'll do it," Anja motioned for her to stay seated, but then, obviously guessing the underlying motive, she smiled. "Or you can help me, sure!"

While Anja grabbed the tray from behind her and loaded it with the bottles of ketchup and mustard, the jars of chutney and mayonnaise, the salt and pepper shakers and the empty bread baskets, D started collecting the plates, piling them on top of each other. The silverware she put aside onto the big serving platter in the center of the table. She had already gotten Tony's plate and Gerry's, Anja's and her own, and was making her way around the table collecting Carrey's and Rick's plates. And then, drawing in a deep breath, she moved on towards Jack. He shot her a *how-are-you-doing?* kind of look as she set the stack of plates down on the table next to him. She just gave him a short shrug and took his silverware while he placed his plate on top of the rest.

Then she let her eyes move over to the next plate, which in that moment Joe picked up with his good hand and held out to her. Her eyes firmly on the plate, she snatched it from him. From the corner of her eye she saw him put his silverware with the rest on the big plate.

"Hey D," that was Sun, sounding like she had a big favor to ask, her speech a bit blurred.

D glanced over at her questioningly. Sun's hand was still resting on Joe's shoulder and she looked somewhat troubled, almost sad.

"Can't you two make peace?" she asked, sounding like a mother that just can't accept that her two kids don't get along. Her hand on Joe's shoulder had moved in what seemed to be a rubbing motion and her expression had turned into a pleading smile at D.

D felt her mouth go dry. "What?" she gasped, still trying to figure out if she may have misheard. Reflexively she had looked over at Joe and found him staring at Sun, totally perplexed himself. His jaws tightly locked, he very briefly closed his eyes and then shook his head as if to clear it. His eyes never met hers.

"You worry too much, Sun!" he said with an exaggerated cheerfulness that didn't quite conceal his irritation. "We're *perfectly* peaceful!" And before Sun could respond in any way, he pushed back his chair, making Sun's hand slide off his shoulder. "Sorry, but I need to get up here for a moment," he said to no one in particular.

As he stood up, his eyes briefly moved over to D, who immediately dropped her gaze.

Joe picked up Sun's silverware, laid it onto the big platter and then took Sun's plate. Plate in hand, he squeezed by behind Jack to get out from behind the table. D quickly moved aside to get out of the way, but Joe stepped right up to her. "Just ignore her, okay?" he said, keeping his voice down, "she's pretty drunk – obviously."

D swallowed, feeling momentarily paralyzed by the close encounter. Finally she shrugged.

Joe had already stepped around her and was just placing the last plate on top of the others.

"Mind if I take that in?" he asked and, without waiting for a reaction, he picked up the stack of plates and walked off towards the door to the living room.

D sucked in a quick breath. Had he just left with the plates that she had collected mainly to get away from *him*? Her hands balled into fists she felt this urge to yell at him to bring back the plates this very minute. Idiotic, of course. She knew that well before Jack looked up at her with this look that seemed to tell her to *please* just let it go.

Taking a deep breath and grinding her teeth a bit, she shot a look around the table and decided that she should probably carry on clearing the table despite the fact that now she had a good chance of meeting Joe on the way to the kitchen. But who cared!? She would just have to ignore him! She reached for the serving platter that had all the silverware on it and pulled it towards her. She considered just carrying the platter in as it was, with everything on it, but with *her* luck, some of those knives and forks would surely slide off with a loud bang somewhere along the way. And then Joe would come by in just the right moment to witness her clumsiness. He might even end up helping her pick everything up, which would make it all the more embarrassing. No, she definitely didn't want that! So she took the silverware in her two hands, her fingers wrapped around it tightly and headed into the living room.

"Hey D," Jack called after her, just as she had stepped through the patio door inside.

D came to a halt. "Yes?" she called back, turning around halfway so she could shoot Jack a look via the window next to the patio door.

"Could you bring a few toothpicks when you come back out?" he asked, while at the same time also mimicking what he meant in case she was already out of earshot.

"Sure!" D nodded and was already taking another few steps in the living room, when she suddenly bumped into an obstacle. Something relatively soft.

As she stumbled backwards, trying not to lose her balance or any of the silverware she was carrying, she realized that she had just fully bumped into Joe, who appeared to have been on his way out.

"Shit – I'm sorry…" he gasped.

"No, I'm sorry," D said reflexively. "Was my fault!"

As she looked at him, still recovering from the unexpected impact, D realized that there was something weird about the way he seemed to be holding his braced hand pressed against his side now.

"I got your hand…" she concluded slowly and wished she could just sink into the ground right here.

"Don't worry about it," he said.

"Guess I wasn't looking…" she admitted grudgingly.

"It's not that bad!" he insisted. "I wasn't looking either, so… And you actually can't do much additional damage there anyway." A crooked smile appeared on his face.

D scrambled for something halfway intelligent to do or say, while his looking straight at her, his face so unbelievably familiar, had all kinds of undesired effects on her system.

"I guess I'm lucky you didn't stab me with all those knives," he suddenly said with a hint of a grin, "or the forks…"

D glanced down at her hands where all the sharp objects were still pointing right at him. She corrected that quickly.

"Would have made me look like a voodoo doll," Joe laughed.

Despite of herself, D felt a laugh creeping up on her – at the thought, or simply as an outlet for some of the tension she felt. But then that laugh got stuck somewhere in her throat. Because standing here, laughing with him like good old friends, just wouldn't have worked.

That somber realization must have been visible in her expression, as Joe's face suddenly turned grave too. Raising his hands, palms up, he gave an exasperated little shake of his head. "Oh, come on, Danny, can't we at least…"

"Stop calling me that!" she suddenly heard herself snap.

It had just spilled out. Uncensored. Angry. Mean. And she wished she could take it back the moment she saw the effect it had on him: his expression seemed to freeze; as if she had slapped him or something. Then, his lips pressed together in a thin line, he huffed out some air through his nose.

"Okay…" he said dryly and nodded. "I'm glad we got that part clarified."

D stared at him, her own heartbeat echoing deafeningly in her ears, her mind whirling. She was scrambling for something to say to defuse what she had done. But then it was too late and that chance had gone.

"*Danielle*," Joe said, dragging the name out with a bitter edge. "I guess I'll get used to it." He shrugged. "Just do me a favor, though, don't start calling me Joseph."

For a moment there, D thought she couldn't breathe. She tried to hold his gaze, but she couldn't. So she dropped her eyes to the floor again and waited for this moment from hell to pass.

"You know," she heard him say in a scathing tone, "that's already been the second really stupid thing I've heard from you in less than two hours, Dann– …whatever!" With a dismissive wave of his braced hand, he turned on his heel.

"Don't you call me stupid!" she hissed after him. "I didn't *want* a steak!"

"No one said you *are* stupid," Joe retorted, shooting her a look over his shoulder. "And you didn't have to *eat* that steak!"

He had already reached the door to the patio, when he suddenly stopped and turned around again, like he had just thought of something. "Oh, my…" he said with mock concern, his good hand pressed against his chest. "I sure hope you didn't just choke down that steak so you wouldn't hurt the cook's feelings!"

With that, he turned around and was out the door.

Gazing down at the silverware in her hands, D tried to keep the trembling under control. She couldn't drop the silverware now! And it was unfortunately too late to throw it!

Trying to pull herself together, she slowly walked to the kitchen. The little match with Joe had left her shaky, exhausted – and feeling *stupid*. She had really lost it and behaved like a total idiot out there! The second time already this evening. Cringing, she realized that that was exactly what Joe had just complained about.

In the kitchen Anja was putting a plate with chocolate chip cookies and two containers of ice cream on a tray. She looked up and smiled as D came in. D smiled back, trying hard to conceal her ruffled state of mind and started putting the silverware into the dishwasher.

"Too bad Sarah couldn't get the evening off," Anja said. "It would have been nice to have everyone together. But it's great that at least during the weekend it'll work out. And the weather looks good."

D swallowed a remark about how much she would have preferred having Sarah here this evening instead of her brother. Of course she couldn't say this out loud! She really, really had to get a grip on how she dealt with Joe or the weekend would be a real disaster.

"The hotel seems really nice," she said. "I've never been there but Pete's parents spent a weekend there last year and they really liked it."

"Yeah, sounds great," Anja said. "And the price Rick's cousin made us sure is unbeatable. Pays off to have one friend with a butchery uncle and one with a hotel manager cousin…" She laughed. "Rick said earlier that for the first evening he's got a little conference room reserved with a projector so we can look at the pictures and films."

"Oh, really?" D tried to sound enthusiastic when the whole picture thing was starting to seem like this looming nightmare. "I'm just really looking forward to the lake," she said. "I've always wanted to be able to just step outside and swim."

Anja laughed. "Yes, I think that's exactly what you'll be able to do. I'm not much of a swimmer, unfortunately, but just having the lake there to look at sounds wonderful. And I guess there's plenty to do. I think Rick has already got some ideas. Like some hike and playing mini-golf..."

When they returned outside it was getting dark. The candles on the table were lit and the terrace light had been turned on.

They had their ice cream and cookies.

D stirred around in her ice cream bowl and made sure to participate in the chatter that was going on around her by throwing in an interested *Ah!, Oh!, Really?* or *I know!* every once in a while. The truth was, of course, that she was hardly taking anything in of what was said around her. Instead that scene in the living room kept playing over and over in her head, each time feeling like a kick in the stomach. And there were all the *should-haves* and *could-haves* that were driving her crazy. If her goal for the evening had been to just float through it, getting along with Joe and giving him her indifferent neutral-friendly attitude, she had failed. Horribly.

"Hey D," Anja suddenly pulled her out of her haze. "Didn't you and Pete take a trip to Lisbon last year?"

"Lisbon..." D stammered, trying to focus and smile. "Yeah, we went there last June."

"Gerry and I've gotten tickets from my parents," Anja explained. "For November. Any tips? Restaurants, sights, secret places...?"

With some horror D remembered that trip and scrambled for something positive to tell Anja. It wasn't that hard, of course. After all, it was a beautiful city and there were a lot of fun things to do, providing the travel companions shared the same interests, which Pete and she had not.

She told Anja about the café with a view and the great fish restaurant they had gone to. (The one where Pete had behaved like an absolute prick, almost bringing the poor waitress to tears.) Once she had started, D suddenly did come up with a lot of ideas of neat things to do and see in Lisbon. It just came bubbling out now. And Anja ended up running inside for a pen and a piece of paper and a small travel guidebook to write down what sounded interesting to her. Sometime during the conversation, Gerry briefly interrupted them, tapping on Anja's shoulder and telling her to pay good attention to what D was saying, but that he and Joe were going to go upstairs to see if Joe could help him with some computer trouble.

With Joe gone, D felt like it was suddenly a lot easier to breathe – and focus, for that matter. She told Anja about a great restaurant that she thought they would enjoy. Because it was a pretty place with outstanding food, not because she and Pete had had an exceptionally good time there. (They had spent almost the entire meal in silence after a fight they had had on the way there over her not wanting to quit her job and move in together. They had still had two days left in Lisbon, but she had already started counting the hours until they would fly home and she could be by herself again.)

Finally Anja had enough information and put the pen aside. And the conversation drifted off to things other than Lisbon. Tony, Carrey and Rick got involved as well. And Jack relocated over to Gerry's seat because he felt somewhat left out over there next to Joe's empty chair and Sun in a state where she just seemed to stare into empty space.

They talked about all kinds of things, one topic popping up after another, and D actually found herself enjoying it.

Around eleven Tony, Rick and Carrey decided that it was time for them to leave, and Anja went inside with them to see them off.

"You wanna go too?" Jack asked D when they were alone – with the exception of a semi-conscious Sun.

Barely suppressing a yawn, D nodded. "Yeah, I think that might be a good idea." And after a short pause she added in a whispering voice. "Preferably before *you-know-who* returns."

Jack laughed out loud. "Oh, you're so bad!"

That outburst shook Sun back to life. "What?" she asked, trying to blink herself awake.

"Oh, nothing. Everything's perfectly peaceful…" Jack chuckled. And then, a bit more seriously he added, "We should get going pretty soon."

While Sun nodded, already drifting off into dreamland again, Jack and D both got up and started clearing what was left on the table. On their way inside they ran into Anja, who assured them that Gerry and she would clean up later. Still, they insisted on getting this done, and ten minutes later all remaining dishes had been transported to the kitchen, the seat cushions for the garden chairs had been stored away and Sun had been motivated to at least drag herself from the patio into the living room, where she was now sitting on the sofa, gloomily staring at Gerry's and Anja's framed wedding picture across the room.

"I'm sorry I'm so useless..." she mumbled as Jack came up to the sofa now. "I'm afraid I may have had too much to drink..."

"You think?" Jack laughed and offered her his hand to pull her up.

She got to her feet a little clumsily, with Jack holding on to her arm until he was sure she was stable. Then the three of them thanked Anja for everything, told her to say Hi to Gerry for them and left.

As they reached Jack's car, D dropped into the passenger seat, her salad bowl on her lap. She still couldn't believe her luck that she had actually gotten out of that house without having to see Joe again. Being around him had been way trickier than she had expected. She was just glad that she would have the whole day tomorrow and half of Friday to recover from this. Recover and hopefully work out some fail-safe strategy that would help her avoid making the same mistakes during the weekend that she had made tonight. Just thinking of them now, made her cringe.

As Jack slammed the trunk shut, she pulled the seat belt across herself. She realized how tense she had been all evening only now that the tension was finally starting to ease a bit. Jack walked by Sun's door, which was still open, and made sure all her body parts, her bag and her purse were inside the car, and that she was wearing her seat belt. Then he closed her door and got into the driver's seat.

"She'll never change," he whispered to D with a nod towards the back seat. "As sweet as she is when she's sober, she's really making a fool of herself when she's drunk like that!"

He pulled out his key and put it into the ignition. "Okay, then," he said. "Let's go." He turned the key. The car made a funny noise, but it didn't start. Unimpressed and probably used to that kind of thing, Jack tried it again. Nothing. And again. And again. And again...

D's heart was sinking with every new attempt. 'Please, let that car start, please, please,' she thought to herself. 'Just for this one ride! Please, please, please!!!'

Jack tried one more time. The result was the same as before.

"Crap!" he slammed his flat hands onto the steering wheel. "Fucking piece of shit!"

D swallowed. They wouldn't be going home in Jack's car, that was for sure. The solution was clear enough. What was he still waiting for?

"You'll probably hate me for this," Jack said as he released his seat belt. Then he got out of the car.

Through the side mirror she could see him walk back to the house.

Three minutes later he came back. With Joe.

Watching them come closer, with Joe just pulling a blue sweater over his head, D growled to herself. Lightly banging the back of her head against the headrest, she cursed Jack's car and Jack and the world. How much bad luck could she possibly have in one day?

"What's wrong?" Sun muttered wearily from the back seat when she heard the trunk being opened and slammed shut again, and then Joe walked by with Jack's cooler.

"Car doesn't start," D said flatly and – surrendering to her fate – unbuckled her seat belt.

Jack had stepped up to Sun's door. "Come on, Sun," he said as he opened it. "Change of plans. Joe's going to take us home."

Slowly and clumsily and with some assistance from Jack, Sun started to climb out of the car. Once she was standing, it took her two attempts to shut her door. Then, with unsteady steps, she headed towards Joe's car, which was parked about twenty meters away.

Taking a deep breath, D got out too. Maybe it was childish, but having to ride in that Volvo for 30 minutes seemed like being invited to walk barefoot over a frozen lake.

"I'm really sorry!" Jack whispered as he came up next to her.

"It's okay," she mumbled and kept walking. "Just don't offer me the front seat..."

# Wrong Chauffeur

When they reached the Volvo, Joe and Sun were just getting in. D was relieved to see that Sun had chosen the back seat on the driver's side and left her the spot behind Jack, where, with a little luck, she might be able to duck out of the view range of the rear view mirror. She had definitely had more than enough unpleasant eye contact with Joe for one evening. No need for any more of that, even if it was just via a mirror.

She settled in her seat, the salad bowl on the floor mat between her feet and her purse on her lap. From the corner of her eye she could see Joe pick up his glasses from the middle console and put them on. And even though she had quickly turned her head and was staring at the damaged street lamp outside, the memory of how he had always used to wear glasses for driving and the movies had already flashed through her head, accompanied by a little sting in her stomach.

As soon as Joe started the car, an annoying beeping noise came on.

"Sun, you need to use your seat belt," Joe called back over his shoulder and turned the car back off.

Sun didn't move or even open her eyes.

"Sun!" Joe shot her an irritated look through the rear view mirror.

Sun still didn't react. She was peacefully dozing in her seat.

"Come on, Suuuuun!" Jack growled and reached back with his left hand to give Sun a little push against her knee. "Buckle up for Christ's sake!"

"Stop that!" Sun muttered and moved her legs over to the left and out of his reach.

"I'll do it," D finally said and released her own seat belt. She scooted over towards Sun a bit, reached across, grabbed the seat belt and pulled it over. Leaning so close to Sun, she couldn't help noticing the smell of alcohol and the impressive view Sun's low-cut dress offered to anyone who cared to look from the right angle. A guy would have to be blind to miss that...

After she had Sun safely strapped in, D moved back over to her own place and buckled up again.

"Thanks!" Joe muttered and pulled out of the parking spot.

153

They drove down towards the main street and D tried hard to concentrate on the view outside her window. Her elbow against the armrest on her door and her chin resting in her hand, she watched the shadows of houses, trees and fences flash by.

With the radio on she could only hear bits and pieces of the conversation Jack and Joe were having in the front – Jack apologizing for making Joe drive such a detour, Joe assuring Jack that it was no problem at all, the two of them discussing what could be wrong with Jack's car, Joe offering to take Jack back there the next morning so they could try to fix it…

D turned away from the window and glanced over at Sun. She seemed to be sound asleep. Biting down on her lower lip, D slowly directed her gaze from Sun towards the front. At the driver. Since he had to keep his eyes on the road at the moment and the rest of his attention was focused on Jack, this seemed like a good time to have a closer look… He was wearing jeans and a blue cotton sweater with narrow white stripes over the light blue T-shirt she had seen him in earlier. The glasses looked like they were new, and the haircut had maybe changed a bit but, in contrast to the time at the funeral, he didn't look much different than three or four years ago. And as much as she hated to admit it, she had actually always liked his style: tidy, plain and classy. Without any need to show off anything really expensive. (Maybe that's why it had been so hard to get used to Pete's constant struggle to show off what he had, including her.)

Sucking in a quick breath, she turned back to her window, feeling edgy. She really couldn't wait to get out of this car. It wasn't a healthy environment!

Outside her window the traffic sign for the highway around town flew by. She swallowed. When she had first climbed into Joe's car, she had kind of hoped that he would feel so uncomfortable transporting her, that he would drive straight to her place and drop her off. Just to get rid of her. Obviously, that wasn't going to happen! The way it looked, he was taking Jack home first. Jack lived across town from Anja and everyone else for that matter. So it did kind of make sense for Joe to drive over there first and then, on the way to Sarah's, take her home and Sun. She could only hope it would happen in that order: first her, then Sun… But she probably didn't really have to worry about that. Joe couldn't want to be alone in a car with her any more than she did with him!

Somewhat comforted by this realization, she allowed herself another glance at him. A glance that somehow drifted off towards his hands. His left hand was firmly wrapped around the steering wheel, while the braced right hand was merely resting on his thigh now. From what she could tell, the brace seemed to be designed to stabilize the middle finger and the ring finger as those were fixed to it with a Velcro strap, while the index finger, the thumb and the small finger were free to move. The supported fingers looked swollen. There was no ring on either hand. Whatever that proved. Especially with the brace, it wasn't unlikely that, if there ever had been a ring, it had had to be temporarily removed until the swelling was gone. But really, what did she care?

After a twenty minute ride they reached the apartment building where Jack lived. Jack wished them a good night, got his cooler out of the trunk and disappeared through the hedge beside the parking lot.

Without a word, Joe backed up the car and drove back towards the highway.

The radio was playing music, Sun was sleeping beside her and D was staring out her window where the reflectors on the guard rail were flying by. She was literally counting the seconds now. With some luck she would be released from this choking cage in less than ten minutes.

Suddenly Joe turned the radio down and cleared his throat.

"Sun," he called back and straightened up a bit, so he could see Sun through the rear view mirror.

Sun didn't react.

"You asleep again?" he called a bit louder. "Sun! Time to wake up!"

D turned her head and looked at Sun. She had opened her eyes and was blinking.

"What?" she mumbled with a dazed expression like she didn't even quite know where she was.

"Do you still live in that same flat?" Joe inquired.

Sun nodded slowly. "Yeah, same place," she said sleepily and pulled her knitted sweater, which had fallen to the floor, back onto her lap.

D felt her throat tighten as the meaning of this conversation was sinking in. He wasn't seriously planning to take Sun home next? Or was he? Maybe he wasn't aware that even distance-wise it would be much smarter to take her home before Sun?

Clearing her throat, she shifted in her seat.

155

"You do know where I live, right?" she asked with as firm a voice as she could muster.

"Your grandma's old place, right?" he responded without taking his eyes off the road.

"Yeah…" D struggled for a neutral tone, her heart beating up to her throat now. Obviously he was doing this on purpose! Her hands cramped around her purse in her lap, she tried to calm down, keep a cool appearance. She could hardly start an argument here about the order in which he had to take them home. She would just have to sit through it. And if *he* didn't have a problem being alone in a car with her, she sure as hell wouldn't let him see that it bothered *her*! And really, it could be a lot worse. At least he wasn't some freaky stranger who might turn into a dangerous rapist. Sure, ten tense minutes with the radio playing and both of them hoping that the other one wasn't a mind-reader would feel like hours, but it would end eventually. She would jump out, say good night and that would be it…

When they reached Sun's building, Sun was asleep again.

"Sun, wake up!" Joe called back as he turned off the car.

Sun didn't move. Shooting her a look through the mirror, Joe exhaled sharply. "Suuuuuuun!" he reached back and tried to reach her leg, but he couldn't.

So he got out of the car and opened Sun's door. One hand resting on the car, the other one holding the door open, he looked down at her undecidedly. "Sun, come on, wake up," he said with audible exasperation. "Come on!" He leaned down and nudged Sun's shoulder.

Only very slowly Sun seemed to be regaining consciousness. "Are we there already?" she mumbled with a hazy look up at Joe.

He nodded. And then his glance suddenly flickered past Sun towards D, who wasn't able to look away quickly enough before his eyes met hers.

"Would you…?" He pointed towards Sun's seat belt. "I think we *do* need some help here."

Nodding, D reached over and pushed the release button. Obviously Joe wasn't in the mood to lean over Sleeping Beauty himself and enjoy the view that was on display.

"Here." D passed the buckle over to him without looking up. And he took it without touching her hand.

D picked up Sun's purse and her knitted sweater from the floor where they had landed once again and put them on Sun's lap. "Here, you might need that," she said.

"Thanks," Sun mumbled drowsily and grabbed the two things. Then she laboriously slid her legs out of the car.

"Okay—" Joe said and offered her his left hand. She took it and let him heave her up into an upright position. Holding her stable, he leaned down again and glanced back into the car. Without a word, D handed him Sun's bag with the salad bowl.

"Thanks," he said and grabbed the handles with his left hand, while his right arm was slung across Sun's back now, basically holding her up.

"Okay, come on now!" Joe said and tried to steer Sun towards the steps up to her door.

Watching the pair of them from the car, D couldn't help noticing how heavily Sun was leaning on him. And then, once they reached the door, Sun suddenly seemed to trip over her own feet. Joe almost dropped the bag as he struggled to keep her from falling to the ground. Sun ended up falling against him instead, in what turned out to look like a distorted embrace.

Obviously not unhappy with this result and unaware of his annoyed expression, Sun slung her free arm around his neck.

"Joe," she giggled. "You saved me!" Her speech was blurred. "It's so great that you're back – I kind of missed you! Always liked you…"

And while he was mumbling something and tried to peel her arms off him, she attempted to kiss him.

"God!" Joe huffed as he turned his head away and freed himself, still making sure, however, to support Sun until she was somewhat propped up against the wall next to the front door.

"You should really come in," Sun chirped and reached out to touch his face.

"I still have someone else to take home," Joe reminded her with open irritation. "And at some point I'd actually like to get home and to bed myself."

He pulled Sun's purse out of her hand and held it up to her. "Here," he said briskly. "Where's your key?"

Obediently Sun took the purse and started digging around in it. Finally she pulled out a bunch of keys. In order to get the door unlocked, she had to try three different ones as she seemed to have forgotten which key it was.

Shaking his head, Joe watched her. When the door finally swung open, he gave her a soft push to make her move inside and set the bag down on the hallway floor next to her.

"Good night now," he told her. "Sleep it off!"

With that he pulled the door closed behind her and headed back to the car, where both his and Sun's door were still open. He pushed Sun's door shut.

"God, she'll never change," he grumbled as he dropped into his seat.

"Your effect on women," D muttered, relying on the fact that he wouldn't be able to hear her anyway while closing his door. She was wrong.

"I knew you'd find the right words!" he scoffed without turning around. "Anyway, that's why I wanted to drop her off first, just in case you were wondering. Needed some excuse why I couldn't walk her any further than the front door."

Her eyes on her purse, D let out a sharp little laugh. "Yeah, because you always have to expect that kind of thing, don't you?" she mocked.

Joe turned and shot her an exasperated look. "No, I *don't* generally expect that kind of thing," he said flatly. "But considering how she's been acting all evening, and the amount of booze she's downed, yeah, I can't deny I was kind of afraid of this."

"No, I *fully* understand," D said sweetly. "Danger's over now! You definitely don't have to worry about anything like this with me!"

Huffing out some air, he shook his head. And D realized that he was – right this second – probably thinking to himself, how this had been the third stupid thing she had said to him in just a few hours.

In the front Joe jerked out the seat belt with his braced hand, his face hard, his gaze fixed on the dash board. He must not have had a good grip on the seat belt, though, because it suddenly slipped out of his hand and snapped back, the buckle lashing against the brace.

"Crap!" he sucked in a sharp breath and clutched his left hand around his braced fingers.

"You okay?" D asked reflexively before she could even think about stopping herself.

"Yeah, just great," he muttered and, with a quick movement, pulled the seat belt out again and buckled it up, this time without incident.

It was dead quiet in the car now.

D was waiting for him to start the engine.

But instead he just sat there for a few seconds that seemed to last for hours.

"I assume you definitely don't want to move up to the front, right?" he asked curtly.

She shook her head and turned to look out the side window again. "No, I'm fine. Thanks."

"Okay then," he said with fake cheerfulness and started the car. "I guess I should turn the radio up, so we don't have to talk..."

D watched the street lights flash by outside her window as they were heading back to the main street. Ten minutes left to go until she would be home.

The humming of the engine and the babbling of the radio host had a somewhat calming effect. Still, being all alone in the car with him made her feel exposed in a weird way. As if her tension or even her thoughts might be tangible to him in this environment. Idiotic of course!

To distract herself, she tried to concentrate on the radio where they were just playing a very shallow love song that she had never heard before and didn't particularly like. As the song ended, there were some commercials for a car dealership, a big furniture store and an insurance company. Finally the radio show host came on again. He had a caller. A very talkative young man, who wanted to send his love to his girlfriend. She apparently lived in a different town and he missed her like crazy...

Grinding her teeth, D wished that guy would just stop babbling. It made her really uncomfortable to have this kind of topic float around here.

The radio conversation continued for another two minutes though, before the radio host finally asked, "So, Will, which song should we play for her?" He spoke in this typical upbeat radio host manner.

D exhaled quietly, relieved that now there was at last going to be some music again.

The caller took a moment to answer. Then he said, "Run to you, by Bryan Adams."

D froze. Dug her fingernails into her purse. Not this song! Not here! Not now!

With the first few chords coming on, she gasped and still didn't feel like any air was reaching her lungs.

"Dammit!" Joe hissed.

And then it was suddenly dead quiet. He had turned off the radio.

Swallowing, D made another, more successful, attempt at breathing, her heartbeat sounding like thunder in her own ears now. She glanced over at Joe, who was glowering out onto the road, his left hand cramped around the steering wheel and his jaw bones hard and prominent against his cheek. Apparently this wasn't his favorite song either!

The silence that filled the car now was almost unbearable. Choking. Pure agony. D was suddenly so aware of her own breathing and the heavy pounding of her heart, that she feared that he could hear it too. Of course, that was crazy. She couldn't hear his heartbeat either. But then again, he didn't have a heart!

Finally Joe turned the radio back on. On low volume and on a different station that only played meaningless instrumental elevator music.

They reached the street that D lived on a few minutes later.

As Joe pulled up next to the sidewalk outside her flat, D hastily freed herself from the seat belt and leaned down to grab her salad bowl from the floor. "Thanks," she said quickly and reached for the latch to open the door.

"Wait–" she suddenly heard him say.

It made her stop in mid-movement.

"*What?*" she asked, shooting him a questioning look.

"Just wait a second, okay?" he said and leaned back in his seat, his head against the headrest.

D let herself fall back into her own seat, her heart picking up speed again.

"I know you hate me," Joe said matter-of-factly, his eyes trained on the windshield, "and I'm perfectly aware that being at the same party, let alone in a car with me, is the last thing you wanted for tonight..."

Totally perplexed, D stared at his profile.

"It wasn't really high up on my wish-list either, to be honest!" He let out a dry little laugh. "But... Well–" Instead of finishing his sentence, he shrugged.

Frantically struggling for a proper reaction, D dropped her gaze to her salad bowl that she was balancing on her left thigh. There were some scratches in the glass.

"I *do* know what an ass I've been," Joe contemplated. "I *do* know that, believe me... And I wish I could change some things, but I can't."

Feeling like someone had just knocked the air out of her, D's eyes darted up at him again. He was still staring out the front window.

"Anyway," he said and straightened up in his seat enough to where he could shoot her a look through the rear view mirror. "I think we need to find some way here to behave like civilized normal people around each other, okay? At least for this coming weekend…"

Staring back at him via the mirror, D swallowed. Nodded. And dropped her gaze.

"So that would mean, for instance," Joe continued and turned around to her, "that you just tell me how you want your steak the next time I ask."

"Well, you know that anyway," D said weakly, unable to look at him.

"Exactly!" he exclaimed and threw up his hands, palms-up. "But that's just the perfect example of how you do these really stupid things just to…" He seemed to be looking for the right words. "…just to get back at me. Either that, or you just flat-out ignore me."

D's expression hardened. "I wasn't–"

"Sure you were," Joe insisted. "And Dann–" He swallowed the rest of her name, making a face like he had just tasted something disgusting.

"I probably deserve it," he said, "but in the interest of everyone around us… – They just want to have a good time, okay? No one wants to deal with our crap…"

Struggling to keep breathing, D stared down at the salad bowl again. She tried to find the scratches because they had something comforting. The leisurely way he had just dropped a personal pronoun connecting the two of them, *our crap*, completely threw her off. That and the fact that unfortunately, what he was saying hit the nail right on the head. (He actually sounded a bit like Robert…)

"Anyway," he said. "Do you think you could at least try to… – you know…"

She nodded and forced herself to look at him "Yeah…I'll try," she said, amazed that her voice still sounded halfway normal.

"Great," Joe nodded, seeming content. Then he turned to the front again.

As he leaned back in his seat, D figured that she was probably released now. She should move. Open the door. Get out of the car.

"By the way," Joe suddenly said, just as she was pulling the latch on the door. "It's actually good to see you. Despite everything…"

With all the strength she could scrape together, D pushed her door open and willed her legs out of the car, her entire body feeling like lead now.

"Thanks for driving me home," she mumbled as she straightened up. "Bye."

She nudged the door closed and directed her feet down the stairs that lead from the sidewalk to the gravel path through her front yard. Everything seemed to be happening in slow motion, and there didn't seem to be any way to speed it up. The fact that she could feel him watching her from the car didn't help, of course. Couldn't he just leave?

When she reached the three steps up to her front door and unzipped her purse with trembling fingers, she finally heard the car being started behind her. And as she turned the key in the lock, he drove off.

D fled inside. Set the salad bowl and her purse on the small side table under the coat rack and stuck the key into the lock from the inside.

She drew in a frantic breath. She wasn't going to let this feeling get to her! Never in a hundred years!

Running her hands through her hair, she headed to the bathroom. To the sink. Avoiding any look into the mirror, she turned on the cold water and leaned down. She shoveled a few handfuls of ice cold water right into her face… She couldn't let ten minutes in a car with him throw her into an emotional mess!

She straightened up, exhaled and opened her eyes, shooting herself a warning look through the mirror. The water had turned her mascara into freaky dark shadows around her eyes, giving her a very unhealthy look. And there was a dark tear-like drop of water mixed with mascara running down her right cheek.

Why couldn't he just behave like the despicable monster she had told herself he was? Why couldn't he just have taken Sun home last? Even if it meant her dragging him into her bedroom… Involuntarily D ground her teeth. No, she didn't really want to think this scenario through any further. Anyway, why the hell did he have to say that it was good to see her? That had actually been the most disturbing thing he had said all evening. That and the weird comment about how he'd like to change things.

She poured some make-up remover onto a cotton pad and wiped off the deadly shadows around her eyes.

What part of it would he like to change?

Crap, why had he thrown that out? Couldn't he just have kept his mouth shut? Let her get out of the car and leave? It wasn't as if she had really needed that lecture on how she would have to drop the hostile attitude for the weekend. She had pretty much figured that out herself by then.

Her reflection was looking back at her. And she watched her own eyes fill up with tears until her vision turned cloudy.

With a quick impatient move she wiped the tears off with her hand so rapidly that she almost scratched her face with her watch.

Clutching the sides of the sink with both hands, she took a few deep breaths. In and out, in and out... If only these last two minutes she had spent in his car would stop replaying over and over again in her mind.

She turned the faucet on again and shoveled some more water against her face. Like there really was a way to just wash this off... It had already started to stick!

She grabbed the towel and buried her face in it. This was crazy! Growling, she threw the towel against the mirror. It landed in the sink and she left it there.

Still shaky she walked into the bedroom and changed into sweatpants and a T-shirt. Then she went to the living room and dropped down on the sofa. She had decided to watch TV for a while because going to bed now was out of the question. Bad dreams were guaranteed, provided that she could sleep at all. Hopefully, the TV would help take her mind off him!

She reached for the remote and started flipping through the channels. All kinds of programs flashed by: a crime series, a drama movie, a documentary about some hospital related issue, a comedy show, some romantic crap, the news, another series of some kind...

Soon she had gone through sixty stations without having found anything that could interest her enough to stop thinking about something she was determined not to think about.

She grabbed the DVD remote and started a new episode of her show. Maybe that would help. She forced herself to stay tuned. She made every effort to connect with the story that was happening on screen. But there was just no way.

With a frustrated growl she turned it all off.

Everything was quiet now.

Tapping the tip of the remote control against her nose, she huffed out a frustrated breath. She might as well face it: a few hours around him and she was all gaga!

She sat there and stared at the black TV screen for another two minutes. Then she got up from the sofa, went back to the bedroom and whisked a large flat cardboard box out from under her bed, almost pulling the handle off in the process. She knelt down on the carpet next to it and, after a moment of hesitation, slid the lid off the box. Chewing on her lip, she dug around in the box between old photo albums, her first baby shoes, an almost hairless doll she had loved as a kid, a bunch of diaries from when she was a teenager and some other things she had kept as memories. Finally she pulled out what she had been looking for: a CD case with Joe's slightly messy handwriting on it.

For a moment she held it in her hand and stared at it... Now, this was a really, really bad idea and she knew it! Still, maybe it was something she just needed to do. She slid the lid back onto the box and pushed it back under the bed with her foot. Then she returned to the living room, took the CD out, set the case on top of the stereo and placed the disk in the player.

She stepped around the coffee table and plopped down on the sofa, her head against the backrest. Turning the remote control around in her hand a few times, she reminded herself once again that this was an absolutely idiotic thing to do. The equivalent of a drug dose for an addict who had been clean and relatively happy for three years. A consciously bad, bad, bad decision! But she really needed to know what this felt like! She just did!

So she closed her eyes, took a deep breath and pressed play.

# Finding a Phone

Pulling out of D's street, Joe turned the radio off. He felt exhausted. This whole evening, even though it had been fun at times, had been a bit much. He had always known that Sun was a handful, but so far he had never had the problem of being the target of her flirting activities. He couldn't say he liked it. And he sure wasn't very good at dealing with it either. Especially when it got on his nerves like that and at the same time he had to try not to embarrass Sun because – after all – she still was a friend.

What bugged him a lot more than Sun, of course, was Danny. He hadn't really been prepared for the hostility she had met him with. Not because it was surprising. It wasn't. Not really. Had he given it any thought at all, he could have easily predicted what their first encounter would be like. But he hadn't given it any thought. Intentionally. Because it would have probably kept him from coming back to Deens. And lately coming back here had been like the bright light at the end of the dark tunnel.

Therefore, he had carefully avoided thinking about Danny. (And it wasn't like blocking her from his mind had been that much of an effort. After three years of practice, it came almost naturally…)

From the moment she had stepped out onto Anja's patio this afternoon, though, there had been no way to further ignore the problem. It had just totally blown him away how she still seemed to be exactly who she'd always been and how (and that had been a brand new experience) she absolutely hated his guts.

The whole thing with the steak had been just silly, he had forgotten about it almost the minute it had happened. But her lashing out at the name had had an entirely different quality to it. It had actually hurt. And it still did.

When he reached the highway now, he suddenly heard the ringing of a mobile phone. He frowned. It definitely couldn't be his because his had been turned off for two days now. The ring tone was amazingly similar, though.

The noise seemed to be coming from somewhere under or behind his seat.

Great! Apparently someone had dropped their phone!

He passed a few more cars and then took off at the next exit. He pulled over into the parking lot of a small bank. The bank was long closed. Some guy was using the ATM and looked over his shoulder now, checking who had just parked next to his car and if there was any danger. Well, it was late at night and one never knew.

Joe turned on the light in the car and searched for the phone. Now that it wasn't ringing anymore, it was hard to locate. He finally felt it somewhere in the back under his seat. Fishing it out, he eventually had to use his braced hand and, of course, he got the brace caught on something under the seat. An immediate flash of pain made him swear and freeze for a moment. Man, he just hated that brace. Cautiously he wiggled his hand free and, the phone clasped between his index finger and his thumb, finally managed to pull it out.

He looked at the phone. Judging from the side he had found it on, it had to be Sun's. Maybe tomorrow, when he took Jack back to his car, they could swing by Sun's place and drop it off. There was no way he was going back there now.

He almost dropped the phone, when it suddenly came back to life in his hand now and started ringing again. The display showed a picture of the caller. Joe's eyebrows snapped together. Pete!?! What an unpleasant surprise!

The picture must have been taken in some park as there were blooming trees and flowers in the back ground. And Pete was smiling his smile.

Joe growled. He knew Pete from a half-year course they had taken together. And even though he didn't know him well, Pete had always annoyed him. He couldn't quite put a finger on why. Part of it was that, to him, Pete just seemed like the perfect example of a stuck-up, rich parents, know-it-all little weasel, who was probably hiding some serious complexes or worse. To think that this guy had somehow managed to pick up Danny, was hard to imagine and even harder to accept. Dear Pete had been to Lisbon with Danny, right? How nice!?! Heart-warming! Maybe that picture had even been taken on that trip to Lisbon… Joe ground his teeth. Once that Lisbon topic had come up after dessert, he had gratefully taken the opportunity to go and help Gerry with his computer upstairs.

With pointy fingers, Joe laid the ringing phone on the passenger seat now. He stared at it with growing disgust, while Pete kept smiling from the display. Finally the ringing stopped and Pete vanished.

Okay. Joe blew out some air with his lower lip sticking out. So this was definitely Danny's phone then. Must have fallen out of her purse when she had helped with Sun's seat belt.

Trying to ignore the thumping pain in his hand, he considered his options. He could always take the phone back home with him and give it to Sarah in the morning. Let *her* return it. It was a safe and reasonable solution. And, so he suspected, the solution that Danny would favor.

Only that his mind had already gotten stuck on the crazy idea of driving back to her place right now and bringing her the phone in person. That idea, he realized with some confusion, had something disconcertingly tempting…

Trying to look at the matter from all sides, it occurred to him though, that – if he decided to keep the phone overnight – it would be impossible for Pete to reach her. That had something very appealing as well. Because, if he was honest with himself, it bothered him quite a bit that Pete smiled from her phone at this time of night. Hadn't Sarah said they had – how had she put it? – *kind of* broken up? What the hell did Pete still want then, in the middle of the night?

Joe reached over and snatched the phone from the seat again. Maybe there were some more pictures or other enlightening photos saved on it? More Pete pictures or even some messages…

Just as he was about to click on the display to get into the photo gallery, the phone started to ring again. And it was Pete *again!*

With an irritated growl, Joe threw the phone back onto the passenger seat like it was a hot potato. His mind had just been made up! Under absolutely *no* circumstances should he keep that phone overnight. He just *knew* that if he did, Pete would call again and smile again, and at some point he would just have to pick it up. And who knew which sick and twisted turns a conversation like that might take…

No, he was going to take that phone to her right now!

# Still up?

The street leading down to D's house was quiet. Most houses seemed dark. Only in the first house on the left the lights were still on. Judging from the many cars that were parked outside, they must be having a party.

Joe remembered being in that house for a birthday party once. He must have been seventeen or so. Sarah had – for some silly reason – taken him along. She had been going out with a guy who lived there, and she had maybe decided to bring her brother so Dad wouldn't ask too many questions. Whatever it was, Joe remembered that he had somehow ended up with Sarah's boyfriend's older sister that night – a girl who had easily been four years older than him. Judy. Yeah, her name had been Judy. He remembered being very bored at the party and hating the music they were playing. He had relocated to the huge overgrown garden to smoke some slightly illegal substance that someone had pushed on him, and suddenly Judy had appeared between the bushes and asked if the joint was any good. And since it had only been his second (and pretty much last) joint ever and he couldn't say much about the quality, he had just let her try it. And somehow they had ended up messing around against that tree. He hadn't been the driving force in this. Not at all. But he could hardly be called an innocent victim either. With the joint and a lot more to drink than he had been used to, he had happily stumbled right into that. Until Sarah had appeared with her boyfriend... Even today Joe was still wondering if they had been looking for him like Sarah claimed, or if they had just been trying to find a place to be alone. Whichever it was, Sarah had been *disgusted* – that had been her exact word, yeah. Disgusted with him, disgusted even more with Judy, who, according to Sarah's interpretation, had taken advantage of her little brother... (Hahaha!)

Judy and he had met again a few more times. He had kind of had a crush on her. Or at least he had thought so. Of course, he had hardly even known her, they had had absolutely nothing in common, and they hadn't exactly spent their time together with great conversations or getting to know each other better, but mainly with physical stuff. It had been quite educational in certain ways, though...

Thinking about it today, he was torn apart between amusement and embarrassment. But then again, he had been only seventeen and people that age should be allowed to make mistakes.

When he passed the little bakery on the right now and D's building came into view, Joe felt his stomach cramp. He suddenly realized that in a movie something like a forgotten phone would never be a coincidence. Maybe he was supposed to act on this? He considered it for a moment and then pushed the idea aside. This wasn't some teenage soap opera but his own messed up life! And he really had enough drama in his life already as it was, or not?

Besides, he wasn't even sure how she would react to his showing up again. She might not open the door. Maybe she wasn't even awake anymore. The house actually did seem pretty dark. He should probably take this as a sign.

He was about to turn the car around and leave, when he realized that the house wasn't totally dark after all. There was a weak flickering light coming through the window next to the front door.

Okay, so she was still up…

Pulling up along the sidewalk, he parked the car.

He reached for the phone and undecidedly held it in his hand for a moment. Then, taking a deep breath, he got out of the car and walked up to the door. After another moment of hesitation he rang the doorbell – and softly knocked at the same time.

"It's me…" he called trying to keep his voice down. "You dropped your phone in my car!"

He knocked again. Then waited. Even though he was almost certain that she wouldn't open. He really should have just brought the phone to Sarah to give back. It had been a really stupid idea to hand-deliver it now. Why exactly had he wanted to do that???

Suddenly he heard the key turn in the lock and the door slowly swung open about halfway.

He was prepared for an aggressive *'What?'* or an angry look, but she just stood there, looking tired and almost fragile – and it wasn't just because she appeared to have washed off the bit of make-up she had been wearing earlier.

She had changed into blue sweat pants and a T-shirt, and she was barefoot. From her T-shirt, a green alligator was grinning, showing a big mouth with lots of sharp teeth, one of which was sparkling golden. Joe realized that he knew that T-shirt...

Trying not to think about where he had seen that alligator last, he looked away – at the salad bowl that was sitting on the small side table next to D half a meter away from him. Right above the salad bowl he saw the print: mountain lake with towering thunderstorm clouds. In the dorm, this picture had been hanging over her bed.

Joe clenched his jaws and exhaled quietly, his gaze briefly wandering past her towards the living room. It was dark except for a candle flickering on the coffee table. Joe swallowed. That shelf next to the sofa looked like the one from the dorm.

He looked back at her starting to feel quite a bit out of balance here...

For a moment D's eyes flickered up at him, but as soon as she found him looking back at her, she quickly dropped her gaze to the phone in his hand. He handed it to her. And this time he made sure he *did* touch her hand, even if just briefly.

"Thanks," she said. "Where was it?"

"What? Oh – It was under my seat."

"Oh, really?" she turned the phone around in her hands.

Joe shrugged. "I just noticed it because," he paused for a moment weighing his words. "*Peeeete* called." The way he overstretched the *eeee* made her look up. She raised her eyebrows and gave him a look that he couldn't quite read.

"Don't worry," he said, "I didn't pick it up. Didn't really feel like talking to him."

Her eyes locked with his now, she blinked, obviously imagining that scenario – his picking up Pete's call. He waited for her expression to turn angry or at least accusing, but it didn't.

"You really didn't have to come back just for that!" she said instead, her eyes dropping to the phone again. "But of course, it's good to have it. I'm meeting Sarah tomorrow and it would be a bit tricky if I couldn't find my phone and she couldn't reach me. So, thanks!"

"You're welcome."

She touched her right eyebrow with her index finger and brushed over it, and Joe suddenly remembered how she had used to always do that... It was at that moment that he realized just *how* good it was to see her. In sweats, without any make-up, barefoot and tired.

Biting down on his lower lip, he slowly exhaled and tried to shake off the weird feeling that was creeping up on him. He was such an idiot! He should go! He had brought back the phone and that had been the point, right? His job was done. Standing around here any longer was really having an unsettling effect.

He had already shifted his weight, ready to take the first step away from the door to return to the car, when he suddenly noticed the faint music that was coming from the living room. One song had just faded and a new one had come on. Despite the very low volume, he immediately recognized the piece. It made his throat tighten. He hadn't heard this song in a long time. Not just because it was hardly ever played on the radio.

As he stood there, somewhat paralyzed and trying hard to tune out the music, he suddenly realized that – when he had handed her the phone and mentioned Pete – there had also been something affecting him in a weird way. Music? He hadn't been consciously aware of it then, but he was almost certain of it now: it had been very quiet after he had dropped the name with the drawn-out *eeee*. Quiet but not totally silent! There had been some music in the background. Definitely.

Staring past her towards the stereo on the shelf in the living room, Joe tried to recall what kind of music it had been that he had heard earlier. He hadn't paid attention then, so he realized it might be impossible to reconstruct. But then – unexpectedly – a short segment of the melody from earlier flashed through his mind. And he immediately knew *exactly* what song it had been.

With the current and the previous song now identified, his head was buzzing. He was weighing the probability of *both* these songs playing anywhere in just *one* single evening in *this* particular order. The probability was close to zero. Unless, of course – and that's when it hit him – she was listening to the CD he had made for her...

# Music and what it stands for...

"Well... Have a safe drive home," he heard her say through the haze that had just come over him. She had straightened up and, despite what she had just said, looked at him a bit undecidedly.

Giving himself a push, Joe nodded. "Yeah thanks," he mumbled. "Good night." And as he turned around and walked down the three steps to the gravel path, he heard the door close behind him and the music stopped.

~~~

Shutting that door, D almost felt like she was trying to shut the heavy metal gate of some giant fortress. She almost couldn't do it. Somehow these last five minutes had cost her all the strength and willpower and composure that she still might have had. And that music that was still playing back there was taking the rest. Putting that CD on had really been the cruelest self-experiment she could have come up with. Did she really have to see how far she could go here? How far she could push herself? Well, maybe this had been just a tiny step *too* far?

Closing her eyes, she leaned her back against the wall next to the door and slid down until she was sitting on the floor. If she had been going for the maximum amount of pain, she had really nailed it. Well done! First accidently drop your phone in his car, then put on the music that could kill you just by itself, and then – to top it all off – get lucky enough to have him show up at your doorstep right in the middle of it. A deadly mix, really!

The evening and the ride in his car had been bad enough, but having him back here, eye to eye, being friendly and nice, had made it so much worse! She didn't want him to be nice! She didn't want him to be any of the things that reminded her of the guy she used to know and that she had tried so hard to ban from her memory. But with everything he'd said or done this evening, there was no denying that he still was *exactly* that guy.

She pulled her legs up and wrapped her arms around her knees. She should turn off that music, of course. But what good would it still do? For tonight, the damage had already been done. Burying her face in her arms now, she was fighting tears. Maybe she should just let go and stop fighting for composure here. She was alone. Even if she cried all night, no one could see her and no one would ever know. It might actually be helpful to get it out of her system. Kind of like an immunization for the next few days.

She hadn't really come to a conclusion, when the next song came on. And that's when – even without her explicit permission – tears started streaming down her face uncontrollably. There was absolutely no way she could have still fought it. Not with this song – and the memories that seemed to be stuck to it like glue.

As the first tears reached her lips, she stuck out her tongue. To check how salty it tasted. And while the taste confirmed beyond doubt that these were really tears, she tried to remember when she had last cried. It had been a few years. But it had been about the same guy.

~~~

Like in a daze, Joe walked back to the car and dropped into his seat. Somehow his head was spinning. With all the wrong ideas.

Rubbing his forehead, he tried to regain some control of his mind. It didn't work. That music had just hit him full-force! Crap! He should never have come here! Really, he should have just turned that stupid phone of hers off and dropped it into Sarah's lap in the morning.

He had totally underestimated what coming back to Deens would mean emotionally. It had been ludicrous to block out the fact that he would have to see Danny and what that meant. It would have been wise of him to not simply dive head-first into this great adventure of coming for the reunion but to at least somewhat prepare himself that this whole thing might be a bit... – confusing? disturbing? unsettling? – and not just for him.

Hearing the music there at her doorstep in combination with having her right in front of him, close enough to touch, had somehow whacked him totally out of balance. There was something about music that could – in a heartbeat – bring back memories and feelings. Even the ones that he had thought were well-buried.

There were some songs that could pass as a soundtrack to his life. And if there was a soundtrack to his time with her, the two pieces he had just heard – and the entire CD for that matter – were part of it. Yeah, and in that respect the Bryan Adams song that the idiot on the radio had ordered earlier, was the score to the final absolute disaster.

Joe took a deep breath. Over the past three years he had been avoiding the songs he had put on that CD at all cost. He had regularly changed the radio station as soon as he heard the first familiar chords. And if any of these songs had come on during a party, he had relocated to the next balcony or patio – anything that had fresh air and a door that could be used to block the sound. Running into this music right here and now seemed like a nasty joke.

Chewing on his lip, he tried to make sense of this. There was something terribly wrong with the picture of her playing this CD. The music was hard for him to take, alright. But if there was one person in this world that – he would have sworn – would have an equally hard, if not harder time listening to that stuff, it was her. So, why on earth was she doing it? Why would she put that CD on? Tonight?

He swallowed as his mind slowly worked its way through this. Yeah – *why?* Joe tilted his head back against the headrest and exhaled. It was just a guess, of course. And he wasn't a trained psychologist. But based on his common-sense psychology, it did make sense in a weird way…

Shit!

His eyes on the car clock, he tried to focus. It was almost one o'clock. He should go home and take one of his painkillers. The thumping pain in his hand that he had briefly forgotten about was getting harder to ignore now. And with some luck those painkillers wouldn't just help against the pain in his hand but also knock him out before he had a chance to deal with any of the issues that were trying to come to the surface here.

He really should go home!

Of course, there was something that was holding him back. Some weird fluffy-cozy-toasty feeling that was firmly connected to the music – and her. It scared him to death. He must be totally brain-dead! She had spent the entire evening exhibiting just how much she detested him, and he came out of it feeling so drawn to her that it hurt. Because that's what it came down to, wasn't it?

He should definitely go home! He had *so* messed it up with her three years ago! He better keep out of her way. He did owe her that. And it was probably best for him as well.

He closed his eyes for a moment. In his head thoughts had started spinning in a dizzying fashion around anything *but* keeping out of her way. He opened his eyes again. Forced himself to look at his right hand. The two broken fingers were swollen and they really hurt. This was a fact and a clear sign that yes, he should quickly go home, take the painkillers and go to sleep. It was a good, safe and reasonable plan. Those other ideas that

174

were swirling around in his head were exactly the opposite of good, safe and reasonable!

He stuck the key into the ignition telling himself that tomorrow was another day. And tomorrow would be a lot easier if he just turned that key. *Now!* He started the car and put it in gear.

And then he turned it off again and got out.

This was playing with fire, of course. He knew it. But he didn't exactly care.

# It's still good music!

Still sitting on the floor behind the door, hugging her knees, D froze when she heard the footsteps approaching outside her door. There were a few soft knocks.

"Danny! Open, up... Please."

Her heart kicked into an unhealthy racing beat and her mouth, and even her tear-filled eyes, went dry.

Joe knocked again.

She forced herself to keep up the vital functions, like breathing and blinking.

"Come on, Danny, open up!"

She could ignore it. Just as he was obviously ignoring that he shouldn't call her Danny! She could play deaf or better dead and pretend for the rest of her life that it had been a wise decision. It would be a wise decision, no doubt about it. Very wise and safe! But could she live with it?

"Danny..." There were two more light knocks.

With a trembling hand D wiped the tears off her face and slowly got up.

Outside her door Joe felt like he had just done a sprint on an empty stomach. His heart was definitely in that kind of mode and so was his stomach. Knocking at her door again – in what he hoped was a non-neighbor-waking fashion – he kept telling himself that this was a stupid, stupid, stupid idea! She would never open up now! She would have to be crazy. Somehow, realizing this had something strangely comforting. It was much better if she didn't open. Really! He should go back to the car and they could both pretend this had never happened.

He had already walked down the three steps from the door to the gravel path, when he heard the key turn. His heart skipping a beat, he turned around again. The door was open. She had opened it about three quarters of the way and looked towards him, a somewhat shocked expression on her face. He wondered if she was shocked because he had returned or shocked because she had actually opened the door.

"What?" she asked quietly as he stepped up to the door again. To his amazement she didn't seem hostile. If anything, she looked a bit lost and helpless – and like she had been crying...

He couldn't help feeling pretty lost himself. Now what? Did he have *any* plan as to what to do or what to say? Her standing in the open door here was so unexpected that part of him was still kind of waiting for her to open her mouth and tell him to get lost. But she just stood there with hanging shoulders, her gaze fixed on the floor between them and said nothing at all.

In an attempt to keep himself from doing anything really stupid now, such as reaching out and touching her face, he placed his left hand against the doorframe.

"What do you want?" she asked shakily, her eyes flickering up at him.

"I'm not sure," he admitted.

Her eyes back on the floor, she just stood there.

"Well…" He cleared his throat. "If you want me to leave, just say so. I'll leave, I promise… and I won't ask why you're listening to *that*…" He nodded towards the room behind her.

He saw her gasp. Then she closed her eyes for a moment and bit down on her lower lip.

"Really," he assured her, keeping his voice down. "I'd just take off and assume that this is your usual going-to-sleep music…"

With an impassive shrug she glanced up at him. She still didn't say anything, though. Joe decided that under the given circumstances this was maybe not all that bad.

"Can I come in?" he asked, his hand tracing the molding around the doorframe.

Instead of any kind of response she exhaled audibly and looked up at him, obviously slightly baffled at the question. Then she dropped her gaze again, maybe considering what to do in such a surreal situation.

Keeping an eye on her, Joe had to fight the strong urge to reach out and tilt her chin back up to him. Instead he took his left hand off the doorframe and shoved it into the back pocket of his jeans.

Suddenly the silence was blasted by the ringing of her phone. When she almost dropped it, Joe noticed that she must have been holding it in her hand all the time. The ringing continued…

Joe swallowed, realizing that this was it. The end of their nice little open-door meeting. That stupid creep Pete! Couldn't he call some other time?

In a rush of frustration, Joe slammed the side of his right hand against the doorframe and took a step back from the door. The immediate sharp pain that flashed from his fingers all the way up to his shoulder now, reminded him that he might want to consider using a different body part next time he felt the need to hit something.

The ringing phone still in her hand, D chewed on her lower lip and glanced up at him for a moment. Joe was prepared for her to give him an apologetic smile or something and close the door. He just *knew* that with Pete calling again now, there was no way it could be avoided.

But then she didn't pick up. In fact, as Joe caught a glimpse at the display, it didn't even seem to show Pete's stupid picture but just a short name that he couldn't read from where he was standing.

"Jack," D said and shot him another quick, slightly uncomfortable look. Then she turned the phone off and placed it beside the salad bowl on the side table next to her.

Joe couldn't believe it. According to his little vision the door should be closed by now. Well, it was still open. And as her eyes locked with his now, her expression almost scared, she gave the door a little push with her bare foot and stepped aside.

It was only then that Joe realized that he wasn't entirely in control of his own movements. He felt momentarily paralyzed and had to give himself a real push to make his feet move across the threshold. But she probably wasn't in any particular hurry to have him step inside anyway.

D watched him come in, still stunned by her own actions. Her hand gripping the door handle, she shut the door behind him and remained with her back to the room – and to him for that matter – for a moment. God, what was she doing? She briefly closed her eyes, and exhaled a shaky breath. Then she slowly turned around.

Following some instinct, Joe headed straight for the stereo. He stopped the music and picked up the CD cover. He squinted. By the way this plastic cover looked, it must have been through some very rough times. But then again, he was surprised that it still existed and hadn't been ceremonially destroyed long ago. He scanned the titles that he had listed on the cover. There were some love songs that – given the circumstances – were absolutely unsuited for this kind of setting. He still couldn't believe that she had put that CD on. That was one crazy thing to do!

As the silence in the room seemed to be getting heavier to the point where it had a choking quality to it – and in lack of any better ideas – he changed his mind. Why not listen to some music here? She had already exposed herself to the worst part of that CD. Why not listen to some more? Maybe something a little less heavy as a warm-up for himself, though. He skipped the CD forward a few songs. Cindy Lauper – *Time after Time*.

D hadn't moved. Her palms pressed firmly against the door behind her, she watched him. It was really all she could do, because with those wobbly knees she couldn't walk, with that dry mouth she couldn't talk and with a totally clouded brain she couldn't even think clearly.

To her great relief he had gone and done what, somehow, she hadn't been capable of: he had turned off that music. Yeah, he probably thought she had gone totally mad to be listening to that. He had picked up the CD case and given her that raised-eyebrow kind of look. Well, yeah, that case had been abused and he was lucky it still existed!

Joe had placed the CD case back where he had found it. And then – to her absolute horror – he had pushed some buttons, skipping through the CD, and had turned the music back on.

D felt her heart miss a beat.

"Turn it off," she said, her voice cracking.

"It's still good music," Joe told her with an almost apologetic shrug.

"It's crap," she breathed, still totally taken aback by the music playing again.

He shook his head. "No, it's not crap!" he said patiently and started peeling out of his sweater, trying hard not to get his braced hand caught in the sleeve. He emerged, his hair a bit messy, and tossed the sweater back towards the sofa. "Okay…" He brushed back his hair with the fingers of his left hand and gave her a cautious look across the room. Suddenly his face lit up as if he had just had an idea. "Wanna dance?" he asked.

D shook her head in disbelief.

He came strolling towards her anyway.

She sucked in a quick breath, scrambling for a flight plan. But she couldn't move. There was just no way.

He stopped two steps away from her. "Come on," he said and tilted his head to the side – with a smile that seemed a bit unsteady.

Unable to hold his gaze, D shook her head again. But even without looking at him, she could feel his eyes on her.

Then he reached out and just took her right hand.

Reflexively her eyes darted up at him. She really wanted to jerk that hand away from him, but somehow she just couldn't.

179

"Danny, come on…" Joe pulled on her hand a little, trying to make her separate from the door.

"You can't be serious," she said weakly. But for reasons she didn't quite understand, she *did* let him pull her away from the door and a few steps into the living room.

"Come on, just dance with me," he said as he placed his braced hand against her lower back.

~~~

From the moment he put his arm around her, Joe was literally holding his breath. This was for sure not going to work! Never in a hundred years would she go along with this. Even if the current dancing position wasn't close by any means. He was giving her more space here than she would have probably had, were she dancing with the Pope. Still, he was expecting her to push him away any moment. Push him away and kick him out. After all, what he was doing here was just outrageous!

"Just try, okay?" he said softly. "Dance with me." It felt a bit like holding a big piece of wood in his arms but he was totally in awe that she even still *was* in his arms.

"Danny, relax!" he told her again. Then he pulled her a little closer and started moving – constantly expecting her to lash out at him and end this.

But then, slowly, very slowly, he felt the resistance fade, and she actually did start to dance with him – if what they were doing could actually really be called dancing. Dancing or not, it made his head spin.

"Danny, just relax, okay," he whispered. "And *do* something about that arm there that's hanging down so limply…"

Scoffing, she raised the arm and, even though he knew it was on his shoulder now, he could hardly feel it. Because she rigidly kept it from fully resting against him.

Well aware that he was pushing it, Joe pulled her closer still into what might actually pass as a close dancing position and desperately hoped that he would get away with this.

Crap, he must be completely out of his mind!

~~~

Staring over Joe's shoulder, D was struggling to suppress the trembling that was caused by a racing heart, irregular flat breathing and him as such. God, what was he doing? And why the hell did she let him? This was all wrong! It was almost like some absurd dream, only that she was pretty sure it was real. And despite being dangerously stupid, it just felt amazing. Which made it even more wrong, of course!

Putting on that music in a masochistic moment and allowing herself to soak in the pain of some silly lost romance was one thing. But letting the protagonist of that romance walk in here, take her into his arms and transport her right back to La-La land was pointing to a very serious mental defect on her part.

And he was doing his best to take her to La-La land here. His hand against her back, his face too close to her temple, his breath in her hair. And during all this, the music had just skipped to another song.

And with that new song Joe seemed even closer. Way too close... She gasped for air. Came to a halt.

"God, stop it–" she croaked, a giant lump in her throat.

Pulling her hand out of his, she tried to break away.

"Wait..." He held her back, his left hand around her upper right arm, his right hand on her left shoulder.

She dropped her head as she felt her eyes filling with tears. God she was just pathetic. She stomped her foot but didn't try to pull away.

"Look at me," he said.

Shaking her head she kept her eyes down.

"Hey..." He touched her chin with the thumb of his braced hand, but she just shook her head again as she struggled to choke down the tears.

"You let me in," Joe said softy, "so I guess we should make it worth it somehow, don't you think?" He moved his left hand from her arm up to her shoulder.

"I have *no* idea why I let you in," she muttered. "But this is just plain crazy!"

"I pretty well know this is crazy," Joe admitted. "But quite honestly, I don't give a shit! *Do you?* Besides, if you really need to do this music thing, you may as well do it properly."

She let out a bitter laugh. "So you're trying to help me torture myself, is that it?"

"Well, yeah, if that's how you want to see it..."

She nodded darkly. "Yeah, that's exactly how I see it."

"Okay. Forget it then..." he scoffed and, his hands raised in a surrendering gesture, he took a step back.

To D, the sudden loss of his touch came as a shock. It left her feeling cold and lost and hopeless. But she would rather die than tell him to please just carry on with what he had been doing.

"Come on," Joe reached for her hand again. "My screwed-up hand won't last much longer anyway."

Unable to look at him, she shrugged. His hand around hers felt so incredibly good... And then his braced hand was back against her back and he pulled her against himself. No, she didn't give a shit either!

"Here we go," Joe whispered, his face dizzyingly close to her ear now. "And about your arm..."

With a fake little growl D moved the arm in question back up until it rested on his shoulder.

"Big improvement!" Joe nodded.

He pulled her close enough to feel her breathe. And for a moment there, that breathing seemed to stop. He kind of liked that effect!

Leaning the side of his head against hers, he started to slowly move his hand up and down her back with the music. He was way past the point where he still cared how this was going to play out and how it might further complicate his life, which it undoubtedly would. This was the best he had felt in years. He was actually surprised that he was even still capable of this kind of emotional high. During the last few months he had been so numb that he had feared that would never change again. Then the little episode with Christine had kind of shown that there might still be some life left in him after all. It had been nothing compared to this, though! This was like flying!

When the second song was coming to an end, Joe was sure that she would pull away. He was prepared to let go and leave. But then she just repositioned her arm against his shoulder and – for the first time since they had started this dancing thing – she actually did seem to relax against him. And that felt even better than flying.

"I meant what I told you in the car," he mumbled. "I–"

When he felt her tense up, he fell silent and held his breath, hoping desperately that he hadn't just blown it.

There was this faint shake of her head against his that he interpreted as a plea to just shut up.

"Okay," he whispered with a short nod.

To his relief she seemed to loosen up after that. And she moved her hand – from his shoulder to his upper back. He could feel the warmth of her palm through the fabric of his T-shirt, and, as the hand moved up further, the tip of her thumb reaching up, gently running over his skin just right above the collar. He closed his eyes.

"I *don't* hate you," she told him quietly. "And I'm *not* ignoring you."

"Well, not anymore," he said, only too aware that her hand had just slid up some more – against the back of his neck, lightly cupping it. That touch that made his head spin.

"Would be close to impossible to ignore you," D muttered.

"Good," he whispered, not even sure himself if he was referring to what she had just said or to what she was doing with her hand.

When the third song was coming to an end, Joe knew that he wasn't going to be able to keep holding his right hand up against her back much longer. The pain was starting to be unbearable. He should get going and hope that he'd still be able to drive – especially shift gears.

But of course, what held him back, and what had made him ignore the pain so far, was the fact that, if he left now, he knew for sure that this – whatever it was – was going to vanish overnight like a stain on a white shirt in a detergent commercial. She would pretend it never happened and stay out of his way in the future. And he wouldn't have the guts to call her on it.

"Your hand?" D had come to a halt. Of course she had noticed the touch on her back getting weaker to the point where it was almost gone.

Not looking at her, Joe nodded.

"Bad?" she asked.

"Pretty bad." A weak apologetic smile appeared on his face as he let go of her. "This just really sucks!"

"Do you want anything for it?" D asked. "Creams, Pills…– or an amputation?"

Joe burst out laughing. "Now *there's* a very progressive approach! But no, I'm not quite ready for that yet. Not while there's still hope. Creams won't help, though." He gingerly touched the swollen fingers with his other hand. "Those two are broken…" he explained. "Normally I'm okay, but today–" He paused. "Well, it seems like today wasn't such a good day…"

"Guess I contributed to that," she said guiltily.

Joe laughed. "Yeah, you landed one hit. But the other three or four were my own fault."

"I've got some pills," she offered. "Nothing really strong, but…"

Even while she said it, she knew that it was silly to try and avoid the unavoidable. This was the end of their little insane get-together. Looking at him now - as he was standing there, chewing on his lip, still kind of fighting it – she realized that he was probably in a lot more pain than he let on. Well, it had to end sometime. Maybe better sooner than later. Because it could only get crazier from here on. Still, just the thought of him walking out the door now and things turning back to normal made her feel like a diver whose mouthpiece for the oxygen had just been ripped out and there was no air…

Bracing herself for what just had to happen, D stood there waiting for him to say it. She was prepared to put on a careless smile and wish him a good night.

But instead of saying anything, Joe strolled over towards the kitchen and sat down on one of the bar stools. His braced hand resting on his knee, he scratched his head and gave her an undecided look. "Well…" he finally said with a little shrug. "I mean – I do have something with me… for emergencies." He pulled a single blister-packed pill out of the back pocket of his jeans and looked down on it, turning it around between his fingers.

Strangely relieved, D went over to the kitchen, switched on the small light above the stove and got two glasses out from a cabinet. She filled them with water, sat one in front of him onto the bar counter and took a sip from the other.

Joe wrapped his hand around the glass, his eyes on the pill that was now lying on the counter next to him, still unwrapped.

D eyed him warily. "Aren't you going to take it?" she asked.

Still not looking at her, he took a sip from his glass. "That's pretty potent stuff," he mumbled evasively.

"Well, that's probably a good thing," D said with a faint smile. What was he waiting for?

Joe glanced over at her with an expression she couldn't quite read. Some of it was just fatigue and pain, but there was also something else.

"There's a little problem," he finally said. "I shouldn't drive after I take this."

D felt her expression freeze as the message reached her brain.

"And that's not some stupid trick!" he assured her with a dry little laugh. "It's only that… – well, after I took one of these in Amsterdam, I…

well, I kind of know that it's not just some over-cautious disclaimer-warning but I *really* shouldn't drive. Or play with a chain-saw. Shouldn't even walk very far probably."

D took a deep breath, still kind of perplexed. That was a twist she definitely hadn't seen coming. Her mind suddenly absolutely blank, she looked back at him.

He gave her a weak shrug. "Yeah... So it's either I leave now and take this at home, or I take it now and drop dead on your sofa in about twenty minutes." Tapping the index finger of his left hand against his glass, he gave her a somewhat challenging look. "It's up to you! Your choice..."

*"My choice?!?"* D gasped. She blinked at him with total bewilderment. "What were the options again?" She frowned. "You leave now and drive home like this, even though you can hardly stand it just sitting here, or you – *stay???"* Her gaze wandered to the sofa.

"I personally would clearly prefer the sofa-option," Joe told her with a crooked smile, very much aware that he was pushing it.

D rubbed her right eyebrow. This was crazy! There was no way she could let him stay! Or could she? Him on the sofa? Unconscious...? It actually seemed like a really cool idea!

"I will deny that I ever said this" she slowly said, "but so do I."

Joe raised his eyebrows and looked at her with wide eyes. "Oh, you *do?"*

"Shut up and just take the stuff, okay?" D growled and took a step back to where she could lean against the kitchen counter across the room from him.

Glancing at his glass, Joe rubbed his chin as if still pondering something. Then he reached for the pill.

"Alright," he said and pressed it out of its packaging.

The moment he put the pill into his mouth, it occurred to him that this might not really be such a great idea after all. He hadn't thought about it so far, but since he wasn't staying in a hotel but with Sarah, his not coming home during the night would most likely not go unnoticed. Sarah would ask questions; she always asked questions...

Of course, maybe he'd get lucky and be able to make it back home before Sarah woke up. But that was a big *maybe*. Whatever! As he washed the pill down with half of his water, he decided that he would worry about Sarah the next morning.

Across the kitchen D had pulled herself up on the counter. Her legs dangling down, her glass next to her, she watched him drink the rest of his water. Then he got up.

"Okay," he said, running his left hand along the bar counter as he stepped around it into the kitchen. "I guess I'll have to stay now."

From her place on the counter D saw him coming towards her. She quickly reached for her water glass and took a quick sip. And then, instead of putting it back down on the counter, kept it in her hand and let the last bit of water squish around inside. Looking at the liquid rather than Joe, who was awfully close now, she tried to focus. Her heart beating like crazy made that very difficult, though. And moving the water around in the glass in a halfway leisurely fashion was becoming harder as her hands were starting to tremble. He should have stayed over there, on the bar stool! If he came any closer...

Holding the glass in front of her almost like a shield, she peered up at him. How was she going to feel about all this tomorrow? Had she gone totally mad?

The music had just skipped to a song that, under other circumstances, would have been real hard to take. Joe had stopped right in front of her, leaving just a few millimeters between him and her knees.

She dropped her gaze to the glass in her hand.

"There are some rules..." she warned him.

Joe nodded. "Oh, I know..." He placed his braced hand on the counter left of her.

She wasn't sure if she was just imagining it or if she could really feel the faint touch of his thumb against the side of her thigh through the fabric of her pants. She glanced up at him. He was looking back at her, his eyebrows raised.

"What?" he asked innocently. "I haven't even done anything yet..."

"You sure didn't have to get up from your chair to do nothing," she said.

He laughed. "Yeah, me getting up from that chair *is* kind of suspicious, isn't it? But don't worry! I'll be knocked out here pretty quickly! Better use the time we've got..."

With this not exactly comforting remark he eased the glass from her hand and set it on the counter far enough away so she couldn't easily get it back.

Her eyes had followed her glass and were still fixed on it, when he reached out and slid his index finger under her chin. She froze. But to his amazement she didn't fight it when he tilted her chin up a little to make her look at him.

She swallowed as her gaze meshed with his.

And then he just leaned in and gave her a short, soft kiss right on the lips.

It was over before she could even blink.

Drawing in a shaky breath she glanced to the side.

"I'm not breaking the rules yet, huh?" He sounded almost surprised as he straightened up again.

Her gaze flashed back to him. Of course this was breaking the rules! But then again, he had been breaking all kinds of rules over the last forty minutes (with her ready assistance), and somehow she didn't want him to stop breaking rules just yet…

From the looks of it, he wasn't seriously considering it anyway, though.

As if to test the limit, Joe leaned closer. Of course her legs were in the way of getting really close.

"Now this is probably breaking the rules, but–" He placed both his hands on her knees and softly pushed them apart just a bit. The cautious look he gave her while he did that indicated that he was ready to jump in case she decided to kick for him.

D closed her eyes for a moment to regain some kind of balance that was about to be lost here.

"Almost," she said.

"Almost what?" she could feel his breath in her ear.

"Almost breaking the rules," she said and moved her knees apart just far enough for him to step up to the counter all the way.

"We'll get there eventually," Joe predicted, his left hand trailing up her right arm.

D could feel that touch tingle all the way through her body. The hand reached her shoulder and finally the side of her neck. Once his fingertips brushed over her jaw towards her ear she flinched.

"Hang on," he said, repositioning his hand to rest firmly against the back of her neck, his thumb on her cheek.

D gasped for air. Through a cloud it occurred to her that this was probably her last chance to pull the brake. She should really pull the brake... But then, as he was leaning in, his nose lightly tipping against hers, she closed her eyes.

"Okay, let's break some rules here," he whispered, his lips already brushing against hers.

Joe knew perfectly well that this whole kissing thing wasn't a good idea at all, but he really didn't care. Not at this point. Not after he'd just placed his lips against hers and – instead of her pulling away – she had slightly opened her mouth. He pressed his lips against hers a bit more firmly, letting the tip of his tongue slide through probingly. He expected her to pull back any second. But then he felt her hands softly on his face, hesitantly sliding to the back of his head, cupping it tightly. It almost made him dizzy. And it took all his self-control to keep this an entry-level kind of kiss rather than just pulling her real close and kissing her for what it was worth as long as she would let him.

Even without his pushing for it actively, the whole thing heated up considerably in no time, though. Her fingers running through his hair, quite a bit of still pretty shy tongue play on both sides, her hands pulling his face a bit closer, his good hand moving from her hip to her back, working its way under her T-shirt, her tensing up briefly as he touched her skin, his hand slowly trailing up her spine...

Finally she broke the kiss and pulled away.

Intuitively Joe took his hand out from under her T-shirt and backed up a step, totally out of breath and well aware that this might have gone way too far.

She was sitting on the counter, giving him a brief puzzled look before she dropped her gaze to her knees. She drew in a shaky breath and ran her hands over her face. "Crap!" she breathed, keeping her hands clutched over her mouth and her nose for a moment. "This can't be happening."

"I'm afraid it just did," he told her, rubbing his chin.

He saw her briefly close her eyes. Then she dropped her hands onto her lap and ran the palms over her thighs, exhaling audibly.

"I could have sworn it wasn't just me, though," Joe said, somehow sensing that her brain had just kicked into gear again and it didn't like at all what had just happened and might want to blame it all on him.

Still not looking at him, she nodded. And slipped off the counter. Joe stepped aside to give her some space. To storm off or whatever else she was planning to do.

Unexpectedly she just stayed where she had landed and leaned against the counter, her eyes on the floor.

For lack of any better ideas, he turned around and leaned against the counter as well, making sure that his arm didn't touch hers.

He was wracking his brain for some good way to handle the situation. Unfortunately his brain seemed to be working at a slower pace every second now as the painkiller was starting to do its thing. He wished her brain was equally drugged. Then they could maybe just both go to sleep now and tomorrow morning they'd pick up where they'd just left off. But since she wasn't under any influence, she would most likely figure out by tomorrow morning (if not right this very minute) that this had all been a big, horrible mistake.

He turned his head to look at her. "I'm sure glad we did this while I was still conscious," he said trying for a joking tone.

She nodded, chewing on her lip. "Yeah, I bet," she said dryly but not unfriendly. "That's as far as it will go, though."

Reaching out he gave her back a gentle rub. "Don't worry. That's about all I can manage right now anyway."

With a weak little chuckle that still reflected disbelief, she pushed herself away from the counter. "I better get you something for the sofa..."

He watched her head towards the living room and finally got moving himself.

"What kind of pillow do you want?" she asked over her shoulder. "Feather or non-feather?"

"Non-feather, if you have one, but mainly just a pillow," Joe said.

Of course her asking him which kind of pillow he wanted was like his asking her how she wanted her steak: their acting as if they didn't know the answers anyway. They would have had to be dumb and blind not to notice these basic preferences in the course of the time they had been together.

Joe had followed her to her bedroom door where she came to a halt, her hand on the door handle. For a moment there, he thought she would tell him to wait outside or something. He didn't know what was customary in this kind of situation, but he assumed that, if anything was way off limits, it was this room.

"My bedroom is a mess," she informed him with a little shrug. She opened the door wide as if to give him a chance to convince himself. "I'm cleaning out my closets."

Joe leaned against the doorway into the bedroom and watched her open the big wardrobe. She got out two pillows that she threw onto her bed. She opened one of the drawers of a dresser and got out two pillow cases and two sheets.

"Two pillows, right?" she asked without turning around.

He nodded. "Yeah, but one is fine too... – and I can really do that myself."

Ignoring him, she had already started pulling the pillow case over the first pillow. And Joe realized that with his hand doing this himself would have been a bit of a challenge, if not a total embarrassment.

Starting to feel comfortably numb, he let his gaze wander around the room. There were a few pictures on the drawer unit, mainly family pictures as far as he could see from the distance. In order to rule out that there were any Peeetes included in that exhibit, he would have had to do a close-up inspection. Maybe not the best idea for tonight. And he was too tired to walk over there right now anyway.

He couldn't help but notice, however, that she had a new bed. Well, the one in the dorm hadn't been hers. It had come with the room. The one here was pretty big. She seemed to be sleeping on the side closer to the window, while the other side was currently buried under clothing and other stuff. Still, the pattern of the pillow case and bedding under the piles seemed to match the pattern of her own side. It was therefore hard to tell if the side covered with clothes had been like this for weeks now, or if it was quickly cleared when Peeete came by. Because really, why would she go through the effort to equip the whole bed with matching comforter covers and pillow cases, when no one ever slept on the other side?

"Here." D handed him the pillows and – two folded sheets under her arm – squeezed by him and headed for the living room. As he trailed behind her, Joe felt that he was getting slower with every minute now.

"Sorry," he muttered, shocked by the weakness of his own voice. "...you really don't have to make my bed."

D laughed over her shoulder. She had just grabbed the two back cushions off the sofa and was leaning them against the side of the coffee table. Then she started putting the bottom sheet on the sofa

"I *do* have to make your bed," she told him teasingly, "because you're an invalid, who is apparently losing consciousness." At the way she said it, Joe felt a sudden wave of warmth wash through him. Hugging his pillow, he sat down on a chair and watched her.

D put another sheet on the sofa and pointed to the wool blanket on the armrest of his chair. "There's a blanket. Do you want to use that?"

"Thanks," he nodded. "Sure…" He handed her the blanket. The pain in his hand had faded into a faint thumping, but at the same time it was getting almost impossible to think a clear thought or focus on anything.

"Now it's really kicking in," he mumbled, sounding almost surprised. Like in a haze, he watched her straighten out the blanket and then walk off towards the bathroom. She came back with a packaged tooth brush in her hand. She popped it out of the packaging and held it out to him like a reporter that was going to interview a celebrity. Slowly he put the pillows that he had still been holding on the sofa.

"Come on now!" D reached for his good hand to make him get up. He slowly rose and took the toothbrush. Only when she pulled her hand out of his now, he realized that he had still been holding on to it. It had felt so nice…

Pointing towards the bathroom, she gave him a little push with her flat hand against his upper back. "Go in there now while you still can," she told him. "There's towels on the shelf – take whatever you like. Come on…"

Slowly nodding, he obeyed and shuffled towards the bathroom.

As the bathroom door closed behind him, D walked over to the big chair he had been sitting on and sank down on it. Staring at the sofa she blew out a breath through her nose. She couldn't believe this was happening.

The CD had almost reached its end, with the Beverly Brothers wanting 'More of you…'

Feeling a little pang in her stomach at hearing this, D reached out and hit the button on the remote to turn off the stereo. She suddenly remembered that on the CD cover this song translated to '*A cheesy one that just fits*'.

Leaning back in her chair, D played with her earring. As strangely thrilling as this whole thing might be at the moment, it was, from an objective point of view, just moronic. Especially because there were a lot of burning questions, the answers of which she probably wouldn't like one bit.

Three minutes later Joe came out of the bathroom.

Looking really faded, he met her eyes across the room. "Let's sleep on it, okay?" he said with a weak smile, obviously having guessed her thoughts despite his condition. "We can talk tomorrow..."

She nodded and watched him head for the sofa.

"Unless you want me to be gone when you get up," he said as he sank down on it.

D shook her head. "Wake me up, if I'm not up, okay?"

"Okay." He nodded slowly. "Same to you. If I'm still asleep when you get up, wake me up, okay?"

"Okay. Good night."

# Just forget about it?

D woke up around 6:30 from some annoying bird. That bird had chosen the tree outside her bedroom window for its high-pitched crazy morning song a few times before. She hated that bird!

Growling, she turned around and tried to go back to sleep. But when the memory of the previous night sneaked into her semi-conscious mind, she was wide-awake instantly. *Oh my!!!*

Flinging her arm over her eyes, she tried to calm down. Her heart was racing and her stomach cramped in a way that made it seem unlikely that she would ever develop any appetite again.

She drew in a deep breath. Her brain was flipping through last night's events in a step by step fashion now – very much like a slide show depicting all the stunning highlights. Suddenly feeling unbearably hot, she pulled back the blanket and turned to lie on her back. Her arms flopped to the sides she stared at the ceiling in the semi-dark room. Out there on the sofa was the guy she had never ever wanted to see again…

This was totally insane! But at the same time it felt so exhilaratingly good. Better than anything had in a long time.

It was just crazy, though. What could possibly come out of this? Why had he come back after giving her the phone? Why had she let him in? How were they supposed to act around each other this morning after what had happened last night? That kiss… God, she really needed to stop thinking or she would go crazy. Stop, stop, stop. Just wait and see. She took another deep breath and closed her eyes. When all she saw was Joe, weary-eyed and destroyed, the toothbrush in his hand, she quickly opened her eyes again.

She was already losing it!

She rolled to the edge of the bed, stretched and got up. She pulled the shades open and shot a quick look into the mirror next to the window. She ran her fingers through her hair to detangle it a bit and then quickly changed from the tank top and shorts she had slept in, into her sweat pants and the alligator T-shirt.

Quietly, she opened her bedroom door and snuck out into the living room. On the sofa a few meters away, Joe was still sleeping. Lying on his stomach, just wearing his boxer shorts, the sheet and blanket half fallen off the sofa. His T-shirt was lying crumpled on the floor; his jeans were folded up on the coffee table with his phone, wallet and car keys on top.

Holding her breath, D took in that picture from where she was standing. This was just... – unreal! She could feel her heart up to her throat now as she considered going over there and waking him up. That's what they had agreed to do, or not? And it wasn't like there weren't several different ways of waking him up that came to mind. But with him lying there, sleeping like a baby and wearing close to nothing, just thinking about getting close to the sofa made her racing heart stop and her throat go absolutely dry. There was just *no* way she could do it. She just couldn't.

As she watched him sleep, she felt a bit like someone who had just paid a fortune to go bungee jumping and now stood paralyzed on the bridge across the canyon, unable to jump.

Finally she turned around and headed into the bathroom.

~~~

Joe woke up from the noise of a shower running. It took him a few seconds to get a grip on where he was and what was going on. For one half-awake moment he had even thought, he was in his hotel room in Amsterdam hearing the shower from the room next-door. But once he opened his eyes, it all came back to him in a flash.

The painkiller had completely put him out during the night. He must have had a somewhat restless sleep, though, judging from the tangled sheet around his legs and the T-shirt on the floor that he must have taken off during the night without even remembering it. And he had had some really weird dreams... His hand seemed to be alright again, though.

As he lay there, staring at a funny looking vase up on a shelf above the stereo, it dawned on him that the plan had been for her to wake him up or the other way around, depending on who happened to get up first. So, she should have woken him up, right? In person and not just by making some noise in the bathroom.

He could easily dream up a few very interesting scenarios for that waking-up-scene. One could always dream, right? He knew it was unrealistic, though. Last night had been unrealistic enough, but her waking him up in a dream-like fashion wasn't going to happen at this point. If ever again.

He sat up on the sofa and reached for his phone from the coffee table. For the first time since he had arrived in Deens, he felt like he could actually deal with it.

When he turned it on and the screen lit up, his hands were trembling. He knew it was going to be bad. And it was worse! There were fifteen missed calls. Thirteen from Liz, two from this Mom. There were five text messages, four from Liz. He wasn't even going to look at them. He could easily guess the content.

The other text message was from his Mom – from Spain. He opened it. It read:

> Joseph,
>
> *just wanted to see how you are. We can catch up when you feel like it. I'll be back on Monday.*
>
> Love you, Mom

He stared at the message for a little longer. He could try to call her in the afternoon. It would be good to talk to her. She had checked on him at least every other week, just to stay in touch – because he had been so bad at writing or calling himself. During these telephone conversations he had always pretended that things were alright and that he was doing fine. In reality things had been far from alright.

The absurd thing was, of course, that in order to even be able to talk to his Mom or Sarah without risking that the whole happy façade was destroyed by Liz screaming or shattering glass in the background, he had usually avoided taking calls with Liz around. He had tried to call back later when he was alone. (Like when he was in the car or on a business trip or out running.) There had been a few times, when things with Liz had been so bad though, that he had almost said something to Mom. But then, he had always stopped himself in time because he just couldn't admit that his relationship, which that most people around him had eyed with open skepticism right from the start, was way more screwed up than even they might imagine. So, he had put on a cheerful tone and kept on pretending. Sarah, of course, had flat-out told him twice to stop the bullshit and that there was *no* way he was really happy with that bitch. (Her words…) Mom hadn't gone quite that far, but he knew that she had her doubts as well. She wasn't dumb. And she knew him better than anyone ever had, except for maybe the girl in the shower.

He deleted all the messages from his phone. There were five voice mail messages too. All from Liz. He deleted them as well. Then he turned off the phone and put it back on the table.

The shower had just stopped running. He looked at his watch. Not even seven…

195

~~~

It took D about 10 minutes to dry her hair, put on a bit of make up and get back into her sweats. All of this happened largely without her actively concentrating on what she was doing. Her mind was too occupied racing back and forth between what had happened last night and how to deal with it this morning.

Chewing on her lower lip she looked at herself in the mirror. What was she going to do? What did she even want? If she could make a wish, what would it be? Shaking her head at herself, she turned away from the mirror and took the few steps over to the door. That's where she stopped again. She couldn't go out there without any kind of a plan, could she? But then again, what did she want to make a plan for? It wasn't like having a really great plan yesterday had served her very well…

As she stepped out of the bathroom, her eyes immediately flickered over to the sofa. And that's when she felt her knees almost give in. The sofa was cleared, the back cushions back in place and the blanket was lying folded on the chair. On the coffee table were the two non-feather pillows piled on top of each other, with the sheets – also neatly folded – draped over them. The jeans and T-shirt were gone. Along with the rest of his stuff. And so was he. He was gone!

She reached out her hand and pressed it against the doorframe next to her. Drawing in a shaky breath, she stood there for a moment. Somehow it felt like someone had just sucked the life out of her. So much about the question what she would wish for. Ha! She coughed out a bitter crazy little laugh. That he would at least still be here when she got out of the bathroom would have been the absolute minimum.

Unable to stop staring at the pile of bedding over at the sofa, she took a step away from the bathroom door. How could he? And why had she not had the guts to go over there and wake him up when she had still had the chance?

She swallowed. Who was she kidding? Her not waking him up had hardly been a question of guts, had it? Wasn't it much more a problem of pride? Yeah, that was her problem, right there. Well, too late now! Chance gone! Boom! Like someone had poked the pretty red balloon with a needle. Bang! Maybe it was better this way!

She forced herself to straighten up. Follow the routine. She needed to go to the kitchen and make coffee. There was a good chance she wouldn't be able to choke down any food for a while though. (She actually felt more like throwing up than eating anything.) But she would make some breakfast anyway and sit and watch her program. Probably best to watch an episode she had already watched, because her mind wasn't capable of processing anything new at the moment.

First of all she needed to clear the sofa from everything that reminded her, however…

She went over there to grab the bedding but then took a quick step to the stereo first and ejected the CD. She stuck it back into its case. The CD case clasped between two fingers, she scooped up the pillows and the sheets and carried everything to her bedroom where she threw it onto the bed. The CD bounced off and slid off the bed onto the floor. Maybe after breakfast she would have the energy to get rid of it!

In the kitchen, Joe's glass from the previous night caught her eye. It was still on the bar counter where he had left it. That needed to go too before she could even think of having a peaceful breakfast!

She was just reaching for the glass when she saw the key next to it. She squinted. It had a small Volvo logo on it.

Was that *his* car key? She glanced up and through the kitchen window across from her. The Volvo was still parked out there on the street. She blinked. That didn't make any sense!

Suddenly she noticed the pen from her magnetic note board lying on the bar stool. It must have rolled off the counter. Why was it not on the fridge stuck to the board? Still holding the glass in her hand, she turned to the fridge. And there, on the note board was the same messy handwriting as on the CD cover:

*I'm getting bread.*

*Joe*

Leaning her back against the bar counter, D closed her eyes for a moment and exhaled. Okay, so that obviously meant that they were going to have breakfast together.

~~~

D was just filling two glasses with orange juice when she heard the front door being unlocked. Feeling her stomach drop, she turned around.

"Hi there," a crooked smile on his face and a paper bag in his hand, Joe pulled the door closed behind him. "I stole your key," he said and placed the key on the side table, where her phone was still lying in the salad bowl.

He came over and sat down on one of the bar stools. On the bar

197

counter in front of him, D had set out what they needed for breakfast; two plates, knives, spoons, milk, butter, sugar and a jar of jam.

Just as he was sitting down now, she brought over the two glasses of orange juice and then quickly turned around again.

"Nice bakery," he said.

"Mhmm, it's been there forever," she mumbled and opened the cupboard above the dishwasher to take out some coffee cups.

"You still like croissants?" he asked.

Maybe he was just imagining it, but for a moment there she seemed to come to a halt. Then he saw her nod. "Yeah, sure."

"Good, because that's what I got." He took the croissants out of the bag and placed one on each plate. It hadn't been lost to him that she seemed to have a serious problem looking at him this morning. Great! Just what he had feared... But at the same time she had set the bar for breakfast!?!

He picked up the jar of jam from the counter and looked at the handwritten label. "Strawberry chocolate," he read aloud and glanced over at her. "Did Robert make that?"

"Mhmm." She nodded and picked up the two steaming coffee cups.

Joe unscrewed the top of the jar and stuck the tip of his knife in to test a little.

"Tastes pretty good," he said.

The two coffee cups in her hands, D turned around and came around the bar. She felt a bit shaky. His remembering that homemade jams with unusual flavor-combinations could only be her brother's work and his still knowing that she loved croissants had made her worry what other, much more personal things, he might remember.

She set the two cups on the bar counter, slid one over to him and sat down on the bar stool to his right, all the time making sure she didn't look his way.

Joe took a sip of orange juice, watching her from the corner of his eye. He just hoped that sticking around here for breakfast instead of just taking off while she was in the shower hadn't been a mistake. The thought of leaving had crossed his mind. It would have been his only chance to make it home to his room without Sarah knowing that he hadn't slept in his own bed. But somehow that had seemed secondary to seeing Danny and figuring out where they stood this morning.

"How is your hand?" she asked with a nod at the brace.

"Much better." He put two spoons of sugar and some milk into his coffee and stirred it. "Seems like it has calmed down again."

"That's good." She let the orange juice swish around in her glass, then lifted it and took a sip. "What happened... with your hand?"

He shrugged and picked up his croissant. "Stupid accident," he said.

"How do you break exactly those two fingers?" she inquired, keeping her eyes on his hand.

"Put them in a place where they got crushed," he responded.

"Where was that?" she asked. And her eyes briefly flickered up to his face.

Hoping she would soon drop the subject, Joe put on a crooked smile and shrugged again. "Car door..."

A tortured frown appeared on her face. "Crap! How in the world did you do that?"

"I don't know," he lied. "Just happened. But as long as these two still work..." He tipped the thumb and index finger together a few times to demonstrate what he meant. "Chances are good that I'll survive."

Her gaze wandering to her coffee cup, she nodded.

Joe picked up the knife, put some jam on his croissant and took a bite.

She sipped on her coffee. "How much longer do you have to keep the brace on?" she asked.

He thought about it for a moment. "Three more weeks if all goes well," he finally said. "I'll have to have it checked sometime during the next two weeks. Maybe Rick's Dad or one of Sarah's doctors can do that."

D shot him a surprised look from the side. How long was he planning to stay? It surely didn't sound like he was going back home anytime within the next two weeks. Quickly dropping her gaze back into her coffee cup, she realized that there was just no way she could ask him that.

He drank half of his orange juice, put more jam on his croissant and took another bite, trying to hold it over his plate, so the crumbs wouldn't all fall on the floor.

From the corner of his eye he could see her trace the rim of her coffee cup with her fingers. He couldn't deny that he was starting to feel a little frustrated here. At home Sarah was probably just getting up and only a few minutes away from detecting his absence. And he was here, making polite conversation about baked goods, jams and his hand injury. It was nice of her to ask about his hand, of course. But, first of all, he couldn't tell her the truth about it anyway, and secondly the topic just seemed to serve as a means to avoid talking about anything else. With the momentum of last night gone and a few hours of sleep, she had apparently come to her senses again. Next they'd surely be talking about the weather and the likelihood of thunderstorms in the evening...

He stuffed the rest of his croissant into his mouth, brushed his hands against each other over the plate and turned his chair a bit, so he could look at her from the side. Pretending not to notice, she reached for her orange juice and took a sip. She hadn't even touched the bread yet.

"Why don't you eat something..." he said.

"I'm eating..." she claimed, grabbed the croissant, took a bite, made a lot of crumbs and then put it back on the plate, giving him a *so-there!* look that almost made him laugh because it was so typical!

"There you go," he said contently and finished his orange juice.

Beside him, she took another tiny bite from her croissant.

"I thought you had left," she suddenly said, her eyes on her plate. "I didn't see your note at first."

Joe looked at her and realized that neither from her tone, nor from her expression he could tell if she was pleased or upset that he had *not* left.

"I was thinking about it," he finally admitted. "After all, you didn't wake me up, so I wasn't sure..." He thought he could see her flinch at the mention of waking him up.

"I was thinking about it..." she mumbled. Then she reached for her orange juice and finished it.

With her setting the glass back down, it became quiet again, the tension almost tangible.

Clearing his throat, Joe picked up his coffee cup and slid down from his bar stool. This wasn't going anywhere. Maybe not sitting so close together would make it easier. He took four steps away from the bar towards the kitchen window. It was a beautiful day. Danny's neighbor with the dog, whom he had met as he had left for the bakery, was just coming back from the morning walk, some little kid was riding a bike on the sidewalk, the guy across the street was dragging an ancient-looking lawn mower out of his garage...

Joe made his eyes change focus until he could see Danny's reflection in the window. She had turned her chair to the side a bit, one arm on the counter and one on the back of her chair and glared towards the living room. He wished he could read her mind.

"So, can we actually talk about it?" he finally asked against the window.

In the reflection he could see her straighten up in her chair and turn her head, shooting him a wary look.

"Talk about what?" she asked slowly. It sounded dangerous.

He shrugged and turned back around to her.

"Well, we could start with last night..." he suggested as he met her eyes.

She didn't say anything, just looked back at him and blinked.

"Or should we just forget about it?" He made it sound like a friendly offer. He knew that this was pushing it, though. Because with some bad luck that's exactly what she had in mind; just forget about last night.

Exhaling audibly, she dropped her gaze to the floor where all her crumbs had landed.

Not letting her out of his sight, Joe leaned against the windowsill behind him. What the hell was he doing here? What did he even want from her? Did he seriously, in addition to the big mess with Liz that was probably still far from over, want to get into this highly complicated constellation? Because really, if he needed some cheering up, why not look for some nice girl out there who was not his ex? Picking up girls had never been a problem...

Regarding Danny, he should probably just be happy and content that they would, hopefully, be able spend the weekend more peacefully than they had spent the grill party. That was something, wasn't it? Wasn't that enough? He cramped his left hand around the ledge of the windowsill as he considered it. No! It just wasn't enough! Not anymore! Even if he couldn't put a finger on what it was he wanted, he was relatively sure that it was slightly more than just peace.

He downed the rest of his coffee.

As he set the cup down on the dining table to his left, D looked up at him. He thought she was going to say something, but then she didn't.

"Okay," he said with a shrug. "So let's not talk about last night then." He paused, not letting her out of his sight. "There are a few other issues, though, right?"

"Like what?" she challenged.

"Well, I would think there'd be some questions or not? Do you want to talk about those?"

"I don't have any questions," she claimed.

"Liar!" he blasted and shook his head at her.

Her eyes narrowed at him calling her a liar. "What questions could there possibly be?" she asked with a little sneer.

"You know exactly what I mean," he said.

She let out a bitter little laugh. "Even if I had any questions," she said, "I can't imagine it would be worth asking because I surely wouldn't like the answers!"

"Grrr, Danny!" Joe shook his head in frustration. "If you don't even ask, how will you ever know?"

She shrugged and looked away.

Joe huffed out a breath and rubbed his left hand over his forehead.

"Great. I'll start then," he announced. "Because, as it happens, *I* actually *do* have some questions!"

She shot him a quick look but didn't say anything.

And Joe realized that it was quite ironic that he, who had often enough tried to avoid relationship talk at all cost, especially with the girl he had before him, was now feeling so frustrated by her refusal to talk it over...

"What's going on with Pete?" he asked curtly. "Are you two still together?" Even to himself he sounded a bit like the public prosecutor in a cross-examination.

She didn't like it, of course – neither the question, nor the style.

"I don't think that's really any of your business," she told him through clenched teeth.

"Maybe not." He shrugged. "But after last night I'd still kind of like to know."

For a moment she glared right back at him. Then, shifting her gaze towards the dining table, she shook her head and quietly said, "No we're not."

Joe scratched his head. That did confirm what Sarah had told him. Still, it didn't really make sense.

"But he *called* you last night," he pointed out.

"Well, yeah, a lot of people call me," she retorted.

"Yeah, but hopefully not all of them in the middle of the night and with such annoying insistence!" Joe said with an acidic undertone.

"I can't stop him from calling if he wants to, can I?" she shot back.

"Guess not," Joe concluded. "What happened anyway?"

"What?" Her mind was still caught up in the issue of Pete's constant calls. *Annoying insistence.* Joe had found the perfect words!

"What did he do?" Joe pressed.

"What makes you so sure it was *he* who did *anything*?" she asked.

A little confused, Joe shrugged. "Let me rephrase it then. What did he *or* you do?"

For a moment she seemed to weigh her answer, then her face hardened. "I didn't find him messing around with his best friend's ex in his best friend's basement, if that's what you want to know."

Joe's expression froze. "Like I...?" It wasn't really a question but a somber conclusion.

D glared back at him, suddenly feeling almost sick to the stomach by what she had just said and his reaction to it. To claim now that that's not what she had meant would be a blatant lie. Of course that was exactly what she had meant! Only now that it was out, she wished she hadn't said it. And she could just see how this might be the thing to tip the scale and make him leave. Because there was probably only so much crap he was going to take from her before he eventually lost his patience.

A few steps away from her, Joe pushed himself away from the windowsill. Chewing on his lower lip, he nodded.

"Great then," he said dryly. "So, given the unforgivable history..." His coffee cup in hand, he came over, snatched his plate from the bar and stepped around into the kitchen.

Frozen in her chair, D watched him put his dishes into the dishwasher. Then he reached over the counter from the kitchen-side and took his orange juice glass and his car keys that had still been lying there.

"I don't know what you expect me to say," D said weakly, not even sure he could hear her while putting his glass into the dishwasher and closing it.

He had heard her. He turned around and leaned against the countertop, stared at the tile floor. Then he shrugged and turned to leave the kitchen area. D could feel her throat tighten as she expected him to leave.

But then he actually came back to his chair. Perched on it, he hung his head and played with his key in his lap for a moment. Finally he looked over at her again.

"So, should we just forget about last night then?" he asked. "We can. Just tell me. Up to you."

Swallowing she looked away.

Suddenly she felt the nudge of his brace against her knee.

"Hey…" he said softly, "you don't know, do you?"

"Well, do *you*???" she asked with a distraught glance at him.

He almost laughed at suddenly having the question back on his side.

"Do *I* know?" he repeated with a trace of amusement. "Yeah, actually–" he weighed his words carefully, his eyes on his key because looking at her distracted him too much. "I'm pretty sure I'd rather *not* forget about it…"

What followed was a moment of total silence.

Finally D sucked in a quick breath that she huffed back out right away.

"What about Liz then?" she challenged, making it sound like she was reminding him of something he seemed to have overlooked. "Do you want to tell me about that? About you and Liz!?! And how last night fits into that…"

Strangely enough, Joe felt a pang of relief at hearing it. Thank God it was out! Even though it sure didn't sound pretty. Especially with the way she pronounced Liz's name.

"Or maybe it's Inga or Susan or whatever by now…" D muttered.

Ignoring the side-kick, Joe shook his head. "Na, that would be… Liz," he confirmed, looking up at her. "And it's over."

Her lips tightly pressed together she blinked, but that was about it.

"I left," Joe said calmly.

The look she gave him was so guarded that it was impossible to read.

"I haven't even told Sarah yet," he informed her, just to say something.

"Why not?" she asked flatly. "She'll love it!"

Joe couldn't help chuckling at the way she had said it. That sarcasm!

And then, totally unexpectedly, a wary, somewhat helpless smile seemed to spread across her face. "Your sister's got a right to know these things" she said sounding not quite serious.

Joe couldn't help laughing, partially out of relief that she finally seemed to have loosened up again. "Well, yeah, my sister would probably fully agree with you there," he said. "And it's not as if I'm trying to keep it from her. There just hasn't been a good time to tell her. Because with Sarah it's not just a question of my quickly telling her the bottom line. She'll want to start a full inquiry regarding the matter. That takes some time," he smiled. "– and good nerves and patience…"

Suddenly his face turned serious again. "Speaking of Sarah, though..."
He sucked in a sharp breath through clenched teeth as if he had just
burned himself. "I think I should get going here pretty soon!" He gave her
knee a gentle pat. "I told Jack I'd come by in the morning and help him
with his car..." He slipped off his seat. "And I still need to go over to
Sarah's first and shower and maybe shave. I sure hope she's not up yet."

"What are you going to do if she is?" D asked slowly.

"Oh, I don't know," he said, a mischievous look spreading across his
face. "How did you put it earlier? That thing you said about Sarah having a
right to know certain things. Does it apply here?"

D swallowed. "No, definitely not," she said, her voice a bit shaky.
"You can make an exception here."

"Oh, can I?" The way she looked at him now, Joe was torn between
bursting out in laughter and kissing her. But then he rubbed his nose and
chuckled. "I guess I won't tell her then," he proclaimed. "Not that she
would believe it anyway..."

Her face lit up and there was a crooked smile.

"I'm sure glad this is a comfort to you," Joe laughed. "Anyway, I really
need to go..." He reached out and gave her shoulder a quick gentle rub.
"You have a good day, okay!"

D nodded gloomily. "Thanks. It's going to be just great. I'm meeting
Sarah for lunch..."

"Oh, yeah, right," Joe said with obvious amusement. "Then, I guess,
we better hope that *you* don't accidently say anything wrong...."

# Waffles or Pancakes...

Sarah woke up at 8:30.

She stretched, yawned and turned over again. It was so nice not to have to jump out of bed right away today! She only had one more late shift tonight and then a three-day weekend. She couldn't wait!

She wondered how D and Joe had gotten along last night. Not that she expected to hear anything about this from either of them, of course. If anyone, Jack might shed some light on how that part of last night had gone.

With another big yawn she pulled back the blanket.

This morning, and that was cast in stone, she wouldn't let her brother get away from the breakfast table before she had a full report and a clear picture of what was really up with him and Liz.

Holding her breath, she listened for any noises from upstairs, but she couldn't hear anything. He was probably still asleep. Who knew when he had gotten home last night? She hadn't heard anything, so it must have been way past the time she had fallen asleep.

She got up and opened the shades. She blinked as the sunshine blinded her. Another beautiful day. And the weather forecast for the next few days was perfect as well.

She went into the bathroom and had a quick shower. While she put some make-up on and kneaded her damp hair a bit, her stomach started to growl. She was getting really hungry. Maybe she should make waffles... or pancakes... with bacon and maple syrup. She never made that for just herself, but with Joe there... He loved that sort of breakfast. And maybe it would make him more inclined to talk.

Back in her room she quickly slipped into Capri pants and a blue T-shirt. Barefoot, she went downstairs to start the coffee. She was still trying to decide whether she should make waffles or pancakes. Maybe she should consult with her brother!

She went out into the hallway.

"Joe?" she shouted up the stairs.

There still was no sound from the bathroom upstairs. No running shower, no nothing. It was 9:30 now. Not really that late, but still... Time for him to get up!

Taking the stairs two at a time, Sarah ran up to his room under the roof. His bathroom across the landing was deserted. She put her ear to his bedroom door. She couldn't hear a thing. He must really still be asleep. She knocked.

"Joe, wake up!"

There was no answer.

"Joe, I'm going to make breakfast." She knocked again, expecting to at least hear some growl asking why she wasn't just *making* breakfast then.

Still nothing. She knocked a few times in a row. "Do you want waffles or pancakes?"

Getting frustrated with the continuing silence from inside Joe's room, Sarah turned it up a notch. "Jooooooe!" she yelled with one hard knock against the door. "Breakfast time! I'm hungry!"

Holding her breath, she listened for a response, like swearing or pillows being thrown against the door.

"Man, wake up!" she called. "Are you deaf?"

She wasn't totally comfortable just walking into her brother's room when she didn't quite know how much clothing, if any, she could expect him to be wearing, but now she just did it. She pressed down the door handle and peeked inside.

One glimpse into the room was enough for her to push the door open all the way and stare inside, her eyes wide. The shades were open, the sun was shining into the room and the bed was empty. And from the way it looked, it surely hadn't been touched last night. It was nicely made and his laptop and a crumpled shirt were lying on it. And there was no trace of him.

Huffing out an incredulous breath, Sarah shook her head. This must be a joke! She slammed the door shut and ran down to her room to have a look through her window facing the street. She hadn't even noticed it when she had first opened the shades this morning, but yeah, the Volvo wasn't there.

Walking back down to the kitchen, she realized that she had lost her appetite for pancakes or waffles.

Absent-mindedly she poured herself some coffee, toasted a piece of bread, put butter and Nutella on it and sat down at the kitchen table, her mind racing. Why had he not come home? Where could he possibly be? Should she be worried? Should she call him? That, of course depended very much on where he was. Somewhere in her sick mind she couldn't help imagining him lying next to some naked girl...

Tapping her foot, Sarah tried to keep her vivid imagination from running wild. Maybe it was all perfectly harmless. Even though, realistically, there weren't a whole lot of harmless explanations for an overnight absence that lasted until now, was there?

Maybe he had had an accident or something? Someone would have for sure contacted her by now, or not?

Stuffing the last piece of toast into her mouth, she went over to the living room to get her mobile phone. Returning to the kitchen, she let the phone dial Joe's number. It kicked into voice mail right away.

With an angry hiss Sarah banged the phone on the table and plopped down on her chair again. It was really none of her business what he did with his nights, of course. He was grown up, at least officially. She was just his sister. If anyone had a right to be mad at him for being gone all night, it was his girlfriend, who – as far as Sarah was concerned – deserved just that! So, maybe there even was a positive aspect right here? He might be out there cheating on Liz!

Still, Sarah found it extremely irritating. She had wanted to have breakfast with him and finally talk about some things. She felt cheated out of that! By some stupid girl he had probably picked up at a bar...

Suddenly her phone rang. She reached for it and took a deep breath, getting ready to yell at Joe, but then realized just in time that it was actually Jack calling.

"Hello Jack..."

"Hi, Sarah! How is it going?" He seemed in a very good mood. He almost always was.

"I'm okay..." Sarah said, still trying to make up her mind if she should mention her missing brother or not. She decided against it for right now.

"How was the party last night?" she asked instead.

"Oh, it was fun," Jack said. "The food was good. They let Joe grill the steaks, which was probably a good thing. Guess after last time when I burnt them all, no one will ever trust me with that again!" He laughed.

Sarah laughed too. "Maybe one day we'll give you another chance," she said in a comforting tone. "But I'm afraid it *will* be a while."

"Hahaha!" Jack pretended to be upset. "Anyway, the food was good and we had fun. Sun got drunk again, of course; Tony showed some baby pictures, loves being a Dad, Carrey seems to be doing much better than when we last saw her, Gerry and Anja are still happy and in love and Rick is going on some sailing trip in three weeks or something, probably has a new flame that loves sailing," Jack paused for a moment. "That's it in a nutshell. The only bad thing was that my car didn't start when we wanted to leave. So Joe ended taking us home. But he probably already told you about that."

Sarah frowned. "No, not really. Joe hasn't told me anything because I haven't even seen him this morning."

"Still in his room, huh?" Jack said slowly. "He just called me that he'll pick me up in half an hour to go over to Anja's and help me with my car. So, I would think he'll be down for breakfast pretty soon. Maybe you could tell him to call again. I can't reach him and I need him to bring jumper cables if he's got any. Just in case."

"He just called you?" Sarah asked as if Jack had mentioned the arrival of the little green men.

"Yeah, just five minutes ago."

"That's really interesting!" She wasn't even trying to hide her irritation. "Because he's *not* in his room, where you'd think he'd be. He's actually not been there all night from what I can tell."

"What?" Jack sounded confused. "Where *is* he?"

Sarah growled. "Are you seriously asking *me*? I just know that he definitely didn't spend last night in his bed. But, fortunately, since he just called you, he must be alive out there somewhere."

There was a silence on the other end, with Jack apparently being a little taken aback by the revelation.

"Any idea where he *could* be?" Sarah asked.

Jack didn't answer right away. "Well, I don't know..." he finally said, "all I can tell you is that, since my car didn't start, he took us home. Me and D and Sun."

"Right. I forgot they'd been riding with you," Sarah said. "I bet D was just *really* thrilled!"

"Well, yeah, sure she was! But I really didn't want to ask Gerry to drive all around town. At least for Joe it was kind of on the way..."

"Did you go out with him afterwards or anything?" Sarah asked.

"No, he actually drove me home first. And then, I'm pretty sure he got rid of D, because, honestly, those two in a car together alone – you could pick icicles afterwards..."

"That bad, huh?"

209

"Well, no, during the party with everyone around it was actually okay, but I'm not sure what would happen if you left them alone somewhere. I mean, D is covering it up pretty well but I wouldn't say she's exactly cool about him being here. She can't be... In fact, Sun made some kind of silly comment about how they should make peace or something, and I thought D was going to have a heart attack. Joe handled it pretty well, thank God..."

"Well, as long as it's not open war."

"It's not. Not at all. But I'm not sure how well she'd keep it in, if she got him alone. Or maybe she'd just ignore him, I don't know. Anyway, I'm sure it wouldn't have been the most pleasant car ride, the two of them together." He paused for a moment. Then he said, "So, then there was still Sun..."

The way Jack said it, made Sarah's ears perk up. "Why are you saying it like that? You don't think he–"

"No, probably not. Just that Sun was – how should I say? – Well, you know Sun. She had way too much to drink again and she seemed very, very drawn to your brother all evening."

"Okay..." Sarah said slowly, still pondering it.

"I really don't know," Jack insisted, "to me it actually seemed like Joe was pretty irritated with her, but what do you know? He drives her home, she's all tipsy and he walks her to her door; she gets all needy and–"

"Invites him in to show him her stamp collection?" Sarah concluded.

"Possibly..." Jack nervously cleared his throat. "Sun has her ways, so I hear at least. But we may be doing them both really wrong."

Sarah exhaled angrily. Unfortunately, it seemed to make perfect sense.

"All men are idiots!" she grumbled.

Jack laughed. "Thanks, Sarah!"

"I didn't mean *you!*" she snapped.

Jack laughed some more. "Great. Which part are you excluding me from? The idiot part or the men part?"

"The idiot part, you idiot!" she clarified.

Jack laughed. "Anyway," he said, "it could also be that he just went to a bar afterwards. By himself."

"Yeah, right! Until almost ten in the morning? Do you know any bars that are open that long?"

"Guess not," Jack admitted reluctantly. "What's wrong with him anyway? He seemed a bit down all evening. Like he actually could use some cheering up. What's going on with Liz?"

Sarah scoffed. "Don't ask me! I'd love to know that myself, but you know him. He doesn't talk unless he wants to, and so far he hasn't been inclined to enlighten me. So, your guess is as good as mine!" She wanted to say something else when she suddenly heard the key in the door.

"Now, guess who's just coming home," she mumbled. "I'll talk to you later, Jack..."

She hung up, laid the phone back on the table and held her breath. The front door fell closed and she heard a key jingle, then footsteps.

"Joe?" She tried to sound halfway friendly, but even to herself she sounded more like the evil guard in an orphanage who caught a kid sneaking in after curfew.

Joe stuck his head into the kitchen.

"Hi," he said with a somewhat cautious expression.

The first thing Sarah noticed was that his T-shirt was all wrinkled. From experience she knew that T-shirts don't get wrinkled unless they are taken off, carelessly dropped and left lying somewhere for several hours. Also, he needed to shave and he didn't look like he had had a night full of healthy sleep...

"Oh, look who's here—" she started.

"Sarah—" he interrupted her, his hands raised. "I really don't want to hear it, okay?" He took a glass out of the cupboard. "Unfortunately I didn't make it back here in time for this to go unnoticed," he said, "but I don't want to discuss it!" He filled the glass with water and leaned against the sink across from her.

"Of course you don't want to discuss it!" she snapped.

"Just stop it, okay?" he shook his head exasperatedly.

Sarah shot him a furious look but realized that she didn't really have a right to press him for answers here.

"Well, I'm just a bit pissed," she said darkly, "because I was going to make pancakes or waffles so we could have breakfast together and talk. But you weren't even in your bed. Do what you want! I don't care what you do at night. I don't care what's up with your girlfriend or why you're even here..."

Joe stared back at her, obviously weighing an unfriendly response, but then he just exhaled audibly and ran his hand over his forehead as if to rub off what bothered him.

"I *will* talk to you, Sarah, I promise," he said trying for a friendlier tone. "Just not right now, okay? I need to take a shower, I need to change and I need to be at Jack's in twenty minutes. His car crapped out last night and I told him that I'd drive back with him this morning and see if we can get it running again."

"I already know all that," Sarah said. "Jack just called..."

"Well, then," Joe shrugged and took another sip from his glass.

"He wants you to call him back," Sarah told him testily. "Couldn't reach you because you had your phone turned off for some stupid reason..."

"Oh, okay." Joe placed the empty glass on the counter and nodded. "I'll call him."

"Don't you want coffee or anything?" Sarah asked. "There's toast too..."

With a quick look at his watch Joe shook his head. "No, Thanks. I'm fine."

Sarah's eyebrows snapped together. "Have you had breakfast *already*???"

Joe drew in an exasperated breath. "Is that a problem?"

"Oh, how nice..." Sarah mocked. But then she stopped herself and took a quick sip of coffee before she could say anything that would really tick him off.

"We could talk tonight," he offered. "We can even go out for dinner..."

"I'm working tonight," Sarah retorted. "From five to eleven. And before that I'm doing something with D."

"Oh, okay, so not tonight then," he concluded. "Tomorrow?"

"Yeah, sure, tomorrow would work..."

"Want to go out for breakfast?" he suggested, still friendly.

"Sure. Breakfast sounds good." Sarah nodded. "There's a new café at the river that's really good."

"Great! Let's go there. I'll pay."

"You'll pay and you'll talk!" She pointed a finger at him.

"Right..." he said with a crooked smile, "I'll pay and I'll talk..."

Sarah managed a smile as well. "I'll reserve a table. Since a lot of people probably have that day off…"

"Yeah, good idea."

"What time?"

Joe shrugged. "I don't know. We could leave here around nine?"

Sarah nodded, her mood obviously improved. "Yeah, sounds good."

With the breakfast plan for the next day settled, Joe left the kitchen and went up to his room, while Sarah finished her coffee and tried to read the paper. Her thoughts kept wandering off, though. To the possibility that her brother may have spent the night with Sun. And stuck around for breakfast!?! Did people usually do that after one-night stands?

Couldn't he just pick up some random stranger from the street if he needed some – how had Jack put it? – some cheering up? That would have been bad enough, of course, but did it have to be Sun? And staying for breakfast!?! Sarah didn't really have anything against Sun as a person. What really bothered her was the fact that Sun was going to be there this weekend and that this little fling might keep on simmering. She could only hope that Joe and Sun had enough brains and tact to handle this halfway discreetly. It made Sarah cringe just to imagine how weird it would be if they didn't. And what kind of effect it would have on D's mood.

# A Talk with Jack

Jack was playing with Sam, his golden retriever, on the green strip in front of his apartment complex when Joe arrived.

"I'll be right there!" he called over and threw the stick for the dog one more time. It took Sam only two seconds to bring it back. "Good boy", Jack patted him on the back. "Now come on, in we go!"

Sam lumbered behind him through the hedge towards the building.

Joe stayed in the car and looked through the glove compartment for something to clean his sunglasses with. Finally he just used his T-shirt.

Jack came back two minutes later, carrying a big leather bag that contained his tools. He put the bag in the trunk and got into the passenger seat.

"How is it going?" he asked.

"Pretty good," Joe said while he backed up the car. "I just hope we can get your car running again! I brought the jumper cables…"

Jack nodded. "Thanks. We probably won't need them, but just in case. It can't be just the battery, though. I *do* kind of have an idea what it might be, and if I'm right it should go pretty quickly…" He went on telling Joe what he thought might be wrong with the car. He had had the same problem twice before with other cars.

Joe nodded, unable to suppress a grin. "You and your cars…" Jack's relationship with his cars (or wrecks) had always amazed him. Jack seemed to never give up on a car unless it was completely dead. And when that happened, he didn't go and buy something newer and more reliable. Joe didn't doubt that Jack could afford a brand new car if he wanted. But instead, he kept getting old pitiful wrecks that, just for the fun of it, he fixed up with lots of love and patience and then held on to until they gave up the ghost. Joe realized that it must be like a game to Jack.

"Sarah said you only got home this morning," Jack interrupted his thoughts.

Joe let out a sharp little laugh. "I'm glad the news travels so fast!"

"Well, yeah, what do you expect?" Jack said with a little chuckle. "Where have you been?"

"Grrr..." Joe growled and shook his head in exasperation. "Can't Sarah ever... Let's just say I was in the park, staring at the stars trying to figure out some things, okay?"

Jack laughed. "Sure, let's pretend that. It doesn't exactly match my little theory, but well..."

Joe shot Jack a baffled look from the side. "You have a theory?" He squinted. "What kind of theory?" There was no way Jack could know, was there?

"Well, with you driving us home," Jack said like that was the key.

Joe felt his stomach knot.

"Oh, come on, Joe..." Jack laughed. "Sun has been quite taken by you all evening. Was plain to see. And then you drive her home and don't resurface until half an hour ago."

Joe couldn't quite follow. "Huh?" Suddenly a frown appeared on his face. "Oh, you mean I–" he paused and frowned some more. He couldn't believe it. "Don't tell me you think I went home with Sun!"

There was a moment of silence in which Jack seemed to reconsider his theory.

"Well, didn't you?" He sounded confused.

"No, I didn't!" Joe retorted. "She was totally drunk – in case you didn't notice – and it was bad enough having to drive her home."

"Okay, okay," Jack said appeasingly. "Sorry then...Wrong theory. It's just... You *did* kind of look like you could use some distraction and so I thought..."

"Yeah, right!" Joe grumbled. "That's exactly the kind of distraction I'd still need! I can't believe you would think that! I'm not *that* stupid..."

"Oh, come on Joe," Jack couldn't help laughing at his friend's indignation. "We both know I've seen you do things that, personally, I consider a lot more stupid!"

For a moment Joe didn't say anything. That had been Jack referring to his getting involved with Liz, of course. Particularly the way it had happened. And *after* Jack had explicitly warned him.

"Don't be mad, okay?" Jack said.

"I'm not mad," Joe retorted. "Really, I'm not mad! Just a bit surprised... And by the way, I broke up with Liz."

Jack let out a little cough. "What? – Ahm... Okay?"

"Sorry," Joe said, with an apologetic shrug and a crooked smile. "I guess I should have made some introduction..."

"Yeah, that would have been helpful," Jack said dryly. "But I understand that you're still practicing, huh? You haven't told Sarah yet, have you?"

"Nope!" Joe shook his head. "She's been wanting me to *talk talk talk* and spill my guts as soon as I arrived, of course. But on Tuesday night I just wasn't up to it and yesterday we had some lovely conversations about my father instead, and since then there just hasn't been enough time."

"You make it sound like you're waiting for the right moment to propose to someone and not to tell your sister that it's over with Liz."

"Well, we're going out for breakfast tomorrow morning and then I'll confess everything," Joe said. "Content?"

Jack nodded with a hint of a grin. "Yeah, very content. Sounds good... And I don't think you'll need to bring tissues. Sarah won't be crying over the loss!"

Joe couldn't help laughing. "You don't say!"

"Yeah, well..." Jack chuckled. "Anyway, it's not as if we haven't been wondering," he said, suddenly more serious again. "At least Sarah and I. I mean... – with your showing up like that, saying that you might stay for a while..."

His eyes fixed on the road, Joe nodded. "I know..."

There was a moment of silence with both of them just staring out the front window.

"What happened?" Jack finally asked, returning to the initial topic. "Why did you break up?"

"A *lot* happened," Joe said. "You don't even want to know all the details. And I don't even quite know *where* to begin. Let's just say it's gotten *really* bad lately. Not that it hasn't been bad for quite a while, but..." he paused for a moment and shrugged. "Anyways, it's over."

"Okay," Jack said. "Knowing the girl a bit myself, I think I can see where you're coming from. Just thought she might have been different with you. After all, you have hung in there for so long..."

Chewing on his lower lip, Joe realized that, just as Liz had said, Jack and he could probably really compare notes here. That was kind of sick...

"Yeah, maybe sometime I'll tell you how the hanging in there worked," Joe said with a humorless laugh.

"Are you okay?" Jack asked sounding concerned.

Drawing in a deep breath, Joe nodded. "Yep!"

"What happened?" Jack asked. "Or do you not want to talk about it?"

Joe thought about it for a moment. And realized that Jack was probably the only person in the world that he could tell at least some of the creepy details.

"Well, the thing is…" he started, still scrambling for a way to say this without slipping into a bitter rant.

"She freaks out," he said as calmly as he could, "like *really* freaks out. About minor things. Freaks out and screams and throws stuff and sobs and smashes something and – …anyway, it's bad." He paused for a moment to gather his thoughts and his composure before he continued. "And then she drinks," he could hear a slightly sarcastic edge creeping into his own voice. "She drinks regularly and a lot, because she's got to go to all these wonderful art gallery parties, dressed up like J-Lo for the Oscars." He let out a humorless laugh. "Yeah, well. And to even it out a bit, she takes pills. To help her sleep, to help her stay awake, to help her with whatever else… I don't know! Oh, and before I forget: She fu– she sleeps around." He exhaled, shot Jack a quick look and found him glaring out the front window, a stern expression on his face.

"*Three* guys I know about for sure," Joe continued. "Probably a bunch more that I *don't* know about." He shrugged "Anyway, we didn't have the most harmonious time lately. And I haven't even been home that much. But when I was home, I tell you…! Well, and then this happened." He held up his injured hand.

Jack looked perplexed. "What do you mean? *She* did that?"

"Yep."

"How the hell–?"

Joe shrugged. "Not *that* hard to do. Just slammed the car door shut with my fingers still in it."

"Eeww!" Jack grimaced at the pure thought of it. "And she did that *on purpose*???"

"Heck, yeah!" Joe let out a humorless laugh. "Definitely not some unfortunate accident. I *do* know the difference, believe me!"

"Crap!" Jack rubbed his forehead. "That *is* pretty bad then…"

"Yeah, I think you could say that," Joe said darkly.

Through the silence that followed, Jack remembered when he had met Liz for the first time. It had actually been he who had made her acquaintance first. He had been biking back from a summer job a little over four years ago, it was getting dark outside and somewhere in a remote area he had come across the hot blonde in a short summer dress who was standing on the side of the bike path, waving him down because she had a flat tire.

Looking back on it now, it seemed like something you would see in a cheaply made movie with a very undemanding script. Here comes the blonde and just sweeps him off his feet. And she really had.

He had jumped off his bike, had a look at her tire and patched it up with something he always carried with him. And while he had been fixing her bike, they had chatted and he had found out that she had just moved to a little flat in Deens and was going to attend some private college for art management.

Two days later they had gone out for dinner and ended up on the mattress in her barely furnished flat. He had been crazy about her (and what they did on that mattress). A week later he had introduced her to his friends. At the beginning she had seemed all chipper and enthusiastic about them and doing stuff with them, but it hadn't taken long before she had started bitching. About Sarah, about D, about the boring hikes and about how she preferred to be alone with him.

For a while he hadn't argued with her (the mattress activities being just too amazing to give up for a hike with friends). But even then he had started to notice that she was quite moody and weird at times.

He had spent a lot of time helping her fix up the flat she was staying at. It was a real dump. Only much later had he found out that she actually came from a fairly wealthy family and could have easily afforded a nice flat or a handyman to fix this one up. To her, this whole thing of studying in Deens had been nothing but a little ego trip; a way to get away from her family and enjoy some adventures. At the time, however, he had thought she had no one but him and gone out of his way to help her and make her happy.

It was maybe two or three months after he had met her that Joe had come into the picture. Liz had bought some used furniture and Jack asked Joe to help him pick it up and put it up in Liz's place. Joe had agreed, even though he didn't like Liz at all. And he hadn't made any effort to hide it. During the time that they had spent working in Liz's bedroom, Liz had been strolling around them and there had been more than one occasion where Jack had felt like she was trying to flirt with Joe. And Joe had flat-out ignored her or even snapped at her a few times when she was standing in the way. Jack remembered it clearly now. Liz and he had had a big fight afterwards. About the flirting with Joe right in front of his nose. He had thought it was tactless. And she had laughed and said he had hallucinations and a minority complex.

Things had gone downhill fast in the coming months. Lots of fights, her high-maintenance, erratic behavior getting on his nerves, her flirting around with other guys... The fact that he hardly got to see his friends anymore was starting to bother him as well. For a while he had still tried to fix it with Liz, but the bitchier and moodier she got, the less sense he saw in staying together.

It had ended right after Christmas without a big bang.

And then, a few months after he had last seen Liz, Joe suddenly told him that he had gotten a call from her. Out of the blue. On his mobile phone. She had asked if he could help her with some computer problem and some other thing in her flat. Supposedly, she just didn't know who else to call.

Even though Joe didn't like her, he wasn't the type to refuse to help when asked. So, he had agreed to go over there. And Jack remembered telling him to watch it. A half-hearted warning masked as a joke. He had said something like, "Joe, just make sure you don't get too close to that mattress, or she'll try to pin you to it!" Joe had laughed it off, of course. At that time Jack had found it laughable too.

Joe and D had both applied for a student exchange year in London and the departure date was just three or four months away. Really, Joe was the last one to fall for the blonde... – or so Jack had thought. And Joe had probably thought so too.

The rest was history. The big crash happened maybe six weeks later. Soon after that, D left for London – alone. Then Liz suddenly disappeared from her flat back to where she had come from. And a few weeks later, to everyone's big surprise, Joe was gone as well.

Jack had been kind of shocked. Sarah had been furious. Everybody else who hadn't been so close to the protagonists and didn't know much of what had happened had just been confused.

Jack had, very much like Sarah, assumed that Joe had just temporarily lost it and was going to be back within a few weeks, laughing about it all. But then it had been almost three months until Jack had heard from Joe again. A short e-mail asking if he could come and stay for a few days while taking his two final exams.

Well, and here they were almost three years later now...

"So, that's why you're here then?" Jack asked.

219

Joe shrugged, his eyes fixed on the road. "Kind of. I guess this whole reunion thing was the inspiration to get out now. Hence the timing... Otherwise, who knows how much longer–" He paused for a moment. "So, thanks for still inviting me even though I haven't kept in touch much..."

Jack let out a friendly little laugh. "You're welcome! I'm glad you came! And I'm sorry to hear about..."

A weak smile spread over Joe's face. "Yeah, well... I should have listened to you! Because, honestly, that whole thing has probably been wrong right from the start. I mean, I can see it now. And I've gotten to the point where I can even admit it."

Jack didn't say anything. He could imagine that admitting that kind of thing to someone who had warned you well in advance couldn't be easy.

"Anyway," Joe chewed on his lower lip, "it could have probably really gone on forever. You kind of get used to things you previously thought you would never ever put up with. It just becomes standard procedure. But recently there have been a few *real* highlights, one of which was the two broken fingers." He cleared his throat. "So, when I packed for my business trip last Saturday, I just threw in a few extra things and left." He had tried to make it sound like a joke, but there was a lot of bitterness in his voice. Suddenly he laughed. "Couldn't you just pedal faster when you saw her flat tire?"

"So, it's all my fault now, huh?" Jack said mock indignation.

"Just kidding," Joe said with an apologetic grin.

"Any hope you'll work it out somehow, though – with her?" Jack asked, suddenly serious again.

Joe shook his head. "Not anymore. I *did* try to make it work for a while. Really did. But unless you're a trained psychologist and or a total masochist, I don't think you can handle it. I'm neither. I can't do it anymore and I simply don't want to. I've had it up to here." The level he showed with his braced hand now was somewhere way above his head. "I need her out of my life!" he said quietly. "I really do."

"Sounds like it," Jack said. "I really think it's great that you came! And we're all happy to see you!" There was a little pause. "Well, with one little exception maybe."

Joe swallowed. "Yeah... well... I know."

"Can't blame her, though," Jack said matter-of-factly. "Just try to keep out of her way. You owe her that."

Joe nodded absent-mindedly. Hearing Jack say that kind of thing stung quite a bit. It made last night suddenly seem even more unreal.

"Hey, and about Sarah," he heard Jack say. "She's just worried about you, okay? She won't admit it, of course, but she's been *really* worried. And she was *so* thrilled when you wrote you'd be coming."

"I know, I know," Joe said. "I just really haven't had a chance to talk to her yet. About Liz. And all the other crap. Like the job thing. I mean, it's complicated too. Because Steve, Liz's brother, and I've got the company together, you know. Most of the money I inherited from Dad is tied up in that."

Jack nodded. "I kind of figured that. So, what are you going to do about that? Does Steve know?"

"Kind of. I mean, he's seen some things. Enough to at least understand that I can't live with her. He told me that. But she's still his sister. So, I'll have to see how to solve this – the business aspect of this break-up. Liz has long enough played that card – that I can't leave because of the company. And I'm attached to it, of course. I like working with Steve, we have a real nice team, it's fun. Oh, and by the way, Liz decided to screw Steve's assistant just two weeks ago..." He laughed without any humor. "It's just bizarre, really. Anyway, it would be pretty hard to give up that job and the company."

Jack frowned. It was tricky to give any advice here but maybe that wasn't even the point. "Tell me if you need help with anything, okay. Like, I don't know... You probably still have some stuff there that you might want to get sometime."

Joe drew in an audible breath. "Yeah, thanks, Jack. I might actually take you up on that. If I decide to pick anything up. Haven't made up my mind yet. Might not be worth it, because by now she's probably smashed everything that's mine. But if I *do* pick something up, yeah, I definitely don't want to be alone with her..."

They reached Anja's and Gerry's house ten minutes later and started working on the car, with Jack burying his head under the hood and Joe assisting as well as he could without endangering his braced hand.

"What about you, though. How's your life going?" Joe suddenly asked. "Any girlfriend? Or happy and single?"

Jack drew in a deep breath, obviously weighing his answer. "Well... I guess, you could say I'm single," he said without looking up from the engine compartment. "And all in all, pretty happy. There've been some flings here and there, of course." He chuckled and paused for a moment. "Nothing really serious for a long time, though. I guess I'm just less and less willing to constantly put up with the crazy tics some of them have. Boy, I tell you! So, once those start showing, I end it fast rather than letting it drag on."

Joe laughed in agreement. "Good idea!"

"But maybe," Jack suddenly sounded more serious. "Maybe I'm just seeing it that way because there actually *is* someone I kind of really like."

Joe gave him a surprised look. "Oh, really?"

Jack kept his eyes firmly on what he was doing. "Yep," he said.

"Someone you *kind of really like*?" Joe teased. "With no tics? Or you just haven't seen them yet..."

"Na, there's some tics but I'm pretty sure I can live with those. They are kind of adorable..."

"Oh, you already figured that out, huh?" Joe said. "Even though you haven't..."

"Well, it's not like I just met her yesterday," Jack said, suddenly a little evasively. "I've known her for a while."

Joe's eyes darted up at the way Jack had said it.

"Someone I know?" he inquired, managing a joking tone even though his mouth was suddenly very dry.

Jack shrugged without interrupting his work. "Yeah, it's definitely someone you know," he said, and for a moment his eyes flickered up at Joe. "But really, it's not worth talking about yet because first of all I need to figure out for myself what I want. It would be risking a good friendship and I'm still evaluating if it's worth it..."

"Oh... okay," Joe muttered, his mind racing. Someone he knew... Someone whose friendship Jack didn't want to risk... Hadn't the last call Danny had gotten last night been from Jack?

# Lunch, Shopping and Borrowing CDs

When Sarah got to the restaurant she felt better. During the twenty-minute bike ride from home she had managed to push the dark thoughts about Joe and Sun and the whole mess to the back of her head.

D was already there, locking up her bike next to the door of the restaurant. She looked up when Sarah pushed her bike in a space next to hers.

"Hi, Sarah! Perfect timing!" D smiled.

"Very perfect!" Sarah agreed surprised by D's sunny mood.

Together they walked through the restaurant to the outside seating area in the back and sat down at one of the tables under the big chestnut trees. A young waitress brought the menus and they ordered something to drink.

"I'm sooo hungry!" Sarah moaned and opened her menu.

"Didn't you have any breakfast?" D asked, realizing that despite having close to nothing in her stomach, she didn't feel like eating anything herself.

"Just a piece of toast," Sarah said. "I was going to make a bigger breakfast, but... then I only had a piece of toast." She had just barely stopped herself in time before it could slip out how her brother's empty bed had destroyed her appetite for waffles or pancakes.

"Oh, that's not much," D muttered almost reflexively. She better not share with Sarah her own breakfast experience and how half of the croissant Joe had bought her, was now lying wrapped up in the fridge because she hadn't been able to eat it while he had been there and even less so after he had left.

"When did you get up?" she asked Sarah over the rim of her menu.

Sarah thought about it for a moment. "Just before nine, I think."

Flipping to the next page of the menu, D tried to remember when Joe had left. Must have been around 8:45. Hard to say if he could have made it. The memory of him perched on his chair this morning, playing with his keys, sent an unnerving heat wave through her body, and she had a hard time keeping a straight face.

"Are you having wine?" Sarah interrupted her thoughts.

"No, why?" D stammered and realized at the same time that she had been staring at the page with the wine list for a while now. She quickly closed the menu.

"I'll have the tomato soup," she proclaimed.

"Soup sounds good," Sarah said, "I'll have that too. But I think I also need a sandwich."

The waitress came with the beverages and took their orders.

D took a quick sip from her lemonade, trying to keep any thoughts of post-grill-party occurrences at arm's length, at least while Sarah was around.

"So, how was the party last night?" Sarah asked.

"Good..." D said a little too quickly, even for herself. She could feel the heat creep up her neck as she looked back at Sarah. She felt like a liar already.

"Well, good," Sarah nodded and played with her glass, obviously wondering if she could request any more detailed information.

"It was nice," D said, as if to prove that she didn't have a problem talking about it. "I sat next to Tony," she babbled on. "Sounds like he and Kim are doing just great. And he's all thrilled with the baby. Who would have thought?"

"Yeah, really..." Sarah agreed. "I'm glad they got that straightened out!"

"Mhmm, me too," D said.

The waitress brought the food.

Sarah dipped her spoon into the soup and stirred.

"Jack called me this morning," she said, her eyes on the soup.

D glanced up at her. "Oh... what did he say?" It was just a question to buy her some time. There was no doubt in D's mind that Jack had told Sarah about his car. The only question was how to best react once Sarah brought it up. So much had happened since she had climbed out of Jack's car yesterday that she wasn't even sure anymore what an authentic reaction would look like. She'd have to wing it...

"He said..." Sarah took her time answering the question as she was struggling to filter out all the parts of her conversation with Jack that were linked to Joe's nightly absence — a topic that was totally unfit for D's ears. "He said that the party was fun even though he wasn't allowed to grill the steaks... And he said that Sun had too much to drink again."

"Well, yeah, Sun had a bit much," D said lightly, surprised that Sun getting drunk at a party was even worth mentioning.

There was a short silence during which Sarah wondered if there was a possibility that D either hadn't noticed Sun's flirting with Joe or that she didn't care. Both seemed unlikely.

"I bet Jack also told you about his car, though, right?" D had decided that it was better to get this over with, even if Sarah seemed to be avoiding the subject for some reason. (Maybe because it involved mentioning her brother, and she was trying to be considerate.)

"Yes, he told me that," Sarah nodded, briefly pondering the oddity of D not having made any sarcastic remarks about Sun and Joe yet. "He told me *that*," Sarah said, trying to focus on how to handle this new, doubtlessly touchy subject. "And about Joe driving you guys home... I imagine you were about ready to kill Jack. Those stupid cars of his!"

"Yeah, I guess..." D mumbled into her soup, clearly remembering now that she *had* cursed Jack. "But since it would have been too far to walk, I didn't really have much of a choice, so..."

Sarah nodded, a sympathetic look on her face. "How did it go with my brother," she asked then, eyeing D cautiously. "I mean in general..."

D swallowed. "Okay," she said slowly, her throat tightening as the memory of Joe squeezing by her with Sun's plate in his hand flashed through her head. "It went okay." She quickly shoveled a spoon of soup into her mouth.

"Well, good," Sarah seemed relieved. "I guess if you just stay out of each other's way, it's okay."

"Right," D agreed with a forced little smile while trying to suppress a shiver that was brought on by her body suddenly remembering Joe pulling her close in an attempt to make her dance with him. If Sarah only knew how staying out of each other's way had worked...

Munching on her sandwich, Sarah realized that, however much the drive with Joe or the sparks flying between him and Sun during the evening might have bothered D, she was obviously not willing to comment on any of it. And in a way Sarah was almost glad about it. She just hoped this façade of impenetrable indifference would hold and wouldn't come tumbling down over the weekend.

They paid and went shopping at a nearby mall for a little while. Sarah needed a pair of new pants, and D wandered through the store more or less aimlessly. Either there really wasn't anything appealing in the store today or she just couldn't focus on that now.

Sarah had meanwhile picked out a few pairs of pants and was on her way to try them on. D trailed behind her and sat on the chair outside the dressing rooms, her mind wandering way off... Sarah came out every once in a while to present the different models and to ask D's opinion. And D tried to make helpful contributions while at the same time things like last night's kiss on the counter or Joe hugging his pillows popped up in her head.

"Hey, can we go by your place later?" she suddenly heard Sarah's voice from the dressing room. The question made her momentarily freeze in her chair. Could they? She quickly considered possible risks of taking Sarah to her place. Were there any traces of Joe having been there? Any way Sarah could tell? She exhaled and relaxed. No, there was nothing. With the bedding, the CD and the breakfast dishes safely stored away, the air was clear.

"Sure," she responded cheerily. "We can have coffee there, if you want."

"Yeah and I might actually need to borrow a few CDs," Sarah said. "If that's alright. There are some songs Jack still wants to use for the slide show and I'm pretty sure you have the albums."

"Sure, no problem," D said, congratulating herself for having removed Joe's CD and its case from the stereo. It sent a shiver down her spine to imagine what Sarah finding this CD on her way to the CD shelf would have triggered. (There would have been a baffled look and then some deeply concerned questions: Is *this* the CD Joe gave you? You still *have* that??? Don't tell me you listened to that last night!?! *D? Seriously?* Shit!)

Trying to shake off that scary image, D got up from her chair.

~~~

"Any news on the London job front?" Sarah asked swiveling on her bar stool as D pushed a cup of coffee over the counter towards her.

"Not a whole lot," D said, suddenly aware that she hadn't even thought about London since yesterday.

"But you applied, right?" Sarah inquired.

"Yeah, I applied," D confirmed, trying to focus on the topic. "I applied on Tuesday. Was going to call you when I got home but then... well, I wasn't sure if you were still alone..." She sat down on the second bar stool.

"Oh, okay," Sarah said, refraining from telling D anything about Joe coming in late that night. "Any reaction yet?" she asked instead.

"Well, Harry called me up right away," D said. "Sounded really thrilled. Said that he'd of course support me if I wanted to go..."

"Good," Sarah said. "That's great!"

"Yeah..." D nodded.

"What's the problem then?" Sarah asked.

"What...? – No problem. Why?"

"Well, you don't seem too enthusiastic."

"Sure I'm enthusiastic," D hurried to say. "It's just all still kind of vague and far away... But June and I are going to London in a week and a half – for a conference and to meet with David, that's Harry's brother, and the other people that work there. We'll just check it out and ask our questions and see. Then we'll know more."

"Wow! Can't wait!"

D nodded with a forced smile. "Yeah, neither can I!" she said. "Should be interesting!" With some alarm she had just realized that the thought of London had somehow lost quite a bit of appeal overnight.

After coffee, Sarah got up and headed for the CD rack. "May I?"

"Sure, go ahead! Take what you need." D went to put the cups into the dishwasher.

Over in the living room, Sarah knelt down on the sofa, so she could have a closer look at the CDs on the shelf behind it.

"I'll leave you for a minute," D told her from the kitchen. "I really, really need to use the bathroom."

Sarah nodded, lost in thought. D's CD collection was extensive. That made it hard to find things if one was looking for something specific. It took her a moment to find three of the four CDs she was looking for. Putting them next to herself on the sofa, she kept looking for the fourth CD until she finally spotted it towards the very bottom of the rack. She reached down and pulled it out, but it slipped from her fingers and landed somewhere under the sofa.

Sarah stepped off the sofa and bent down to reach for the CD. As she picked it up, something else under the sofa caught her eye. It looked like a piece of clothing. She reached back and pulled out a blue sweater. Must have slipped off the sofa sometime. Maybe Pete's. She brushed a bit of dust off it and laid it over the armrest of the sofa.

With the CDs in hand, she stepped around the coffee table and returned to the bar, unaware that behind her the sweater had just slipped off the sofa again.

Perched on one of the bar stools, Sarah opened one of the CD cases to check out the lyrics of a song she had been looking for. When D reappeared, Sarah was just flipping through the CD booklet, humming to herself.

"Did you find what you wanted?" D asked.

"Yeah, thanks!" Sarah said and slid the booklet back into its case.

"You're not letting Jack drive again, are you?" she asked D as she closed the case. "No, this time I'll take *my* car," D said. "And Jack and Sun are riding with me!"

"Oh, okay…" Sarah said, a bit baffled at the causal mention of Sun. Well, maybe D had really not noticed anything after all.

# An Afternoon Alone

Fixing Jack's car had taken until noon. When it was finally running again, Jack had to hurry over to his parents' house where he was expected for lunch. It was a holiday and they had his grandma over from the retirement home. Jack usually tried not to miss that.

With nothing else to do, Joe decided to go to the mall. To get a bite to eat and look for some things he needed, especially some more clothes. It was either that or washing all the time.

As he walked by all the shop windows twenty minutes later, he realized that he hadn't been shopping forever. He had just not been in the mood for it. Well, he was in the mood now. And it was about time he got some new stuff anyway.

He spent almost three hours wandering through at least ten different stores and ended up getting some T-shirts, a new pair of jeans, two sweaters, two long sleeve shirts, some socks, more underwear, a pair of sneakers... It was fun. He was on a roll.

As he packed the bags into the car, he remembered that he had also wanted to get something to read. So he went back into the mall and looked for the book store. He got a magazine and two books that sounded interesting and not too hard to digest.

On his way back to the car he came by a sports store and decided to get some new running stuff as well. He had always liked running as a means to get out of the house and keep himself balanced. He hadn't done it much lately because Steve had talked him into joining a gym. He had tried to go there once or twice a week. But somehow moving on some machine surrounded by other gasping, sweating people, even though it may keep the body in shape, more or less, had just never done it for him. It didn't have any liberating effect on the mind. Not like running outside alone did.

He went into the sports shop, got some running shoes, shorts and long jogging pants and a navy blue fleece jacket.

Feeling almost exhilarated, he strolled back to the car. He hadn't spent that much money on himself in ages. It had been kind of fun. And however much he had spent, he would bet it was still less than Liz spent on one of her cocktail dresses and a pair of high heels...

When he got back to the house around four-thirty, Sarah wasn't home. But he hadn't really expected her to be there anyway. She was probably still out with Danny.

He decided to go for a run right away. It turned out to be more of a mix of running and walking, of course, but that was fine for a start. It felt good. And it helped clear his head.

When he got back home, he felt exhausted but really upbeat.

Sarah must have been home while he had been gone, but had already left again. There was a note on the kitchen table:

*Joe,*

*There's a lot of food in the fridge if you want.*

*Also, please finish the tiramisu. Won't keep much longer.*

*Have a good evening!*

*See you tomorrow for breakfast,*

*Sarah*

Humming to himself, Joe hopped upstairs to his room. He peeled out of his clothes, went across the hall and had a shower. He still hadn't shaved and was kind of playing with the thought of skipping it for today altogether. It was already late afternoon. But then he decided to do it anyway.

Back in his room he slipped into his jeans and a T-shirt. Then he sat down on his bed, legs stretched out, grabbed his laptop and turned it on to check his e-mails.

With some relief he noticed that there was *no* e-mail from Liz. That was a good thing. There were two e-mails from Steve and two newsletters from online shops but nothing else. He opened the first e-mail Steve had sent.

*Joe,*

*guess you have your phone turned off. It's too bad it's come to this, but I can't blame you. Take your time and let me know if you need anything.*

*In the meantime, I already need something from you: Can you please forward the presentation for the Swedes. I can't find it and I think you had one of the last versions on your laptop. No rush, though, I don't need it until next Thursday.*

*Thanks and good luck,*

*Steve*

Joe pressed *Reply* and sent back an e-mail with the presentation attached.

The second e-mail from Steve had just some information on the exact times that Steve was going to be on vacation. It was two weeks from now. Steve was going to be gone for ten days. Joe had promised to be there, at the office, and cover for him.

> *Hi Joe,*
>
> *Here are the dates that Susan and I are going to be gone: Sept 2nd to Sept 12th. I know you'll be in Amsterdam from the 2nd to the 4th (Mon to Wed). Should be fine if you just cover for me Thursday and Friday of that week and then maybe Monday to Thursday the following week. With things being as they are with Liz, I imagine you don't want to be around here for too long. (You could stay at our house if you want. Just let me know.)*
>
> *Steve*

Joe pressed *Reply* and typed.

> *Hi Steve,*
>
> *Thanks for the offer with the house. I think I'll just stay in the office, though. Days you mentioned sound fine. I'll be there. We can talk before you leave. Tell Susan hello. I'm sorry everything is such a mess!*
>
> *Joe*

He closed the e-mail account and surfed the internet for a while, reading the news and playing a silly shoot-the-bird game. Then he turned off the laptop.

He picked up the phone from the bedside table and turned it on. 4 more missed calls, one from Steve (probably about the presentation), the rest from Liz. No other messages.

Joe decided to finally call his Mom back. She was still in Spain, but it might be easier to tell her the news on the phone while he felt as good as he felt right now, rather than face to face when she was back and he might not be in the mood to talk.

He pressed the call button and let it ring. Eventually it kicked into voice mail. Did he want to leave a message? Why not?

"Hi Mom, this is Joe, I'm at Sarah's, everything's fine. I'll try to call you after the weekend. You'll be back soon anyway. I'll still be here, so we can meet then. Love you. Bye."

He hung up and considered calling Liz back and getting it over with. For some reason it seemed strange that she hadn't sent him any nasty e-mails yet. Not like he would have read them, but since she couldn't reach him on the phone, it was surprising that she hadn't tried the e-mail route. But maybe what she had to tell him came across much better in spoken than in written language. There were just so many more options – yelling, screaming, sobbing, hissing...

He drew in a deep breath. He really didn't want to wreck his good mood now, but being alone in the house might actually be a good time to call her back. And he could always hang up when it got too much.

He scrolled through the contacts to the L's and stared at her name for a while. He was about to press call when he decided against it. No, he really didn't want to talk to her. There was absolutely nothing he had to tell her and he sure as hell didn't want to hear her screaming and ranting. Not tonight. It would just drag him down again.

He turned off the phone and stretched out on the bed. Lying there, everything completely quiet around him, he tried to relax. But then his stomach growling made that impossible. He was getting really hungry.

# Finishing the Tiramisu

Downstairs in the kitchen Sarah's fridge had a lot to offer. It was a wonder the door still closed. There was leftover lasagna, all kinds of cheeses, vegetable soup, cut meats, some antipasti in glass jars and the leftover tiramisu covered with foil.

Joe stared at the well-stocked shelves undecidedly. His stomach was growling, he was starving and all he had to do was reach in there. But just as he was going to reach for the vegetable soup – something light to start with – a scrap of memory from last night flashed by and sent a wave of warmth into the pit of his stomach. He swallowed. He wondered what Danny was doing.

Maybe they could go out to dinner...

Tonight...

Before he could stop himself his mind had already started going through some options and scenarios and they all sounded just perfectly fine.

As he contemplated if he even dared calling her and how likely it was that she would pick up and agree to meet with him, it hit him that he didn't even have her new phone number. Crap!!! Well, Sarah had it, of course. And Jack... But he could hardly call them and ask.

So, that was that. Joe blew out an exasperated breath. Now that the idea had already taken on some shape, just giving it up was frustrating, to say the least.

Reluctantly focusing on the food in the fridge again, Joe involuntarily kept pondering the issue in the back of his mind. That's when he suddenly remembered an e-mail he had received a few weeks earlier. Something from Rick, with an attachment – a word document with a rough schedule for the coming weekend and a list of everyone that was going to be there. Hadn't there been some phone numbers as well? Not all of them, though, because hadn't Rick explicitly asked in his message that everyone who didn't find his or her phone number on the list should please get in touch and help complete the list?

Joe pushed the fridge door shut and went up to his room, taking two steps at a time. He turned the laptop back on and impatiently waited for it to boot up again. Once it was ready, he accessed the e-mail account and scrolled through his e-mails. He should probably clean out his mailbox at some point!

He scrolled up and down through the messages of the past few months several times, but he couldn't find even a single e-mail from Rick. That was impossible! He hadn't deleted it, had he?

He was about ready to give up the search when it occurred to him that he hadn't actually received the e-mail directly from Rick. Sarah had forwarded it to him.

Once he did a search for e-mails from Sarah, he found very quickly what he was looking for. He clicked on the e-mail and opened the attachment. Slowly he scrolled through it from top to bottom. And there was Danny's mobile phone number…

He stared at the screen, his throat feeling a bit tight all of a sudden. So, there was her number. Nothing standing in his way now! Scratching his head, he reached for the phone that was still lying on the bed next to him and drew in a deep breath. Did he seriously want to do this? Was it really such a great idea to call her? Maybe he should just have his soup and see what the weekend would bring.

He exhaled in one big huff. The weekend wouldn't bring anything – at least not in that regard. He shouldn't have any illusions there. If he wanted to see her up-close and personal, it would have to be tonight! But maybe two evenings in a row was overdoing it a bit? His mind was going back and forth, trying to come to some decision. To call or *not* to call?

Then it occurred to him that, even if he called her, she might not pick up because she didn't recognize the number. So, why not let fate decide? If she picked up, great, if not, he was going to have his soup and watch TV.

His hands not quite steady, Joe turned on the phone and typed in the number from the computer screen. He could feel his heart beating up to his throat as the phone started ringing. She probably wouldn't pick up anyway. Maybe he should just hang up…

But then she *did* pick up.

"Hello?" she sounded cautious – no wonder with the unknown number.

"Hi Danny, it's Joe."

He thought he heard her catch her breath.

"Oh… Hi…." It sounded almost like a question.

"How are *you*?" he asked.

"Good," D replied reflexively. *A totally confused wreck* would have been much closer to the truth, of course. Ever since Sarah had left, that kiss on the counter had been flashing through her mind in half-hour intervals, making it hard to breathe whenever it happened. And hearing his voice now had just triggered the whole thing all over again.

"Do you want to go out for dinner?" Joe asked. "I mean..." There was a little pause. "...it's probably a bit spontaneous and maybe inappropriate but..."

"I'm actually already cooking something," she said uncomfortably.

"Oh, okay," Joe was scrambling for a way out. "Well... that's okay. It was just a spur of the moment kind of idea. Didn't think it'd work anyway. We can do it some other time." (Of course he knew that they wouldn't.)

There was a short moment of silence.

"Well..." D finally started. "I guess you could just... Do you want to just come over here? I'm making pasta with garlic and ham cream sauce. So, if you want..."

It took Joe a moment to react.

"Are you sure?" he asked, sounding a bit perplexed.

D barely kept herself from scoffing. How could she possibly be sure? This was, of course, nothing she had come up with after proper considerations but just a spur of the moment kind of idea as well.

"There's enough for a whole family," she said, amazed at the halfway normal sound of her own voice.

"Okay," Joe said slowly. "I guess I could. Actually sounds really good! When?"

"Well, anytime," she said. "The sauce is done. I just need to cook the pasta. And I can wait with that."

"Okay," Joe cleared his throat. "I think I could leave here in a few minutes. Is that alright?"

"Sure. Then I'll put in the pasta in ten minutes..."

"Yeah, that should work fine. Ahm – and Danny – there's still some tiramisu that Sarah made and that I'm supposed to finish. I'll bring that. For dessert..."

She laughed. "Okay, perfect! See you then!"

When she put down the phone, D felt like a small meteorite had just hit her. Like in a haze she wandered to the stove and turned off the boiling water. Then she went over to the dining table and dropped down on one of the chairs, trying to digest the overwhelming adrenaline rush the adapted dinner plans had just triggered.

As she traced the edge of the table with her hand, her eyes came to rest on the blue London folder that was lying before her, several loose pages with e-mails pertaining to her application sticking out.

After Sarah had left, she had been browsing through the printouts, looking for the exact dates and times that June and she were supposed to fly over there. Chewing on her lower lip now, she reached for the folder, pushed the loose pages back inside and got up. With the folder in hand she went to her bedroom, pulled open the drawer of the bedside table on what used to be Pete's side, let the folder slip inside and pushed the drawer shut again. She walked out of the bedroom refusing to think about possible motives for what she had just done and got busy in the kitchen.

By the time she turned the water back on ten minutes later, she had prepared a bowl of mixed salad and the table was all set. Red placemats, white plates, red and white striped napkins, glasses for water and some for wine. She had made sure there was no candle on the table or anything else that would give the wrong impression. The table wouldn't have looked any differently if she had been expecting Sarah or Robert.

When, through the kitchen window, she saw the Volvo pull up outside, she resisted the urge to rush to open the front door. Had it been Robert or Sarah, that's what she would have done. Instead she waited. When the doorbell finally rang and she opened, her hand annoyingly unsteady, she found herself looking right into Joe's smiling face.

"Hi, there," he said. "I hear you serve dinner... I brought some dessert." He held up Sarah's tiramisu dish, covered with aluminum foil. "Here, my contribution."

"Yours?" D raised her eyebrows, barely suppressing a grin.

"Well, actually..." He laughed. "It's Sarah's *involuntary* contribution."

As he stepped inside, he gave her a quick peck on the cheek, very much like the ones she got from Robert or friends like Jack or Rick. Coming from him though, it stung in a weird way.

"Almost done," she nodded towards the stove. "Just five more minutes on the pasta."

She headed to the kitchen, the spot on her cheek still tingling, and put the tiramisu dish into the fridge while Joe sat down on one of the bar stools behind her.

"So, how was it with Sarah?" he asked.

D turned around. "Good," she said – only to add a little quieter: "Or actually, a bit awkward and… well, not exactly very relaxing."

Joe chuckled. "Yeah, I guess…" He had both his forearms resting on the counter, his left hand cradling the braced hand.

"Did you make it back in time?" D asked.

"Nope," Joe shook his head, dropping his gaze to his hands.

D was waiting for him to maybe elaborate, but he didn't.

"I was kind of wondering," D said, turning back to the stove. "But from her mood I really couldn't tell."

Glancing over at her, Joe remembered that Sarah had mentioned during the lasagna dinner that she and Danny didn't talk about him.

"How did it go with Jack?" D asked, stirring her sauce. "His car running again?"

"Yeah. He got it fixed pretty quickly. Seems to be a routine for him."

D let out a little laugh. "I bet it is…"

Behind her, Joe chuckled. "Yeah, I'll never understand why he doesn't just get a proper car," he said. And then he decided on a little experiment: "I think he should get a functioning car and a girlfriend that lasts," he said lightly. "Seems like he's always single."

D kept stirring her sauce. "Oh, I kind of thought he was going out with someone," she contemplated. "Well, maybe that's over already."

"Must be," Joe said.

Turning down the temperature for her sauce, D shrugged. "Well, I'm not always up-to-date on his girlfriends," she said, "Somehow they hardly ever seem to make it long enough to be introduced to me." She chuckled.

"Well, it doesn't sound like there's been anyone serious in a while," Joe said. "But I mean, he's a cool guy, Jack. Or what do you think? I mean, how's his effect on your species?"

"My species???" she shot him a look over her shoulder. "Is there such a thing?" She laughed. Then she said, "Sure, Jack's great! Jack's about the nicest, friendliest most patient guy I've ever met. And optically, he's got something as well…"

Behind her, Joe decided not to push this any further. He might get to hear stuff that he really didn't want to hear, and it did seem as if she was enjoying this quite a bit. It didn't sound like she was currently in love with Jack herself, but since she obviously saw Jack's many qualities so very clearly, it probably couldn't be completely ruled out for the future…

As he kept watching her stir the sauce – even though it probably didn't need any more stirring – he couldn't help remembering how he used to visit her in the dorm and they would cook something together. She had made pasta with cream sauce a few times there too. And it had been nice. The cooking, the dorm, her room… – her bed… Shit, he really shouldn't go there! Focus on something else, for God's sake! The food for instance. He hadn't had pasta with cream sauce for a long time. Liz was definitely not the best cook in the world. And when she had cooked, she had usually surprised him with incredibly healthy stuff that left him hungry and grouchy. No butter, no real cream, no whole milk – never chocolate. She had seldom ever cooked, though. He would have to say that was a good thing. She had liked to go out instead, always happy to use this opportunity to show off her new dress or purse or shoes or whatever. And she had been pissed if he didn't feel like dressing up as well. Or if he just wanted to go to some laid-back comfy restaurant with good food instead of one of those fancy places she loved so much. And no matter where they went, she would never order what was on the menu. She always had those special wishes and sometimes he really thought he could hear the chefs cussing in the kitchen after the waiters had put in Liz's order.

D had just gotten a strainer out from under the stove and turned off the timer that showed ten more seconds on the pasta, when her phone started to ring.

Joe saw her bite her lip. Was she thinking what he was thinking? He shot a look at the phone that happened to be lying at the end of the bar counter to his right. He was expecting to see Pete's picture on the display, or Jack's name for that matter. The photo showed a different familiar face, though. One that he hadn't seen for a long time.

He grabbed the phone and held it out to her over the counter. "Here, it's your brother. I can strain the pasta."

She took the phone but then hesitated to pick it up. Finally she did.

"Hi, Rob…"

Joe stepped around the counter, pulled the strainer out of her hand and went over to the sink.

"I'm fine, how are you?" he heard her say as she took his seat at the bar counter. She did sound a bit impatient.

He picked up the pot from the stove and drained the pasta.

"Oh, yeah, the website… – Well, I haven't really had time yet, but I'll give it a look after the weekend, okay?"

There was a short pause in which she was listening to whatever Robert was saying on the other end.

"No, I..." She interrupted herself. "Yeah, I sent it off. On Tuesday. It was – ... ahm... It was well-received."

At the sink, Joe frowned. What was that all about? That seemed pretty cryptic language!

"Well, we'll see what happens," she told Robert, sounding almost a little irritated now.

Joe opened a few cabinets, looking for a bowl for the pasta. When he couldn't find anything that would nearly match the dishes she had set the table with, he shot her a questioning look, pointing to the noodles in the strainer.

"Sure, it's a chance," she muttered, her eyes meeting Joe's. She pointed to the cabinet above the stove. Joe opened it and she nodded.

"I'll know more after I've been there and looked at it," she told Robert, obviously picking her words very carefully so that anyone unfamiliar with the context wouldn't have a clue what she was talking about.

Pretending not to be listening, Joe reached up and got a stack of three bowls down from the cabinet. He took out the middle one and put the other two back.

D had strolled over to the sofa, giving some short *'yes/Mhmm/I guess'* answers to whatever Robert was saying.

Joe let the pasta slip from the strainer into the bowl. Glancing over at D, he saw her plucking around one of the sofa cushions while she listened to Robert. Suddenly, and only very briefly, she seemed to come to a complete stop. "Oh that..." she stammered and quickly resumed readjusting the cushions.

"It was okay," she assured Robert, her light tone not quite masking how uncomfortable she seemed to be. "Yeah...– exactly. Nothing exciting..."

There was a pause in which Robert was obviously responding, and Joe caught her shooting him a quick cautious look via the living room window. A look that he met with a deliberately clueless and harmless expression while at the same time he was wracking his brain what this was all about.

"No, she had to work..." D said, clearly eager to end the subject. "Well... Yeah... Yesss... No, it was fine, really!"

Joe suppressed a grin. So this was about the party last night?

"Rob," D said, struggling for a calm tone. "I'm kind of in the middle of cooking... No, not a really good time. Actually it's ready now. Gotta strain the pasta. Sorry! Yep. I'll call you sometime tomorrow, okay?" she cleared her throat. "Right. Say Hi to Ann! Bye!"

She hung up.

As she returned to the kitchen, Joe pretended to be totally immersed in the demanding chore of tossing the pasta with the sauce. He had hesitated for a moment before he had poured the sauce over the noodles. Liz had always hated it when he did that, but he liked it. And since it had been Danny who had first introduced him to this kind of tossed pasta dish, this was definitely the place to toss the pasta...

"So, yesterday was okay, huh?" he glanced over at her, barely suppressing a grin.

She gave him a semi-frozen look.

"It was really not all *that* bad, right?" he didn't make much of an effort to mask his amusement.

"Stop grinning!!!" D blasted, pointing the phone at him like a laser weapon ready to strike if he didn't cooperate. In response Joe put on an exaggeratedly serious face.

With a little growl she squeezed by him to get the bottle opener and a parmesan grater out of the drawers. Then she took the parmesan and the wine out of the fridge.

"Here, I'll open it," Joe had already picked up the bottle opener from the counter and reached for the bottle. As she handed it to him, their eyes met and he raised his eyebrows at her challengingly. She quickly looked away.

"So, are you going to tell him about this?" he asked as he peeled off the plastic covering the top of the wine bottle. "I mean, Robert."

She shot him a dark look. Then her mouth curled into a sweet smile. "I won't have to if I kick you out before we eat!"

Joe laughed out loud. "Well, as far as I'm concerned, you don't even have to tell him if you keep me here until tomorrow morning," he said and pulled the cork.

D stepped around him and carried the pasta bowl and the parmesan grater to the dining table. Then she picked up the water pitcher that was already there and filled the two water glasses. She couldn't even imagine how she would ever break the news to Robert. After all the bitching she had done about not wanting to see Joe, and now here he was… Robert would have a ball making fun of her!

Joe had come up beside her with the wine bottle. He leaned in a bit. "I think it's better not to tell anyone," he said, his voice dropping to a whisper. "You and I eating together, that's *real* bad…"

"Shut up or you'll leave without any food!" she said, forcing herself to hold her ground and not flee, even though feeling him right next to her made her slightly dizzy. Finally, Joe straightened up, took a step back and started pouring the wine.

"Looks really good!" he said with a look at the pasta bowl. "Thanks for the invitation."

"You called at the right time," she said and pulled a chair out to sit down.

"Oh," he tilted his head and raised his eyebrows. "So, you would have just invited anyone who called at the right time?"

"Sure, that's what I do…" She gave him an angel's smile.

"Right," he said and sat down across from her.

He had just unfolded his napkin, when she jumped up again.

"Oh, I forgot the salad in the fridge! I'll be right back… Just need to put the dressing on."

When she returned with the salad, Joe had dished up some pasta for both of them and had grated some parmesan on his and a lot on hers.

"Lots of cheese for you," he grinned.

"Thanks – just the right amount," she said, a funny feeling spreading through her stomach.

"I haven't had cream sauce forever," Joe told her as he watched her divide the salad into their two bowls.

"I have it sometimes," she said, careful not to mention that, whenever she made it, it automatically made her think of him and the dorm and their first few weeks together. And that usually spoiled her appetite.

"Reminds me of the dorm," Joe said.

D gasped for air and hoped he hadn't noticed. "The dorm, yeah," she muttered, pretending like it had occurred to her just now. "I just wish Richard could be here with us…!"

For a moment Joe gave her that *Are-you-serious* kind of look, then he just burst out in laughter. And she did too. She hadn't thought of her impossible, unusual, messy dorm-mate for a long time.

"Man, he was such a basket case," Joe sighed.

"Oh, but he was such an inspiration," D giggled suddenly on a roll. "I miss him…"

"I don't," Joe said with a mock frown. "He freaked me out. Really, really freaked me out. And I don't think he liked me very much…"

D glanced up from her food. "Oh, was he not nice to you? Why would that be??? Maybe he had a seventh sense there…"

Joe squinted at her as if to decide how to take this. Then he shrugged. "I don't think he had a seventh sense. As far as I could tell he didn't have any sense at all. And no tact, no taste… and the stuff he ate. I'm sure glad you didn't prepare any of his delicious recipes today."

It made her laugh some more. "If I had only thought of it earlier…" she said with fake regret. "We could have had his famous pizza, unthawed and aged in the box for three days, topped with chili con carne poured from a can and ketchup on the side!"

"Thank you for the very detailed description," Joe said with a disgusted look, pretending to lay down his fork. "I just lost all my appetite… And you haven't even mentioned the beer served in a chipped coffee mug yet." They both laughed. It was just such a liberating, almost exhilarating feeling – a welcome change from the tension.

"I wonder what he's up to these days," Joe chuckled.

"Oh, if he ever finished his law degree, he's probably got a high-paying job in his father's law firm."

"I didn't know his father had a law firm."

"Yeah, it's been there for four generations. I saw his father only once, with his grandma… real upper class high society kind of people. I think there's some aristocratic streak in there as well. At least that's what Richard let slip once…"

Joe laughed. "Hence his regal behavior. Still, can't picture him in a suit behaving like a decent human being."

"Well, if he didn't get into the law firm he's probably working for his Mom – parents were divorced. She runs the pub halfway up Mount Hunt."

"Oh, really? How come you know all these intimate details about him?"

"I just pieced them together from things he said, I guess."

Joe took a sip of his wine. "I wanted to go up Mount Hunt sometime anyway while I'm here, so I guess I'll have to check out that place. Who knows, with his talent in the kitchen, his Mom may have hired him as a cook."

D laughed, even though her throat had tightened with his casual mention of *while I'm here.*

"Yeah, you should check it out," she said with a smile that almost hurt.

Across from her, Joe nodded, chewing on his food.

D reached for her wine glass and took a sip.

"So, what's your plan?" she asked over the rim of her glass. "For *while you're here.*"

Joe shrugged. "I don't know. I don't think I even have a plan…"

"How long are you going to be here for?" She managed a cheerful amicable tone.

"Oh, I'll just see how long Sarah can take having me around," he said jokingly, "and how some other things play out."

D swallowed. Was he talking about Liz? Yeah, what else? She scooped up some noodles, her mind whirling.

"How do you think it's going to play out?" she asked lightly.

"What?" Joe glanced up at her, looking confused.

"Well, how's *what* going to play out?" she asked, barely able to keep her voice from cracking. "What would it take for you to go back?" She hadn't thought it possible, but she actually sounded like a well-meaning friend.

He frowned. "Back to Liz?" It sounded like she had just inquired what it would take for him to jump into a pool of piranhas.

D shrugged, embarrassed. "Well, yeah. What else is supposed to play out?"

He gave her a short, slightly irritated look and then dropped his gaze to his food.

"Well… I'll have to figure out stuff such as what I'll do about my job, about a place to live…" he suggested.

"Sure, right…" D felt stupid for not even having thought about that part. She had been so preoccupied with Liz.

"What's the deal with your job?" she asked slowly, suddenly aware that she knew absolutely nothing about his current life except for the name of his girlfriend and the town they had been living in. She had made it crystal-clear to Sarah right from the start that she didn't wish to be informed about anything regarding Joe. And Sarah hadn't tried to convince her otherwise. Now, D realized, it would be kind of helpful to have some basic knowledge at least.

"I own a company together with Liz's brother," Joe enlightened her. D could feel her jaw drop. "Oh, I didn't know that," she stammered. "Yeah, I know…" he said curtly. "Anyway, that's kind of tricky."

Momentarily unable to say anything, D nodded.

Joe stabbed some salad leaves with his fork. "And I'll just have to see how that's going to play out."

"I see…" D mumbled, feeling like an idiot.

"It's hard to tell, how this thing with Liz is going to affect my working with Steve in the long run," Joe contemplated, his eyes on his plate. "Steve's a nice guy and he's not even Liz's biggest fan, but I can't rule out that it'll turn into a problem after all. But maybe not. I'll see. And then there's the flat, of course…" He picked up his water glass and drank out of it, all the time avoiding looking at her. "It's not like she can't easily afford the flat without me," he said, setting his glass back down on the table and picking up his fork again. "If necessary, Daddy's going to subsidize her a bit and things will be fine." There was an edge to the way he said it. "Of course, I still have a lot of my stuff there, though. Not that I'm even sure at the moment that I want it back. Still kind of making up my mind. Jack has offered to help me pick it up if I decide to…"

Poking around in her noodles, D registered that apparently he had told Jack.

Across from her, Joe straightened up and she could feel him look at her. She glanced over at him and found him giving her a crooked smile. "So, it's all a bit of a mess right now." He shrugged. "But you're hardly the right person to be whining to about this!"

"Well, you're not exactly whining," she said slowly, her mouth dry. "I asked you…"

"Yeah, I guess," he played with the stem of his wine glass.

"Why did you leave?" she somehow managed to keep any kind of emotion out of it. She wouldn't even have dared to ask that question if he hadn't made the same inquiry this morning about Pete as if that were the most normal thing in the world.

At first Joe didn't quite believe his ears. He hadn't expected her to go there. Not when this morning he had almost had to force her to ask if he was still with Liz – something that he had just absolutely needed her to ask. But with that having been clarified, he would have been perfectly happy to ban the topic from their conversations for the next hundred years. There was just no way he could discuss with her the problems he had had with Liz.

D misinterpreted his hesitation. "You left for someone else..." she concluded.

Joe swallowed. Great. They were heading for very, very thin ice here. He had no clue how to handle this properly.

He shook his head and looked at his half-full water glass. "No," he said slowly. "There's no one else." And then, just wanting to get it over with he added: "I left because it didn't work..."

"Oh, it didn't?" It was impossible to miss the sarcastic edge in her voice.

"No, it didn't!" Joe shot back. His face hard now, he gave her an unblinking look. He really needed her to let this go now!

Unable to hold his gaze, D dropped her eyes to her napkin. She was battling conflicting emotions mixed in with the realization that the way this was going, it could only end badly. And as if to prove herself right, she said something she knew was wrong the moment it rolled off her tongue.

"How come it didn't work?" Her voice had taken on this somewhat acidic, almost mocking tone. "I thought you were such a perfect match!?!" The moment she heard herself say it, she wished she hadn't.

It took Joe a moment to overcome his perplexity. Not just at what he had just heard but particularly at the tone. It actually felt like a slap in the face. He stared at her for a moment as she stubbornly looked down on her plate. Huffing out a breath through his nose, he finally shook his head and reached for his wine glass.

"What was I even thinking getting into that kind of discussion with you?" He let out a sharp little laugh, not even trying to hide his irritation. He could have sworn he could see her flinch, even though her expression stayed this well-controlled mask. "Do me a favor," he said with a sneer. "Let's try not to talk about anything remotely personal again because I don't think we can handle it."

D swallowed, feeling as if someone had just knocked the air out of her. Petrified she stared down on her plate. This dinner had just gone very, very wrong.

Across from her, Joe resumed eating. She didn't dare to look at him, but from the corner of her eye she could see him finish the last bit of his pasta and eat the rest of his salad. There was no doubt in her mind that he was just dying to finish his food and get out of here.

Her hands were trembling as she scooped up a few noodles with her fork. She needed to at least pretend like she was still eating. Keep her head up, sit straight, and keep her face neutral. Even though she felt kind of nauseous, she shoved a forkful of pasta into her mouth and then chewed on it endlessly, afraid that – if she tried to swallow now – it wouldn't go down. Finally she washed the food down with water. There was no way she could eat any more.

Maybe what had just happened showed that they should have done what everyone had advised: stay out of each other's way. Because – how had Joe just put it? – they just couldn't handle it. She would always be mad at him and hurt and mistrusting and sarcastic, and he would probably always feel guilty and assume that she hated him. Which unfortunately she didn't.

"Hey…" His voice pulled her out of her dark considerations. Swallowing hard she looked up. He was looking back at her with a wary expression. Then he glanced to the side and exhaled audibly. "I'm sorry, okay?" he said and cleared his throat. "I didn't… – it came out the wrong way, okay?"

Feeling a giant lump in her throat, all D could do was shake her head and drop her gaze.

With the tense silence that engulfed them now and neither of them moving, D could hear her own heartbeat in her ears.

"It wasn't your fault," she finally said, her voice unsteady. "I shouldn't ask questions that are none of my business and then I mock you when you answer them…"

She could feel his eyes back on her, but she didn't look up. "It's just that sometimes…" for a moment there her voice failed. "Sometimes it just still bugs me!"

Joe could feel his jaw drop a bit. He had been prepared for her showing him the door or snarling how well-deserved his unhappy ending with Liz was. The one thing he definitely hadn't been prepared for was her telling him that it still hurt. Because that's what this was, right?

Looking at her frozen, almost shocked face now, he realized that what she had just told him hadn't been meant to be said out loud. It had slipped out. And now that it had, she probably already hated herself for admitting it and him for being around to hear it. Shit. What now?

With him still looking at her, D was desperately trying to choke down tears that she felt creeping up on her. She needed to pull herself together. Gain back her composure. God, why had she just said that? How pathetic could she possibly get! Justifying being a bitch with the fact that she still wasn't over him after three years? She wished she could just run and hide.

She heard him suck in a quick breath and exhale. There was no way she could even look at him now. She didn't want to see the shock and the pity in his face. She had just made a total fool of herself...

Joe downed the sip of wine that had been left in his glass, his heart beating heavily and his mind somewhat blank.

The moment he set the glass back on the table, D pushed her chair back and jumped up.

"Danny, listen..." Joe started half-heartedly, not even sure what he was going to say but well aware that it might be crucial to say something to defuse this.

"Don't," she scoffed and shook her head, picked up their two plates and her wine glass and headed around the bar into the kitchen. Her knees were rubbery, but she made it somehow. She set the wine glass down and opened the dishwasher with such force that the door almost flew back up again. Inside, some glasses were rattling dangerously. She pulled out the bottom tray and slid the plates in, dropped the silverware into the basket and whisked around to reach for the wine glass from the counter. She came to a halt when she found Joe standing right behind her, his empty wine glass in the braced hand and the salad bowl in the other.

The abruptness of her movement in combination with the look she gave him, made him take a step back reflexively and just place the dishes on the counter. Raising his hands in surrender, he backed up and got out of her way.

Her hands shaking, D grabbed the salad bowl that still had some salad inside, pulled open the door under the sink, picked the few salad leaves and cut up tomatoes out of the bowl with her bare hand, dumped them into the garbage and shut the cabinet door with her foot. She placed the glass bowl in the dishwasher more or less gently and then washed her hands, splattering water on the counter around the sink and even on herself. She didn't care. In the overall context of making a fool of herself this little clumsiness wasn't even worth thinking about.

Joe had gone back to the dining table and was moving all the remaining dishes over to the bar counter from where she could take them or not.

Avoiding looking his way, she snatched the dishes from where he placed them and, one after the other, put them into the dishwasher. She was glad that she could spend some more time staring into that machine. She still felt like in a state of shock. She couldn't even remember when she had last embarrassed herself like this. She just wished they weren't in her own flat. Then, at least, she could have just grabbed her stuff and run away...

Joe had put the parmesan back into the fridge and decided to just stay in that area as it was kind of out of her way. His back against the wall, he kept an eye on her. He was feeling a little helpless here. He still didn't quite understand how exactly the surprisingly relaxed conversation that they had at the beginning, had – within just a few seconds – spiraled into this solid hostile something. Sure, the choice of topic had been an extremely dangerous one and he had contributed his part to wreck the fragile harmony by getting so upset about her silly remark. Now there didn't seem to be any way to save the evening. No matter what he said, it would either be wrong or a lie. Maybe it would be best if he just left and went home. The only problem was that he couldn't quite imagine how, under the given circumstances, he would be able to manage a halfway civilized departure. It might just make things worse, if that was even possible.

As he pondered the issue his gaze fell on some invitation on the refrigerator. An invitation to a 15-year anniversary party of some company with a swan logo. Must be the one she worked for.

He glanced back over at her. She was leaning against the closed dishwasher now, stubbornly staring at the floor, her arms crossed over her chest. He tried to imagine how she would react if he left now. Would she be relieved? Angry? Inconsolable? It was really hard to predict what effect it would have on her. Maybe she was actually desperately waiting for him to get out of her place, though. Whichever it was, one thing was for sure: if he left now, that was going to be it. There wouldn't be any more spontaneous get-togethers, maybe not even a normal conversation. His taking off now would be accepting defeat – for both of them. Accepting that they didn't work at all, not even on the most basic friendship level.

Maybe it didn't matter, though. Or did it?

Heck, yeah! As much as he hated to admit it, it did matter a great deal! He simply didn't want to leave! Did he seriously have to? Because really, if he put into perspective what had just happened there at the dinner table... Compared to the fights and scenes he had had with Liz, this didn't exactly qualify as drama. And there were worse things than her telling him that it still bugged her!

Taking a few deep breaths, he pushed himself away from the wall.

"Okay," he said as he opened the fridge, "now that we have survived the real uncomfortable part, let's have some tiramisu!"

Even though she had heard what he had said, it took D a moment to grasp that – unexpectedly – he hadn't informed her that he was going to leave. It was so unexpected in fact that her brain was still lagging a bit behind while her body already kind of reacted. Like in a haze she got out plates and small forks and set them on the counter. She still couldn't bear to look at him.

He was just taking the tiramisu dish out of her fridge.

"Do you have a big spoon?" he asked. And amazingly he sounded like he had his cool back.

Her hands still not quite stable, she got a serving spoon out of the drawer under the bar counter. She pretty much had to look at him as she handed him the spoon or she might – instead of steering it towards his hand – have stabbed him with it. For a moment there, their eyes met, Joe looking back at her a bit wary but otherwise normal. Then he turned his attention to the tiramisu and the demanding job of dividing it evenly between the two plates.

"We could sit outside," he suggested without looking up.

D shrugged. "If you want..." It sounded more like 'I don't care'.

Ignoring her obvious lack of enthusiasm, Joe picked up the two plates and headed across the living room out the door to the deck.

D placed the tiramisu dish in the dishwasher. When she turned around again Joe was just coming back inside, went over to the coffee table, grabbed the candle and the lighter and, with that in hand, headed for the balcony door again. One foot already outside on the deck, he stopped, turned around halfway and shot her a look across the room.

"Danny," he said softly, "turn off that brain and come on outside! We can both use some fresh air!" He nodded towards the deck. "Come on!"

Shaken by this irresistible invitation, D left her spot in the kitchen and followed him.

He set the candle in the middle of the table and, holding the lighter a little clumsily in his left hand, lit it.

Slowly lowering herself onto the chair across from where he was standing, D watched him, her mouth absolutely dry. What was this going to be? She had been so careful earlier to avoid having a candlelight dinner and here he was, setting the table for dessert under stars and the moon and with a candle?

Joe had sat down. He picked up the two forks and handed her one. "Here. Eat. It's great…" There was a hint of a smile on his face.

D couldn't quite tell if it was a friendly, encouraging smile or a *God-I-feel-sorry-for-you* smile. Maybe she should just follow his advice and really shut that brain off. Because if she wasn't even able anymore to take a smile for a smile, then that brain was really making her life a lot harder than it had to be.

The fresh air actually felt good. Cleansing. Calming. It wasn't as warm as she had expected, almost a little cool. It wasn't a clear night anymore either. Almost looked like thunderstorm clouds were moving in. The candle was flickering.

Joe cleared his throat but then, instead of saying anything, he just took another bite of his dessert. D glanced over at him – and found him looking back at her.

"I know it bugs you," he said, his gaze drifting off towards the garden that lay in the dark now. "But I don't know what to tell you. There's absolutely nothing I can do to change what's already been done, or is there? I know I messed it up. But brooding over it won't help. So…"

D looked at her plate again, her heart racing and her throat too tight to even swallow. And to her absolute horror she felt tears creeping up on her again. To cover that as best as she could, she kept her eyes on the plate and quickly shoved a big portion of tiramisu into her mouth. The sweet taste of it had something unexpectedly soothing. She relaxed a bit.

"I don't know…" she heard him say, his voice not quite steady, "maybe I'm glad it *does* still bug you."

Her eyes darted up at him for a moment and then back down to the table. She could see him running the very tips of his fork over the thick layer of cacao on his tiramisu, creating some wavy lines.

"And about your question, how long I'm staying," he said, picking up the conversation somewhere before it had derailed earlier. "I think I'll be around for a while." He paused for a moment. "That is, of course, if Sarah can stand me that long…" He stopped carving patterns in the cacao layer and took a bite instead.

"Sarah's thrilled that you're here," D mumbled without looking up.

"I know that," he said patiently, "but it's still not that easy… I mean, me and her as house mates. I already got a taste of it this morning. She wasn't pleased at all that I didn't sleep at home. She almost reminded me of my Dad." He rolled his eyes and took another bite.

"That bad?" D glanced up at him.

Joe let out a breathy laugh. "She was pretty pissed, I can tell you that."

"Well, who knows who you spend your nights with…" D said with a weak smile.

Joe laughed out loud. "Yeah, really – who knows!"

The ice suddenly seemed to be broken, but D still found it hard to look at him. So she focused on her dessert and ate a few small bites. Suddenly she felt his knee gently pushing against hers under the table. She glanced over at him and he smiled at her, definitely the friendly, not the sympathetic kind of smile.

"Come on," he said and gave her knee another push. "Don't look so grim." The grim face he made for her as a demonstration now made her laugh.

"Very good." He seemed content with his achievement. "I see you've got the idea. Now keep that up!"

Holding on to that smile, D slowly nodded. "I'll try."

Joe scooped up his last piece of dessert with his fork. "How's Robert doing by the way?" he asked.

"Good," D said, relieved about the neutral subject. "He's good. Lives ten minutes away from my parents with his new girlfriend. Well, not that new anymore, actually. Just new for you, I guess. They've been together for two years or so. Her name is Ann."

"Great. So, he's not with that weird girl anymore… – what was her name? Maggie or something…"

D laughed. "*Mary*. The weird one was Mary."

"Right." Joe nodded, seemingly lost in thought for a moment. "He was studying English and History to be a teacher, right? Is he really teaching then?"

D shook her head. "No, he tried that for only half a year after he graduated. He hated it. He isn't really a kid person, I guess. And there he was surrounded by them! I'm not sure why he thought that would ever work if he doesn't really like children. The best thing that came out of this experiment was that he met Ann at that school. She's still teaching."

"So, what is *he* doing then?" Joe sounded genuinely interested.

D laughed. "He has followed his *real calling* as he calls it," with her fingers she indicating quotation marks.

"He's making jam!" Joe burst out as if he was a competitor in a TV quiz show.

"Almost," D said with a chuckle. "He started a catering business. Still in the beginning phase but it seems to be taking off. Works with two other guys and a young woman. And Mom is helping sometimes. He took quite a risk with it, but it seems like it's going well."

"Wow." Joe sounded impressed. "Sounds great. It's good that he found something he likes."

"Yeah. He just loves it."

"I bet." Joe remembered one of the dinners at D's parents' house when Robert had experimented with a goose and some very unusual ingredients, and they had all been laughing about the mess in the kitchen and Robert's desperate face. And then it had been just absolutely fabulous.

"Does he have a website or something? Because, you know, Steve – the guy I..."

"Liz's brother," D interrupted with a nod that indicated that she knew now who Steve was and there was no need to beat around the bush.

"Yeah..." Joe said, somewhat relieved. "Steve and I have a customer down there that's always looking for a good caterer for all kinds of occasions. Hasn't found one yet – judging from the food they had the last time I was there. Might actually be a good match. And it's kind of in the area where your parents live."

"Oh it is?"

"Yeah... Does Robert have a website?"

"Yes. Not quite finished yet – in fact, one of these days I'm supposed to proof-read some changes he just made to it. If you want I can send you the link of the part that's already up and running, though."

"Yeah, sure, send that to me. My e-mail address..." Joe hesitated for a moment. "Actually it hasn't changed." He suddenly looked insecure.

D swallowed. "Okay," she scratched her left eyebrow. "I think I can still piece it together then." The truth was, of course, that she still knew it by heart. Not that she had expected to ever need it again.

She watched him scrape the last remains of his dessert from his plate and finally put the fork down. Giving her a somewhat undecided look, he leaned back in his chair.

The wind on the deck was picking up. In a distance, there was already some lightning and thunder.

"So, were you and Pete actually living together?" Joe suddenly asked without any introduction.

D almost dropped her fork at the sudden change of topic. Obviously he had given up his earlier idea of steering clear of anything personal. She blinked a few times – her eyes fixed on what was left of her dessert – and considered her options. She could, of course, tell him it was none of his business. In a way he probably even expected that kind of reaction. It wasn't hard to guess, however, that after that sort of a response, he wouldn't stick around much longer. The evening would be over.

Slowly she shook her head. "Not really," she said and sucked in a quick breath. "Or only on the weekend. Depends on how you want to see it. Pete works in Sastown. He's got a flat there, in his parent's house. I've got this place here and my job. So, on the weekends he came here or I went there." She decided to skip the part where she had come up with all kinds of excuses to boycott even those weekend get-togethers.

"I see," Joe said and picked up his fork again. "That kind of explains it, I guess," he said, trying to balance the fork on the index finger of his right hand.

"Explains what?"

"Well, I just kind of noticed that this place doesn't look like there's any furniture missing and there's no trace of him either." Joe decided to zone out the matching sets of bedding on her bed. "Not even a toothbrush!" It seemed worth mentioning, as – after all – he had one since last night.

D shrugged. "Well, as far as the toothbrush is concerned – if you really need to know – he had two. They are just not in my bathroom anymore. I put them in the bag with all the other stuff he's still got here."

"Ahm... – Okay." Joe put his fork down and pushed it around on his plate. Somehow Pete still having stuff here and his toothbrushes and all the other things just being stored away somewhere, most likely in one of those closets in her bedroom, had an unpleasant taste to it.

"Any new candidates?" he asked as casually as he could.

"Huh?" she gave him a puzzled look. Then her eyes narrowed.

D was scrambling to come up with a proper reaction. She had been absolutely unprepared for him to flat-out ask her things like this. But then it dawned on her that, back at the dinner table, she had asked him basically the same question in a much nastier way. So, instead of telling him to stick to his own business, she shook her head. "No, no new candidates," her eyes trailed off to the railing around the deck. "Besides, I think I need some time to breathe for a while."

There was a moment of silence.

Watching her closely, which he only dared because she was looking away, Joe couldn't help feeling a little aggravated. Even if there didn't seem to be anyone else right now, what she had said in regard to Pete could mean pretty much anything. He wasn't even quite sure how and why the relationship with Pete had ended. Judging from their conversation this morning, it had been at her initiative. Just recently or months ago? Why exactly? He had to admit that he was just dying to know these things. But asking her about this right now was surely overstepping a red line.

"Do you want that?" D pointed at what was left of her dessert. "I can't eat any more..."

"Sure." Joe reached over and took her plate. Two bites and it was all gone.

Silence again...

"What do you do?" Joe asked her. "I mean, workwise."

"I work for Swan..." she said.

"They do export and import, right? I saw the invitation on your fridge. 15 year anniversary!"

D felt a sting. Thank god she had put away the London folder or they would be discussing that.

"I handle some of the purchasing and exports – some with India, a lot via Great Britain. I like it. It's fun and there's always something going on. Sometimes I bitch about it but overall, I like it. It's a fun job, and the things people do remind me of a soap opera sometimes..."

Joe laughed. "Same at our company." He wondered how she would view the story of Eric, who had slept with a girl who was one owner's sister and the other owner's girlfriend. That surely qualified as soap opera material, didn't it?

"What do you do... exactly?" she asked with a shy glance up at him.

"It's a small software company," he said, "relatively specialized. Steve and I developed a few programs. We got some pretty good and reliable customers, mainly in the Scandinavian countries and the Benelux, one in Hungary, two in Italy. It was hard work getting them all set up to the point where things are running relatively smoothly. A lot of trips back and forth, but it was fun." He skipped the part where he had personally taken every possible business trip just to get away from Liz.

There was a heavy silence again. Joe didn't feel like elaborating any more on his job as it would inevitably take him to the point where he had to mention that he had to cover for Steve two and a half weeks from now and that he had another trip to Amsterdam scheduled in two. Somehow he didn't want to think about that right now.

D nodded, deep in thought. She had just realized that Joe's job problem was probably even trickier than he had admitted during dinner. And there were obviously a few things on his mind that he didn't want to talk about. He had put so much work and so many ideas into that company – and probably also a lot of money. There was no way he could just let that go and start over.

From the corner of her eye she saw him check his watch. It was a few minutes past ten. D tried to recall what kind of neutral reaction she had planned last night when she had expected him to say that he had to go. She would need it now…

"It's pretty late," she heard him say.

She nodded. "I guess." She bit down on her lower lip as her eyes met his for a moment. Joe dropped his gaze and set the two plates on top of each other. Then he reached over and picked up her fork that she had just set on her napkin when she had offered him the rest of her dessert earlier.

A sudden gust of wind blew the napkin out of his hand onto the deck, but he managed to step on it before it could get very far. He picked it up and stuck it under the forks on the plates. Finally he looked up again. Running his fingers over his chin he gave her an undecided look. "I guess I should go, huh?"

D swallowed. She could hardly tell him to stay…

The way the wind was picking up, it would probably start raining soon.

Across from her, Joe leaned back in his chair again and stared towards the outline of the apple tree.

"What if I didn't want to go home?" he asked a little stubbornly.

Despite the cool wind, D felt like a heat wave had just hit her. What now?

"Sarah would be mad," she said, that being the first thing that came to mind.

Joe looked back at her a bit baffled. Then he rolled his eyes. "Ask if I care!"

"I guess you don't," D concluded. "In any event, you would have to find some place to sleep... – like a garden bench or something."

Joe laughed. "Right. Well, what about that sofa in there?" With his thumb he pointed at the window to the living room behind him.

Pursing her lips, her eyes locked with his, D blew out a breath through her nose.

"It's pretty comfortable, I already tested it," he told her. "So if it's still free…"

D swallowed. Oh my, what was she doing? Before she even knew it, she nodded. "Yeah. Still free, I guess."

"Can I book it then?" Joe asked. "I mean, since I've already been assigned a toothbrush and two pillows?"

Instead of an answer, she glanced over at him with a weak smile. Her head was spinning.

"And you know, it's starting to rain now, too, and it would be very dangerous for me to drive home in such crappy weather…" Joe batted his eyes at her.

"Right," she slowly said, feeling strangely out of breath. "So, you're staying on my sofa for safety reasons?"

He shrugged with a grin. "Do I have to answer that? – You're right about Sarah, though. She'll be mad. *Very* mad. And that breakfast tomorrow is going to be real fun. I better make sure I at least get there in time."

D nodded, a giggle creeping up on her. "Yeah, you better!"

"That's not funny!" he scolded, but couldn't help grinning himself. "I have to make sure I get there in time and I have to appear to be starving because she didn't take it too well this morning when she realized I had already had breakfast somewhere. God knows what kind of scenario went through her head there…"

D bit her lip, somewhat glad to know that – whatever Sarah had imagined – was very unlikely to have included her.

It was almost eleven when it started raining and they fled inside. They put away the dishes and then stood around in the kitchen a little undecidedly until Joe proposed that they watch a movie. He picked out something funny and they sat on the sofa next to each other but not close enough to touch.

About half an hour into the movie, D was starting to get really tired. When she had nodded off for the third time, Joe finally turned off the TV. Ironically the sudden silence made her open her eyes again. She blinked with confusion.

"Is it over already?"

"No, but maybe you should go to bed," he said, his head turned her way.

"Maybe…" she nodded weakly.

Joe got up, took her hand and pulled her up. "Come on."

As he watched her stumble into her bedroom to give him his pillows and sheets, he had to admit that he could have thought of much better ways to end this evening than his telling her that she should go to bed (alone). Why exactly had he wanted to stay here?

He took the bedding that she handed him.

"You can keep watching TV," she told him.

"Yeah, I know. I might." He watched her disappear into the bathroom.

He returned to the sofa, turned the film back on and tried hard to concentrate. When the bathroom door opened again a few minutes later, he looked up.

"Wake me up tomorrow morning, okay?" she said tiredly as she pushed open the bedroom door. "Don't just leave."

Joe laughed from the sofa. "I never just leave… Good night!"

"Good night."

# Alligator Attacks

After D had closed her bedroom door, Joe turned off the movie and flipped through the channels without being able to focus on anything. Somehow this evening had been a bit of a mess. He really couldn't quite say what had made it so important to stay, when it was purely his staying on the sofa and her sleeping in her bedroom. Not that he was even sure he would have wanted it any other way. Or maybe he would... Well, not worth thinking about right now.

He turned off the TV and suddenly remembered that he better send Sarah a message. He could only imagine what that would set off, but he would just have to deal with it tomorrow.

He typed,

*I'll come right to the café at nine. See you there. Don't be mad!*

Since he had the phone turned on, he couldn't help checking his messages. There were two missed calls from Liz, three text messages from her as well and one message from Christine. Chewing on his lower lip, he deleted the info on all the missed calls. He did read two of Liz's messages:

*You fu... assh... Call me back!*

followed by

*I hate you! Call me!*

He decided he could do without reading the third message and just deleted all three.

Finally he clicked on the one from Christine. He hadn't really expected to hear from her.

The message just said,

*I just had some ice cream which made me think of you. How are you doing? Let me know when you're back in Amsterdam if you want to get together. nsa.*

*Christine*

Joe turned the phone around in this hand. *nsa* must mean *no strings attached.* He rubbed his chin as he tried to decide if he should respond. Then he did.

*I'm fine. Hope you are too. I'll be in Amsterdam Sept 2 to 4. I'll get in touch.*

*Joe*

Once he had clicked on *Send*, he turned the phone off and laid it on the coffee table. That's when something on the floor between the sofa and the big chair caught his eye. Was that his sweater? He leaned down and picked it up. He hadn't even missed it. Must have fallen off the sofa last night. He laid it on the coffee table next to his phone.

It was almost midnight when he went into the bathroom.

As he brushed his teeth, he let his gaze wander around. So far he had resisted the urge to open any of the drawers or the mirrored cabinet. He had been way too tired and out of it the previous night, and Danny had been waiting outside. Tonight was different.

He looked at his own reflection in the mirror and suddenly realized that he didn't really *have* to open anything. This wasn't some stranger's place where, if you peeked around a little, you would be surprised or shocked at what you'd find. He had known the girl who was sleeping next-door long enough. He didn't have to pull out drawers because he could easily guess that they contained some brushes and that great-smelling lotion she had always used (and that he was sure he had smelled during the dance yesterday) and her make-up – a certain amount of bottles, mascaras, pencils, eye shadows and nail polish and all that cosmetic stuff. He was well acquainted with all the technical terms by now. And even though he had no idea why anyone would need all that, Danny's stash here would for sure be nothing in comparison to what Liz used to carry around in her purse as an emergency kit.

He could open the mirror cabinet, but he already knew that what he was probably going to find, were some creams, dental floss, eye makeup remover and maybe a package of birth control pills… He pushed that last thought away quickly as it inevitably reminded him of Pete. And the fact that Pete had been standing right where he was standing now, brushing his teeth and then walking right into that bedroom. Grrr… Joe didn't want to think this through…

He spit out the toothpaste, rinsed his mouth and, instead of just laying his toothbrush on the shelf next to the sink where he'd left it last night and this morning, he stuck it into the cup with *her* toothbrush.

His eyes still on the two toothbrushes, he sat down on the side of the bathtub and ran his hand over his forehead. The whole thing with Pete was starting to drive him nuts, really. Somehow it seemed increasingly important to gain some clarity as to what was really going on. Was it just a

259

half-hearted trial-separation *to have time to breathe* or the definite end of a relationship?

Whatever it was, it still seemed quite fresh. From the little he had heard, it appeared as if she still communicated with Pete one way or the other, and like she had neatly packed up Pete's stuff, so he could pick it up sometime at his convenience.

Joe growled to himself. This was actually very confusing and, if he was quite honest, extremely annoying and disconcerting. He was relatively sure that three years ago she hadn't even thought about neatly packing up his toothbrush, shaving kit and the few clothes he had in her dorm so he could come get them. If he had to make a guess, he would say she had probably broken the toothbrush in two and ripped or cut his clothes into pieces. And she surely hadn't picked up the phone when he had tried to call her. So, whatever was the cause of the breakup with Pete, it didn't seem nearly as unforgivable and unmendable as what he had done.

On the shelf next to the sink, three perfume flasks caught his eye. The one to the left looked familiar. Painfully familiar. From her little bathroom in the dorm...

Out of some crazy mood he reached for that flask and took the cap off. Holding the top up to his nose he inhaled.

The scent hit him so instantaneously that, even though he had expected it, it came as a shock. There was a weird sudden flash of weakness that he could feel all over. Swallowing, he closed his eyes. And experienced a total mess of emotions and memories that made him catch his breath and press the cool glass bottle against his forehead. He felt a bit like falling. Free fall... From high altitude... With scenes of a relationship flying by – Danny going shopping with him for Sarah; first evening in her dorm room; the concert; biking, with his borrowing Sarah's bike; a few days of trying to get her out of his head; waking up in the hospital; her showing up a few days later; his escaping his parent's house on crutches; first night together in her dorm room...

He forced his eyes open and sucked in a desperate breath. Crap! He better stop thinking before he overdosed... He quickly put the cap back on the perfume flask as if there was an evil ghost inside that had to be contained. Hastily he set the perfume back next to the other two flasks, got up and turned around.

Feeling a little shaky, Joe left the bathroom and walked back towards the sofa – by D's bedroom door. He came to a halt. Stared at the closed door. What if…? What if he went in? What if he woke her up? What if…? He imagined reaching out, placing his hand on the door handle, pressing it down…

He shook his head, irritated with his own mind game. If he really did that (enter that room), it would – even if for some stupid reason she didn't kick him out right away – end in total chaos.

He went back to the sofa, took the two back cushions off, put the bedding down, took off his pants and his T-shirt and slipped under the sheet and the blanket. He switched off the light and tried to go to sleep. Unfortunately he was wide-awake now...

After half an hour of tossing and turning he switched the light back on and got up. He went over to the fridge and poured himself a glass of milk. Maybe that would help him go to sleep. Leaning against the sink, he took a few sips.

He hadn't heard the bedroom door open, but suddenly he became aware of D standing a few meters away from him, barefoot and wearing a striped red and white tank top and red pajama shorts.

"Sorry. I didn't want to wake you up," he said trying not to stare at her bare legs or the area of her top where he could guess the outline of her breasts.

She shook her head and came over. "You didn't wake me up. I couldn't sleep."

"Oh, okay," Joe felt pleasantly surprised that he was obviously not the only one with this problem.

"Do you want some milk?" He held up his half full milk glass.

"Sure…" Without thinking about it, D just reached for his glass and drank some. Then she handed him back the glass, carefully avoiding his eyes.

Joe downed the rest of the milk. Then, shooting her a look over the rim of his glass, he tried to gauge the situation. She was staring at the floor with an undecided expression, one bare foot rubbing against the other. Impossible to know what she was thinking… It was kind of nice that she had reappeared, but Joe wasn't sure at all what to make of it or what to do, for that matter. And from the way it looked she wasn't going to be much help.

He put the glass into the dishwasher wracking his brain how to proceed. Finally he had an idea.

"I saw you have some ice cream in there," he said lightly as he turned around to her. "Since we both can't sleep, we could have some midnight dessert. I can offer you a place on the sofa and a piece of blanket..." He was just winging it.

D blinked, obviously weighing the idea. Then her face lit up and she slowly nodded. "I'm glad you know the contents of my fridge so well..." she chuckled as she squeezed by him to get some bowls out.

Joe went over to the sofa, picked up his T-shirt and put it back on. Then he grabbed the back cushions and placed them back on the sofa.

When he turned back toward the kitchen, D had both ice cream containers open and was holding the ice cream scoop in her hand, looking a little hesitant.

"Here, *you* do that!" she finally said and held the ice cream scoop out to him.

He laughed and took it out of her hand, intentionally brushing his thumb against hers. "Sure, just exploit me," he said, "I'm big and strong."

"Hahaha!" she mocked and watched him as he started scooping out the ice-cream. It was a little tricky to do this with his left hand.

"How much do you want?" he asked her.

"Two scoops please," she said and leaned against the sink half a meter away, twisting the top of a dish-soap bottle between her fingers.

Joe dished up the ice cream and realized at the same time that during his three years with Liz they had never been able to agree on any kind of ice cream they both liked (she preferred the sour sorbet stuff, he was more into chocolate, caramel and everything rich and creamy). But then he came here and all he had to do was just blindly reach into D's freezer and fish out what turned out to be his favorite ice cream flavors. Some things apparently never changed! It was kind of nice – and at the same time plain scary.

A minute later they were in the living room. With Joe sitting on the sofa and D sitting on the chair beside the sofa...

The second she had (for some idiotic reason) sat down in that chair and Joe had shot her that *Do-you-really-have-to-do-this?* look, D realized that she had just messed it up! 100 points! She should have just stayed in her bed! He had invited her onto the sofa and she had sat down in the chair. Just to make a point. Of what??? Well, there was no way to correct it now.

Joe started digging his spoon into the ice cream, his eyes fixed on something in his bowl. He just couldn't figure her out! Why on earth had she come out of the bedroom and seemed all thrilled with the ice cream/sofa idea, only to run straight for that chair then?

"You know…" It did sound a little nasty, but he couldn't help it. "You *really* don't have to sit here with me. Feel free to just take the ice cream and go back to your bedroom." He knew that he was pushing it.

D bit her lip. For a moment he expected her to jump up and follow his sarcastic advice. But sometimes miracles still seemed to happen. She rose from her chair, although with a stubborn expression.

"Okay, I'll sit with you then," she muttered.

"Great idea!" Joe laughed, lifting the blanket. "I thought that had been the plan anyway…"

She slid under the blanket. But of course, even now, sitting next to him, she made sure to leave enough space between them so they didn't touch. Not exactly what Joe had had in mind, but he decided it was a good start.

For a while they just ate their ice cream and didn't say anything. Finally Joe broke the silence. "Can I ask you something?" he asked, pointing his spoon at her.

Her jaw seemed to drop a little. "What?"

Looking at her, Joe realized that she was obviously expecting the worst. He wondered what that could possibly be.

"What did Pete want last night?" he asked. From her expression he could tell that the question took her by surprise and that she didn't like it too much, but it was obviously *not* what she had feared he'd ask.

"I haven't called him back yet," she retorted.

"Oh you haven't?" Joe gave her a surprised look. "That's kind of mean, isn't it?"

She shrugged and kept eating her ice cream, trying hard to keep a straight face. Thank God his question hadn't been what she had expected. He could ask about Pete all he wanted. That was fine. No problem there. She would answer more or less truthfully – whatever she saw fit – and that was it. But she just hoped and prayed that he wouldn't start asking her anything that had to do with him or the way she felt about him. Because it was one thing to let him into her flat and let him stay and possibly even let him kiss her (which so far he hadn't even tried this evening), but it was something entirely different to discuss the meaning of such insane actions with him.

"So, *why* is he still calling?" Joe seemed to be genuinely interested.

"He's calling because – …we're still friends, I guess," she said keeping her eyes on her ice cream.

"Oh, *are* you?" Joe raised his eyebrows. "Does that really work?" It didn't sound like a serious question.

D stirred around in her ice cream. What the hell did he want?

"I can't say yet if it works," she mumbled, "but I can hardly refuse to try, can I?"

Instead of a response, Joe shrugged.

With her spoon D ploughed a straight line in the middle of the ice cream mush that was still left in her bowl.

"Well, maybe he just wanted to know how last night was," Joe suggested, still not ready to let the topic go.

D bit her lip. "Could be," she said dryly, "and *no*, he *doesn't* know that *you* were there. If that's what you're indicating!"

"I'm not indicating anything," Joe said saintly.

Spooning up the ice cream to the left of her dividing line, D cleared her throat. "He probably wanted to tell me something about the stupid company party I need to go to with him next week." She wasn't really sure why she had just put that out, but somehow she had just had to say it.

If Joe was surprised or annoyed or anything, he hid it well. He finished his ice cream and then leaned forward a bit to set the empty bowl on the coffee table. And he used this opportunity to inch over a little closer to her. So, as he leaned back again now, his upper arm *did* touch hers. And if he just moved his leg a tiny bit, his knee would actually be against hers…

Even though he refrained from doing the knee-part for right now, D felt the hot flash run through her from top to toe just from his sitting so close. Thank God she was having ice cream here and not hot soup!

Glad to have something to occupy herself with, she ate what was left in her bowl at the slowest possible pace (which naturally made the ice cream mush turn to soup). Once she was done, she licked the spoon, let it slide back into the bowl and tried to decide if she should just keep the bowl on her lap now or put it on the coffee table, which would mean she would have to move. And she just knew that, if she moved now, she would never dare to sit as close to him again as they were sitting now.

Joe must have guessed the dilemma. Without a word he reached over, took the bowl out of her hand, leaned forward, put the bowl on top of his own and then leaned back again – this time sitting even closer than before. And he decided to just go ahead and do the knee-thing while he was at it.

264

So, he did, but only for a brief moment. Then he pulled his legs up on the sofa, his feet resting on the edge, and casually draped his arm over the back of the sofa behind her.

Trying hard to ignore the warmth that seemed to be radiating from his arm (even though he wasn't even touching her) D stared at her hands in her lap.

"This whole thing is so stupid..." she mumbled.

"What's stupid?" Joe was confused. "This?" He gently nudged his arm against her shoulders.

Sucking in a shaky breath, D shook her head. "No, that thing with Pete..."

Joe let out a little laugh. "Oh, *that*! What part of it? That he keeps calling you? That you go to some company party with him? That you're still friends?"

D felt her throat go dry.

"Actually," Joe said calmly without waiting for an answer, "I never liked Pete, so I'm kind of biased here – in more than just one way."

He turned his head and looked at her from the side. And then he said in a perfectly friendly tone, "So, I guess I'm probably the last person that should give you advice or even an opinion on this matter. Sarah might be a lot better!" (That wasn't to say that he wouldn't have just *loved* to give her some advice, of course!)

"I've talked to Sarah," D said flatly, "she thinks it's idiotic..."

Joe laughed out loud. "Well, then, there you go!"

His laugh and words still echoing in her ears, D suddenly felt his arm slide down against her shoulders and her heart seemed to miss a beat. She resisted the immediate urge to jump up and flee. And she struggled to keep her expression neutral because she could feel his eyes still on her.

Finally, he turned his head and they were just sitting next to each other, both staring at the coffee table.

Biting her lip D, forced herself to stay put and keep breathing.

Joe, for his part, was immensely relieved – and surprised – that the slipping arm hadn't chased her away. He was very tempted to proceed with pulling her closer and kissing her, but he was afraid that he wouldn't get very far if he tried that. Plus, he had just remembered an incredible piece of advice he had once read, "*...you need to go at a pace that's even too slow for her, in order for her to figure out that she wants it too...*" For some reason that seemed just extremely fitting in this particular case – move so slowly that even *she* would eventually get frustrated. No kissing unless she started it, and definitely nothing beyond that.

So, they just sat there in silence for a while, his arm around her back and his thumb softly stroking a spot of exposed skin on her shoulder.

When, after a few minutes of this, D slid forward to the edge of the sofa, Joe just pulled back his arm and watched her get up.

"I think I better go back to bed," she said without looking at him. She picked up the two bowls from the coffee table and, cradling them in both her hands, stood there, giving him an undecided look.

Obviously she wasn't even quite sure herself that leaving now was what she really wanted. Joe knew that it was definitely not what *he* wanted. He wanted her back here on the sofa, preferably lying down this time... But then he took a deep breath, put on a friendly smile and said, "Okay, I guess it's really late." He was impressed with himself at how calm and well-meaning he sounded. "Good night, again."

"Good night."

She dropped the bowls off at the bar counter and then disappeared into her bedroom, quietly closing the door behind her.

Alone in the living room again, Joe pulled his T-shirt over his head and thrust it across the living room with a frustrated growl. He snatched the two back cushions off the sofa, dropped them next to the coffee table and turned off the light.

Lying in the dark again, he suddenly had a scary idea: what if she was following the exact same grand piece of advice not to make a move unless he did? Was it even likely that she would ever make a move, given their history? Wouldn't she rather die than do *that*? Whatever! He should go to sleep now. Tomorrow was another day.

He had almost nodded off when the noise of the bedroom door snapped him back into consciousness. He was instantly wide awake again, his heart beating wildly.

"Joe?" he heard her whisper from the end of the sofa where he had dropped the back cushions. "You still awake?... *Joe?*"

He realized that this was the first time she had actually said his name since he was back in Deens. Hearing her say it tugged at something inside him quite a bit.

"Oh, you're back!" he teased. "How did that happen? Are you scared all alone in your room?"

"Yeah, right..." she grumbled.

It was too dark to really see anything except her silhouette, but it looked like she was scratching her head. Joe was lying there, just dying to know what her plan was, if she had any.

"Do you still have space under your blanket?" It was hardly loud enough to hear.

"Sure," Joe said trying to hide his surprise. Any possibility that he had misheard? He watched her step over the cushions and come up to the side of the sofa and realized that no, this could hardly be a misunderstanding.

"Come on in," he lifted the blanket.

Now she hesitated. Stood there, motionless, and looked down on him.

"Do I have to put my T-shirt back on for this?" he asked. "Or would that defeat the purpose?"

Instead of an answer, she sat down on the edge of the sofa. He had moved back as far as he could to give her some space. Holding his breath, he was waiting for her to actually lie down.

When she finally did, he had to keep himself from laughing out loud, though. Because she stretched out – facing away from him, of course – lying so far out towards the edge of the sofa that there seemed to be worlds between them. How did she even *do* that? The sofa wasn't *that* deep!

Rolling his eyes behind her back, Joe draped the blanket over her and, after a moment of hesitation, draped his left arm loosely on top of the blanket. As the arm came to rest somewhere around her hip, he heard her draw in a breath. And then she slowly and quietly exhaled.

With her just lying there, not nearly close enough to feel comfortable with, Joe was torn apart between his very good resolutions and the suspicion that some assistance on his part was crucial here to get things going.

"Okay, Danny," he said and propped himself up on his right arm a bit, "if you seriously intend to stay like this, you'll fall off the sofa. And I doubt that's what you came back here for."

He pushed her a little with his bent knee against her lower back to prove his point.

"Stop it!" She reached behind herself and pushed his knee back with her hand. Then, to his surprise, she actually did slide back his way a bit, but it was only enough so she wasn't in danger of falling off the sofa anymore. Not enough to touch.

With a little snort, Joe let himself fall onto his pillow, his right arm now bent under his head. He put a little more force behind the left arm that he had draped over her, holding his flat hand firmly against the blanket where her stomach must be. He felt her tense up. But he didn't care. In contrast, it actually confirmed that he was doing something right here!

He inched a little closer – close enough to where his chest actually touched her left shoulder blade. And, keeping his left arm on top of the blanket firmly wrapped around her, he made sure she couldn't move away when he slid his knees against the back of her slightly bent legs now. He felt her flinch, but to his surprise she didn't try to escape.

"So, and now you need to relax!" he told her.

"I *am* relaxed," she lied, sounding a bit out of breath.

Joe let out a little laugh. "No, you're not!" He moved his face close to her ear. "You're not relaxed at all," he whispered and ran his flat hand over the blanket right above her belly.

"Well, are *you* relaxed?" she growled.

"Mostly," he lied.

"Oh, *are* you? *Really???* " She leaned back against him, sliding into his lap a little further.

Joe closed his eyes and swallowed. "I just have an anatomical problem here," he admitted, "but, yeah, I *do* find this pretty relaxing. Keep going…"

"You better keep this anatomical problem under control," she scoffed shakily and quickly moved back into the initial position.

"Don't worry, I will," he chuckled and rubbed his chin against the side of her neck. "Relax, Danny," he told her again and softly blew into her ear, well aware that this totally defeated the purpose of making her relax.

She gasped for air. "*What* are you doing?" she moaned.

"Just making it up as I go along," he admitted. "But I could ask you the same thing, *What the hell are you doing?*" He imitated her accusing tone. "This isn't meant to be some sort of nasty experiment by any chance?"

She didn't answer right away.

"Answer please," he nudged her shoulder with his chin.

"It *is* kind of an experiment," she finally admitted.

"Well, great!" Joe exclaimed, "and you just lie here and flat-out admit it?" He let out amused breath, intentionally close to her neck again.

"That's pretty shocking! But well, since we're here, I guess I will just conduct my own experiments too, if you don't mind."

Without waiting for her reaction – or permission for that matter – he pulled back his left arm and slid it under the blanket. He could feel her freeze as soon as his fingertips touched the fabric of her shorts right above her hip.

"Relax," he whispered and laid his hand on her waist. She didn't relax but she also didn't tell him to stop. So he moved up his thumb, sliding it under her shirt and slowly brushed it over the small area of bare skin he could reach. He felt her catch her breath, but at the same time her back seemed to relax against him. Finally! Pleased with this result, Joe decided to proceed, sliding his entire flat hand under her shirt, his palm slowly skating from her waist over to her other side. He could feel her stomach retract for a moment, as she gasped. But then, as she exhaled, her soft skin met his palm again.

Keeping his hand there, he realized that he could actually feel her breathe. He closed his eyes and just let that feeling sink in for a few seconds, only his thumb gently moving up and down in the rhythm of his own breathing that seemed to have adapted to hers.

Amazed that she hadn't pulled away yet, and feeling both dizzy and inspired, Joe decided to carry on with the experiment while he still could. Slowly, very slowly, he started moving his hand up. It would be interesting to see how far he would get.

"Joe," she gasped. "Stop that." She caught his hand about halfway between her belly button and the area of interest and held it there.

"Oh, you don't like my experiment?" he said with fake surprise.

"Well, you don't like mine either." She sounded shaky.

"That's not true," he told her patiently as he pulled his hand out from under hers and laid it back on her belly. "I'd probably even give your experiments a thumbs-up, but somehow they *do* seem to have a pretty cruel element to them." He placed a kiss on the side of her neck.

"You don't *seriously* expect me to have mercy with you of all people?" she asked breathlessly.

"I didn't ask for mercy," he let his hand slide across her belly over to her waist again, his arm draped across her now. "I just think that, if you step into the alligator's cage and try to run your little experiments, you *do* have to be prepared that the alligator will try to bite off your hand or head or whatever part of you it can get ahold of!" He playfully bit her ear lobe before he buried his nose in her hair for a moment. That's when it suddenly hit him that he was straying way off the path of his good resolutions here. He was on the best way of pushing this too far. Realizing that, he took his hand off her, raised his arm and slid away towards the very back of the sofa.

The sudden loss of his touch took D by surprise. For a moment she just lay there, maybe expecting some new experimental approach. When nothing happened, she reached back with her hand and realized that he had moved away and was lying on his back.

"What's wrong?" she asked and turned around to him.

Staring at the dark ceiling, one of his arms bent under his head, the other lying across his stomach, he shrugged. "Well, don't tell me this wasn't breaking the rules," he said darkly.

D swallowed, taken aback by the somber tone. Like rules still mattered at a point like this!?!

"Breaking all kinds of rules," she confirmed and lay on her side, facing him.

When, instead of any reaction, he kept staring straight up, she propped herself up on her arm and reached over to brush a strand of hair from his forehead. As her fingers softy touched his temple, she thought that she saw him close his eyes. Forcing herself not to retract her hand, she traced his left eyebrow with the tips of her index and middle finger until she reached the spot right between his eyebrows.

"So, is the alligator pretending to be asleep now?" she asked as she ran her fingers down the back of his nose with that same soft touch.

"It's still very dangerous," Joe breathed, struggling to keep his eyes shut. "You better make sure you don't provoke it. Even when it's sleeping it's an unpredictable threat!"

"Oh really?" she chuckled as she let her fingertips dance over the tip of his nose for a moment as if to really tempt the alligator. When there was no reaction, the touch wandered down towards his mouth.

Despite the fact that he was feeling increasingly light-headed with her newest experiment, Joe tried to keep perfectly still and pressed his lips together. Of course, the alligator should snap for her fingers here any second, but he didn't want this to end – not just yet. He let the touch pass over his lips and down to his chin without trying an attack. It just felt so good.

The light touch passed his chin and trickled down over his neck to his collarbone. That's when he caught her hand and – his hand on top of hers – held her palm pressed against his skin. She didn't fight it.

He opened his eyes and turned to face her.

"This is where you kiss the guy!" he told her with a little smirk.

"Is it?" she croaked.

"Man, Danny! If this was a movie, the audience would be rolling their eyes in frustration by now."

His hand that had been on top of hers, was now trailing over her wrist up her arm, over her elbow towards her shoulder.

She looked down at him with a torn expression.

"You'll have to start this time," he whispered, giving her shoulder a gentle encouraging squeeze. "I'll help you then, but you'll have to start. You're the one in charge of this experiment!"

"I can't do this if we discuss it in detail beforehand!" she complained.

Joe burst out laughing. "That was by no means in detail! Do you want me to really go into detail here how this is supposed to work?"

"No thanks!" she mumbled.

"….there is a bunch of good scenarios that come to mind, and each of them will work just fine," he teased, "like for example, you could–"

When he felt her thumb running over his lower lip, he fell silent.

Taking a deep breath, D moved a little closer and, pushing herself up on her arm a bit more, looked down on him.

"Okay then," she said. "Seems like there's only one good way to make you shut up." She placed her free hand against his cheek and brushed her thumb over his mouth for a moment. As she leaned in, Joe closed his eyes.

Lightly placing her lips on his mouth, she kissed him.

As promised he did his best to help carry this further. His lips, opening a bit, he kissed her back, his tongue gliding over her lower lip, while he wrapped his arms around her; his lips sliding against hers, one of his hands in her hair, pulling her face closer; his tongue somehow finding hers.

Somewhere in the course of this, he managed to pull her down against himself – a move that made the kiss gain even more momentum.

Immersed in what felt like a pink, fluffy cloud that was just too good to be true, Joe was trying to ignore the red flashing alarm light that had come on somewhere in the back of his clouded mind. This thing was about to spin out of control. He knew it. And part of him wanted it to do just that. There was hardly any clothing between them and his hands were just itching to remove the little there was. And the way this kiss was going he was almost positive he would get away with pretty much anything right now.

It took all the self-control he still had left, not to push up her shirt but loosen his embrace instead and break that kiss.

Like a rag doll D sank against him, her face buried somewhere between his neck and his shoulder.

"Don't get me wrong," he told her, stroking her back, "I would *love* to carry on with this but... well, I'm pretty sure if this got out of hand, you'd blame *me*."

She lifted her head a bit. "Well, who else could I blame?" she asked weakly, totally out of breath.

Joe couldn't help chuckling. "Oh, that's alright! Just blame me, then," he said, "rumor has it, though that this kind of thing takes two. And as far as I remember you started it!" He resisted the urge to bury his face in her hair. "It wasn't me!"

Chewing on her lower lip, D huffed out a breath through her nose and he felt her nod against his neck. Then, slowly, she pulled away and rolled over to the other side.

As he turned to face her, he saw her sit up and run her hands over her face.

"You okay?" he reached out and put his hand on her knee, giving it a gentle rub.

"I don't know," she muttered and slightly shook her head, "feels like some fuses just blew."

"Sorry about that!" Even to himself he didn't sound very sorry.

She shrugged, looking kind of helpless. "Are you still going to wake me up tomorrow morning?"

"Sure. If you want, I'll make sure the alligator bites your toe around eight." The thumb and index finger of his hand bent playfully, he clawed her knee, imitating the bite of the alligator.

"Okay," she chuckled wearily and gave his clawing hand a quick pat. Then she got up. "Good night."

As she closed the bedroom door behind her, Joe threw his arms to his sides. What the hell was he doing? Did he have *any* idea what a mess he was getting himself into? Or did he even care?

Maybe until half an hour ago he could have still said there was nothing, no harm being done... It would have been a blatant lie even then, but he might still have gotten away with it. But the whole sofa thing had definitely been crossing the line. No use denying it!

He might be able to sleep with Christine and get lucky enough to find that there really were no strings attached. But kissing Danny was an entirely different state of affairs. Just plopping a steak on her plate could have some very severe consequences.

Was he ready for any of that?

Hardly!

He couldn't roll around with her on her sofa half naked and pretend that this was the normal, harmless way to spend an evening.

Even though, quite amazingly, it had been *she* who had started the sofa thing, there was no denying that he had been pushing it all evening and he had contributed a big part to it getting this far. He had called her about going out for dinner, he had told her he wasn't up to going home... He had been pushing it full force. And then he had the nerve to complain about her experiments!

# Garbage bags

Joe would have loved to ignore the wake-up signal from his watch. His first impulse was to turn it off and just go back to sleep. But then Sarah and the fact that he was supposed to have breakfast with her this morning, snuck into his dreamy mind and made a peaceful continuation of his sleep impossible.

With an unwilling groan, he rubbed his eyes and then lay there for another minute, his arm over his face. Crap, he was absolutely not in the mood to face Sarah and the unavoidable questions she was going to ask. But there was no getting out of it this time.

Slowly he sat up and ran his fingers through his hair, drawing in a deep breath and slowly letting the air escape through his nose. The whole experimenting last night on the sofa seemed like a crazy dream this morning. He wasn't even quite sure how he felt about it. Part of him wanted to quickly forget about it, the other part – by far the stronger one – cursed him for having pulled the brake on the experiment when he had. If he hadn't done that – who knew? – he might have woken up with her beside him. The idea made his stomach churn. Could have, should have, might have.

He got up, grabbed his clothes and went into the bathroom. He had a quick shower, brushed his teeth and got dressed. And just before he left the bathroom, he took another sniff from that one perfume flask – with a similarly unbalancing effect as the previous night.

He stepped out of the bathroom hoping to find Danny up and about in the living room or the kitchen. But she wasn't. He hated to admit it but he actually dreaded going into her bedroom and waking her up. He had this very bad feeling that, however close they had gotten last night, he might not find a trace of it when she opened her eyes this morning. And he simply didn't want to see that. Instead he imagined that, if she woke up by herself and emerged out of that room after having had a few minutes alone to come to terms with the sofa experiments, they might be fine.

To gain some more time, he went over to the sofa and folded the sheets and the blanket, put everything in a pile with the pillows on top and replaced the back cushions on the sofa.

Still, there was no trace of Danny and no noise from the bedroom either. He checked his watch. It was getting too late to wait it out.

Exhaling tensely, he went over to the bedroom door and knocked. Without really waiting for an answer, he opened it.

To his surprise the shades were already open halfway.

"Hi," D was sitting in bed, her back against the headboard and her comforter over her lap. Scratching her head, she shot him a wary smile. "Are you feeling as well-rested as I am?"

Joe laughed. "Yeah, you can rely on that," he said and stepped around the bed to her side, feeling immensely relieved. Judging from what she had just said, she wasn't trying to deny that a good part of last night had been spent with other activities besides getting rest and sleep.

"You'll have to go pretty soon, huh?" she said with a quick glance at the alarm clock on the bedside table.

"Still got ten minutes," he said with an undecided look down at her. She moved over a little. He took that as an invitation to sit down on the bed.

"I hate to tell you this," he said with a wink, "but I'm almost glad I'll be spending the next two nights in a room with Jack. Maybe I'll get some sleep then..." He draped his right arm over where her legs were stretched out under the comforter.

D managed a half-hearted chuckle. "Poor you," she teased and secretly wished that she was equally looking forward to sharing her room with Sarah. At this point she was almost dreading it because, after all that had happened, she hadn't the faintest idea how she was going to be able to behave normally around Sarah.

Joe registered how she had absent-mindedly dropped her gaze to her lap. The sun was illuminating the side of her face and her hair.

He imagined kissing her. He really wanted to. Kiss her and pull her down on that bed and continue where they had left off last night. He knew it was idiotic, though. He had to go soon and there wasn't enough space on this bed anyway.

He glanced at the piles of stuff that were sitting next to her.

"What's up with all that stuff?" he asked pointing to the collection of pants and shirts and whatever else (that mustard colored thing couldn't be clothing!?!).

She shrugged. "Mostly stuff I need to take to the clothes container sometime," she said. "Except for the small pile on the floor. Those are curtains for Sarah."

As he glanced over to the pile for Sarah, Joe felt this little stab in the pit of his stomach. He knew that fabric. Those were the curtains from the dorm. He couldn't even say how many times he'd opened and closed those...

"And the small collection there on the pillow," D continued her detailed explanation of each individual pile. "There are a few things I'm still not sure about. Maybe I'll keep them, maybe not."

"Okay." Joe got up from the bed. "I can take the stuff to the container if you want. There's one right where I get off the highway." He shot her a cautious look.

She hesitated.

"We'd just need some big garbage bags to pack this up," he told her.

D squinted at him a bit warily, but then she pulled back the comforter and got up.

"Sure... I just haven't gotten around to it yet." She stepped around him and left the bedroom towards the kitchen. After a few seconds she returned with a roll of big black garbage bags. She tore one off and handed it to him. "Here, be my guest." She tore another one off for herself. Then, pretending to consider pulling off another bag, she shot him a quick look.

"Do you want to maybe bring Sarah her stuff too, while you're at it?" There was an angel's smile on her face.

Joe cocked his head at her. "Sure, I can do that," he said coolly. "I might have to explain to her how these things got from your bedside into my trunk, of course, but sure, I don't have a problem with that if you don't. Just give me another bag..."

She stared back at him, obviously unsure if he was just bluffing or there was a possibility he would seriously do it. Finally, having come to the conclusion that he was bluffing, she laughed. "Okay. You win!" she told him and placed the remaining roll of bags on the bed.

"Oh, okay." Joe grinned. "You *sure* about that? I mean, it would give Sarah and me something to talk about at least." That was plain sarcasm.

"I think you've already got more than enough to discuss as it is," D said with an encouraging smile.

Rolling his eyes a bit, he nodded and started putting stuff from the piles in front of him into his bag.

"I know it's a mess," she said apologetically and grabbed a few shirts from the other pile. "You probably think I've turned into one of these messy people…"

"No, that's not it," Joe responded a little evasively, his gaze on the bag.

Something in the way he had said it, made her look up at him.

"What is it then?" she asked and stopped her bagging-activities.

"Nothing," he shrugged and dropped a pair of pants into his bag.

"Is this about *clearing* the bed?" she pushed.

He didn't respond. Just kept picking up things from the bed and dropping them into his bag. He could feel her staring at him from the side, but he ignored it. Because he couldn't think of anything to say that would qualify as a smart move in this situation. She had guessed right: of course this was about clearing the bed.

"I'm not going to sleep with you," he suddenly heard her say. And in a way it almost sounded like an apology.

Joe coughed out a baffled humorless laugh. "I'm glad we got that clarified," he said dryly, his eyes trained on her now. "How nice that your experiments last night yielded some usable results!"

He could see her swallow and blink.

"That's not fair," she growled and looked away.

"Well, like *you're* being fair," Joe shot back and reached for the flashy cocktail dress, the disposal of which he absolutely welcomed. (Why had she ever gotten *that* thing???)

"I'm not trying to clear your bed because I expect you to… – whatever!" He threw his left hand up in exasperation. "It's more that… – well, … *if* I come back here and *if* I happen to stay overnight and *if* you – by any chance – feel like sleeping *next* to me, it would be kind of nice if we didn't have to both try and fit on the sofa, okay? And please note: there are three *ifs* in that sentence!"

He grabbed the last two pieces of clothing that were still lying on the bed in front of him and shoved them into his bag. Then he tied it up and leaned it against the bed.

"I'm sorry," D said weakly and continued packing her bag.

"It's fine," he said flatly and picked up a shirt from the top of the small pile she had said she wasn't sure about. He unfolded it, had a quick look at it and then placed it back on the bed. Then he did the same with a red summer skirt, a blue dress and some striped Capri pants.

D was just putting the last piece of her pile into her bag.

"I think you should keep these," Joe held up the blue dress and the red skirt. "I like them."

"Okay." D grabbed the T-shirt and the striped pants he hadn't declared worth keeping and stuffed them into her bag. Then she closed it.

Joe picked up his bag and reached for hers. "I'll just take these outside," he said, "then I'll come back in and get my other stuff."

When he came back into the house D was waiting in the living room, the tiramisu dish that she had just gotten out of the dishwasher, in her hand.

"Right, I better not forget that," Joe said. He picked up his phone and the sweater from the coffee table and took the tiramisu dish from her.

"I must have forgotten my sweater yesterday," he told her, "probably slid off the sofa. Found it last night on the floor."

"Oh really? I didn't even notice it," D said, suddenly remembering how he had taken it off before the dancing. Had that really been only yesterday? Seemed like so long ago already.

"Well," he finally said, giving her an undecided look, "I guess I'll see you at the hotel tonight, huh?"

"Yeah…" she nodded, not quite sure what an appropriate good-bye scene included.

"You're hopefully not riding in Jack's car again," Joe said, interrupting her thoughts.

"No," D she shook her head, trying to focus on the question. "This time I'm driving *my* car, and they are riding with me."

"Good." Joe reached out and, with a gentle rub against her back, leaned in just enough to give her a quick kiss on the cheek.

"Have a safe drive," he said as he let go of her.

"You too!" she nodded, baffled by the totally unsatisfying kiss. But what did she expect after what she had just told him in the bedroom?

"Bye!" he said and headed out to the car.

"Bye…" She lifted her hand in a little wave before she shakily closed the door behind him.

# Breakfast with Sarah

Sarah's alarm had first gone off around 7:30. She had ignored it and stayed in bed for a while. Finally, at a little before eight she stretched, rolled to the edge of the bed and got up.

She had a quick shower, put on some make-up and – wrapped in a towel – she returned to her bedroom where she cracked the shades open to have a look at the weather outside. Her eyes widened as she glanced up and down the street. Joe's car wasn't there – again!?! She almost dropped her towel.

When she had come home the previous night, she had noticed that his car wasn't parked outside yet, but not in her wildest dreams had she expected that he wouldn't return all night – again. Especially since they had agreed to go out for breakfast this morning.

Furiously Sarah glanced around the bedroom, looking for her phone. She was sooo mad!!! She grabbed the phone from the night stand, plopped down on the bed and was about to call him, when she saw his text message.

"What the hell?" she snorted after she had read it. She pressed the button to call him back. When it kicked into voice mail right away, she angrily thrust the phone onto the bed with so much force that it bounced right back and would have landed on the floor had she not flung herself across the bed and caught it in mid-air.

Pacing up and down in her room a few times, she tried to calm down. He was going to be there for breakfast, so there wasn't much she could complain about. At least *he* would see it that way.

It was almost 8:30 now. She better get dressed or *she* would be the one to be late.

~~~

Pulling into the café's parking lot, Joe was relieved to see that Sarah's car wasn't there yet. He was six minutes late after going by the clothes containers to drop off D's stuff.

He parked the car and decided to just go inside instead of waiting for Sarah at the car.

It was a cute little café that must have opened sometime over the last few years. He had never been there before.

The waitress led him to a small booth in the back at a window. He sat down and stared at the two unopened menus on the table. He was really hungry, but he couldn't say that he was looking forward to the next half an hour or however long this was going to take.

When Sarah arrived five minutes later, she was angry. He could see it when she walked up to the table. And he wasn't surprised. She threw her purse onto the bench across from him and gave him a furious look as she sat down.

"You must be completely–" she fumed.

"Well, good morning!" he interrupted her, keeping his voice down.

She stared at him and was just opening her mouth to say something else – judging from the look on her face it wasn't going to be anything very friendly – but she stopped herself when she saw him raise his hand and give her a warning look. "Calm down Sarah, okay?" he said, "I know you're mad, but I really don't want to get into the *'where have you been?', 'How dare you?'* discussion right now, alright? And maybe we should have something to eat before we talk at all."

Sarah grabbed the menu, flipped it open and stared at it, trying to swallow her anger. It was stupid, of course. What did *she* care how her brother spent his nights?

"Can I get you anything yet?" An eager young waiter had stepped up to their table and looked at them expectantly.

Sarah ordered coffee, orange juice and pancakes.

Joe ordered coffee and an English breakfast.

From his choice Sarah concluded that, wherever he had been, he had obviously not been fed breakfast this time. She kept herself from commenting on that.

Once the waiter was out of sight, they looked at each other again; Joe wondering why she was so upset, and Sarah realizing that his mood didn't appear to be as splendid as it had been the previous morning. But just like yesterday he didn't seem to have slept much – and he needed to shave. Unless this was going to be his new look. Didn't look too bad…

"I'm sorry, okay?" he said with a hint of a smile. "It's *not* what it looks like!" He let out a surprised little laugh. "Oh man, I never thought I'd ever be saying *this* kind of thing to my own sister!"

Sarah shrugged, giving him a dark look. "Well, you don't have to tell your sister anything at all," she grumbled. "It's your life. *Totally* your business. Just do what you like! But that's what you're doing anyway, right?"

Giving her a slightly frustrated look, he exhaled. "Sarah, come on..."

She raised her hands, showing her palms. "You don't have to *tell* me anything, you don't have to *justify* yourself... I don't give a shit!"

Joe leaned back into the cushion of his seat and rubbed his chin. "There are some things I would actually like to tell you, though," he said in a conciliatory tone, "and that's what we're here for as far as I know. But then there also are some other things that really *are* my business. And that's the stuff we *won't* be talking about."

Sarah shrugged. "Sure... just feel free to pick and choose what's right for my ears and what's not," she told him angrily.

"Thank you, I will!" Joe retorted dryly.

A waitress brought the coffee and the juice. And while Sarah shot her an irritated look, annoyed by the constant interruptions, she found Joe thanking the girl with one of his best smiles. Sarah had to keep herself from kicking him under the table. Was he trying to pick up the waitress next?

Oblivious to the fact that he had just committed another major crime, Joe took a sip of his coffee and then glanced over at his sister.

"Okay," he said, "what I actually *did* want to tell you, is that I broke up with Liz."

Sarah almost spilled her orange juice. What was that? Had he really just said it?

"Broke up as in *take a break* or break up as in *that's it* ?" she inquired, just making sure she wasn't getting ahead of herself with joy here.

"Not just *taking a break* as far as I'm concerned," Joe answered.

"Wow!" Sarah looked baffled. "Guess that explains it."

"What?" He couldn't quite follow.

"Oh, nothing. Just the part that we *won't* be talking about," Sarah said with an acidic smile, "the part where you're out and about all night..."

He shook his head, his expression darkening. "Sarah, if you don't drop that attitude, I swear I'm out of here."

Sarah swallowed. "Yeah, okay. I get it... Sorry... Sometimes I just can't help it."

"Obviously!"

"Why did you–" she interrupted herself, obviously having changed her mind about what to say. "Did you just leave, as in *walk out on her*?"

"Pretty much."

"Wow. Why now?"

Before Joe could say anything, the waitress brought the food. And even though Sarah wasn't pleased with yet another interruption at a crucial moment, she realized how hungry she was. And the food looked really good. Joe was right, food might help to improve the mood considerably.

"You can have a pancake," she offered.

"Thanks, but I think I've got enough here," he said. "Do you want some of mine, though?"

"No, thanks, I'm fine," Sarah said and poured some maple syrup over her pancakes.

For a while they ate in silence. Then Joe picked up the conversation again. "Okay," he said, "you wanted to know why *now?*"

Her mouth full, Sarah nodded.

Joe thought about it for a moment.

"Well,... and I'm sure you'll be delighted to hear this: I guess we'd finally reached the point where it couldn't have gone on any longer – or at least I had reached that point." He arranged a piece of sausage and beans on his fork. "It's been pretty unbearable for a long time, actually. But instead of calling it quits, I just went on every possible business trip to get away and have my peace." He paused for a moment and took a bite. "That only made it worse once I got back, of course."

"I see," Sarah said, eyeing him cautiously. "I can't say I find it very delightful, though. More disturbing."

Joe glanced up from his plate for a moment – mainly to see if she was mocking him. But when that didn't seem to be the case, he ate some more of his breakfast and then continued. "Anyway", he told her, "lately... well, I guess some things happened that made it hard to ignore that it just *couldn't* go on. And then you sent me the invitation for this weekend, of course. So, at some point, when it was just really bad again, I kind of decided that it's now or never."

Sarah gave him a long look, not quite sure what to say. Especially what to say that wouldn't include any form of *'I could have told you so'.*

"She changed," Joe said as if he was reading her mind. "After about half a year of living together she changed pretty drastically..."

Sarah frowned. "And there's no way she might have always been that way and you were just too blind to see it?"

Joe's expression turned defiant. "I don't think so, but well, if you say so, who knows, maybe I'm that big of an idiot that I really just didn't see it."

"God, don't be so touchy!" Sarah muttered. "It's just...– if she already turned into an evil witch after the fifteenth kiss you gave her, why did you wait until now to run? I don't get that. She didn't have you locked up in a tower!"

"No, she didn't," he admitted, "but as I said, I was gone a lot. And maybe I didn't want to deal with all the crap of a split-up. And for a long time I just didn't want to accept that I totally fucked up getting involved with her in the first place..."

Sarah raised her eyebrows. "Well, that's a surprise hearing it from you..."

Joe rolled his eyes. "Well, you hear it now. Hope you're content!"

Slowly Sarah shook her head. "Not really, no," she said quietly. "I love to be right, of course. But in this case... – you're my brother and I would rather see you happy! Sure, I never liked her. But I thought – or hoped, for that matter – that there was something nice and good in her that I just didn't see. I was hoping that for *your* sake."

"Well, thanks," Joe said with a hint of sarcasm. "But no, there's not a whole lot of nice and good... at least not anymore."

Sarah stuffed some pancake into her mouth and chewed on it, scrambling for an appropriate reaction. She wanted to ask what had really happened, but his being so vague was a clear indicator that he probably didn't want to talk about it in much detail. "So, that's why you said you'd stay for a while?" she said, giving him a wary smile, "...because you left her?"

"Yeah, basically," he confirmed. "It's probably stupid to run and stay with you, but I kind of need some time away from her and the job to sort things out. And it just sounded really good to see you and the others."

Sarah put down her fork, but then resisted the urge to reach out and touch his hand. She picked her fork back up.

"I'm glad you came!" she told him with a little smile. "Even if it's three years too late. Just *please* don't go back to her! *Please, please, please!*"

Joe couldn't help laughing. "Don't worry I'm not planning to!"

"And you can stay as long as you want. Really. It's your house too... And while you're around I might just exploit you for yard work and cleaning out the attic and setting up my computer properly and fixing some things on the car and the house…"

"Oh my," Joe chuckled, "that sounds like a life-long engagement."

"Exactly!" Sarah laughed. "Maybe in two weeks you'll be longing for your old life with Liz…"

"I kind of doubt that," he said with a crooked smile.

A few minutes passed with both of them just eating their breakfast and following their own trains of thoughts.

When Joe put down his silverware on his empty plate, Sarah looked up at him again.

"You know, to me it's still hard to understand how you ended up with her in the first place," she said. "She so didn't seem like your type. More like the type that you'd always joked about."

Picking up his coffee cup, Joe shrugged and took a sip.

"And it wasn't as if you just had this little quick thing with her," Sarah pressed on. "I mean, you literally dropped everything and everyone here and ran off to be with her. And not until three years later you–"

"I already told you that I was gone a lot and it wasn't exactly the happiest three years, okay," Joe said a little impatiently, his gaze drifting off towards the window to his left.

Sarah kept her eyes on him. "Were you in love with her?" she wanted to know. "I mean, *seriously?*"

Staring at something outside the window, Joe chewed on his lower lip for a moment.

"Well, you probably wouldn't have left from here otherwise, right?" Sarah tried to answer the question herself because he didn't seem to be willing to.

Across from her, Joe glanced her way again and shrugged. "In retrospect, I would say that there were some other decisive factors as well," he told her.

Sarah raised her eyebrows. "You mean apart from your burning love for Liz?"

Ignoring the sarcasm, Joe gave an affirmative little shrug-nod. "Yep."

"Such as?" Sarah demanded.

"Such as… timing…" he suggested, "– and our father."

"Dad?" Sarah was confused. "Because you didn't want to be around him?" She frowned. "That's kind of a sick reason to hook up with Liz, though."

Joe huffed out an irritated breath. "I didn't say he was the reason I hooked up with her. But he wasn't exactly an incentive to stick around here. Getting away from him was definitely a bonus in the whole thing."

"Great!" Sarah said darkly.

"Well, yeah, I didn't say it all makes a lot of sense," Joe mumbled stubbornly.

"Good, because that doesn't make any sense at all," Sarah shot back. "If you had just needed to get away from Dad, you could have just gone to London with D. As far as I know that had been the plan, right? And you totally wrecked that!"

His face hard now, Joe turned to look out the window again, obviously unwilling to comment.

"I mean, one day you were planning a student exchange year in London with D and were hardly ever home for that matter because you were sleeping more in D's dorm than in your own bed, and the next day it's all over and you're off with Liz…"

Across the table she could see him draw in a long breath. Finally he turned to look at her.

"I don't think it all happened quite that quickly and in exactly that order, or did it?" he challenged. "Anyway, the London thing had something to do with it too, I'm afraid."

"What? How could that have had anything to do with it?"

"Well, it's hard to explain," Joe said looking uncomfortable.

"Try it anyway!" Sarah said through clenched teeth.

"Well… Danny really wanted to do that London thing," he started a bit evasively, his eyes shifting towards the window again.

Raising her eyebrows, Sarah watched him. It was a bit of a surprise to hear him call D that. Funny how he still did that.

"She was pushing for it. And I kind of went along with it, but…" He paused and took a quick sip of his coffee. "Anyway… I mean, it would have been a good way to get away from Dad, of course, but I really didn't want to go and live in London for a year. Looking back it seems pretty stupid, I know, but at the time… it just scared me, I guess. The whole London thing… – and the implications – I mean, living there together and stuff like that…"

Sarah frowned. This was getting confusing now.

"What implications???" she asked sharply even though it was already starting to dawn on her. "Did you think you'd have to marry D afterwards or what?" Sarah shook her head, still looking totally bewildered.

Instead of answering, Joe bit down on his lower lip and drew in some air through his nose. Sarah took this as a confirmation.

"You're such an i–" she caught herself before she said it. "And since when did you not want to go to London?"

He shrugged "Right from the start."

"Why the hell did you fill out all the forms then and… pretend and make plans…?" She was getting louder now.

Joe shrugged again and made sure he didn't look at her.

"*JOSEPH!!!???*" Sarah barked.

With a defiant look, he turned back to her. "I guess I hoped it wouldn't be approved or something else would happen," he said. "Man, Sarah, don't look at me that way!"

Sarah shook her head in disbelief. "I thought that year in London was as much your idea as hers," she snapped. "So, help me out here, Joe, did Danny–" She dragged out the name and watched him while she did. "Did D even *know* you didn't want to go? Or did you just play along, hoping something would happen…"

"I guess…" he admitted, uncomfortably staring at the salt shaker now.

"Ah, I see!" Sarah exclaimed. "And when it didn't happen by itself, you *made* it happen…"

She saw him close his eyes for a moment and take a deep breath. Good, at least he was suffering!

"That's not true," he finally said quietly.

Sarah grabbed the salt shaker he was still looking at and squeezed it hard. She would have liked to bang it on his head, but instead she set it back down on the table with a lot of force.

The young waiter had reappeared at a distance, probably intending to come by and ask them what else he could do for them, but he changed his mind when he witnessed how the salt shaker was banged on the table.

Sarah turned and stared out the window herself now. Three years later she was finally getting to the core of the drama! She felt like yelling at him, but given the location she hissed instead, "You hooked up with Liz because you weren't able to tell D that you didn't want to go to London, and because you wanted to hurt Dad? And maybe even because you seriously thought D was just waiting to marry you? Is that it?"

"Could be, I don't know," he muttered. "I know that sounds stupid today. But yeah, in a nutshell that's probably what it was. Of course, it's a lot more complicated, though... And, like I said, a big part of it was timing."

Sarah's eyes narrowed. She didn't have any doubt that Liz had timed it to perfection.

"This is sick, you know!" she leaned across the table, forcing him to look at her. "I can just see it now. You go over to Liz's place because she *really, really* needs you to help her with whatever it was you helped her with. And you didn't just go over there once. And while you're there you two get into talking about the more personal stuff, and she's the *only* one in the *whole* wide world who understands that you'd rather *not* go to London. And with *her* you can discuss all the other things that are wrong in your life, including your relationship." She paused only to catch her breath. "This is such bullshit, Joe!" Angrily she shook her head. "And of course you two get a little closer! How sweet! And then we make sure, D stumbles across how close this has really gotten and – voila! – you're free as a bird and don't have to go to London. And then you stupid idiot decide to run away with Liz to cast the mess in concrete. Just idiotic! But no, sorry, you said you actually were in love with her, didn't you?"

Joe drew in an irritated breath. "I don't think I *did* say that, no; but yeah, I guess I wouldn't have left with her if I hadn't at least *thought* I was in love with her. I'm not *that* stupid."

Sarah nodded, biting her tongue so she wouldn't say anything that would really piss him off.

"Let's blame it on the timing then!" she exclaimed with sarcastic generosity. "The timing and Dad and D for being oh-so-pushy and – oh, I almost forgot – probably some incredible sex on the side. Right? I mean, you didn't explicitly mention it, but judging from the woman involved, I assume sex played a role as well, didn't it? I *do* have enough imagination to picture what Liz can do for you in *that* department! And that's when you guys just absolutely lose it!"

The frozen look Joe gave her now, made her realize that she was about to go too far. She better drop that subject because it was clearly overstepping the line. And if she was honest, she was highly uncomfortable with the topic herself. Maybe even more than he was. It made her feel sick to her stomach to just think it through. Yeah, she better not make him really angry by pushing the sex-theory because he might retaliate by throwing some graphic, hard-to-digest details at her. So, yes, she better let this go.

But that didn't mean she was done with him!

"Man, you must have been so screwed-up," she insisted. "Now I finally know why you didn't lose any time before you cancelled the London thing." She shook her head. Even now thinking back to those days made her cringe.

"Liz must have had you spun around her finger so well! Grrr! And at the same time I – stupid me – I was trying to talk some sense into D. Ha! I was so convinced that it could only be a horrible misunderstanding. *You and Liz? No way!?* No, my brother couldn't be *that* dumb! Little did I know, huh?"

One look at Joe showed her that she was again (or still?) operating very close to the limit. His face was hard and it seemed to contain a clear warning: he wasn't going to listen to this all morning. But certain things needed to be said while there was a chance.

"I will never forget," Sarah said, trying hard to contain her irritation, "when Jack called me that night... – I was staying with grandma because she was sick and Mom and Dad were on a trip or something, remember? I should have let you play Granny's nurse that evening. Then you couldn't have screwed up like that!"

"Jack called you?" Joe suddenly seemed confused.

Sarah nodded with an angry look at him. "Yeah, Jack called me," she said flatly. "And he told me what had happened. And at first–" She let out a shrill little laugh. "At first I didn't get it! Stupid, huh? Jack had tried to reach D, but she just wouldn't pick up. And he was worried. So he called me, and I called her, and I couldn't reach her either. Well, sometime during the night she called me back, though." Sarah kept an eye on Joe just to make sure she wasn't going too far. He had a defensive look on his face now, but it seemed as if he had decided that he would just sit through her listing his sins and get it over with.

"For D it was already over at that point," Sarah told him, "I know that. She was ready to drop you right there. And she *should* have! But I told her, '*No, you can't do that. You need to at least talk to him!*' Stupid, stupid me! I think D had the much better judgment there."

The defiance was fading from Joe's expression, giving way to something between fatigue and frustration.

"I talked her into giving you a chance to explain…" Sarah let out a bitter little laugh. "I could still kick myself for that. I wish she hadn't listened to me. But she did. And she calls you the next morning and then Liz picks up your phone and tells her 'Oh, he's in the shower.' "

Suddenly Joe's face seemed to freeze. His eyes went from wide to squinting. He straightened up and leaned forward a little.

"*What???*" He looked totally perplexed. "When was that?"

"Well, the morning after that freaking party," Sarah said, a little confused by his reaction.

Joe blinked, blank-faced and rubbed his chin. "She called on my *mobile?* And I was in the shower? I mean, *Liz's* shower???"

Sarah shrugged. "Where else?"

Joe still looked baffled. "I was at home that morning," he finally said, his eyes locked with hers. "I *definitely* was at home. By myself. And I tried to call Danny from Mom and Dad's landline because I couldn't find my phone."

Suddenly he turned pale and looked like he had just had a very scary vision. "Crap…" he breathed.

His gaze dropping to his plate, he swallowed. For a moment he just sat there, obviously trying to catch up with whatever was going through his mind. Then, with a defiant look, he glanced back up at Sarah. "For your information," he slowly said, "I did *not* go home with Liz after that party. I may have done some really stupid things that night, but *that* would have been just sick! I actually went to the dorm, but she didn't answer the door or she wasn't even there, I don't know. And I didn't cancel London until weeks later when… – well, Danny wasn't talking to me anyway." He fell silent and let his head fall back, briefly closing his eyes.

"Great, thanks to your cancelling, Pete got to go instead," Sarah stated.

Ignoring her comment and somehow lost in his own thoughts, Joe shook his head. "Shit… – I really didn't know about the shower thing," he said. "Liz must have had my phone."

Sarah bit her lip, feeling stunned. This had just totally caught her by surprise. She had been so sure that he had… With an increasingly hollow feeling in her stomach (despite all the pancakes), she watched him stare out the window.

"The shower thing is not even the main point, Joe," Sarah said trying for a softer tone. "You screwed up *way* before that."

He kept staring out the window, huffing out some air through his nose. "I know that," he said dryly and shook his head. "Shit, I just can't believe she did that." His tone indicated, however, that he didn't find it unbelievable at all.

"Well, if you were really not there – in her shower, I mean – then it means a) she had your phone, and  b) she picked it up when D called, and c) she lied to D, and therefore d) she's even worse than I thought! And I really didn't have a high opinion of her to begin with."

"Yeah great," Joe growled, shooting her an irritated look. "We already know that last part, thank you! And, you'll be happy to know – you were *so* right!"

"I wish I wasn't," Sarah said quietly. "And I mean it…"

"Yeah, I know," he muttered with an exasperated shake of his head, his mind obviously whirling with all kinds of things now.

"Joe, really…" Sarah reached out and touched his arm, giving it a gentle rub. "Brooding over the shower thing now is like… – I don't know…" She was scrambling for a comparison that would make him feel at least a little better (and herself as well). "It's like worrying that you accidently stepped on the broken pieces of a vase that you had personally flung against the wall full force ten seconds earlier. The shower thing was bad, yeah, but in the overall-context, I don't think it made that much of a difference. Just made me and D look like idiots."

His eyes on his coffee cup, he nodded, but he didn't look convinced at all.

"Come on now," Sarah said, struggling for an encouraging tone. "Stop thinking about it, okay? I'm sorry I even brought it up. I didn't know that you didn't know… Just take it as a sign that you definitely did the right thing. Three years too late, but right nevertheless"

Joe rubbed his left temple, still looking withdrawn. "I didn't exactly need *this*, to know that I did the right thing," he mumbled, "but well…"

Finally his eyes trailed up at her again and he straightening up in his seat. He blew out some air with his lower lip sticking out and slightly shook his head as if to shake something off.

The next time the waiter peeked around the corner, Joe waved for him and paid for their breakfasts.

# Parking Lot Reflections

Out in the café's parking lot, Joe told Sarah that he needed to go by an electronics store on the way home to buy a charger for his phone.

That was only half the truth, of course. Even though he hadn't brought his charger, he still had the one for the car. And with his phone currently being turned off most of the time anyway, there wasn't exactly an urgent need to charge it.

His main reason for this little detour was that he needed some time to think. Alone. Because the shower story that Sarah had just sprung on him at the café had pushed him considerably off balance.

Driving down the highway now, he tried to remember the details about his lost phone three years ago. He had never given it much attention – so far. It had been gone and then it had reappeared three days later. No big deal.

Now that he really thought about it, though, he remembered that the phone hadn't just suddenly turned up in his room or a jacket pocket or some place you would expect it to. It had actually been Liz, who had pulled it out from under the seat of his car. With some comment like, "Hey, there's a phone. Is that yours?"

He remembered it clearly now. He had just assumed that the phone must have been lying under that seat for the three days it had been missing. Even at the time he had been a little surprised though, because he could have sworn that he had searched the car relatively thoroughly. But with all hell having broken lose after the party, he hadn't been entirely sure, and there had been no reason to be suspicious.

Finding out now that Liz had had that phone (and what she had obviously done with it), was something that would take a while to digest. In fact, each time he thought about it, it sent a hot wave of fury through his head.

His left hand cramped around the steering wheel, Joe tried to calm down and repeat to himself what Sarah had told him: that in the overall-context his having gone home or not having gone home with Liz after that party really didn't make much of a difference. He just wished he could believe that!

At the parking lot outside the electronics store, he pulled into the next-best spot, turned off the engine and just sat in the car for a while, staring into space.

If someone had told him three years ago about the shower thing, he would have undoubtedly called them an evil liar. Now, after his eye-opening time with Liz, he had no difficulty at all believing it. It was just so *like* her. He had just been too naive and too blind to see it then. Sarah was quite right about that.

He pressed the fingertips of his left hand against the bridge of his nose as if that would help stop his mind from spinning dizzyingly around the issue of Liz having the phone.

The shower thing was bad enough but it inevitably lead to a whole different issue: The question of *when* Liz had actually gotten hold of his phone. How long had she had it?

He had always wondered why Danny had just showed up at that party without any previous notice like a text message or a call. She had been supposed to be out of town for some three-day seminar. They had had a fight before she had left.

Now, with the shower information, he was seriously wondering if maybe Liz had already had the phone earlier. The day *of* the party. He did vaguely remember wanting to use his phone that day, but not finding it right away and not pursuing it any further. He had completely forgotten about that.

Things had been very hectic that day leading up to the party, and he had been tired and confused. So, yes, there was a possibility that Liz had had his phone the whole day of the party without his even knowing that it was missing.

If that were the case and Danny had called or left a message about coming back earlier or even about going to the party, then Liz would have known about it while he didn't know a thing. And Danny would have been pissed because he hadn't picked up his phone or called her back. Or- who knew? – maybe Liz had actually even sent a message back in his name, suggesting that they meet in the basement. Anything seemed possible…

He had himself to blame for what had happened, though. First of all, if Liz had the phone, it was his own damn fault! He had spent the night with Liz. First time. And he had been late for class, and in the hurry he had probably left his phone at her place.

He had been at Liz's flat several times during the month leading up to the party. Only the first three times had really been purely to help her with her computer troubles.

She had kissed him when he had been about to leave after the third visit. He had been shocked at first, but already on his way home he had come to the conclusion that this was actually a cool twist.

The next time he had gone over there, he had officially wanted to finish something. That's when Liz had told him that she was in love with him. She had made it very clear that she didn't care that he had a girlfriend whom she even knew personally.

He had been confused but also flattered, and – unfortunately – very tempted to just stay there. He had liked her and she (Sarah was right about that) had somehow made him feel like she understood him. Not regarding his Dad – because that was something he had only ever discussed with Danny, not with Liz. He had talked to Liz about London, though. He had dropped a frustrated comment about it sometime, and Liz had immediately picked up on it. And she had pushed the topic further and further and made him feel like she could totally see his point. She had understood how he felt about the London thing, and she had seen how he might feel trapped with Danny. From today's point of view he was seriously wondering, though, if maybe he had only started to feel trapped after Liz had suggested that he was. And she had suggested it. He clearly remembered that. More than once.

All this was no excuse for anything, of course! He had been a complete idiot. Part of it (Sarah had guessed correctly) was that Liz had had something that – at the time – had really turned him on. And she had done her very best to play that card.

That evening, when she had talked about being in love with him, he had still had the brains to leave before things could go too far. Not that they hadn't already gone much further than was advisable, especially with that steamy kiss in the hallway. He remembered Liz holding on to his arm after that kiss, a pouting look on her face, asking what was holding him back, when in reality he wanted to get out of that relationship and the London thing anyway. She had tried to convince him that he had no obligations whatsoever towards Danny and that there would be absolutely nothing wrong with his staying. Still, he had somehow managed to leave.

After that, he had kept out of Liz's way for a while. He hadn't felt really comfortable with the effect she seemed to have on him, particularly on his good judgment.

Then there had been a few fights with his Dad, and at the same time things weren't going well with Danny either. She was bugging him about some stuff he still needed to do for the London application. He had been dragging his feet for weeks on that. She had insisted that if he had some kind of a problem, he tell her. They had been at her dorm and she had been angry. And he had denied that there was any problem. Ha! He had told her that everything was just fine and that she was seeing ghosts. She hadn't bought it, though. And she had said that he should probably go home and sleep there that night because they might both need some room to think. The next day she had left for her three-day seminar.

That had been two days before the party. He had had some classes the next day, early in the morning, and he had run into Liz on his way to the university.

Today he wondered if this encounter had been a pure coincidence or if Liz had maybe been waiting for him behind some shrubbery and just jumped out in the right moment. He couldn't rule it out. At this point there was absolutely nothing he would rule out.

Anyway, there she had been, purring like a cat, batting her eyes and persuaded him to meet her later for dinner.

Over the course of that dinner he had had way more to drink than he should have. Right in the middle of the dinner he had received a message from Danny saying that he needed to contact the office that organized the London thing. She had written that, according to an e-mail she had received, there was some serious problem with something in his application and if he didn't straighten things out the next morning, they might not be able to stay in the same dorm or his whole exchange year might fall through altogether.

He remembered hearing the text message come in just as the dinner had been served. He had fished out his phone and Liz had leaned over and read the message with him. She had put her chin on his shoulder and run her fingers along his collar at the back of his neck, whispering something like, *Oh my, she's sooo pushy!* He had turned to her, not quite comfortable with that statement and the situation as such and already a bit under the influence of too much wine, and Liz had given him this seductive smile and kissed him on the mouth right there in front of the waiter who had been deboning her fish for her.

He had been mad at Danny for pushing the London thing (or he had simply been scared), he had been drunk, and Liz had been there, playing the understanding friend who was just dying to be more than just a friend… She had been coming on to him strong that evening. The kiss before the main course having been a relatively harmless introduction of what still was in store.

Thinking about it now, literally made him cringe. Man, he had been *so* stupid! It would have taken an absolutely clear head and a lot of strength and determination to keep this evening from ending in Liz's bed. He had had neither. That couldn't be an excuse, of course, but it was an explanation.

He had gone home with Liz.

The bits and pieces he remembered about that night, made him grind his teeth now. It had been an absolutely wild night. He had woken up a little shaken, hung-over and too late for a class he couldn't miss.

On his way out, Liz had been hanging around his neck, giving him one of the most demanding kisses he had ever gotten to that point.

He remembered sitting in his class half an hour later, not sure what had hit him and wondering if he even ever wanted to get close to Liz again. But while part of him had been freaked out, another (bigger) part of him had felt thrilled, fascinated and elated.

He should have felt guilty. Or he should have at least been thinking about a fair breakup with Danny. But everything seemed blocked by his paralyzed brain. And he had just let the crazy wave carry him…

Somewhere in the back of his head he had, of course, known that he was heading for a big crash. But maybe that's what he had wanted. Who knew? Maybe that had, even if just subconsciously, been the driving force behind it all. He really couldn't say anymore.

In a way he had maybe let the Liz thing get so far out of hand that Danny would have to find out eventually and (as Sarah suspected) he'd be free. Not that he had planned it or consciously wanted it, but he had let it happen.

That night he had gone to Jack's party. By himself.

He had actually not even been in a party mood. He had mainly gone because it had been Jack's birthday, and with both Sarah and Danny not being able to come, he had felt that at least he should be there. Looking back on it now, he should have told Sarah to attend instead of him, and he should have stayed with Grandma. Could have, should have, would have...

About half an hour into the party, Jack had asked him to get some drinks from the big fridge in the basement. So he had gone downstairs.

And then, just as he had been about to leave the room with the fridge and the big freezer, there had been Liz.

She was standing in the doorway in that red dress.

First, he had been baffled. He hadn't expected (or even wanted) her to be there. He had been pretty sure that Jack hadn't invited her, and he himself had (for safety-reasons) avoided telling her about this evening program.

Eye to eye with her now, he had figured that she was downstairs to get drinks as well and that they would just have to try and get through the evening pretending that they hadn't seen each other for weeks.

"I've locked the door upstairs, just in case..." Liz had told him with a smile and in a tone that didn't leave much room for interpretation. That's when he had finally made the connection...

Unfortunately he remembered it much more clearly now than he wanted: the music from upstairs; Liz taking the bottles he was still holding and setting them on the shelf next to herself; Liz slipping the straps of her dress off her shoulders and letting the top fall down to her waist; Liz assuring him in a whispering voice that she had skipped the underwear for this evening, since it had kind of been in the way the previous night...

He recalled that he hadn't been all that thrilled with the whole thing. Especially the location had seemed *very* wrong. Having sex in adventurous places might be a nice thing for books and movies, but messing around in Jack's parents' basement – especially with anyone that wasn't his girlfriend...

He had put up some sort of (maybe not very decisive) resistance, basically proposing that they at least wait until they were back at her place. But Liz had had her way of convincing him that here and now was just fine...

A set-up? Maybe. Perfect timing? Definitely! She had slung her arms around his neck and whispered something about how that song, which was audible from upstairs, was *exactly* how she felt about him. It was Bryan Adams' *Run to you*.

Then she had started kissing him while pulling his shirt out of his pants. One of her hands had started unbuttoning his jeans, applying a

296

disarming kind of pressure, making sure he knew exactly where this was going, in case he still had any doubts – which, really, he didn't have.

And he had gone along with it. Not with the greatest enthusiasm maybe, but with way more cooperation than he should have. She had pulled herself up onto the freezer, so she could sit on it and wrap her legs around his waist.

Well and then, halfway through the song, the music had suddenly gotten louder. At first he had been so preoccupied with Liz that he hadn't even noticed it. And when it had finally dawned on him that someone upstairs must have opened the (obviously unlocked) door to the basement, and was coming down the stairs, it had already been too late. He had pulled away from Liz's embrace and turned around towards the stairway. And there had been Danny. Standing there – frozen, startled, staring.

The music had kept on playing. *Run to you* by Brian Adams…

It had been almost surreal. Not at all like in a film, though, where the betrayed girlfriend bursts into tears and runs off, while he hastily pulls his pants up, so he can run after her and assure her that it's not at all what it looks like…

First of all, his pants hadn't been down yet, but it had been close enough. And Danny hadn't run off. And there hadn't been any tears either. She had just stood there – at the top of the stairs – and looked at them, like a scientist studying a virus that she has just discovered and finds extremely horrifying.

Then, even though she must have had a sufficiently good view from where she was standing, she had come down the stairs two more steps as if to have a closer look.

After another moment of glaring at them like this, she had shaken her head in disgust and said something like, 'Wow. So, that's what you want, huh?' And then she had turned around and walked up the stairs in no particular hurry.

He could have caught up with her easily if he hadn't been so dumbstruck.

Upstairs she had taken out the key from the inside of the door, switched off the basement light and slammed the door shut as hard as she could. And then she had locked it from the outside.

He hadn't seen her again or even gotten a chance to talk to her until two and a half years later at his Dad's funeral – where she had showed up hand in hand with Pete.

Liz and he had been freed from the basement a few minutes later by Jack. He had never dared to ask how Jack had ended up with the key, and how he had known or been informed which door to unlock with it. Joe could kind of picture it, but he had never actually had the guts to ask Jack for confirmation.

He just remembered standing there, in the total darkness of the basement, and hearing the door being locked upstairs. He had felt like someone had kicked him in the stomach. In a state of utter shock. Liz's giggling had brought him back to life. Even then he had been unable to figure out what she found so incredibly funny. He had told her to get dressed, for God's sake, and shut up.

He had buttoned up his jeans again and tucked his shirt back in.

He hadn't been able to see if Liz was actually pulling up her dress because it had been pitch dark, but at least – at some point – she had stopped giggling and he had heard her slide off that freezer.

He had just left her standing there and, like in a haze, he had tapped towards the stairway in the dark. He had made it up the stairs about halfway when he had heard the key being turned. For one crazy moment he had actually thought it could be Danny. But then he had found himself eye to eye with Jack.

Jack had switched on the light and, after a confused look at him, had shot a glance down the stairs. Joe still remembered Jack's expression freezing as he had spotted Liz, who unfortunately had still been fumbling with the shoulder straps of her dress – and giggling again.

"Crap, Joe," Jack had scoffed and shaken his head with that look that said it all. "This is *really* bad. I just can't believe this!" And then he had turned around and walked off.

From what Joe knew now, Jack must have tried to call Danny right afterwards. A reasonable reaction after Jack had discovered the disturbing thing she had locked up in the basement. When she hadn't picked up her phone, Jack had ended up calling Sarah.

Joe remembered Jack and himself avoiding each other for weeks after that. The same with Sarah. She had tried to yell at him once or twice right after it had happened, but he had just walked out on her and slammed the door shut behind him. And as a result she had shunned him for a while and he had been perfectly happy about that. (Little did he know that hearing Sarah out might have yielded some very valuable information regarding not only the whereabouts of his lost phone but also the fact that some pretty nasty stuff was being done with the help of that phone.)

He had always thought that D had just stopped talking to him after the party. All attempts he had made to talk to her had failed. He had gone over to the dorm right after the party, but she hadn't opened or just not been there. He had tried to call her the next day and the day after, but she hadn't picked up, or probably just pressed *reject-call* instead.

He had also gone to the dorm again two days later, but again, she had either really not been home or pretended not to be.

Sitting in his car now, Joe huffed out an angry breath. The more he thought everything through, the more he realized that the enlightening breakfast talk with Sarah had opened up an entirely new (but disturbing) perspective on the days after that party. Obviously D *had* tried to call him! And Liz had told her that he was in her shower....

Joe growled to himself and balled his left hand to a fist that he slammed against the side of his seat.

After the party he had had no intention of seeing Liz again anytime soon (if ever). But then she had somehow tracked him down three days after the party, just as he had been getting into his car outside the university. She had jumped into the passenger seat and delivered a heart wrenching performance of how madly in love with him she was, and that she knew how bad it looked, but that she was convinced they were just made for each other and he shouldn't throw it all away...

He had told her he needed time. Because at that point he didn't know *anything* anymore. He had just wanted to hide somewhere and be alone.

He remembered driving Liz home, though – since it had been pouring rain. And when she had gotten out of the car, she had miraculously pulled his phone out from under the seat. Until then he had assumed that he had lost his phone in Jack's basement and he had dreaded contacting Jack about it.

A few days later he had given up trying to get in touch with Danny. He had packed some stuff and taken off to spend some time in his aunt's cabin – an excellent place to hide from the world and everyone. He had stayed there for almost two weeks.

When he had returned to civilization, he had heard that Danny had prematurely moved out of the dorm to stay with her parents until it was time to go to London.

He had made one more attempt to contact her: he had called her brother. Robert had been nice enough, given the circumstances, but Danny had refused to talk to him.

Somewhere around that time he had cancelled the London thing. Even if he had still wanted to go he doubted that they would have still let him. Not with all the things he had failed to fill out and forward to the office, and with the funds that he hadn't transferred for the advance payment on the dorm room.

He had started keeping more to himself. Part of it had been that everything with his friends reminded him way too much of Danny – which had been somewhat painful (even though he wouldn't have admitted it then).

Jack had very slowly gotten back to talking to him again, with both of them carefully avoiding the topic. The other friends had behaved a little cautiously, but otherwise normally. All they seemed to know about the issue was that there had been a break-up, and as his friends they acted accordingly – by tactfully not asking about it.

As for Sarah, she had *not* gone back to normal routine. Far from it! Even after she had finally accepted that he wasn't going to listen to her shouting at him, being around her had been a real pain. She had somehow decided that if she couldn't yell at him, she would at least be his constant silent reminder of what a jerk she thought he was. She kept shooting him those looks or scoffed and growled at everything he did or said. And then there was still Dad, of course, who made life at home additionally unpleasant...

Joe remembered having hooked up with Liz again maybe six weeks after the party. She had tried to contact him several times over the previous weeks, but he had ignored it and she had eventually given up.

She had been surprised when he had called her out of the blue and asked her out. It had been either that or killing his Dad or Sarah (or taking the next plane to London and making a fool of himself)...

Seeing Liz again had felt good and comforting. Maybe because she had been the only person around him that didn't make him feel as if he was an incredible idiot. From today's point of view, he would have to say that she had played her part really well. She had managed to appear to be *exactly* what he thought he needed at that time. And he had bought it – happily. For a while he had really thought he was in love with her. No denying it.

A few weeks later – it must have been the middle of November – Liz had suddenly told him that she was moving back to where she was from, a town about two hours away from Deens. Her brother had just moved into a small house with his girlfriend and Liz was going to take over the rental contract of the flat her brother had just moved out of.

She had been raving about that flat, and she had pointed out that there would easily be enough space for two... So, if he wanted to get away... She had actually really pushed for him to come with her. And he, more or less head over heels, had done just that.

The first few months of living together had actually been great and fun and liberating. (A bit like when he had lived with Peer during his first year of university, just with a little more going on in the bedroom...) But looking back, he realized that even *then*, at the very beginning, there had been some occurrences with Liz that, in hindsight, had been indicators of problems to come. But he had been a bit distracted. Not only with the bedroom activities but also with preparations for his last two exams and increasingly also with the plans of starting a company with Steve. Maybe without all that distraction he would have noticed much earlier that his relationship with Liz was heading for disaster. But he hadn't paid enough attention. Especially once the company idea was taking shape. He had been so into that and it had been so much fun and exciting...

And even later, when it was hard to miss that Liz and he were just one big mess anymore, he had still not wanted to admit it – not even to himself.

Staring at the people walking in and out of the electronics store, Joe drew in a deep breath. What was he doing, brooding over all of this? Stuff that he couldn't change anymore...

Finally, he gave himself a push and got out of the car.

# My Dish, Your Sweater...

When Joe got back to the house, Sarah was sitting at the kitchen table, flipping through some advertisements that had come in the mail.

She looked up as he walked in from the hallway, the bag from the electronics store and his sweater in one hand and a square glass dish in the other hand.

First she squinted, but then her eyes widened. Was that her tiramisu dish? Had he just brought that in from the car? It was empty and it was clean...

Sarah straightened up.

"Where is that coming from???" It sounded dangerous.

Joe stopped in his tracks, suddenly realizing that it had been stupid to bring the dish in now.

"Don't tell me you took that with you last night!?!" Sarah just couldn't believe it.

"Well, you told me I should finish it," Joe said a little stubbornly. "It's gone now."

One look at Sarah told him that this had definitely not been a smart thing to say. But he had simply not been able to help it.

With an icy face Sarah got up, snatched the dish from him, put it into the cabinet under the stove where it belonged and slammed the cabinet door shut.

"Are you crazy or what?" she hissed. Sure, she had told him to eat it. But that was meant to comfort him over an evening at home all by himself. Instead he had taken her dessert along with him as he spent the second night in a row with Sun or who knows who. Just unbelievable! And he obviously didn't even think there was anything wrong with it!

With clenched teeth Sarah leaned against the kitchen counter behind her. She reached for her car keys that were lying on the countertop close-by and started playing with them. Click click click. She didn't let her brother out of her sight.

With some bewilderment, Joe looked back at her, glad that she had chosen to play with her keys instead of one of the knives from the knife block behind her.

For a while they just stared at each other, Sarah giving him a dark disapproving look, Joe countering it with a raised-eyebrow *what-do-you-want-from-me-now?* glare.

He would have loved to just go up to his room right now and evade the predictable thunderstorm. He really wasn't in the mood for any more than he had already had for breakfast. But then again, he didn't want to make her even angrier than she already was. Especially since they still had to survive a two-hour drive to the hotel together. And really, in comparison to Liz's tantrums, Sarah's outbursts, even the really bad ones, were something he should be able to deal with relatively easily.

"I can't believe this!" Sarah hissed, introducing the second round.

With an exasperated sigh, Joe laid the small bag and his sweater on the chair in front of him. He placed his hands on the back of that chair and leaned forward a bit on his outstretched arms. "*What* exactly is your problem, Sarah?" he asked. "Can you even *tell* me what your problem is?" He gave her a challenging look. He knew *exactly* what her problem was, but he was just dying to hear how she would phrase it. He imagined it could get a little tricky for a smart person like her to admit that she was just plain jealous.

Click click click. Sarah was still angrily playing with her keys.

Joe tilted his head at her. "So? Is this really about the tiramisu now?"

Sarah growled. "No, it's not just about that," she snapped. "Well, or yes, in a way..." She was obviously getting a little confused herself. That made her even angrier, of course.

"That tiramisu..." she said through clenched teeth, "I made that for when you came, and it's personal and you just take it to some..."

"Huh?" he raised his eyebrows and tilted his head her way a bit as if to understand her better. "It's personal????" He had to keep himself from laughing out loud. "Sorry Sarah," he said just barely hiding his amusement, "that tiramisu was really good, it really was... but you make it sound like I took your very secret diary with me and recited it to my date during some wild sex scene."

Sarah swallowed. She pointed her finger at him with a warning look. "I do *not* want to hear that," she croaked. "I mean, what you do – the sex part... It's like imagining my Teddy bear in bed with Barbie... Just sick!"

"Yeah, that is *very* sick!" he agreed, really laughing now. When he saw her furious face, he immediately fell silent.

Tense silence.

Then Sarah cleared her throat. "You just told me half an hour ago…" the suppressed anger was clearly audible as she slowly spelled out her words, "…that you left Liz not even a week ago. That's *very* good news as far as I'm concerned. Congratulations! But it *is* kind of surprising to me that instead of taking some time to – how should I say – reflect on your past mistakes and learn from them, it takes you exactly two days and you start some new adventure…"

"A new adventure?" He raised his eyebrows and looked slightly amused. "With your tiramisu?"

Sarah's eyes narrowed. "Well, I assume you didn't sleep in the park the last two nights?" she snapped.

"Which park would you recommend?" He grinned. "No, I didn't sleep in the park and eat your tiramisu all by myself." He couldn't help pushing it a little.

Sarah stopped jingling her keys and clenched her fist around them.

Joe watched her, wondering how long she could keep doing that without hurting her hand.

"I guess I just don't understand you," she growled and relaxed her hand around the keys again.

"Well, I'm sorry!" he scoffed. "I didn't know you had a curfew here and some kind of moral code that I'd have to stick to."

Sarah gasped for air. "Great, now I'm the…" She threw her hands in the air. "No, I don't have a moral code," she snarled, "but some common sense wouldn't hurt!" Her lips tightly pressed together she dismissively shook her head. "But just do what you want!"

Joe rolled his eyes but didn't say anything. This was kind of absurd.

Sarah slammed her keys back onto the counter and brushed the strands of hair away that had fallen into her forehead. She was well aware that her freaking out about the tiramisu dish had been silly. What really bothered her, of course, was that he seemed to fall from the arms of one tramp into the bed of the next one. Why did men have to be such idiots? Couldn't at least her brother be an exception? Well, she should know by now that he wasn't!

But it was just idiotic to let this bother her so much. It wasn't really her business, she knew that. Amazingly enough, *he* hadn't even pointed that out to her yet. It actually seemed like he had a considerable amount of patience. More than she remembered him ever having. In the old days he would have never stuck around for an argument like this. He would have long ago kicked a chair and/or stormed out slamming the door. Not today. He didn't even seem to take it all too seriously. Maybe she should just be happy about that.

"I'm sorry," she finally said with a stubborn look. "I guess I just can't help it."

Joe nodded. "I know…" he said generously, "but you'll have to get a grip on that, okay? Because I'm not going to have this discussion with you now every time I come home later than you think is morally justifiable. It's my life and I make the decisions, even if they are idiotic sometimes." He paused for a moment and gave her a crooked smile. "And if you can't deal with my horrific life-style, you have to tell me. Because then I'll just have to move to the park…"

Sarah swallowed at the same time as she felt a smile sneaking onto her face. "No. Sorry. I do *not* want you to move to the park!" she said. "This is your house too. And I know I shouldn't get so upset about that kind of thing. Part of it is that I'm worried… and a little jealous, I guess."

He shrugged. "I know. And it's fine; I sometimes feel the same way. Like with Andy. But maybe you could keep it under control a little better. I did with Andy…"

"Maybe you shouldn't have," she said, "and maybe I should have bugged you more about Liz…"

"Yeah, maybe." He considered it for a moment. "I don't think that would have helped much, though. For either of us."

Sarah shrugged. "Guess not." She scratched her head, looking at him a little undecidedly. "Can I ask you something, though?"

"Sure…"

"Is it Sun?" She tried to sound like an understanding sister. "I mean, in a way I can see that you might need some… distraction."

"What?" Joe grimaced at her with obvious frustration. "Man, Sarah. Give me a break! Not you as well…" He rubbed his forehead and then suddenly his expression changed from frustrated to mischievous. "Wait," he said in a tone that was just a tad too sweet. "I've had this exact same question before! Where was it?" Pressing his index finger to his lips, he pretended to ponder the question. Then, an enlightened smile spreading across his face, he raised his index finger. "Ah, right," he exclaimed, "it was Jack! Yesterday. Right after he talked to you on the phone…" he made a theatrical pause. "Could there be a connection?"

Sarah looked back at him, her expression a bit embarrassed now. But Joe was on a roll. Like a comforting parent speaking to a scared kid, he folded his hands together and tilted his head a little. "Has Jack not called you back yet and told you what I told him?"

Sarah shook her head, realizing that now she would just have to deal with the consequences of her stupid question.

"Nooo, Sarah," Joe said, his tone still slightly mocking, "it's *not* Sun. Can you please stop investigating now! I really don't want to talk about this anymore! Okay!?!"

With a forced smile, Sarah nodded. "Okay. Yeah, I know… Sorry!"

She pushed herself away from the counter, came over and sat down on the chair across from where he was standing.

Watching her, Joe hoped that she would let it go now. Because there was just absolutely no way he could tell her where he had been the last two nights.

She looked at him, an apologetic smile on her face. "I can't live with not knowing what happened to my tiramisu, though…" she insisted jokingly.

"Poor Sarah," Joe laughed. "I'm afraid you'll just have to live with it, I'm afraid…"

"But if it's not Sun…" she made another half-hearted attempt.

"If it's not Sun then someone else ate your tiramisu," Joe shot back. "Deal with it!" He took his hands off the back of the chair and straightened up. "When do you want to leave?"

Sarah shrugged, obviously okay with the change of topic now. "I just need to pack some stuff," she said. "Won't take me more than half an hour."

Joe looked at his watch. "I still need to check my work e-mails, I need to pack, I should probably shave," he rubbed his scruffy chin. "Is it okay if we leave around three? Takes two hours, right?"

Sarah nodded. "Something like that. A little less, I think. So, yeah, leaving at three should be fine! You're driving?"

Nodding, he picked up the bag and his sweater from the chair in front of him. "Okay, I'll go upstairs then," he said and headed for the kitchen door.

Sarah had just pulled the newspaper closer and was watching him walk away, when something caught her eye. She blinked. Where had she seen that sweater before…?

"That is *your* sweater?" she blurted out after him.

This outburst made Joe stop in his tracks and turn back around to her, a baffled look on his face. What was that? Had she lost it now, just when he had thought she had come to her senses again? Leaning against the frame of the kitchen door he squinted at her.

"*What* is it with my sweater?" He didn't get it.

Sarah still looked at the sweater as if it was a piece of evidence from a murder scene and he was the main suspect. Joe looked back at her like a worried doctor looks at a sick patient.

"Do I need to call a doctor?" he mocked.

With a weird expression she looked up at him again. "I fished that sweater out from under D's sofa yesterday…" she said flatly, obviously not quite believing herself the indications of what she was saying.

Joe suddenly felt like someone had dumped a giant bucket of ice-cold water over his head. Holy shit!

When he now saw Sarah slowly shake her head, still looking quite stunned, he knew she was done adding two and two together. And she had probably also double-checked the result and made sure that there was *no* other possible interpretation.

He bit his lip. No use denying it now. Because, as much as he wanted to find one, there *was* no other plausible explanation!

"Great, Sherlock Holmes," he said dryly, "I guess you just solved the mystery then."

Sarah's eyes widened as she gasped for air.

"You were with *D*???" she shouted.

A stubborn look on his face, Joe stared back at her and shrugged.

Sarah hit her forehead with her flat hand. "How the hell did *that* happen???" From the way it sounded, it was clearly an accusation and not a question.

Instead of an answer, Joe just held her angry gaze, his good hand rubbing his chin and his mind still racing. This was the worst imaginable coincidence! Why had Sarah not given the sweater to Danny after she had found it? Then at least he would have been warned not to wear it or wave it around in front of Sarah's nose anytime soon. But since it had, for some stupid reason, wound up on the floor again, there was no way he could have known.

"*JOSEPH!?!*" Sarah shouted angrily.

"What?" he shot back. "What the hell do you want me to say?"

"I want to know…" Sarah spoke very slowly through clenched teeth now. "I want to know if you were at D's place the last two nights!"

Joe exhaled with audible frustration, rolled his eyes and shrugged. "Yeah, I was there. Content?"

Sarah still looked puzzled. "You slept there???"

From the way she looked at him, her brain was currently scanning through all the imaginable scenarios. Joe could just see it. And he knew she had a vivid imagination. He decided to stop that thinking machine before it could come to the wrong conclusions.

"On the *sofa*…" he took a step towards the table and snapped his fingers in her direction to make sure she was listening. "I slept on the *sofa*, Sarah. Okay!? Both nights. Do you hear me? I didn't…"

Looking very troubled, Sarah raised one of her hands to make him stop.

Joe shrugged. He had had no intention to finish his sentence anyway.

"Okay. Then I guess I *won't* tell you what your Teddy bear and Barbie *didn't* do…" he mocked.

"Don't call D *Barbie!*" Sarah snapped angrily. "I just can't believe you did that!"

"Did *what?*" Joe blasted. "Share your tiramisu with her?"

"No, you idiot," Sarah's eyes narrowed. "You know *exactly* what I mean!"

"Not exactly, no!" He gave her a challenging look.

Scrambling for words, Sarah glared back at him furiously. "You must be completely out of your mind!" she snarled.

Joe's expression darkened. "Yeah right! Sure... I'm completely out of my mind!" He gritted his teeth. "Well, Sarah, as shocking as it might come to you, I didn't exactly use a gun to get into her flat!"

"No, just my tiramisu!" Sarah shot back. "But that was already the *second* night anyway, right?"

Instead of an answer, Joe huffed out an angry breath through his nose, his gaze trailing to the side. The very last thing he needed now was Sarah pointing out to him, that his activities during the previous two nights were indeed a little questionable. He knew that perfectly well himself.

He saw Sarah briefly close her eyes and blow out some air, shaking her head.

"Crap! Now I almost wished it was Sun…" she said more to herself. "Or at least someone I don't know!"

"Well, thanks," Joe grumbled, "if I had only known that, I might have considered your preferences... So sorry!" He took a step away from the table again and turned around to head upstairs.

"Yeah, just go upstairs," Sarah snarled after him.

His palms turned up, he turned around again.

Sarah was sitting in her chair, her arms stretched out on the table, her hands twisting the edges of the newspaper in front of her. She didn't look at him. Just stared gloomily at the little paper rolls she was producing. Finally she tore off one, made a small ball out of it and flipped it across the table. Then she glanced up at him, looking drained.

Joe gave her a crooked smile and a helpless shrug. "I don't know myself what to make of it, okay?" he said conciliatorily. "It wasn't some evil plan. It just happened."

Sarah slowly nodded. To her own surprise her anger was evaporating.

"So that's why you're so cheered up all of a sudden," she said.

Joe gave her a surprised look. "Oh, am I cheered up?"

"Well, you seem like you're in a lot better mood than when you arrived."

He shrugged and looked away. "I guess..."

Sarah leaned back in her chair without letting him out of her sight. "If you hurt D, Joe, I'll kill you," she said. "I just want you to know that! D even talking to you is mind-boggling as far as I'm concerned."

He held her gaze, but didn't say anything.

"If you dare to mess with her again," Sarah insisted, "I'm done being your sister. And this time I really mean it."

"I don't go around hurting people on purpose, okay?" he retorted. "You should know that!"

"Well, okay. Maybe you don't," Sarah said. "But in this particular case you better make absolutely sure, you don't even hurt her by accident!"

Stone-faced Joe glared at the table.

"I really think I must be dreaming!" With a crazy laugh, Sarah threw her hands in the air. "Two days ago I thought, the worst that could happen to me this weekend, was being caught in the middle when D and you openly avoid and mock and hate each other. Not in my *wildest* dreams could I have imagined this!"

"I know it's a shitty constellation," Joe admitted.

"*Very* shitty!" Sarah said. "Especially for me because I'm sharing a room with D and I can only imagine how totally weird this is going to be.

My pretending that I don't know about any of this, and you two pretending to have nothing going on."

"There really isn't much of anything going on, alright?" Joe said sharply. "For her it's more of a crazy self-experiment anyway."

"Oh, poor Joe," Sarah mocked. "How can that be? I wonder why D is so hesitant about this and won't give you her heart on a silver platter."

"Oh, just cut it out, Sarah!"

Sarah scoffed. "Well, I'm sorry, but did you expect me to cheer you on here?"

He let out a bitter laugh. "Nope! If I had had my way, you wouldn't even know about this! But since you do, and since you don't approve of course, why don't you just go ahead and have a talk with Danny. Get it out of your system! Make sure she doesn't make the same mistake twice. Come on, Sarah, you can do it!"

"Argh!!!" Sarah glared at him angrily. "I just... Grrr... I just *hate* the situations you get me into!"

Shaking his head, Joe turned around to finally go upstairs.

"I won't say anything..." Sarah told him weakly. "I promise."

"Whatever..." he said and headed for the stairs.

Sarah looked after him, rubbing her temples. She felt a headache coming on. No wonder! All the things that had happened this morning would make anyone's head spin.

She got up and took a pill with some water. With the half full glass she returned to the table.

How in the world had Joe managed to spend two nights at D's place? She tried to remember what exactly D had said about the party and the ride home. D hadn't been very specific, that was for sure. And she hadn't jumped on the *Sun-was-drunk* issue either. She had been a little absent-minded, now that Sarah thought about it. And she hadn't really wanted to talk about London much anymore all of a sudden. Great!

# Calls

Around 1:10 pm D was done packing for the weekend and more or less ready to go. She wasn't supposed to pick Jack and Sun up for another hour, however. There was really nothing left to do for her in the flat. She had been very productive if not to say hyper-active since Joe had left. She had watered the plants, vacuumed, dusted, cleaned the bathroom and unloaded the dishwasher. She had even almost finished cleaning up her bedroom, too. The ironing pile was still lying on the chair but that was about it. She had stuffed the curtains for Sarah in an Ikea bag but then decided not to bring it with her on the weekend trip because they would need all the trunk space they had. Sun wasn't famous for travelling light and neither was Jack. D herself had a little trolley and a small bag with a pair of shoes and hiking boots.

Since she still had an hour to kill, D decided to do the unavoidable: make some calls.

First she called Robert. He told her they were just having breakfast.

"We were out late," he said while munching on something, "went to see the new James Bond movie. I thought it was crap. Ann liked it... And then we ran into some friends and went to their place for a while. What's up with you? When are you leaving for your weekend thing?"

"Oh, in an hour. Jack and Sun are riding with me, so I've still got some time and..."

"...you thought you could call your only brother..." Robert said theatrically.

"Exactly. Since I cut my only brother off so coldly last night."

"Yeah, that was heartless," he chuckled. "What were you cooking that couldn't wait?"

"Oh, just pasta. But you called right when I needed to strain it. Sorry." She was pacing around the living room and over to the kitchen like a panther in a cage.

"No problem... – So, is there anything else to report about the party on Wednesday?"

"Not really," D said lightly, relieved that it had come out so naturally. "It was okay. I actually had a good time overall."

"Well, good. And how was it with Joe?" Robert asked, of course not willing to let her get off so easily. "Did he really show up?"

D was glad he couldn't see her because she was almost certain that she was blushing.

"Yes, he was there," she confirmed in an almost bored tone. "It was okay. Not *that* bad."

"See, I told you," Robert said, "and it was probably good for you to see that you're *so* over him."

D bit her lip. Yeah right. That was exactly what that evening and the following one had shown very clearly...

"Yes, I guess," she mumbled. "We'll see how the weekend goes."

"It'll be fine," Robert predicted. "Make sure you enjoy it!"

"I will! Thanks and have fun testing your new barbecue!"

When she hung up, she was sweating. Lying to Robert was something she usually didn't do. But then again, she hadn't actually lied to him.

She went to sit on the swiveling bar stool Joe had been sitting on last night. Scratching her left eyebrow, she looked at the phone in her hand. She still needed to call Pete back. Now might be a good time.

It rang a few times. Her heart was racing and she was getting her hopes up that he might actually not pick up. But then he did.

"Danielle. Hi..." He seemed a little distracted. Normally he would have started the conversation with a complaint about her not having called him back earlier. Surprisingly he didn't seem up to it now.

"Bad time?" D asked, wishing he would say yes.

"No, I'm just having lunch at Mom and Dad's, but it's not ready yet anyway. Let me just go outside."

There was a silence in which he obviously went to a place where he could talk freely.

"Mom and Dad say *Hi*, by the way," he told her, sounding surprisingly calm and friendly. D wondered how much his parents knew about the split-up. Maybe they also thought it was just a temporary thing? Or they didn't know anything about it at all?

"How was your party?" he interrupted her thoughts.

"Good... – Fun."

"Who was there?" D knew that he was just making small talk. He wasn't really interested in the answer and probably not even listening because he thought he knew anyway.

"Everyone except for Sarah," D said. "She had to work."

312

She knew Pete wasn't going to catch what *everyone* meant in this particular context and she didn't want him to. But she had just had to say it – while she was sitting on Joe's chair. It had felt weirdly exciting and liberating to put it out there.

"Hey, about that party at work…" Pete said on the other end.

D felt her stomach cramp at the mention of this. "Yes?" she tried for a tone that didn't sound too irritated. She had promised to go, so…"Next Friday, right?"

"Right…" He hesitated, cleared his throat. "There's this… – well, this year the whole thing is a little bigger because it's the 25-year anniversary, you know… Most of the others are staying there overnight since there's going to be some fireworks around eleven and a brunch on a boat the next morning. So… I kind of thought I'd reserve a room for us too."

"Are you kidding?" She suddenly felt nauseated. Of course he was *not* kidding. "You reserved a room for us to stay overnight?"

"Well, it would really be weird if we left while everyone else… And everything is paid for by the firm."

D was squirming on her seat. Had she seriously believed it would be just a painless evening with his colleagues and she would just be there as a *friend?*

"Well, I didn't really put the news out yet that we… you know," Pete admitted sounding a little embarrassed. "It's really nobody's business."

D cringed. "Of course, it's nobody's business, but if that means we'll have to be hugging and kissing and whatever else you've got in mind to keep up appearances, I–"

"Of course not!" Pete interrupted her.

"Well, but we'd have to share a room, right?"

"Yeah, well…"

"I don't *want* that," she told him as firmly as she could. "I don't *want* to stay overnight. I don't feel *good* about it!"

"My God, Danielle, this is *one* night in a hotel room with me," he pointed out, his irritation tangible. "It's not like it's the first time we've ever slept in a bed together. Don't be so… I'll leave you alone, I promise."

"I didn't realize that this was an overnight thing," she insisted, ignoring his hint that it wouldn't be a big deal. "Why did you not tell me about this last time?"

313

"Because I just found out about it myself," he claimed. Somehow it didn't sound honest. Maybe she was doing him wrong, but in a way she suspected that he had planned this all along.

"Can't you do it as a birthday favor?" he urged.

D swallowed. Right. His birthday was coming up too. And she had broken his heart. Shit.

"I really don't want to stay there overnight!" she repeated weakly. "I'm going to go to the party with you, but you need to come up with some excuse why we – or at least I – have to leave before midnight. I'm sorry! Just tell them I turn into a pumpkin…"

"Okay, thanks a lot!" The way he said it, it sounded like she had just denied him the most harmless little wish out of pure spite. "I need to go back inside now. Lunch is ready. I'll call you sometime next week."

He hung up.

Her hands shaking, D let the phone slip back into her purse.

# Lakeside Hotel Arrivals

"Man, Sun, you were really drunk Wednesday night," Jack chuckled as he leaned forward from the back seat. "You may wanna watch it a bit tonight."

Sun giggled sounding a little embarrassed. "Yeah, I know!" She looked over her shoulder at Jack. "You don't want to know how I felt the next morning! I hardly remember how I got home."

"Well, that's how it goes..." Jack laughed.

"I *do* remember that your car crapped out, though," Sun said like that was a real achievement. "And that when I woke up, I was in Joe's car and D unbuckled my seat belt and Joe was pulling on my arm to actually get me out of the car. Right?" With a glance over at D, she laughed.

D managed a relatively authentic laugh as a response, hoping desperately that Jack hadn't gotten the implication of what Sun had just said. Of course he had. As she shot him a quick look through the rear view mirror, she caught the questioning, concerned look he gave her. A look that seemed to say, *'He drove Sun home first?'*

"Don't look so concerned," Sun groaned, misinterpreting his face as concern for herself.

"Oh, I'm not!" Jack assured her with an uncommitted laugh and turned to look out the side window. He suddenly felt bad. Sun's memory of Wednesday night might be a little blurred, but if she remembered D unbuckling her seat belt, D had most likely *been* there. Which meant that after Sun had gotten out, D and Joe had been alone in the car.

Why in the world would Joe do such a thing? Jack realized that there were two possible explanations. One was that Joe was so desperate to get rid of Sun or too uncomfortable to drive in a car alone with her, that he actually preferred D's cold indifference. The other explanation – and this didn't seem unlikely either – was that Joe had wanted to get D alone to talk to her. Jack could only imagine how that must have gone. No matter what the motives, Jack was sure that D had probably cursed him and his car more than once in the course of this undoubtedly delightful ride. No wonder she hadn't even picked up her phone that night when he had called to check on her and apologize again.

They reached the hotel around 4:30 pm after driving the last twenty minutes on a narrow, winding road that was built into the mountainside about a hundred meters above the lake. This last part of the drive had been slow, but once they had come around the last curve, there had been a stunning view of the lake and the surrounding mountains, one of which had a snow-covered top. There were two little towns tucked between the foot of the mountain and the lakeside, and their hotel was located right at the lake on a little peninsula that made the building look as if it were floating in the water, with boats and swimmers around it. Despite its size the hotel seemed to fit perfectly into the area, without being overwhelming.

"Wow," Sun exclaimed as they were driving the last few hundred meters down to the hotel. "That looks even better than in the pictures on their website!"

"Yeah looks great," D agreed as she tried to follow the signs pointing to the underground garage. "I'll definitely have to go for a swim tomorrow."

In the garage they got their luggage out of the trunk and then took the elevator up to the lobby. At the reception they ran into Gerry and Anja who had just checked in.

"Some of the others are already outside," Gerry said and nodded towards the outside seating area that was visible through the sliding glass doors of the lobby. Rick, Carrey, Tony and his girlfriend, Kim, were sitting out there under a big umbrella, some beverages on the table in front of them. They appeared to be immersed in a heated conversation.

"We'll just go upstairs and drop off our stuff," Anja said as she stepped aside from the reception, making space for Sun to move up to the desk.

"Yeah, let's just meet out there later," Sun said.

"Sarah and Joe aren't here yet, huh?" Jack called after Gerry and Anja.

Gerry turned around and shook his head. "Not yet."

Jack fished out his phone and checked for messages.

"Here's something from Sarah," he said. "You probably got it too, D. Says they're running a bit late because of some traffic problems. They should be here in half an hour at the latest, though. That'll still give them a little while until dinner..."

"They'll get here in time," Gerry predicted with a smile over his shoulder and followed his wife to the elevator. "See you later..."

As she waited for the check-in behind Sun and Jack, D let her gaze wander around. Across the lobby she could see the entrance to a big, bright dining hall with a large window front overlooking the lake. This was probably where tonight's dinner would be. Easy to find. And after dinner, the plan was to look at the old photos and films. Rick had said he had reserved a small conference room with a projector for that.

Sun was done with her check-in and Jack told her to just go ahead upstairs. He quickly filled out his own paperwork and handed the receptionist his credit card. Once he was finished and it was D's turn to check in, he stuck around to wait for her.

As she filled out her name and address on the form the lady gave her, D realized that she would prefer it if Jack just went ahead. She had a feeling that she knew exactly why he was waiting around for her.

Two minutes later they were on the elevator together. They had just pressed the button for the sixth floor that both of their rooms were on, when Jack cleared his throat – always a sign that something was bothering him. Pretending not to notice, D kept her eyes on the display above the door that showed their progress in ascending.

"I didn't realize Joe took Sun home first," Jack said without any introduction.

"Well, yeah…" D shrugged, not quite sure how to respond.

"I'm really sorry about that," Jack said guiltily.

D turned to look at him. "Well, it's not your fault…" she said as reassuringly as she could while wracking her brain how to just kill the topic very swiftly.

"Yeah, sure…" Jack didn't look convinced. "But I know that this was about the worst replacement taxi I could have waved down for you."

D let out a little laugh. "Don't worry about it, Jack. Really!" She meant it. "He got me home and that's what counts, okay? Besides, I've survived far worse."

Jack nodded, as the memories of the *far worse* she was referring to, flashed by. "I know," he said. "Still, I feel kind of bad."

"It's fine, really," D assured him. "I'm already over it. Now, please, stop worrying about it!"

"Okay," Jack nodded, seeming relieved.

They had reached their floor and the elevator doors opened.

"What's your room number?" D asked.

"643," Jack read from the folder that had come with his key card. "And yours?"

"647."

They walked down the corridor together. Finally Jack stopped.

"643. Guess that's right here." He pointed to the brass numbers on the door.

"And mine is there..." D headed to the next door on the same side of the corridor and fiddled with her key card. "Do you just want to meet downstairs later?" she asked over her shoulder where Jack had just unlocked his door.

"Sure," Jack nodded and then disappeared into his room.

Stepping into her own room, D exhaled and briefly closed her eyes. She definitely needed to hide in here for a few minutes. Hide and recover. That elevator ride had left her uncomfortable, tense and hot. Accepting Jack's apologies under the given circumstances seemed sickeningly dishonest. And she had the distinct feeling that this had just been a little taste of what the weekend could still bring in awkward situations.

She set the trolley next to one of the two beds and dropped the bag next to it. It was a nice, bright room and tastefully furnished. There were separate beds, a desk with a chair, a built-in closet, two comfortable little wing chairs, a TV on a side-board and a coat rack between the entrance and the bathroom.

D opened the door to the bathroom and flipped the light switch on inside. It was a spacious bathroom with a large sink, a toilet, a rainfall shower and giant mirrors that would put every dimple in the right horrific light. Next to the sink there was an assortment of little bottles with shampoos and body lotion along with an egg shaped bar of soap. D picked up one of the bottles, smelled it – and frowned. God, that was sweet...

She turned the cold water on and let it run for a while. Then she took one of the two glasses from the shelf above the sink and filled it with water. As she took a swig, she looked at her reflection in the mirror, giving herself a questioning look. How exactly was she going to handle tonight and the next two days? Maybe it was about time she gave it a serious thought?

It would have been wise to coordinate with Joe – even if just roughly – how to act with friends around. But of course they hadn't coordinated anything. Because discussing this kind of thing would have meant that they would first a) have to acknowledge that something had actually happened between them and b) at least vaguely analyze the meaning of what had happened. D, for her part, was determined to do neither a) nor b) until it absolutely couldn't be avoided anymore. Just thinking about the last two evenings and nights made her stomach feel very funny and her knees wobbly. Butterflies!? Great! She better not let this feeling surface to the point where it could leave any traces in her expression, because Sarah had a scary talent of detecting butterflies from far away. Not that Sarah would ever think of her brother as a possible cause, of course. D felt relatively safe in that respect. Still, if Sarah noticed anything out of the ordinary (a dreamy smile, an absent-minded sigh, a quick hopeful look at the phone...) she would start to ask questions. Questions good friends were entitled to ask. Such as: *Wow, you look like you're on cloud 9... Who is it? What do you mean, it's nothing? Just look at yourself!*

Given Sarah's strong dislike of Pete, she would be absolutely delighted by any sign that a replacement for Pete might have already been found. She would undoubtedly insist on a full report. *Who, where, why, what and since when?* D wasn't prepared to even think about how to answer any of that. She generally didn't feel like lying to Sarah, just like she normally didn't lie to Robert, but in this particular case telling the truth was out of the question. So, for the moment the safest thing was to keep a straight face and make sure Sarah didn't notice anything.

Lost in thought she left the room, strolled back to the elevator and pressed the button to call it. The dingdong that sounded as the elevator doors opened made her glance up. And she found herself looking right at Sarah – and Joe.

"Oh, you're here," she stammered.

Sarah growled, as she pulled her suitcase out into the hallway. "We could have been here much earlier," she said in a scathingly sweet tone, "if he..." With her thumb she pointed over her shoulder towards her brother. "If he hadn't tried to get around the traffic jam on the *stupidest* detour."

Stepping into the hallway right behind Sarah, his bag over his shoulder, Joe just shook his head and shot D a brief look loaded with frustration.

"You better ask for something for your headache, Sarah," he said darkly and squeezed by behind his sister. "Because with that mood of yours..."

"I can take care of myself, thank you!" Sarah snapped in his direction.

"Sure, sure…" he mocked from behind her, rolling his eyes. Then he headed down the corridor towards his room.

"Just for your information, though," he called back over his shoulder, "we could have easily made it here in time if you had just let me drive *my* way!" He unlocked the door to his room.

"Right," Sarah hissed after him, "we'd probably be lying in a ditch if I had let you do that…"

He kicked the door open. "Oh, give me a break, Sarah!" He didn't even turn around. "Just do us all a favor and take something against that headache and then lie down until you feel better because you're just…" instead of finishing his sentence he threw his hands in the air and disappeared into his room, the door falling closed behind him.

Still standing in front of the elevator that had, of course, left by now, D and Sarah looked at each other.

"So, you have a headache?" D asked, glad to have a topic that didn't contain anything she could trip over.

Sarah scowled. "Yeah, I have a headache and I've got him. Ask me if there's a connection!"

D laughed.

Even with a paralyzing headache Sarah realized that this was definitely not the reaction she would have gotten three days ago. If she had as much as mentioned Joe in this way, D would have met it with tense silence and an evasive look – definitely not with a spontaneous laugh! Just the fact that D hadn't turned into Miss Ice Queen as soon as Joe had stepped out of that elevator, spoke volumes. It was just little things. And Sarah wasn't even sure she would have noticed them without having been tipped off. But she clearly noticed them now.

"I brought my headache drops if you want them," D offered with an encouraging smile.

Sarah nodded. "Yeah, the drops would be great. I've already taken one of my pills but they are useless!"

She followed D down the corridor.

In front of their door D stopped and waved the key card until the little light on the lock turned green. "Really nice room…" she predicted and opened the door wide to let Sarah in.

The bright light in the room made Sarah squint. Her head was just killing her now.

"Do you want me to close the curtains?" D asked and, without waiting for an answer, just pulled them closed.

And Sarah watched her, suddenly having this vision of her saying, '*Do you want to sleep on my sofa?*' God, she really needed to stop thinking about this now. If she kept pondering it, her head would surely explode. And even with a clear and painless head, she would probably not be able to figure out how in the world Joe had managed to make D scrap all her principles within just a few hours. Sarah set her trolley down next to the free bed.

D was already pulling her toiletry case out of her own luggage. She unzipped it and fished out a little bottle. "Here." She held it out to Sarah with a sympathetic smile. "Take the magic potion and you'll feel better in no time – hopefully. Always helps me."

"Yeah, hopefully..." Sarah took the bottle. "Thanks."

She shuffled to the bathroom where she filled one of the glasses with water, let about twenty drops drip into her mouth from above and rinsed them down with water.

D appeared in the doorway, and they looked at each other through the mirror. "Maybe you should lie down for a while," D suggested. "Just until it kicks in. You still have forty minutes till dinner. We'll make sure to get you in time – in case you fall asleep."

Sarah nodded weakly. "Yeah, maybe I will. Thanks."

After D had left, she sunk onto the bed, her arm over her eyes and waited for the headache to subside.

~~~

Walking back to the elevator, D wondered if Joe was still in his room. For a moment she considered checking, but then she forced herself to just walk past room 643. It was no good exposing herself to yet another dose of emotional turmoil!

"Danny..."

She stopped in her tracks and whisked around when she suddenly heard his voice.

The door to his room was cracked open and he was peeking out, one hand on the door, the other one on the doorframe.

D shot a nervous glance up and down the corridor and then back at him, her mouth suddenly dry. "What?"

"Come in for a second, okay..." Joe opened the door wider. He reached out, almost as if to take her hand and pull her in, but when she didn't seem to need any further persuasion or assistance, he stepped aside and retracted his hand, rubbing his forehead instead.

Feeling slightly shaky, D pulled the door closed behind herself and leaned against it, hands behind her back. For a moment she stood there, staring down at her shoes as that had something calming. And she *did* need calming right now. Because she felt as if she were caught up in a tornado! First an uncomfortable elevator-talk with Jack, then a few weird and nerve-wrecking minutes with Sarah, now a one-on-one with Mister-turn-my-world-upside-down himself and then next, right back to a happy gathering with the oblivious friends...

She glanced over at Joe, who was leaning against the wall a few steps away from her now, looking a bit tense.

"So, did you sedate Sarah, I hope?" he asked in a joking tone that sounded a bit forced.

"Well, I gave her the magic drops, and with some luck she'll be better for dinner..." D babbled, finding her own voice hollow.

Biting down on his lower lip, Joe slowly nodded. "That's good, I guess..." He paused and shook his head, exhaling sharply. "Sometimes she just drives me absolutely crazy!"

"Seems like that works both ways," D said with a smile. "Sarah didn't use those exact same words, but I think it was something very similar."

He rolled his eyes and reached up to massage the back of his neck.

"Your breakfast didn't go really well then, huh?" D asked.

"Nope, didn't go well at all..." He shook his head.

"Because you were gone at night?"

Joe let out a humorless laugh and nodded. "That was part of it, yeah..." His eyes drifted off to the floor as if to avoid her gaze. Then he pushed himself away from the wall and took the three steps over to the desk.

D watched him perch on the side of the desk and run his left hand over the side of the wooden desktop, obviously pondering something. She was just about to ask what was going on, when there suddenly were noises in the hallway outside. Noises of footsteps, approaching fast.

D intuitively took a step away from the door and then froze. What if Jack came back now? Or if Sarah came knocking?

She tried to keep track of the noises outside, literally holding her breath. And when her eyes met Joe's he seemed to be doing exactly the same.

Finally the footsteps passed their door and the noises faded. Briefly closing her eyes, D exhaled. At the desk Joe had dropped his gaze, still looking tense and somewhat absent-minded. Suddenly he looked up.

"Do you think there's any chance I can get you alone sometime this weekend?" he asked.

"We *are* alone," D pointed out the obvious.

"I actually meant for more than three minutes and without having to pray that no one comes by," Joe clarified.

"Might not be the best environment," D said with a pang of regret.

"I realize that," he grumbled. "But still..."

"What's going on?" D asked, trying hard for a steady voice. "Why do you have to get me alone?

He didn't answer right away, dropped his gaze for a moment and then looked up again. "It's not about me renting a room so we can make out, if that's what you're worried about," he finally said flatly. "I understood perfectly well what you told me this morning."

Staring at him, D swallowed.

"I just need to..." he started, then paused and chewed on his lip for a moment. "During that talk with Sarah this morning, some stuff came up... and... I need to talk to you."

D felt this cold, choking wave hit her as possible topics he might be referring to, started flashing through her head.

"I don't want to talk..." she stammered, her mouth suddenly dry, "...at least not about...*that.*"

"You don't even know what I–" he said half-heartedly.

"I have enough imagination..." she mumbled, her voice cracking.

"Okay," Joe said quietly.

What followed was a moment of tense silence, with D looking at her shoes and Joe looking at her.

"And if we just skipped the talking?" he suggested.

Her eyes darted up at him and she found him giving her a somewhat challenging look. Then a crooked smile started spreading across his face.

Her eyes locked with his, D swallowed.

He cleared this throat. "A whole weekend of keeping an unsuspicious distance just doesn't sound real great," he said with an apologetic little shrug. "But then that's just me, of course..."

Looking back at him, D could clearly feel the side effects of that look he gave her, and that smile, and that shrug and what he had just said.

There was this very distinct tingle in her stomach. And it was undeniably butterflies... Talk about guys manipulating her! Pete could learn from this one here!

"It's not just you..." she admitted grudgingly.

"Oh? Really?" Joe raised his eyebrows, obviously amused. "Not just *me*, huh?"

"Forget it," she said with fake fury. "It's definitely only *just you*!"

That made him laugh. "No, no, no! Too late now!" he chuckled, pointing a finger at her. "It's definitely *not* just me!"

Obviously a lot more cheered up than before, he got up from his desk and came strolling towards her.

Suddenly there were footsteps outside again.

D froze – and saw Joe come to a halt two feet away from her, his eyes flickering from her to the door behind her. As the footsteps came closer, he kept staring at the door. But then the footsteps passed their door and his face lit up.

"Oh, you're so jumpy!" he teased as he took the two steps that still lay between them.

"Oh, I'm jumpy and you're not?" she retorted.

"No, I'm very calm," he lied and stepped up to her with a wide grin. "And if someone comes," he said, already dangerously close, "I'll just hide you in the closet."

"Wow, that's just ingenious!" she said, trying to hold his gaze and sound serious.

"That's what they do in the movies..." Joe told her with an innocent bat of his eyes.

D nodded, dropping her gaze. "Yeah, yeah..."

"Anyway," he said and raised his right hand to where he could brush the side of his thumb over her cheek. "If you don't flat-out reject the idea of getting together alone..."

"I don't," D mumbled, glancing up at him again. "But I really don't know how that's going to work without..."

"I know," he said, his voice dropping to a whisper. "It would have to be *top secret*..."

"Mhmm..." She nodded, struggling for a serious face and the strength to hold his gaze even though it was starting to wear her out.

"I'll try to come up with something *top secret*," Joe promised with a smile. "Just keep your phone around, so I can let you know when something pops up."

She nodded. "Okay…" It came out more like a question.

"It'll be okay," he assured her with a smile and placed his left hand on the door beside her head. D blinked up at him and swallowed.

"I guess I should probably let you go before someone really comes," he whispered, leaning a bit closer to where the tip of his nose almost touched hers.

"Oh, is this you letting me go now?" D asked shakily.

"Mhmm." He leaned in for a soft, warm kiss right on her lips. It didn't last quite long enough for her to kiss him back. She had closed her eyes, though. When she opened them again, her head spinning, she found Joe looking back at her, his head tilted.

She shrugged and blinked and huffed out a breath. "How do we do this?" she asked warily. "I mean, not the getting-together-top-secret part, but …in general… *downstairs*… with the others. How do we…?"

"You mean, how do we act?" Joe asked just to make sure he understood correctly.

She nodded.

Joe let out a little laugh, his braced hand resting on her shoulder now, the side of this thumb brushing up against her neck. "Let's just try to re-enact Wednesday night," he suggested teasingly. "I'll be nice, polite and friendly, and you'll be alternating between pretending to ignore me and being cold, snappy and testy."

D drew in a shaky breath and rolled her eyes at him, even though he was already dangerously close again.

"One more for the trip downstairs," he announced and tipped his nose against hers before he kissed her again, this time giving her a little more time to contribute to it.

A short kiss, then he pulled away and stepped to the side.

"Okay, you better go now before we get caught here or die from a heart attack imagining it," he said and gave her shoulder a gentle squeeze. "I'll be down in a few minutes and you can start ignoring me…" He grinned.

"Hahaha!" D retorted with a somewhat tortured smile. She turned around and cracked the door open to take a quick peek outside, just to make sure the coast was clear. Then, shooting Joe one more scolding look over her shoulder, she slipped out, briefly feeling the light touch of his hand against her lower back as she did. Then the door closed behind her.

Walking over to the elevator D tried to compose herself. How in the world had she gone from initially really looking forward to this weekend, to dreading it because she had found out that Joe was going to be there, to now almost wishing it could be only him and her? Man, that was just sick. Really! And it was crazy and totally unfair to all the nice people downstairs! She better focus on what this weekend was all about: having a good time with old friends!

~~~

After closing the door behind D, Joe went over to his bed where he had dropped his bag earlier. In order to waste some time, he started unpacking a few things.

He felt a little better now, but his mind kept flashing back to all the crazy things that had happened in the morning – the breakfast with Sarah, the revelation of the shower incident and Sarah's epiphany upon recognizing his sweater. These things just kept popping up in his head, and every time that happened, he could feel his stomach drop.

On the drive over from Deens he had felt as if he couldn't even breathe properly before he had a chance to talk to Danny. It had seemed absolutely urgent a) to give her a head's up that Sarah had found out about them and b) to make clear to her that he had *not* spent the night after the party with Liz.

For a moment there, when she had been in his room, he had seriously considered just getting it over with and telling her right then. That would have probably been a disastrous move, though. He could see that now. Because from what she had said, she would have probably just run and screamed and refused to talk to him again if he had pulled those topics out of the hat. The way it looked, he would just have to deal with it himself for right now. At least with the shower thing. Because really, what difference did it still make so many years later? Maybe he should just let sleeping dogs lie altogether. Maybe he would.

The fact that Sarah had figured out where he had been the last two nights, was a different story. He needed to tell Danny before it came out some other way and the damage would be done.

~~~

326

D found the group still seated in the garden, their glasses mostly empty. They were immersed in some discussion about a new TV show. Rick and Carrey were reciting some scene they had found especially funny.

D sat down next to Jack, who had reserved some space on the bench next to him. He leaned over. "Did you see Sarah?"

"Yeah, she's got a headache and took some drops and lay down."

"Oh, okay..." he said, obviously careful not to ask her about Joe next. Little did he know that she could have given him very exact information on that as well. Just as she was pondering this paradox, Joe came strolling out of the building.

Approaching their table, he avoided looking at her, but when he pulled over another chair between Anja and Rick – just right across from her – their eyes met for a fraction of a second.

"Sarah's got a headache," he said to no one in particular. "We're supposed to get her when we're ready for dinner..."

The mention of dinner prompted everyone around the table to check their watches.

"Almost time," Gerry diagnosed, his arm around Anja. "I'm pretty hungry."

Anja nodded. "Me too."

They stayed for another fifteen minutes and then paid for the beverages. As they wandered inside, Carrey and Sun excused themselves to go up to their rooms for a moment, and Jack offered to get Sarah. Neither Joe nor D made any attempt to stop him. They were both secretly welcoming the fact that they didn't have to do it.

"Thanks Jack," Joe even said, jokingly patting Jack's back. "She might be less grouchy if *you* go..."

Jack laughed. "Oh, are we having a little family trouble?"

"Yeah, you could say that," Joe grumbled and followed the others to the dining area.

# Dinner from Hell

The dining room was bustling. There seemed to be quite a few people from town who came just for Saturday dinner. A lot of couples, some families.

D tried to stay around Tony and Kim while, from the corner of her eye, she was aware of Joe talking to Gerry. She just couldn't seem to get him off her radar...

Their table was in the far corner of the dining room, at the window; a big oval table for eleven.

Just as they sat down, Sarah and Jack appeared from upstairs. Sarah looked better. She shot D a weary smile across the table. "Drops helped..." she mouthed and sat down between Jack and Joe.

The waiter came to take the orders for what they wanted to drink. Since they had a fixed menu for dinner, there were no decisions to be made in that regard.

Soon the conversations picked up where they had been interrupted before they had moved inside from the garden. D tried hard to concentrate on what Rick was telling Tony about some sort of new implant that was just being tested for the hearing-impaired. Keeping her eyes on Rick or Tony or her napkin or her hands, she made sure her gaze didn't flash over to Joe. This was harder than she had thought. She heard him talk to Jack and growl at Sarah, which Sarah countered with some hissed comment.

When the waiter brought the drinks and everyone was hopefully distracted, D allowed herself to briefly glance over to the other side of the table. Joe was absent-mindedly staring into his glass, and next to him, Sarah was laughing about something Jack must have said. Suddenly Joe looked up and met her eyes. It literally made her stomach knot. He gave her a little crooked smile before he dropped his gaze again and started playing with his glass.

Finally the soup came. It looked really good and D realized how hungry she was. As everyone ate their soup, the conversations around their table died down, except for the occasional praise that it tasted really good.

Ten minutes later the second course was served. A fish dish with potatoes and fennel root. D hadn't had a lot of fennel in her life, except for maybe in tea. She was surprised at how perfectly it went with the fish and the potatoes and the dill in the sauce.

They were about halfway through the second course when Anja's phone rang in her purse. With her mother being quite sick, she had the phone turned on day and night so the hospital or her Dad could reach her in case of emergency.

Turning pale, Anja dropped her silverware and fumbled with her purse, her hands shaking. "I'm sorry, but... "

"It's okay." Gerry patted her thigh as she fished the phone out.

She looked at the number on the display and frowned. "No idea who that is," she said.

She picked it up. "Hello?"

Anja was just about to get up to leave the dining room for the duration of the call, when her jaw seemed to drop and she sank back onto her chair – all eyes on her.

"Hello, Liz..." she stuttered with audible disbelief. Then there was a short pause, Anja's expression a mix between bafflement and irritation.

"Fine, how are you?" she said politely. "...yeah, we're just starting dinner here..." Tensely holding on to her phone, she listened to whatever was said on the other end.

"Yeah, he's here..." Anja said, shooting Joe a questioning, almost accusing look.

Stone-faced, Joe shook his head. "Tell her I will call her." he said, his voice trembling.

Anja nodded, Liz obviously still talking on the other end.

"Hey, Liz... ahm – can he call you right back?"

"Yeah, but... I think it's better if you just talked to him directly."

"No, he's definitely going to call you back right away..." The way Anja pointed her finger at Joe while saying that, was a clear warning that if he didn't do what she had just promised, she would personally kill him.

Liz seemed to keep talking on the other end, making Anja frown and squirm on her seat uncomfortably.

"Sure..." Anja finally said, shaking her head in exasperation. "Yeah, sure I can give him a message too, but if he calls you right away, why don't you just..." There was a moment of silence again in which Liz obviously responded. Whatever she said, made Anja suck in a breath and briefly close her eyes. "No, alright…" she said soothingly. "Liz, you need to calm down, okay. I can hardly understand you… Sure. I'll give him a message…"

Two seconds passed then Anja's eyes widened. "What?… No, I understood, but – that's really something you should tell him personally. That's nothing I should be… – Liz, calm down." Her jawline hard, Anja shook her head. "It's okay," she finally said with audible exasperation, "I'll tell him. Yeah. I promise. Bye…"

With a shocked expression, she hung up and put the phone on the table. "Shit…" she breathed and leaned her head back for a moment. Blew out some air through clenched teeth. "I can't believe she called *me!*" she said, her voice suddenly sounding shrill.

Everyone was staring at her. She was staring at her plate as if to briefly digest what had just happened.

Gerry frowned. "What's wrong? Who *was* that?"

Anja shook her head. "I'll tell you later."

She turned to look at Joe, who was looking back at her with a frozen expression. "Just say it," he told her with a shrug, "since we're all here. I mean, that was the whole point of it all, I'm sure…"

Anja shook her head. "I can't believe she drags me into this! All of us, actually!" She drew in a deep breath. "She wants me to tell you here and now…" she started, but then paused and cleared her throat. "She says she's pregnant. And you have your phone turned off all the time… And she says you can't just run away when she's pregnant."

Joe felt like someone was pulling the rug from under his feet. "Shit!" he breathed as he leaned back in his chair, his gaze turning unfocussed. He didn't have to look around, to know that everyone was staring at him – with shock, concern, disbelief, sympathy…

From the corner of his eye he saw Danny push back her chair, get up and walk out. It seemed to be happening in slow motion, through a thick fog. And there was absolutely nothing he could do about it.

He reached into his shirt pocket and pulled out his phone. His hands were trembling. It was still dead quiet when he got up.

"I'm really sorry about this!" he mumbled, his throat feeling tight. "Excuse me…"

Trying not to look into all the serious and worried faces, he squeezed by Jack's and Sarah's chairs to get out behind the table. Then, like in a haze, he made his way out of the dining room, through the lobby and out to garden into the fresh air.

~~~

There was an eerie silence around the table after Joe had left. No one said anything. Anja, still shocked, was poking around in her food just like everyone else who still had any.

"I still can't believe she called *me*!" Anja finally said. "That's just the most bizarre thing to do. I don't even know how she got my new number. I'm not even friends with her or anything..."

Carrey nodded. "Yeah it's really weird. She must be pretty desperate."

"A bit of a lunatic, if you ask me..." Gerry commented.

"Yeah, but that he doesn't pick up the phone when she calls," Carrey pointed out. "I mean, that's just...When she's dealing with something as important as that..."

Jack glanced over at Sarah.

She was just sitting there, staring at her plate, one hand cramped around her knife, the other one pressed flat against the table top as if to grant some stability. When she felt his eyes on her, she weakly shook her head without even looking up.

Jack looked at the faces around the table. The mood had dropped to zero.

"Maybe he didn't know," Gerry contemplated.

"Well, what she said to Anja doesn't exactly sound like he didn't know," Kim said, obviously reminded of her own experiences. "Sounded more like he—"

"He *didn't* know!" Jack interrupted her sharply and saw all heads turn his way as a consequence. He shot another quick look at Sarah, hoping she would come back to life at some point and say something in her brother's defense as well, but the way it looked, he wouldn't be able to count on her.

"I had a talk with Joe yesterday," he slowly said. "Up close and personal." He paused for a moment and glanced around the table. He could only hope he'd make things better here and not worse! "He told me that they've split up – him and Liz – or actually: he left. Because... ahm – there were some *serious* problems. From what I heard – and I'm not going to go into detail here – I definitely don't blame him. I can *guarantee* you that when he left, he had *no* idea whatsoever of this pregnancy thing. He would have told me. And sorry, but pregnant or not, delivering this kind of news with timing like that to an audience like us is kind of sick if you ask me..."

There was some mumbling and nodding around the table.

"Well, I sure hope they can work this out," Kim said.

"Maybe it's not even true..." Rick suggested.

"Oh, come on..." Carrey snorted with an angry frown at Rick.

"Yeah, why would she do *that*?" Anja asked, also challenging Rick.

"Not unheard of..." Gerry said, coming to Rick's aid. "If he left her, as Jack said, and she didn't like it... Some women take drastic measures..."

"I can't imagine she'd do that..." Carrey insisted.

"I can!" Jack let out a bitter little laugh. "And allow me to remind you that I know her a little..."

Carrey shrugged with a sour look at Jack.

"Come on, come on..." Raising his hands in a calming gesture, Gerry shot a look around the table. "You don't want to get into a fight about this, right? We don't know all the facts, so let's keep out of it, okay? And don't let *that* ruin the weekend."

Jack shot Gerry a grateful look across the table, and there was a lot of nodding and some murmurs of consent to what Gerry had said from the others. Then the waiter appeared to see if he could clear anything off the table yet.

"I think I'm ready for desert," Anja sighed with a look at her unfinished plate.

"Yeah, so am I," Kim pushed her silverware to the side of the plate and let the waiter take it.

Even though no one had finished their food, they all decided to move on to the next course.

"Can I take this away?" the waiter had gotten to D's abandoned chair with a plate that had hardly been touched.

"I don't know," Rick said with a confused look at D's plate next him. "I guess you can take it... I don't even know where she went."

Sarah's brain finally kicked into gear when she saw Rick shoot her a questioning look, obviously assuming that if anyone knew where D was, *she* would. And even though she had no idea where D could be, the reason for her disappearance was crystal-clear. And so was the fact that there was no way, D was going to come back and actually still finish her food.

"Yeah, I'm sure you can take it," Sarah stammered, trying to pull herself together. "She probably went to the bathroom or upstairs. She didn't feel that great even this morning. Probably migraines..."

Sarah was amazed at herself, how easily and believably that had come out. When at the same time she felt like screaming or throwing something. She could feel Jack's eyes on her. Ignoring that, she slowly pushed back her chair and got up.

"Are you alright?" Jack asked, keeping his voice down.

"I need some air…" she said with a quick shake of her head. "I'll be back…"

She stumbled out behind Jack's chair and into the big lobby. She headed for the lounge area she had seen during the check-in. It was located at the far end of the lobby, somewhat hidden behind some giant plants. There were several cozy couches and coffee tables and dimmed lighting. The only other people there at the moment were a young man and woman sitting on a loveseat in the very back, totally immersed in each other.

Sarah stopped at the first couch and sank down on it.

That's when Jack caught up with her.

"Mind if I join you?" he asked and, without waiting for an answer, sat down on the seat across from her.

For a moment they just sat there. Sarah staring at the coffee table between them and Jack watching her.

"What did he tell you?" she finally asked without an introduction. The topic was clear enough.

Jack drew in a deep breath that he slowly released before he spoke. "He told me that he had, and I quote, *left her*. And that she was drinking and…" He paused for a moment to sort his thoughts. "…that she's sleeping around and somehow not quite all there. Sounded pretty grave. And knowing him – *and her* – I don't think he was exaggerating."

Sarah stared at him, waiting for him to continue.

"He didn't tell me a lot of details," Jack said, "but the bit he *did* say was enough for me to agree that it's good he got out of there…"

Silence.

Jack frowned. "Well, but you talked to him too, right? What impression did *you* get?"

Sarah's expression darkened. "I definitely didn't get as many details as you did," she said flatly, "but that's probably because we kind of got stuck on the question why he had gotten involved with that bitch in the first place."

Jack scratched his head. "Oh, okay. So, you chewed him out before he could get there…"

"Well, yeah. Poor Joe," Sarah grumbled.

"He told you about his hand, though, right?"

Sarah squinted. "What *about* his hand?"

"Well, sounds like it wasn't just some accident but *she* did it."

"What?" Sarah's eyes widened in disbelief. "Liz?"

"Yep. Just so you know what we're dealing with here," Jack said with a shrug. "I sure hope he doesn't run back to her now!"

He leaned forward in his seat and reached for a glass ball that was lying on the table for decoration. "But this changes things, of course," he admitted.

Sarah nodded a grim expression on her face. "God, this is such crap!" she moaned. "I was *so* glad this morning when he said he had left her! And now that! I don't even want to *imagine* him and her and a baby… That's the absolute worst case scenario as far as I'm concerned! "

"Well yeah, it's pretty drastic," Jack said and rolled the glass ball around in his hands. "We can always hope that it's not true," he said slowly, "but I guess if it *is* true and she wants to keep it, he won't be able to just wash his hands of her. Not that he's even the type to try that…"

Sarah slid down in the sofa until she could lean her head against the back. With a deep sigh she shook her head. "He's sooo stupid!"

Jack cocked his head. "Well, in the right moment even the smartest guy will fall for the *don't-worry-I'm-on-the-pill* assurance. *I* have. Just got lucky, I guess…" The apologetic grin that had started spreading across his face faded when he saw Sarah scowl.

"All I'm saying is that she may have tricked him," Jack hurried to say, "or it might have been an accident. It's crap either way."

"No kidding!" Sarah briefly closed her eyes and exhaled. Then she opened her eyes again and watched Jack pass the glass ball from one hand to the other.

"It just drives me crazy, though," she huffed. "Here he comes, with all that Liz chaos still looming over his head – and I don't care if he knew it or not – the first thing he does…" Something made her stop before she could say it.

Jack let out a little laugh. "Oh, is this still about Wednesday night?" he asked. "I don't really know *what* he did, but it definitely didn't sound like he was with Sun. I'm not even sure he was with *anyone*... or messing around for that matter..."

Sarah bit the corner of her lower lip. She really would have just loved to enlighten Jack that what Joe had done Wednesday night was way more idiotic and harmful than screwing Sun or whoever else. She really wished she could share this with Jack. Simply because he might be able to make her feel better. Somehow he always did. But she knew she needed to keep this to herself. Not because it would undoubtedly destroy Jack's faith in Joe's intelligence and integrity (she did not care about that) but because it would mean adding D to the picture. And she just couldn't see how that would benefit anyone. Having seen D get up from dinner, all color drained from her face, Sarah knew that D was at this very moment cursing herself and wishing she could turn back time. If D had any idea that anyone (even if only her closest friend) knew about the little secret of the last two nights, she would probably freak out. Therefore, Sarah decided, the thing to do, was to quickly try to forget this and not spread the information.

"Don't be so mad at him," Jack said. "He's got enough problems as it is..."

"I know that! But I'm still mad!" Sarah grumbled, her gaze locked with Jacks. "Thanks for the psychological support, though!"

Jack smiled. "Anytime you need me..."

Managing a weak smile herself, Sarah nodded. She knew he meant it. He had proved it often enough. All the times he had come over to the house when the Andy-problem had gotten bad. And afterwards when she had been crying and ranting. Jack and D had seen it all. And Jack had comforted her and cheered her up – and one time he had held her.

"Ready to go back?" Jack asked, rubbing his hands over his thighs.

"I guess..." With a little shrug Sarah rose from her seat.

Jack stepped around the coffee table up to her and put his hands on her upper arms. "Stop worrying, Sarah. He's grown up. You can't save him from anything..."

Caught in Jack's gaze, Sarah nodded, totally taken aback by the weird feeling that had just rushed through her. And the tingle she had felt when her eyes slipped to his mouth and she suddenly wondered what it would be like to kiss him. Jack? *Oh my!* Thank God he couldn't read her mind. He would be shocked.

Jack took his hands off her arms and nodded towards the lobby. "Okay, let's go back..." he said, his hand lightly against her back as if to make her move into the right direction. It wasn't an unusual touch between them. He'd done that a hundred times before. And still, this time it did feel different...

~~~

In the luxurious lobby bathroom, D was sitting on a closed toilet seat in one of the stalls, oblivious to the chatter outside, the flushing of toilets and the occasional howling of the jet-engine hand dryers.

She wasn't sure how she had made it here. It was all blurred from the moment she had realized who it was that Anja was talking to. And when Anja had put out the disastrous p-word, her mind had gone absolutely blank for a moment. And her throat had felt like a giant cotton ball was stuck in there, making it impossible to breathe or swallow.

Somehow a basic emergency survival program must have kicked in, however. She only remembered it through a haze, but somehow she had managed to get up and, one wouldn't believe it, move her feet. Walk straight. Make another frantic attempt at breathing. And succeed. Set one foot in front of the other, make it out of the dining room. Into the lobby... Half blind already with tears, she had stumbled through the bathroom door that someone else was holding open for her.

There had been a free stall towards the end, and she had fled inside. She had locked the door behind herself, closed the lid over the toilet and sunk down on it.

Breathing shakily, she tore off a piece of toilet paper, her hands anything but steady, and dabbed the corners of her eyes before any tears could flow over, mesh with her mascara and leave traces on her cheeks.

She tried to choke down the tears. She absolutely couldn't cry here! Everyone would notice. She couldn't have a breakdown. Not here, not now, not ever again – at least not about this guy!

She sat up straight, her hands flat on her knees, breathed in and out, in and out... She tried to concentrate on the grain of the painted wood of the door in front of her. The white tiles around the doorframe. With every breath the urge to cry seemed to subside. She felt herself getting calmer. And her brain booting up again.

She desperately needed to reprogram that brain. Delete everything her memory had recorded since Joe had driven her home. Put her world back in an upright position after it had literally been turned upside down since then and drowned in a tsunami three minutes ago.

She pressed the index and middle finger of her right hand against the spot between her eyebrows. She'd be alright. She needed to be alright! Rewind, rewind, rewind...

Thank God she had slept in her own bed last night!!! It had been so close. If *he* hadn't... Shit! She closed her eyes, swallowing hard, choking down another bout of tears. She tried to make those pictures go away. Joe in just his boxer shorts, the glass of milk in his hands, Joe pulling her into his hotel room this afternoon...

She gasped for air as the question crossed her mind: Did he already know it then? Was that why he had wanted to get her alone? To tell her about *this?*

Pressing the back of her hand against her mouth she closed her eyes. Calm down, calm down! She felt like screaming. Or smashing her own head against the tile wall for being such an idiot! Such an incredibly naive, stupid idiot.

Her throat was burning with the tears she was trying to keep from welling up. Breathe in, and out...

Outside a group of women must have just barged in. Talking loudly, giggling, slamming doors shut. Someone tried her door but then accepted that it was really locked.

It took another few minutes of intense struggle and breathing exercises to regain some balance. She glanced at her reflection in the shiny metal cover of the toilet paper holder and realized with incredible relief that – to the oblivious crowd – she would look alright. She would just claim she had had a spell of migraine. It would be okay.

Still feeling somewhat shaky, she finally got up. Took another deep breath. Flushed the toilet as an alibi and unlocked her door.

As she slowly walked back to the table, she braced herself for whatever she would find. Fortunately it didn't seem like anyone had noticed her absence much.

Seeing Joe gone was both a great relief and a nauseating shock. She tried not to let it get to her. Maybe he was already on his way to be with his pregnant girlfriend. He should! And they should get married soon...

~~~

Joe had walked out of the hotel and followed a sign towards the lakeside promenade. His mind was racing. He felt sick to his stomach as the bizarre situation at the dinner table kept flashing through his head again and again. He had caught a glimpse at Danny right before she had

337

gotten up. She had had that look on her face that he would never forget. Her expression had, within not even two seconds, gone through the emotional stages of disbelief, horror, shock, disgust, fury, confusion all the way to a strange kind of determination. And then she had gotten up and left.

The lakeside promenade was taking him along the lake behind the side of the hotel that was facing east. There weren't many people out walking anymore now that it was getting dark. Almost everyone was probably either at home by now or having dinner in the hotel. There were lamps along the path every thirty meters, with bugs and moths buzzing around them. Up ahead, Joe spotted a boathouse and across the path from it a small hill with a few benches. He decided to walk up there. It seemed like a good place to be alone.

He reached the benches two minutes later. Through a haze he took in the view from up here for a moment. The lake lay very still, like a big black sheet of glass. Around it he could see the outline of the mountains and at their base, tucked between the mountainside and the shore of the lake, the glittering lights of the two little lakeside towns. Below him a little to the right the hotel sat on its peninsula, many of the windows illuminated. He thought he could see the big window front of the dining room with people still enjoying their dinners. Towards the tip of the peninsula, there was a brightly lit glass construction that reminded him of a gazebo. Probably part of the spa area. In fact, there seemed to be people in bathing suits in there and a bunch of lounge chairs arranged against the rounded glass façade.

Reminding himself that he wasn't here to enjoy the view, Joe turned to the benches behind him and sat down on the middle one. He sucked in a shaky breath. Crap! This really just couldn't be happening! He leaned forward, his elbows resting on his knees and rubbed his eyes. Maybe, if he just rubbed them hard enough, he would wake up from this freaking nightmare.

He should have known that Liz would come up with something. Something mean. Something sick… He felt the anger get the upper hand. Sliding his left hand up through his hair, he dug his fingers into his skull until it hurt and let out a growl that felt rough against his throat.

Finally he straightened up, his hands on his lap. He needed to pull himself together! This was just Liz! He thought he had learned to control himself in the three years with her, but in situations like this he would have liked to smash her face. He took another deep breath, brushed his hair out of his face and looked at the phone that he held clasped between the thumb and index finger of his braced hand. Time to face the unavoidable!

He turned the phone on. There were five more unanswered calls than yesterday afternoon. He should have called her back then. He should have known… What devilish idea to call one of his friends and put that kind of news out in front of everyone!

He took another deep breath and pressed the button to return the call. It rang twice then she picked it up.

"Hello?" she always answered her phone as if she didn't see on the display who was calling. He squeezed the phone hard enough that he was afraid it would crack. It didn't.

"Joe?" she asked sweetly like she wasn't entirely sure.

He didn't say anything.

"Well, Honey," she said delightedly. "That was quick!" She giggled.

"You must have really lost it completely…" he started, the suppressed anger surfacing.

"You didn't pick up your phone," she said as if that explained or justified it all. "And I needed to get ahold of you."

"And that justifies calling innocent bystanders like Anja and telling her stuff like that?" he tried to keep his voice down.

She laughed. "Well," she said, "since I couldn't reach you."

"I didn't want to talk to you…" he retorted sharply, "and you pretty well know why."

She clicked her tongue in this annoying *too-bad-for-you* kind of way.

"You better change your attitude, though, Honey," she told him sweetly. "Because I'm pregnant."

Joe closed his eyes and sucked in a breath.

"You have to come back to me…" she said like a mother talking to a kid that just didn't get it.

"No, I don't," he corrected. "And I *won't*, Liz." He finally managed to keep his voice under control. Sounded almost calm even though he absolutely didn't feel like it. "It's over. How many times do I have to tell you until you understand… – I'm *not* coming back."

There was a moment in which he thought he could hear her catch her breath. Then, she started to cry.

His jaws tightly locked, he stared down towards the water.

"You can't do that!" she finally screamed when, despite of her

339

sobbing, he didn't say anything

"Cut it out, Liz!" he growled.

On the other end of the line he could hear glass shatter. She must have dropped something on the floor. He could just picture it. He had seen it often enough.

"I'm pregnant!" she hissed.

"Oh, really?" he said through clenched teeth. It had just now occurred to him that it might not even be true.

"It's true!" she screamed, and he held the phone away from his ear.

"Well, maybe it is," he said dryly, "but I'm pretty sure it's not from me. You know as well as I that since your little escapade with Mr. fucking Bob Sorelli we've had a layer of rubber between us!" He let out a bitter little laugh. "So, if you're really pregnant, maybe you should talk to Bob or Phil...or Eric? Help me out here, was there anyone else? Do you even know?"

"You asshole!" she screamed.

"There you go," Joe said. "Now we're talking…"

She started sobbing again. "You need to come back," she cried, suddenly sounding like a begging little child, whose mother had left. "We need to talk…"

"Talking won't help," Joe said darkly. "It never has…"

She was sobbing uncontrollably now.

"Liz, please... – I'm miles away and honestly I think that is a good thing. You've got some friends. Talk to them. Tell them what an asshole I am. That's fine. Just get a grip on it, please. It just can't be me!"

The sobbing stopped for a moment and there was this freaky little laugh. Mixed with it, Joe thought he heard another, somewhat familiar noise that he couldn't quite place right away. It sounded like glass clicking against glass. He squinted. A bottle against a glass, and then the pouring of a liquid.

"Are you drinking?" he blasted. This was just unreal!

She snorted. "Well, what do you expect...?"

"Right... what do I expect!?!" Joe closed his eyes for a moment and sucked in a shallow breath.

It was quiet on the other end now, and he could just picture her taking a big sip out of that glass.

"You know, Liz," he just couldn't stop himself. "If you really *are* pregnant and you're thinking of keeping it, you should probably stop

340

drinking!"

Suddenly she laughed; another shrill, freaky laugh that just sent shivers down his spine. He sat there, biting down on his lip, his braced hand pressed against his thigh as he tried not to lose it here.

"You know what?" he heard her say, and she suddenly sounded strangely calm again. "I may just want to mix this glass of whiskey, my second one, by the way, with some of the great pills you left here…"

Click.

She had hung up.

Joe let the hand that was still clamped around the phone sink into his lap. He swallowed, his whole body slightly shaking now. He tried to pull himself together, concentrate on his surroundings. The air was cool now. It had gotten dark and there was a soft breeze.

He stared out at the lake. God, he felt as if three big guys had just beaten him up.

He forced himself to consciously take in the view he had in front of him. Under normal circumstances this would have been the perfect night and the perfect location.

He tried to decide how serious Liz's threat with the pills had been. Could he just ignore it? He wished! That girl was a nightmare come true! He ground his teeth in frustration. No, as much as he wanted to, he *couldn't* just ignore a thing like that! He couldn't risk it.

He touched the screen of his phone, opening the contacts. He scrolled down. For a moment he hesitated. Then he tapped on the number he was looking for and, his hand still not quite steady, put the phone back against his ear. It rang three times and then Steve picked it up.

"Joe? Hi! How are doing?" Steve sounded surprised.

"Not so good actually," Joe admitted. "I'm really sorry to call you on a Saturday night but… there's kind of a problem."

"We were just watching TV," Steve said. "What's up? *What* kind of problem?"

"Well… – I'm here at a hotel with some friends and," Joe huffed out a humorless little laugh because this was just so unreal. "Liz just called one of my friends here..."

"Oh crap…" Steve said, apparently well aware that that could only be a bad thing.

"Yeah, you can say that," Joe agreed darkly. "She called this friend, whom she barely even knows and told *her* to tell *me* that she's pregnant."

341

He heard Steve gasp for air. "You're kidding!?!"

"Yeah, I wish!"

"God, she's so screwed up…" Steve sighed. "She told that to your friend?"

"Well, yeah, because – and I quote – she couldn't reach me. I have to admit I had my phone turned off…"

"Do you think it's true?"

"What? That she's pregnant? I don't know. Maybe, maybe not. Only, that it can't really be from me…"

There was silence on the other end, with Steve obviously trying to decide how to respond to this.

Joe drew in a deep breath. "I'm really sorry to even bother you with this – and I definitely don't want to drag you into the question as to who might have gotten her pregnant. It's just… Well, she wants me to come back, of course – don't ask me why! – and I told her that I wouldn't and that she should stop drinking – because seems like she's downing some whiskey as we're speaking…" He paused for a moment. "She just hung up on me a moment ago, threatening to mix the whiskey with some painkillers I got for my hand – some really potent stuff…"

"Shit!" Steve exhaled.

"Yeah…"

"It's probably just another one of her stunts," Steve contemplated, "but what do we know…"

"That's just it," Joe said uncomfortably. "I mean, she's already drunk and she's mad as hell. So, I don't know. I wouldn't really rule out anything."

On the other end, Steve drew in a deep breath. "Do you want me to go over there?"

"Could you?" Joe asked. "I hate to do this to you, but the only other thing I can think of is calling the police. Because I'm four hours away."

"Even if you were here, Joe, I don't think it would be such a good idea if you went near her. This whole thing seems a little too explosive right now."

"I know…"

"I'll take care of it, don't worry," Steve assured him. "Maybe I can just sort it out over the phone and if not, I'll go over there."

"Thanks, Steve… – I'm really sorry!"

"Well, it's not really your fault that my sister seems to be a total wacko!" Steve said dryly.

"Yeah, well…" Joe didn't quite know what to say. He was just glad Steve saw it that way.

"I'll send you a message later," Steve said.

"Okay. I'll check my phone in about an hour. But I'll turn it off right now because if she calls again… My talking to her just makes it worse!"

"I understand," Steve said. "Don't worry. It'll be fine."

After Steve had hung up, Joe stayed on the bench for a few more minutes. Then he got up and walked back to the hotel.

# As if she had planned it...

When Joe returned to the dining room, their table was deserted. The others had obviously moved to the other room with the projector that Rick had talked about earlier.

Joe went to the reception and asked for directions. They told him to go over to the other building and up the stairs.

As he walked over there, he knew that he wouldn't be able to concentrate on any pictures or conversations at the moment. Still, he didn't want to be by himself either. Maybe he could just sit there and zone out.

He was so deep in thought that he first walked by the room he was looking for and only realized it when he had reached the end of the corridor. He turned around and walked back. He quietly opened the door and snuck in.

The room was dimly lit. It had a big screen in the front. They had hooked a laptop up to the projector and were watching some film that Rick or Jack must have put together from different trips they had taken. Great! Joe clenched his jaw. That was *exactly* what he had still needed! Memories of a wonderful past that he had totally screwed up.

Some of the heads turned when he came in. Rick gave him a sympathetic smile, Gerry nodded at him with an *I'm-sorry-buddy* look.

Joe couldn't help scanning the room for D. He spotted her over at the opposite side of the room in the very front – in the seat that was the furthest away from the door.

She was staring at the screen with a frozen expression. Had it not been for this expression, he might have thought she hadn't noticed him coming in. But she had noticed. Because, slowly now, she turned around and met his eyes across the room. She looked straight at him with a provokingly cold narrow-eyed look. Joe shrugged and, with a slightly exasperated shake of his head, he looked away. He felt drained. Absolutely drained. As if the maximum amount of drama that he could possibly process in one day had been reached and everything beyond that just overflowed. So, no matter what kind of looks Danny decided to shoot him here, it just didn't get to him anymore.

Right in front of where he was standing, Sarah had just turned around and glanced at him with a mix of bewilderment and real concern. And Jack, who was sitting next to her, nodded towards the empty chair behind them. Joe sat down on it and leaned back. Man, he felt so numb.

Shooting him a worried look over her shoulder, Sarah reached back with her hand and gave his knee a somewhat clumsy, encouraging pat. He managed a forced little smile, placed his hand on hers and gave it a gentle squeeze in return.

The film showing on the screen now had probably been taken five years or so ago – by someone with quite an unsteady hand. Joe was starting to feel dizzy just trying to get into it. He remembered some of that short camping trip to a mosquito-infested area at a little lake. Not that he really wanted to remember it.

After a few minutes, the film was over and Rick was fiddling with the computer in the dark, probably about to start some other film or slide show. Joe decided to take this opportunity to leave.

He leaned forward to Sarah. "I'm going upstairs," he whispered and rose from his chair. When Sarah shot him a worried look over her shoulder, he gave her a crooked smile that was meant to assure her that he was okay. Then he snuck out of the room.

Sarah caught up with him in the hallway that connected the conference wing to the other building.

"Joe! Wait!"

He stopped, giving her a weary look. "Just go back in there, Sarah, okay?"

"Like I can still concentrate on that? And like you can go to sleep now?"

Looking back at her, he shrugged. Of course she was right. There was no way he could sleep. But that hadn't been the point anyway. He had just wanted to get away.

"We could go and have a drink together," Sarah suggested, giving him an insecure smile. "Come on..."

Defensively he raised his hands. "Just let me be, Sarah, please... I'd rather be alone. I'm not good company right now."

"That's fine," Sarah said softly, patting his upper arm. "You don't have to be good company! But I think you definitely shouldn't be by yourself brooding..."

"Yeah, whatever!" he grumbled while heading down the corridor. "Let's go and have a drink then...!"

Relieved, Sarah followed him.

In silence they walked over to the bar.

Joe picked a small table in a corner with no one else around.

The waiter came to take their order.

Joe shrugged at Sarah. "Order anything," he said. "I really don't care what I have..."

Sarah ordered two cocktails that she knew they both liked.

"I can't believe she did that..." she finally said.

Joe let out bitter laugh. "Neither can I. But I guess I shouldn't be surprised by anything she does anymore. She..." he paused when the waiter brought the drinks. He took a sip and then picked up the orange slice to chew on it.

"Did you call her?" Sarah asked over the rim of her glass.

"Yep! Probably made it worse. But I really don't want to talk about this now." He leaned back, his head resting against the wall behind him.

Sarah stirred her drink with the straw. "What are you going to do? I mean, if she's really pregnant?"

"I don't care if she's pregnant or not," he said sharply.

Sarah gave him a baffled look. Not that she wanted him to make up with Liz, but still... He didn't care?

"Don't look at me like I'm some sort of monster," Joe growled. "I don't care because it can't be from me, that's all."

"You're sure about that?"

"Yesss!"

"How come?"

Joe let out a humorless little laugh. "Are you seriously asking me that? Aren't you the one who freaks out just imagining her Teddy bear possibly having some kind of sex life...?"

Sarah blinked at him with irritation. "I'll get over it," she assured him.

"Okay," he shrugged. "Well, you know, Sarah," his tone resembled that of a mother talking to a little child. "There are those rubber things, okay... Now don't put your hands over your ears because that's not my favorite topic either, but since you insist on knowing..." He paused for a moment. "Anyway, no sex with Liz without those rubber things. You understand? In the last – let's see – eight months or so. I'll spare you the details why. Let's just say it was *my* choice and for *my* protection."

Sarah nodded warily. That had already been more than she ever wanted to hear on that kind of subject. She took another quick sip of her drink to hide how awkward she felt about this conversation. She was starting to feel the alcohol. Maybe a good thing in this situation.

She looked at Joe, who was playing with his glass, turning it around on the table, shifting it between the lines on the table's surface. He had hardly touched his drink.

"I really don't understand how she got Anja's new number, though," Sarah said. "Anja said it just changed two months ago. And that *timing!*"

Joe looked up at her and nodded grimly. "Yeah, that timing... Couldn't have been more perfect, could it? Calling at a time where she got *everyone's* undivided attention..."

"Yeah, it's almost like she had planned it, sitting at home and thinking like..." Sarah did a nasty imitation of Liz. "Like *'let's see, when will it have the worst impact? How could I do the most damage?'*"

Joe nodded tiredly and took a sip through his straw. His eyes strayed off towards the bartender and he just stared into space for a moment, reflecting on what Sarah had said. Then his eyes suddenly widened and he sucked in an abrupt breath. "Crap!" he hissed. He almost knocked over his drink as he straightened up in his seat, looking a shade paler than before.

Sarah stared at him. "What's wrong *now?*"

Joe blew out some air with his lower lip sticking out. Finally he shook his head. "I need to go back to the house," he said, his voice suddenly loaded with urgency.

"Why? What's wrong?" Sarah didn't get it.

"I just realized something *really* scary," Joe said slowly. "Maybe she *did* actually plan it. And I think I may even know how. The timing is just too perfect to be a pure coincidence!"

Sarah frowned. "What?"

"Remember that list that you e-mailed me a while ago, the one Rick made? Had names, telephone numbers and a draft of the program for the weekend..."

Sarah's eyes widened as it dawned on her what he was getting at. "God... she's such a..."

"That's the list she's been working off, I bet," Joe said with a fake little smile.

Sarah shook her head, still in awe.

"But it's not like I had this list lying around somewhere," he said, obviously still in the process of working through it himself. "I never even printed it out. For obvious reasons."

"How did she get it then?" Sarah frowned.

He did the fake little smile thing again and made a swirling movement of his hand, as if he was going to introduce something grand and lovely. "Yeah, how did she get it?" His expression turned grave again. "Here's the real problem: the only place where I've got that list, is in my e-mail account. I just had to look for it myself yesterday to... well, to look for a number." He swallowed. He would probably not need that number ever again. "Anyways, if she's got the list, that means she's been in my e-mail account."

Sarah raised her eyebrows. "Okay... So she's reading your e-mails," she concluded darkly.

"I guess," he shrugged. "The password is not all that challenging. And the e-mails I get really aren't all *that* exciting. At least I thought so."

"Okay," Sarah said again. "Guess she found an interesting one after all... Why do you want to go home though? The damage is already done anyway. And that password... well, you can probably change that on your phone too, can't you?"

He nodded. "Yeah, sure! I don't care about that e-mail account, though. It's more that... well, if she took the effort to get into the e-mail account and pull off what we've just witnessed, she's up to no good. And the talk on the phone I had with her is not exactly going to appease her, trust me," he drew in a deep breath before he continued. "My problem is that I've got a list saved on the computer that's in the flat with her. A list with *all* my passwords. Passwords for online banking, savings account, eBay, Amazon, some other online things, all with my credit card saved as payment type... You name it..."

"Crap!" Sarah was starting to see the big picture.

"Exactly!" Joe said. "That could be real crap! It doesn't have to be. I mean, I'm not even sure if she ever turns that computer on anymore. She's got her laptop and an IPad. But still, it's there and if she wanted to find something else to hurt me with, she might start looking there as well. And if she comes across that list before I have a chance to change all those passwords, I'll be screwed." He paused for a moment. "Maybe it's far-fetched, I don't know. And the file name of that list is not flashing red *Passwords*. I did have the brains to give it some deceiving title. But still. I need to change those passwords and I'd rather not lose any time. I can't do it from here, though. I need to go home and get on my laptop. I have a copy of that password list saved there as well. Then I can just work off that list and change everything. You get me?"

Sarah nodded darkly. "Yeah, I think so…" She would have liked to tell him he was overreacting, but there was a good chance he wasn't.

Joe pushed his drink over to her. "Guess you'll have to drink the rest of that. I better not. And can you tell Jack?"

"Sure, I'll tell him," Sarah said as she watched him get up. "Are you coming back here then? Tomorrow?"

He thought about it for a moment. Then he shook his head. "I kind of doubt it," he said slowly. "I honestly don't think I can take any more of this happy get-together. Not with everything that's going on with Liz…"

"Yeah, I understand," Sarah said, rolling her straw between her fingers. "I'm sure I can drive back with…" she fell silent when she saw his expression harden. It made her swallow D's name.

Avoiding her gaze, he stepped out from behind the table.

"Joe…" Sarah said.

Leaning his side against the table he looked down at her, a cautious look on his face. "What?" he asked darkly. And she just knew he was already guessing what she was going to say.

She drew in a deep breath. "Do you want me to talk to… Should I say anything to D?"

He let out a bitter laugh. "Are you kidding me? No, please don't! You should have seen the look she gave me in there… She's *so* pissed at me."

"Okay." Sarah nodded, angry at herself for even bringing it up.

Joe's expression softened a bit. "It's not just that," he said sounding tired. "I just don't think I've got the energy to deal with that right now. Everything is just too screwed up. I can't handle one girl who's plain crazy and one that will never forgive me for running off with the crazy one." There was a little humorless laugh.

"Yeah, I see your point," Sarah said. She got up and gave him a spontaneous hug. "Drive safely, okay and send me a message when you get there."

Patting her back, he pulled out of her embrace. "I will."

~~~

D heard the door of the conference door open and close. From the corner of her eye she saw Sarah come back alone and sit down next to Jack. They were sticking their heads together, briefly whispering.

D tried to concentrate on the pictures. But instead her mind kept spinning around that exchange of looks she had had with Joe twenty minutes earlier. Her mouth went dry as she remembered it. She had given him that *Go-to-hell* look and he had countered it with his best *whatever* shrug. She tried to tell herself that he had just gone up to his room and to bed. But the nauseating feeling in her stomach told her that he had left the hotel.

# Dark Road Home

Joe threw his bag into the trunk and the small backpack on the backseat and then got on his way. He had only been gone two minutes when he realized that he had left his glasses in the backpack. How confused was he already that he didn't even remember the most basic things? He would have to pull over as soon as there was a chance and put the glasses on. His vision without them wasn't too bad, only things at a distance were a bit blurry, but with twenty kilometers of narrow, winding road ahead of him, he better make sure he had both a clear head and good vision. That road might make for a fun ride in daylight, but in the dark it was really tricky to navigate. And it almost looked like there was some fog farther ahead too. Great! That was just what he needed!

He slowed down. To a speed that he would normally call Grandma-speed. Under the given conditions it seemed like the only safe thing to do.

The car plunged through a patch of fog and another one and then out into the clear night again.

He was still keeping his eyes open for a place to pull over, when suddenly somewhere up ahead a big shadow appeared out of nowhere. He hit the brake, his backpack flying from the backseat against the back of the passenger seat. And he saw the silhouette of the deer standing in the middle of the road right ahead. The outline of this obstacle was becoming clearer and clearer the closer he got. It was big, with impressive antlers and eyes that were staring right at him – petrified. It was one of these moments that just drag on like in slow motion. And you see it coming and there's nothing you can do. The car was still moving towards the deer, the brake pedal pushed all the way down, tires screeching, his hands almost crushing the steering wheel as he tried to get the car as far to the right as he could without going over the edge. And he was still sliding towards that massive body...

Finally the car came to a halt. Only a fraction of a second before the expected moment of impact. He found himself literally eye to eye with the animal which was still staring back at him with something resembling curiosity. Then, with an almost dismissive shake of its head, it took a quick jump across the road and up the steep, sloped mountainside straight into the forest. And it was gone.

Sinking back into his seat, Joe was panting. With trembling fingers he pushed the button to turn on the hazard lights. His heart was racing. That had been so close!!! His mind had already been jumping back and forth between imagining the impact upon hitting that thing, and picturing diving off the road towards the lake...

Thank God nothing had happened! He almost couldn't believe it.

His hands were still trembling when he reached back for his backpack, unzipped it and fished out the case with his glasses. He put them on and took a few deep breaths. Then he steered the car from the narrow shoulder back onto the road, turned the hazard lights off and continued his drive at an even slower speed than previously.

It took him another twenty minutes on the curvy road, with thick fog in places, until he finally reached the main road to the highway. About that same time, the fog lifted.

Once he reached the highway, the rest of the drive would have been uneventful and easy, had it not been for the heavy fatigue that was coming over him, making it hard to keep his eyes open.

He tried to focus on staying awake, but after he had jerked up for the second time after almost nodding off, he turned on the radio. On high volume... He wasn't really in the mood to listen to music, but he realized that he might need it to keep him awake. The trick was finding a radio station that he could listen to. (If there was one thing he definitely didn't want to hear right now, it was love songs.) He pushed the tuning button a few times. There was Classical, but just three seconds of that would put him to sleep for good. There was Hip hop... Eeww! He kept pushing the tuning button until a Jazz station came on. He didn't exactly like Jazz but decided to listen to it anyway. At least it would keep him awake without being emotionally charged or sleep-inducing or flat-out annoying.

~~~

D had sat through the second round of pictures, experiencing everything through a thick haze.

Thankfully, everyone who had contributed photographic material seemed to have – consciously or not – avoided including anything that would show Joe and her in any kind of constellation that would indicate romantic involvement. Maybe it wasn't so much that they had avoided it, but more that there simply wasn't a lot of these kinds of photos outside her own collections and maybe Sarah's. Joe had always been reluctant to display any kind of affection with an audience present or with a camera pointed at him.

With one picture after the other flaring up and then fading into the next, D had started to feel the full effect of what had happened over dinner. It felt like a giant bruise somewhere inside that hurt with every breath she took. A pain that surely wasn't going to kill her, but that was going to take a while to ease.

Finally the picture show ended and there was a lot of laughter about some especially funny photos of Jack and Carrey that had come on towards the end – and a bit of teasing how apparently no one had dared to submit the really embarrassing shots of Rick and Tony pulling down their pants on New Year's five years ago… When Sun insisted that she was sure she had sent at least one of these shots to Rick, everyone burst out laughing and Rick was accused of censorship – an accusation he rejected adamantly.

Jack got up and turned the light back on.

"I'm going to bed," Carrey proclaimed while stretching her arms into the air. "I'm sooo tired."

"Yeah, me too," Kim had actually nodded off during the last half an hour and was blinking sleepily.

"That was great," Tony said and gave Kim's back a rub. "I think I'll call it a night too." He got up and then pulled Kim up as well.

"Yeah, aren't you some wimps!" Rick laughed, fiddling with the computer, unhooking it from the projector. "Once the clock strikes eleven, they drop like flies, huh? I'm going to go to the bar and have a drink…" He looked around. "In case anyone wants to join me."

D saw Gerry and Anja exchange looks and whisper to each other, the body language indicating that Anja wanted to go to bed but encouraged Gerry to go ahead and keep Rick company.

When D looked across the room to Sarah and Jack, Sarah suddenly glanced over at her, giving her a somewhat weird look. It was that look that made D spontaneously decide that, whatever Sarah was going to do about the bar-or-bed decision, she was going to do the exact opposite. Because she simply couldn't imagine how awkward going upstairs and being alone with Sarah right now would be. When both of their heads were buzzing with everything that had happened over dinner, while at the same time they would both be struggling to keep it inside because they simply couldn't talk about it. At least not to each other… It would just be

353

horrible. And the worst part of it, D realized, was that Sarah might actually suspect her of enjoying that Joe was in trouble. With all the hostility she had expressed a few days ago when Sarah had first told her that he was coming, it wasn't far-fetched that Sarah might think that...

Across the room, Sarah had just turned to Jack beside her. He was giving her a *Come-on* kind of look, and for a moment Sarah seemed to consider it, but then she shook her head and got up.

"I'm going to bed too," she announced tiredly.

D drew in a deep breath. That was it then. She would have to go to the bar and sip a drink until there was a good chance that Sarah was either asleep or would pretend to be asleep.

"I'll join you," she heard herself say in Rick's direction.

"I will too," Sun called over from the other side.

"And Gerry is too," Anja said, giving Gerry a smile that he countered with a shrug and a grin.

Rick grinned contently. "Great!" He glanced at Jack. "What about you? You coming?"

Jack still looked as if he weren't sure. Finally, he nodded. "Yeah, I'm just going to go upstairs and change my shirt. Got some sauce on it..." he pointed to a small stain on his chest.

"Are you serious?" Rick laughed. "No one will care."

~~~

Alone in the elevator with Jack, Sarah glanced up.

"You're not seriously just going upstairs to change your shirt, are you?" she asked.

He shook his head, his eyes locked with hers. "No, not really," he admitted. "I kind of wanted to have a quick word with you."

"Yeah, me too, actually," she said. "It's hard to tell you anything with everyone around." She knew that her very, very short whispered summary in the conference room had probably left him more confused than enlightened. After all, she had only told him that Joe had left for Deens because he desperately needed to take care of some stuff on his computer.

"Do you feel any better after you talked to him?" Jack asked.

"A bit." Sarah managed a weak smile. "Since he assured me that I won't be the auntie of some kid that has his smile and Liz's piercing blue eyes, I *do* actually feel better."

"So, he's sure about that, huh?" Jack sounded pleasantly surprised.

They had reached the sixth floor and the elevator doors slid open.

"Sounds like it," Sarah said as she stepped out into the hallway.

"Well, that's at least something," Jack said as they walked down the corridor.

"And it sounds like he thinks she got into his e-mail account and found the document with the schedule for this weekend and the phone numbers. You know, the one Rick had made. I forwarded that to Joe…"

Jack leaned against the wall next to the door to his room, his eyebrows raised. "Hence the perfect timing," he said darkly.

Sarah nodded and dropped her gaze to the floor. That carpet had quite a pattern.

"Do we have to worry about D?" Jack suddenly asked.

Sarah glanced up at him, sucking in a quick breath. What did he know?

"About D?" she asked as innocently as she could. "Why?"

"Well, you covered for her nicely when she walked out during dinner," Jack said with a smile. "But we both know she was perfectly fine when we got here this afternoon, no trace of any medical condition. I would say that that call *really* got to her…"

Sarah stared back at him.

Jack held her gaze and shrugged. "I guess no matter how much you're over someone," he contemplated, "getting that kind of thing served for dinner would still be hard to digest."

"Yeah – sure," Sarah agreed, relieved that obviously Jack was just worried in general.

"You should probably talk to her," Jack said, "make sure she's alright."

Shaking her head, Sarah raised her hands defensively. "No, I don't think that's a good idea."

"Why's that?" Jack seemed confused.

"Because we can't talk about my brother… Never could. Never did. Probably never will."

"What?" Jack frowned at her. "You're kidding, right?"

"No. Not kidding. Didn't you know that?"

Jack shook his head. "No. I thought you two talked about everything."

"Yeah, everything but Joe," Sarah said. "It's just… the constellation, I guess. We just *can't* talk about him. It's just too awkward. Even when they were still together…"

Jack swayed his head from side to side, obviously thinking about it. "Guess it does make some sense," he finally admitted.

355

Sarah nodded. "That's also why telling D that he was going to be here this weekend was a bit of a problem in itself."

"Oh, is that why you waited for weeks?" There was a teasing tone in Jack's voice now.

"Yes, that's exactly why!" Sarah retorted.

"Okay…" Jack still seemed to ponder the issue. "But you did talk… well, after he and Liz… After my party."

"Yeah, well, it was kind of unavoidable then. But even then it was mainly *me* talking. *She* didn't say a whole lot. If you hadn't already given me a heads-up, I'd probably still be tapping in the dark as to what exactly he had done and why they suddenly weren't together anymore. She never even told me *what* exactly she saw in your basement. I mean, not that I don't have a vivid enough imagination, but…"

"Right," Jack agreed. "And it's not like we really need to know this in any more detail. And by the way, that's the one thing *he* and *I* have never talked about and hopefully never will."

# Safety Measures and a Bad Night

When Joe reached the house around eleven-thirty, he was very relieved that the drive was finally over – safely. He felt exhausted and the Jazz music was starting to really get on his nerves.

As he carried his stuff in and closed the door behind him, he realized how weird it felt to be here all by himself.

Trying not to let the feeling get to him, he walked into the kitchen and, perched on the table, turned his phone on. There was a text message from Steve.

> *She's okay. Mad and irrational but not suicidal.*
>
> *Didn't say anything about being pregnant.*
>
> *Steve*

Joe typed,

> *Thanks!*

Then he sent Sarah a quick message:

> *Drove like a grandma. ;)*
>
> *Just got here.*
>
> *Joe*

After he had turned the phone back off, he went to the fridge, made himself a sandwich and poured a glass of milk. Then he walked upstairs to his room.

Sitting on his bed, munching on his sandwich, he started the laptop. By the time it had booted up, he was almost done eating. He quickly finished his sandwich and his milk, then grabbed the mouse and got to work.

The file with the passwords was named *Car parts*. Liz might not even open it if she came across it on the home computer, but he didn't want to rely on it. Especially after she had just proved what she was capable of given the opportunity. He huffed out a sharp breath and shook his head as the scene at the dinner table replayed in his head yet again. It still made him dizzy just to think about it.

Trying to focus on the essentials now, he scrolled through the list on the screen. There were about fifteen passwords and connected usernames listed alongside the accounts they applied to. He would have to change them all.

First he opened the website that lead to his online bank accounts. These were really his main concern. If Liz got into his bank accounts, who knew what sick ideas she would come up with.

He checked the balances. Everything looked okay. Thank God! He went into the area with the personal data and made the necessary changes. Afterwards he adapted his list accordingly before moving on to the next site.

During the following half an hour he changed the passwords of every online service on his list. His savings account, the site for his credit card statements, Frequent Flyer account, Amazon, eBay, Dropbox...

He also made sure that no orders had recently been placed with the online retailers that would be charged to his credit card. Fortunately there was nothing suspicious.

About ready to shut down the computer, he remembered the e-mail account. He should change that too. Not that the damage hadn't already been done, but he still needed to make sure that Liz wouldn't be able to get into the account ever again.

It took half a minute to change that password. And since he had the account open already, he decided to quickly check the e-mails as well.

There were two unread ones. One from Steve just saying *Thanks* for the presentation he had forwarded.

The second e-mail was from a customer. Joe forwarded that one to Steve to take care of.

Suddenly he noticed that between these two mails there was actually another one. Strangely enough, that one showed up as read, even though he couldn't remember ever seeing it, let alone opening it.

One look at the sender and he knew for sure that it hadn't been there last time he checked. It came from Danielle123@...

Danny. The e-mail had been sent today just before noon.

Titled *Robert's link*. The e-mail was short:

*Joe,*
*here's the link to Robert's website.*
*D*

Staring at the letters on the screen, Joe pressed his lips together. Liz had obviously opened this – and then either forgotten to switch the status back to *unread* or simply not bothered to. His throat feeling very tight, he leaned his head back against the wall. No doubt now that Liz had been in his e-mail account...

He suddenly felt like smashing something! This was just... Grrr! His eyes shifted down to the screen again where the e-mail was still open. He swallowed. It suddenly seemed like something incredibly precious. Like the sole remaining proof of something probably lost forever. She had sent that when they had still been talking and he had been... happy? Well, he could frame that e-mail because there wouldn't be any more to come!

He hated Liz! He could feel all his anger and frustration balled up in the pit of his stomach like a rough, big, heavy stone. There was a good chance that this very e-mail had set it all off. Liz would have been just absolutely furious to see it. And the very least she would have done, was scroll down further to see if there was either any more of that or anything else she could hurt him with. That's when she had probably come across the schedule for the weekend and the list with all the telephone numbers.

Thinking about it now, he was almost surprised that Liz had called *Anja* and not Danny. She could have. The number was on the list. But she had probably realized that, if she called Danny, she would undoubtedly get cut off by Danny hanging up on her long before she could get the delightful news out. No, calling Anja had been a much smarter move.

Scrolling down through his e-mails again, Joe made an effort to see them through the sick eyes of Liz. Was there anything else that could be dangerous?

When, even after going through the list of e-mails from the last two months, he couldn't find anything dangerous, he clicked on D's message again and stared at it for a while longer. Wishing he could turn back time. Back to the point when this had been sent. It made him sick to think about it! Could have been... Finally he closed the e-mail.

He was about to sign out of his e-mail account when he suddenly noticed the little arrow that was next to Danny's message. He squinted. What the hell? Had Liz sent a response? His hand trembling, he clicked on the sent folder, expecting the worst. But there was no message to Danny. There was one to Liz's own e-mail address, though. She had forwarded Danny's message to herself? Why would she do that? Still pondering the significance of his latest, doubtlessly disturbing discovery, Joe shut down the computer and set it on the bedside table.

He felt beat. And exhausted. And maybe even still a bit shocked at what had happened. He better try to get some sleep. Maybe tomorrow things would look a bit less bleak. One could always hope. Only that he didn't quite believe it.

Sitting on the edge of the bed, he unbuttoned his shirt and slipped out of his jeans. He didn't bother to brush his teeth. It really didn't matter tonight.

~~~

D was playing with the little umbrella that had come as a decoration with her drink. Her second drink. She never had two drinks. Because even after just one, she usually felt the alcohol. Tonight was no exception in that respect. She *had* felt the alcohol (clearly) even before the first glass had been empty. But then she had ordered another one. Because she had suddenly started to feel so nice and cozy – and numb. She was sitting in this comfortable chair, everyone around her was chattering, sometimes saying something funny that even got through to her and would make her giggle. Alcohol normally just made her tired, not relaxed and giggly. Today it did. She was actually enjoying it.

When she had first decided to come along to the bar, mainly to avoid being alone upstairs with Sarah, she hadn't expected to stay long. Because it seemed only too predictable that sooner or later a discussion about the dinner-incident would start, and she knew that she wouldn't be able to sit through that.

But then, right as they had sat down, Jack had returned (in a new shirt) and had laid out the rules for their bar visit, namely that he didn't want to hear anything about the dinner interruption anymore because it would really spoil the rest of his evening. Everyone had agreed.

So far, the conversation had gone from praise for the picture show, to the question of what to do tomorrow (take the cable car up the mountain if the weather allowed, play some mini golf, go out for dinner), then Rick had talked some about his experiences working in his Dad's doctor's practice that he was going to take over soon, and finally Gerry told some stories of all the troubles they had had remodeling their house.

Unexpectedly D found herself really captured by the conversations. And even though Joe did flare up in her mind a few times – each time with a feeling of her stomach knotting – she managed to push these thoughts away quickly before they could drag her down.

She took another sip from her drink and finally ate her pineapple slice. She checked her watch. It was past midnight already. Across from her, Jack was looking tired. Suddenly he looked up and met her eyes giving her a searching look. She managed a weak smile in return and then quickly dropped her gaze to her drink and the ice cubes that had by now shrunk to the size of peas. She stirred them with her straw and watched them swirl about.

Around her, the conversation carried on. Sun was talking about a new neighbor that had just moved in next to her and seemed to be Mr. Grouch himself. This prompted Jack and Rick to dig out their best neighbor stories, some of which D had heard a few times already. Already familiar with the stories, D couldn't keep her mind and her attention from drifting off. She glanced over to the bar where the barkeeper was doing something artistic with the shaker. While she watched the content of the shaker being poured into two fancy glasses, and while the chattering around her continued – still circling around the neighbor topic – she became aware of the song that was playing in the background. Older song. From some animated Christmas movie. Kate Winslet? Touching melody. She had heard the song before, but she had never really closely listened to the words. Tonight the refrain seeped into her consciousness whether she wanted it or not. It was about a lost love, with the singer wishing she could turn back time. Wondering if the guy she'd been in love with would still be the man she used to know if she hadn't let him go. Despite the fact that she knew she had had to draw the line, she was still wondering what might have been different if they had given it another try and if she hadn't left. Would he still be the same guy today? They would never know...

D tried to keep her expression from distorting. This song just hit the nail on the head. The melody and the lyrics... Just hurt like hell. Because this was exactly what it came down to with Joe. Maybe, if she hadn't dropped him like a hot potato and left for London, things would have been different. They'd never know...

Taking a deep breath and putting on a tired smile, she looked up and found Jack giving her a concerned look.

"Are you okay?" he mouthed while Rick kept talking.

She gave a short nod, her ears still tuned to the music in the background. When the song was over and Rick paused for a moment, she placed both her hands on the table, cleared her throat and proclaimed that she was going to go to bed. And while the others were still debating if they should do the same or get another drink, she got up, wished them a good night and left.

She had almost reached the elevator when she heard footsteps behind her.

"D, wait..." That was Jack.

She slowed down and turned around, giving him a half smile from the side. "Going to bed too?"

"Yeah. I better…" he said.

They got on the elevator.

"How are you doing?" Jack asked.

"I'm fine," she claimed.

"Well, good," Jack said not exactly looking convinced.

D sucked in a quick breath, dropped her gaze and nodded. The effects of the alcohol made it hard to think clearly and she could only hope that Jack wouldn't start an in-depth talk about things she wanted to keep buried in numbness at least until tomorrow.

For a moment she could feel Jack still looking at her, and she really thought he was going to say something. But then he didn't.

Up on their floor they said good night and separated.

D walked down the corridor to her room, feeling her pulse heavily in her ears. She heard Jack's door close behind her. The key card in her hand, she waited outside her room for a moment, taking a few deep breaths. That music down in the bar had somehow stirred it all up again. She felt like crying. But that wasn't an option! She choked down the tears. She was *not* going to cry! She would quickly go to bed and try to sleep. She was tired enough! And with some luck sleeping on it might make it better.

Quietly she opened the door to her room and slipped in.

Sarah was sleeping – or at least pretending to be.

# Awakenings

Joe was blasted awake at two in the morning by an ambulance racing by outside his open window with the sirens howling. It took him a moment to recall that he was at home in Deens in his bed.

He sleepily opened his eyes and stared into the dark. He felt weird. Usually when he woke up, he didn't have the faintest idea what he had dreamt. But now, with the very sudden interruption, something from the last dream seemed to still be clinging to him, leaving him with this amazing feeling. He closed his eyes again and tried to recapture of that dream as much as he could before it vanished into nothing. In his dream he was lying on his back on a blanket or something outside, under a tree. It was a sunny day. He was only wearing swim shorts and was looking up at canopy of leaves above him. As he felt someone stretch out next to him, he closed his eyes. And felt that someone cuddle up to him; someone's knees nudging the side of his thigh, a bikini top brushing up against his bare upper arm – just a layer of fabric between his skin and soft breasts. An arm being draped across him, the gentle touch of a palm coming to rest on his stomach just above the waistband of his swim shorts. A warm, soft touch – breath-taking, exciting and at the same time immensely comforting. Fragments of a dream that hadn't quite evaporated yet.

In a desperate attempt to keep it from fading away, he placed his own hand on his belly. He could feel his own accelerated heartbeat, his belly rising and falling with every breath. And then, as the dreamy feeling finally vanished, the heartbeat slowed down and the breathing became quieter. He knew exactly who this dream had been about. It had been the exact same feeling as last night on the sofa...

A part of him wished he could just go back to sleep and maybe catch up with this dream again. He could enjoy it some more, maybe carry the dream a little further... Another part of him was awake enough to realize that dreaming any more along these lines would only make it more painful to wake up tomorrow morning. Given the circumstances, these kinds of dreams weren't exactly healthy.

He turned to his side and switched on the bedside lamp to check the time. It was 2:20 am. He switched the light back off and turned to lie on his back again, one arm draped behind his head. He wanted to go back to sleep, not think about anything, but then the talk he had had with Sarah in the bar flashed through his head again. She had asked if she should talk to Danny. Even now it made him cringe to imagine what that conversation would have been like.

He had claimed that, considering everything that was going on with Liz, he didn't have any energy or any interest to deal with Danny on top of it. And he had even believed it, too. But judging from the dream he had just had, and the way it had made him feel, he might want to reconsider. Who was he kidding?

And it wasn't as if his dream had just been some pathetic far-fetched fantasy that could never happen for real! Last night on the sofa had been just as good, if not better. He swallowed as the realization that there would never be a follow-up made his throat go dry and his lungs ache for air. He drew in a sharp breath and told himself that he shouldn't think about this now. Things always seemed more dramatic and painful during the night.

Determined to try and go to sleep, he closed his eyes. Forced himself to think of something nice and relaxing. Like a field of flowers, some sheep jumping over a fence... one, two, three, four... twenty-two...

He opened his eyes again and growled to himself. He threw his arms to his sides. There was *no* way he could just bury this and refuse to think about it! He needed to deal with it! Find some solution! He just absolutely *needed* to try and fix this thing with Danny. *Somehow.*

It was total bullshit what he had told Sarah. That he didn't have the energy!?! What really drained his energy, and he could see that clearly now, was to imagine that it had all slipped away already. He couldn't let it go like this!

The question, of course, was *how* to fix it. And if it *could* even be fixed. When Liz's call had landed like a wrecking ball.

He huffed out some air through his nose, his mind whirling. In order to have even the slightest chance of success with whatever he might come up with, he needed a minimum of two things: getting Danny alone and getting her to listen. Either would be a major challenge. Because she would undoubtedly do her very best to avoid him. And even if he somehow managed to get anywhere close to her, she would never hold nice and still and patiently listen to what he had to say.

And what could he even say? Any good ideas in that department yet?

He rubbed his eyes and stared into the dark. There was another problem too: even if he caught her by herself, and even if he came up with the perfect thing to say, and even if she decided to hear him out, her pride would get in the way. Big time! So, no matter how much she might want to just sink into his arms in that very moment, she would still deliver a convincing performance of how much she despised him and that she *never* wanted to see him again. Only by coincidence had he ever figured that paradox out. And despite the fact that he knew about it now, it was – in a heat of the moment situation – extremely tricky to properly determine if what he had before him was heartfelt resentment or just extremely good theatre. Telling them apart was close to impossible.

Joe thought about this for a moment. That was the biggest problem of them all. But then again, there wasn't much to lose at this point. So, why not just assume that any form of rejection he would encounter was just an act. If, in the course of his endeavor, he happened to mistake authentic resentment for well-disguised affection, so be it!

Having come to this conclusion, Joe felt relieved. It might be a stupid plan, but at least it was a plan. And now that he had a plan, he could try to go back to sleep. He would definitely need all his energy come tomorrow.

Turning to the side, he yawned and closed his eyes. Another one of those dreams might not be bad – just as an inspiration…

~~~

D woke up when Sarah closed the bathroom door.

And as soon as her memory kicked in and the last evening flashed by, her stomach felt like she had swallowed a monstrous piece of chewing gum.

She threw her arm over her eyes. She wanted to sleep and forget. If she could only pull the blanket over her head and hide here for a day or two – or until this horrible feeling subsided.

If someone had told her yesterday morning how she would feel today… Just thinking about yesterday morning made her want to cry. Joe stuffing clothes in the garbage bags, handing her the two pieces he thought she should keep. She would need to get rid of these as soon as she got home.

For a moment she considered driving home right after breakfast. She could claim that she was sick and leave. But then she pushed that thought away very quickly. First of all, it would be slightly suspicious to everyone, especially Jack and Sarah, who usually had a very good eye for suspicious things. Secondly, being home alone was probably only going to make things worse as she would sit and brood until Monday morning. She was much better off staying here and getting all the distraction she could; participate in all the fun stuff the others had planned for today and try to immerse herself in it.

When Sarah came out of the bathroom fifteen minutes later, her hair still a little damp, D had halfway pulled herself together and was sitting on her bed, reading (or pretending to read) a book. She glanced up at Sarah.

"Good morning," she said trying for a smile.

"Hey," Sarah said, "When did you get to bed?"

"Around twelve-thirty," D said lightly and put the book aside. Then she stretched and yawned.

Watching D pull back the blanket and slide her legs out of bed, Sarah tried to evaluate the overall condition her friend was in. It was hard to tell. Had she not known what she *did* know in regard to Joe's blue sweater, she would probably think D was in the best mood and just a bit tired from having been up late. So, if it was just acting, the acting was good. It really was. And in a way Sarah was glad to find D up and about and smiling (even if with questionable authenticity) because she had no idea how she would handle anything else.

"Why don't you go ahead for breakfast?" she heard D say. "It's going to take me a while. "

"Sure..." Sarah realized that that probably *was* a good idea. For both of them. "I could wait, though," she offered anyway.

"Na, go ahead," D insisted.

"Okay..." Sarah kneaded her hair between her fingers a bit more. "I'll see you downstairs then."

After Sarah had left, D went into the bathroom and locked the door. She was going to give herself 20 minutes to get ready and appear in the breakfast room with a smile and stable enough to get through the day without any glitches or breakdowns. She needed to pull this off!

She slipped out of her pajamas and stepped into the shower. The temperature turned to something that was neither too hot nor too cold, she just let it rain down on her. She was doing her best not to lose control over her thoughts, but her mind had already started to race. Rewinding her brain to a point before the grill party hadn't worked at all. The scenes from her two evenings with Joe were flaring up now, one after the other, having a choking effect. The fury she had felt last night had given way to something much more complex. There was still burning anger but it was more at herself for tapping into this situation in the first place. Then there was pure hate for Liz. And as much as she wanted to say the same for Joe (that she hated him), she realized that it just wasn't true. She would have loved to hate him. She tried to convince herself that he had just been playing a mean and stupid game in order to trick her into what had happened on the sofa. The only problem was that a small part of her had serious doubts about that theory. That small part even kept insisting that he may have been honest…

She placed one hand against the tile wall and tipped her forehead against it. It was just the hardest thing to accept that she had lost it yet again. That thing… That rare something that she had only ever had with Joe. Something she had managed to forget even existed. Something she had never ever had with Pete – or anyone else for that matter. Living without it had been okay and would have probably continued to be okay if she hadn't, over the past three days, been reminded of how it felt. From the moment when Joe had asked her Wednesday night if she wanted to sit in front, it had been there. Boom! This chemistry that could just knock you off your feet. Casual touches that made your skin tingle and your heart stop. An amazing closeness that was intense and relaxed all at once and that just worked – without words.

She gasped for air and softly banged her head against the tile wall a few times. She needed to get him out of her head! As fast as she possibly could! And who knew, maybe she would eventually find someone else whom she clicked with even more. Or she would just, over time, forget again what it felt like and would be content with a lot less…

Feeling the bile creep up her throat, she gave up fighting tears. If there was a time and place to let go, it was here in the shower where no one could see her and the tears would just be washed away by the water. And with some luck she would get this out of her system for the rest of the day.

~~~

On her way down to the breakfast room Sarah checked her phone. There were no new messages from Joe. He had arrived alright and that was the main thing, of course, but she had a really bad feeling. It wasn't good that he was all by himself at home. He wasn't exactly the kind of person who easily got depressed, but she could see how the current developments could get even him down pretty badly.

She stopped just outside the breakfast room and sent him a short message.

*Let me know how you are. Don't let this get you down! Do something fun! Let me know if I can do anything.*

*Sarah*

In the breakfast room Anja, Sun and Rick were already in the midst of having breakfast. Sun looked very tired, and Sarah concluded that she must have been at the bar too long last night.

Sarah got some coffee and then went back to the buffet. She piled a roll, some ham and cheese and scrambled egg on a plate and joined the others.

"Jack isn't up yet, huh?" she asked.

Rick shook his head. "I'll wake him up when I go upstairs. Because if we want to take the cable car up the mountain and go for a short hike, we should probably leave in an hour at the latest. Is D up?"

Sarah nodded, chewing on her roll. "She's coming."

"Good," Rick said. "Carrey, Tony and Kim have already had breakfast, so we're in good shape!"

"Have you heard from Joe?" Anja asked Sarah, a concerned look on her face.

Sarah shrugged. "Got home alright. Nothing else. But that's just him."

"So, he just went home to *your* place?" Gerry asked, sounding somewhat relieved. "Not back to that crazy girl?"

"No," Sarah shook her head. "Just back home."

Gerry nodded with a sympathetic smile but didn't press for more details. And neither did anyone else.

They spent the morning taking the cable car up a mountain, took a forty minute hike to a small restaurant with a great view, had lunch there and then returned and took the cable car back down again. Around one o'clock they arrived back at the hotel and decided to go and play a round of mini-golf on the course next to the hotel.

During their trip up the mountain D had overcome the dazed state she had been in during breakfast. The walk on the mountain had felt good. And with everyone around her chatting and laughing and joking, her mind had cleared and she had sometimes even found herself laughing along. All in all, she had managed relatively well to keep at bay the choking feeling that she felt each time Joe crossed her mind.

As they lined up around the first mini golf obstacle now, D found herself briefly struggling again to keep her thoughts from drifting off to the dark side of her mind, but once Carrey, who was the first to try her luck on hole number one, took her third horrible shot, her attention snapped back to the fun side of the day. One would have had to be dead not to find this funny.

With the exception of Jack, everyone in their group played unbelievably badly, which was commented on by the ones not currently swinging the club with scathing, teasing remarks and lots of laughter. And the worse they played, the more they laughed. And when Rick had such a bad shot that he actually had to dive into the bushes to find his ball, D found herself laughing so hard that it left her feeling light-headed. It was just the most liberating thing. Laughing until you couldn't breathe...

It took them a while to finish the course. Once the last ball finally landed in the last hole, which was actually up a pipe and into a small bucket, Rick was hooked. "Let's play another round," he urged excitedly. "We're getting better all the time! Come on...!"

"I didn't see any improvement," Carrey said with a frown, "and I think I need to go and get something to drink and maybe I'll lie down for a while."

"Yeah, me too," Sun said. "You guys are wearing me out. I'm not used to so much exercise in one day. And of course, I didn't get to bed until two in the morning."

"Neither did I," Rick pointed out. "But do you see me giving up? No! I can still play!"

In the end, Anja, Gerry, Tony and Jack decided to stay and play another round with Rick, while everyone else headed back to the hotel.

D trailed behind Sarah, Sun, Kim and Carrey, who all seemed to be immersed in a conversation about food. Or at least Carrey and Sun were.

They all got on the same elevator up to their rooms, with Sun and Carrey getting off on the second floor and Kim on the third. Alone in the elevator now, D and Sarah found themselves engulfed in a tense silence.

"Well, that was fun," D said just to say something.

"Yeah, really," Sarah managed a laugh. "Neither of us are mini golf talents, but it was great fun."

"I don't think I would call anybody – except for maybe Jack – a *talent*." D said.

Sarah slowly nodded. "Yeah, I guess, he did alright," she said a little absent-mindedly.

As they got to their room, Sarah sat down on her bed and D disappeared to the bathroom. When she came back a minute later, a glass of water in her hand, Sarah was just putting her phone back on the nightstand. Their eyes met for a brief moment.

D took a quick sip from her glass and walked over to her bed, put the glass onto the nightstand and kicked off her shoes. She sat down on her bed, her back against the wall, her legs pulled up.

Across from her, Sarah had kicked off her shoes as well and stretched out on her bed, her arm draped under her head. She closed her eyes.

D knew that Sarah had probably checked her phone to see if there was any message from Joe. Feeling her own stomach knot, D wondered if there was. Of course it was impossible to tell from Sarah's face.

Trying to distract herself and to avoid the impression that she was brooding over something, D reached into her nightstand and fished out the tourist magazine that was supplied by the hotel. Lost in thought, she started browsing through it.

# If it means anything to you...

They had been like this for three tense minutes now, D sitting on her bed, flipping through the magazine, and Sarah stretched out on the other bed, her eyes closed.

No one had said a word.

Sarah was caught in a fierce internal struggle. On one side there was Joe's orders for her not talk to D about anything regarding him, on the other side there was her own extreme and growing edginess in this matter – a strange feeling of urgency that something absolutely *needed* to be done... She was having the hardest time keeping her eyes (and her mouth) shut.

From the other bed she could hear D flipping through the pages of her magazine. And from the speed at which those pages were turned, it seemed highly unlikely that D actually looked at them. If Sarah had to make a guess, she would say that D was just aimlessly flipping through pages here, her mind probably occupied with something entirely different... It was driving her nuts. That D just sat there sulking with her horrible little secret and that there hadn't been any sign of life from Joe all day. He couldn't just put his head in the sand and lick his wounds and let D think about him whatever she wanted (which currently probably was, that he had driven straight back to Liz).

Throwing all her good resolutions overboard, Sarah drew in a deep breath and cleared her dry throat.

"Hey D," she said, opening her eyes and looking over to her friend on the other bed. "About Joe..."

Upon hearing her own name, D had questioningly glanced up from the magazine. The moment Sarah had dropped Joe's name, D's expression had frozen into a guarded mask.

Keeping an eye on that mask, Sarah turned to lie on her side and propped herself up on her elbow.

"He only went back to our house," she said plainly.

What followed was an eerie silence and a staring contest of sorts. Sarah could feel her heart like a drum inside her chest, but then decided to just carry on. "He didn't..." she interrupted herself, suddenly having changed her mind regarding what to say. "Seems like Liz has gotten into his e-mail account," she said matter-of-factly. "And he had to go home and straighten things out on his computer before she could do any more damage."

When there still was no reaction whatsoever from D, Sarah gave her a closer look, just to make sure she was still breathing. She definitely was. And one of her hands was balled to a fist and she was looking increasingly angry.

"He didn't go back to *her*, if that's what you're thinking..." Sarah said while she still could.

D's eyes had narrowed. "Why exactly are you telling me that?" she asked sharply.

Holding D's gaze, Sarah shrugged. "I don't know..." she said making it sound more like a question.

"*Why* are you telling me that?" D asked a little louder. "Why would *I* care?"

"Well, if you don't care, then just forget it!" Sarah retorted and flopped back on her back again so she could stare at the ceiling.

From the other bed she could hear D gasp for air. "I don't give a shit what he–" D started.

"Good for you!" Sarah interrupted. "I just wanted to make sure we're all on the same page..."

D slammed the magazine onto the bed and huffed out an angry breath.

It made Sarah turn her head and look at her.

"What did he tell you?" D demanded, her eyes flickering angrily.

Sarah didn't answer right away. Simply because she was still trying to put together a viable response.

"*What* did he tell you?" D asked sharply.

Sarah let out a little humorless laugh. "Oh, he would have rather died than tell me *anything*," she said, turning to the side and propping herself up on her elbow again. "But since he was carrying around a sweater that a day earlier I had fished out from under *your* sofa, he probably didn't see much sense in denying it!"

D swallowed, her expression changing from anger to some form of shock. "Great," she breathed, her gaze shifting to the side for a moment. "Absolutely fabulous!" Suddenly her eyes darted back towards Sarah. "He slept on the sofa, okay?"

Sarah rolled her eyes. "It's kind of funny how you both seem to think that's really important information for me," she said. "It was the very first thing Joe came up with too."

D looked confused. "Well, it's not like we—"

"Grrr," Sarah interrupted, grinding her teeth. "God, are you and Joe actually acting from the same script? I don't care *where* he slept, alright? Or if he slept at all." She shook her head to get rid of the pictures that the *we didn't* had provoked in her head.

"Well, I just want to make sure we're all on the same page here," D retorted.

"Yeah, thank you," Sarah grumbled. "To me it's hard enough to imagine how he even got inside your flat. In that context it really doesn't make a huge difference if he spent the night in your bathtub, in a lawn-chair on your deck or in your bed. One is just as hard to believe as the other."

D bit down on her lower lip and blinked a few times. "Yeah, what was I thinking, right?" she finally said, and there was a real bitterness in her voice. "I must have totally lost my mind there! The *stupidest* thing I've ever done. I agree...."

"That's not what I meant, D," Sarah said with some exasperation. "I was just surprised because I really thought you'd never speak to him again, that's all."

D laughed. A sarcastic laugh. "That was the plan, yeah! Actually, a pretty good plan in hindsight. I should have stuck to it... But—" She paused for a moment. "Shit, I'm *so* stupid!!!" Shaking her head at herself, she scooted to the edge of the bed and got up. She went over to the window and looked out.

"It doesn't have *anything* to do with your intelligence," Sarah said softly.

Her back to the room, D just gave a shake of her head.

"Guess it's not so easy when you're face to face with him, huh?" Sarah said. "Sticking to the plan, I mean."

At the window D threw her hands in the air. "I don't know... No, it's not! Especially when he's..." her voice was cracking. "God, I hate him!"

Silence.

Even though she could only see D's back at the moment, Sarah had a feeling that her friend was probably fighting tears. But she might actually win that fight – because there was *no* way she would ever let anyone see her cry over this particular guy again.

"Anyways," Sarah said, "all I'm saying is that he's only gone back to Deens and not to Liz, okay? That's all. End of message."

Still with her back to the room, D nodded. Then she turned around and leaned against the windowsill behind her. There were no tears…

"Is he…," Her voice sounded a bit choked up. "He's not coming back here, is he?" she asked.

Hesitantly Sarah shook her head. "It didn't sound like it last night, no."

Dropping her gaze to the carpet, D drew in a long breath that she subsequently slowly released through her nose. "That's fine," she finally said with a dismissive little shrug. "Probably a good thing!"

Sarah gave her a worried look. Nothing was fine here! Or good… No use pretending otherwise!

"D, listen…" Sarah was scrambling for words. "I really hate to get into any new messes between you and my brother but… if it means anything to you that he comes back here…"

D's expression froze. Then she shook her head, letting out a laugh that sounded a bit shrill. "No, Sarah, I'm not going to call him, if that's what you're saying."

Sarah opened her mouth to respond, but then she didn't.

"I can't…" D said as if she was waiting for some kind of absolution from Sarah.

"I hear you, D," Sarah said through clenched teeth. "But the way I see it, he's pretty sure right now that you hate him. Which, of course, you say you do, but … Well, like I said, if it means anything to you, you might want to consider letting him know. Send him a message or whatever."

For a moment D seemed to seriously consider it, but then she shook her head. "I can't do that."

Sarah huffed out a resigned breath and shrugged. "Whatever you say!"

"What do you expect me to tell him, Sarah?" D demanded, her hands in the air, palms up. "Something like, '*Oh, please come back!!! I've learned absolutely nothing from the past, and I don't give a shit that the bitch you dumped me for is pregnant now*'…?"

Sarah stared at her for a moment and then just shook her head. As much as she wanted to, the paternity issue and what Joe had told her in

374

that regard, was nothing she could possibly discuss with D. That was just way too intimate. She had already stuck her head out way too far as it was.

"Forget I even said anything," Sarah said flatly and let herself flop back onto her back again, her arms to the side like in surrender.

"Yeah, right," D muttered angrily. "Like I can just forget that now!"

Instead of any response, Sarah just lay there, her lips tightly pressed together as if to keep them from saying anything else.

She clasped her hands over her belly, suddenly aware that she was experiencing a deja-vu. Only that last time they had had this kind of conversation, she had actually managed to convince D to call Joe. And then Liz had picked up the phone...

D had turned to look out the window again. "I think I might go for a swim in the lake," she said.

"Yeah, you should..." Sarah mumbled. "I'll have a nap in the meantime..." She closed her eyes.

She heard D walk over to her bedside table, pull something out, probably her bikini, and disappear to the bathroom. She came out two minutes later. Sarah opened one of her eyes halfway and glanced over at where D was just tying the belt of her bathrobe.

"Okay, I'll be back," D said quietly and slipped into her slippers. "Enjoy your nap."

"Yeah, thank you very much," Sarah grumbled, "and you enjoy the cold water!"

# Going Swimming

She must have nodded off after D had left. When there was a knock on the door, it took Sarah a moment to wake up.

Still drowsy, she rose from the bed and stumbled over to the door. D had obviously forgotten her key.

Her eyes widened when she opened the door and found herself looking right into her brothers' eyes. "Joe?" she blinked, her brain slowly coming up to speed. "I thought you weren't coming back."

"Changed my mind," he shrugged a tense expression on his face. "Sorry I didn't call."

Sarah opened the door wider to let him in.

But he just leaned against the doorframe and shot a look over her shoulder into the room. "Danny's not here, huh?"

Sarah shook her head. He surely didn't lose any time with small talk. And he surely didn't beat around the bush why he was back. Maybe a good thing.

"She went swimming," she told him.

"When?"

"I don't know." She looked at her watch and thought for a moment. "Maybe ten minutes ago."

"Where?" he asked and Sarah felt herself reminded of a cross-examination in an American court movie.

"What?"

"Lake or pool? Do you know?"

"Lake…"

"Okay." He chewed on his lip. "Did she go alone?"

"Yeah," Sarah nodded, following his train of thought now. "She went alone."

He nodded, obviously still pondering it.

Then he gave her a crooked, apologetic smile and took a step back into the hallway. "I'll talk to you later, Sarah, okay?"

"Yeah, whatever!"

She closed the door.

~~~

Jack had been watching TV when he heard a knock on the door, followed by the little click of the key card being used, and then Joe appeared.

"Joe! You're back? Great! I thought you were…"

"Well, yeah, I'm back," Joe seemed a little taken aback by the euphoria. "Hey, did you bring any swim shorts that I can borrow?"

"What?" Jack was confused. "You want to go swimming?" He shot a skeptical glance towards Joe's braced hand.

"I can go into the water with that," Joe claimed.

"Okay. If you say so…" Jack frowned. "And you want to go right this minute?"

Joe nodded. "It's kind of an emergency. And I can't explain right now…"

"Okay…" A questioning look lingering on his face, Jack got up and pulled blue swim-shorts out of his bag. "Here." He handed them to Joe.

"Thanks," Joe had already pulled his T-shirt over his head. "You don't need these right now, do you?"

"Nope. I wasn't planning on going swimming right now," Jack said, still not quite sure what to make of this.

Joe headed to the bathroom and reappeared a minute later, wearing Jack's swim shorts and just pulling one of the white hotel bathrobes on.

"I'm sorry about this, Jack," he said as he pulled the belt tight around his waist. "You probably think I'm insane."

Jack didn't contradict.

"Okay, I'll be back…" Joe announced and gave Jack another quick apologetic smile over his shoulder. Then he hurried out of the room.

Scratching his head, Jack watched the door close. What had *that* been? Had Joe lost it now? An emergency to go swimming in someone else's swim shorts and with a hand injury that could probably use some rest?

Jack reached for the phone and called Sarah's mobile.

"Jack?"

"Hi, Sarah! Hey, did you know that Joe's back?"

Sarah hesitated. She had thought Joe had gone right down to the lake. Must have run into Jack somewhere along the way.

Jack misinterpreted her silence for an inability to talk freely. "You probably can't talk with D around, huh? Do you want to come over here for a sec? I'm in my room."

"No, that's fine," Sarah assured him. "I can talk. D isn't here. She went swimming…"

"Oh, *really*?" Jack said. "*Swimming*, huh?"

"I know that Joe's back," Sarah said quickly. "I mean, he just came by a few minutes ago."

"Oh, okay. And you didn't notice anything… – strange?" Jack asked in a weird voice.

"Did you run into him?" Sarah asked instead of answering the question.

"No, he's just blown through here," Jack reported. "Said he needed to borrow my swim shorts out of some emergency to go swimming right this minute." The way he said it, it sounded like a question.

In the silence that followed, Sarah was well aware that there was just *no* way Jack hadn't made the connection. And she was scrambling for what to tell him if he called her on it.

But then he only cleared his throat. "Well, I just wanted to let you know that he's back…" he said a bit too lightly.

"Yeah, thanks."

"Well, I guess we unexpectedly have him back for dinner, then," Jack contemplated. "That's good."

"Mmhh," Sarah agreed, lost in thought. "Let's just hope no one gets any mysterious calls this time…" she added in a weak attempt at joking.

Jack laughed out loud. "Well, I for my part just won't pick up." He paused for a moment and then laughed again. "But I'm probably the last person she would call anyway."

On the other end Sarah swallowed. That's right. She had almost forgotten or intentionally blocked out that Jack had been with Liz for a little while too.

~~~

Joe made it to the elevator and down to the spa area without anybody crossing his path. That was a relief because the fact that he was running around barefoot may have been frowned upon by some hotel guests.

The spa area was larger than he had expected. There were three saunas in the back, a small inside swimming pool and a big hot tub. Up towards the front was the glass-façade construction with the lounge chairs that he had seen from the hill the previous night. Located right at the tip of the peninsula it offered a perfect view all around.

Joe didn't really pay much attention to any of that, though and left the sun-flooded lounge area through the sliding glass doors. Outside he headed across the lawn between the many lawn chairs and towels that were spread out on the grass. People dozing, getting a sunburn, playing cards, chatting, cuddling... He took the stairs down to the lake and stepped onto the pier that was built along the shore here. There were a few rental boats tied to it to his left. To his right was another wider pier leading far out into the lake, with kids jumping off at the very end and swimmers climbing up and down on the four metal ladders on the sides.

His hands tucked into the pockets of his bathrobe, Joe walked about halfway out, his eyes scanning the people on the pier and the heads of the swimmers in the water. There were a lot of them. Some close-by, some further away. With that many heads to choose from (several of them submerging here and re-emerging somewhere entirely different), and with some boats floating around in-between, it could get tricky to spot Danny.

The initial rough idea had been to just catch her while she was swimming somewhere close to the pier or anything else they could hang on to while having a fruitful conversation. The way things looked out here, he could as well just forget about that. She could be anywhere! He walked back towards the stairs and glanced around once more, feeling discouraged. Even if he suddenly managed to make her out somewhere, how could he possibly catch up with her with that hand of his?

He passed the rental boats again. Undecidedly he looked at them. Had he brought his wallet, he could have probably rented one, but he wasn't even sure how much good that would have done. Leading a constructive conversation from a boat with a swimmer who was busy trying to swim away from you, didn't seem promising.

He climbed back up the stairs. This had been an idiotic idea to begin with! He better face it! Unfortunately it was an idea that was extremely hard to give up. Because the way he saw it, here and now might be his best or even *only* chance to get Danny alone and accomplish anything. Once she was back in her room or even at dinner, surrounded by friends, it would be too late. They would automatically slip right back into the routine of shooting each other cold looks and there would probably be no way out of it.

As he stepped back into the spa area, the lounge chairs sitting against the windows in the glasshouse caught his eye. Maybe he should just wait *here*. She would have to come through that door sooner or later, wouldn't she? In fact, one of the bathrobes hanging on the rack next to the door might be hers. Trying to catch her in here was less than ideal, of course. Because chances were that, as soon as she saw him, she would storm off. And with so many other guests around, he would hardly be able to hold her back without causing a scene. Still, for lack of any other ingenious ideas, he decided to stick around.

He walked over to a chair which was parked with its back against the window looking out towards the tip of the peninsula. This chair seemed to be positioned strategically well, as it had a perfect view of the sliding door. At the same time it wasn't the first thing people would see when coming in.

Still standing next to the chosen chair, Joe glanced through the window behind it. Past the lamp and the flag post with the hotel's flag, out towards the water. There was a single person swimming out there. He squinted, his heart suddenly beating faster. Could that be her? He would have needed his glasses to tell for sure at this distance. He ran his left hand through his hair and tried to focus on the little head. Could be her. It did kind of look like her.

He glanced out the window to his left, facing the hill from where he had called Liz last night. All the benches were taken now. At the base of the hill he could see lots of people on the lakeside promenade today. Only around the boathouse the path didn't lead directly alongside the lake but behind a big hedge. Right in front of the boat house there was a small pier with a metal ladder. He hadn't seen that pier last night. But with the hedge and the boathouse it had probably been obstructed from view. His eyes shot back to the lonely swimmer. If this was really her, he would bet that she was heading for that pier on the other side. Glancing back and forth between the swimmer and the pier, he gauged the situation. That was still quite a distance to swim. And even though she had always been a good swimmer, she would definitely need a break once she got there.

His mind racing, Joe considered his options. Running out to the flag post, throwing himself into the water and trying to catch up with her swimming, was an option he immediately dropped. He glanced towards the path again. He could always walk. Take the elevator up to the lobby, rush out to the promenade, run over to the boathouse, crawl under, over or through that hedge… It wasn't far at all. He could probably make it. Of course, running around barefoot and in a white hotel bathrobe would get him some interested looks from the nicely dressed pleasure walkers out there, but he couldn't care less about appearances at the moment.

# The Stalker

Swimming with strong, regular strokes, D slowly ploughed through the water, glad that she had made it away from the area with the boats and all the other swimmers and the screaming kids.

She had almost reached the tip of the peninsula with the flagpole that she had seen on her way through the spa area earlier. Initially she had planned to swim to this point and then get out here. But she had just spotted the small pier in front of that boathouse over there. It lay in the full sun and there wasn't a single soul anywhere close-by. So, why not just swim there? It looked inviting. And right now the swimming felt great. The water was just right, not too cold, amazing green color and totally clear.

Somehow swimming always relaxed her. It had something liberating. And right now it seemed like the ideal way to work off the frustration and anger that had built up inside her since last night. Yeah, and that conversation with Sarah just fifteen minutes ago... That had really almost blown her away. It absolutely sucked that Sarah knew! And then for Sarah to seriously suggest that she should get in touch with Joe!?! The agitation that came with the unpleasant memory made her automatically swim faster. She only noticed it when her arms were starting to get tired. So she slowed down again, concentrating on her strokes and on her breathing. She still had quite a ways to go. The distance to the pier seemed to be a little further than expected. She would definitely need a little rest over there before swimming back.

As she was getting closer to the pier and her arms were starting to feel sore, she considered turning onto her back and just floating the rest of the way with her hands and feet paddling a little. That would have meant getting her hair all wet though, and she wasn't really in the mood to do a hair-drying-styling session before dinner with that pathetic hotel hairdryer. So she kept pushing ahead, holding her head above water and doing her strokes. Finally she was close enough to reach the metal handrail of the ladder that lead up to the pier.

Huffing out a relieved breath, she grabbed the handrail and pulled herself closer. For a moment she just clung to the ladder, panting and feeling totally wiped out. Her heart was beating like crazy and her upper arms felt like rubber.

When after a minute her breathing calmed down a bit, she probed with her foot how deep the water was. She could reach the sandy ground with her toes, but at the same time she had to cling to the handrail, stretch her neck and tilt her head up or she would be in the water up to her nose.

So she climbed up the ladder and sat down on the pier with her legs dangling down. It felt good. The wood was warm, the sun was shining on her face and the birds were singing on the trees around her. Only from a distance could she hear the voices of the people who were enjoying a Saturday walk on the lakeside promenade. She turned around, but she couldn't see past the hedge and the boathouse. That was convenient because with some luck this meant that none of the passers-by could see the pier from the promenade either...

Her hands wrapped around the edge of the wooden planks, her legs swinging back and forth, D looked down into the water. It was so clear that she could see the rocks on the ground and some fish swimming around.

She lifted her head again and, squinting against the sun, she glanced over towards the hotel. It looked really pretty – especially with the mountains behind it. Shielding her eyes from the sun with her hand, she tried to identify the mountain they had taken the cable car up to this morning. The one with the bare top kind of looked like it. She even thought she could see the cables glinting in the sunlight.

Keeping her face in the sun, she dropped her hand and closed her eyes. It was a relief to know that all the rooms of her friends were facing the other way. So, there was no danger of Sarah looking out the window right now and watching her with concern.

Thinking about Sarah made D grind her teeth and try to quickly steer her thoughts into a different direction. To London. Yeah, she should think about London. That upcoming trip to London suddenly had something immensely appealing again after having been banned to the back of her mind and the bottom of her priority list for the past few days. Things changed quickly... Now she was actually really looking forward to it. Only eight days to go and she would be on the plane. She couldn't wait to get there, have a few nice and interesting days, maybe make plans for a new exciting future, have some good food, meet new people... (This did feel a bit like a deja-vu, though...)

The sudden creaking of wooden planks and the whole pier starting to slightly swing under somebody's footsteps made her click her jaws together in irritation. Obviously this pier wasn't hidden well enough after all! She let out a little sigh, frustrated that the very minute she had started to relax a bit here, some stupid swimmer or walker or fisherman or whatever had to jump out of the bushes and come stomping onto her pier! Determined not to let this ruin the moment, she kept her face in the sun and her eyes tightly shut. She would just ignore the intruder until he either disappeared again or she had regained her strength and was ready to swim back.

The swinging increased as the person kept coming closer. With her eyes closed, D was aware of the motion even more. And then there was the point where the swinging suddenly stopped and it felt as if the person had come to stand somewhere right next to her.

"Hi there," she heard someone say.

Her eyes flying open, she jerked around.

And found Joe looking down on her.

Her jaw dropped and – for the moment it took her to process what she was seeing – both her heart and her lungs seemed to briefly stop doing their jobs.

"What the hell?" she hissed. "I thought you were gone!"

"Well, sorry, but I'm back." Joe said and shrugged.

Without another word, D pushed herself off the pier and submerged in the cool, green water. When she resurfaced, her hand reaching for the handrail to pull herself to the ladder and her eyes still blinking away water (yeah, now her hair was all wet!!!), she saw Joe's bathrobe drop and then there was a big splash of water right in front of her.

His head popped up just a few feet away from her – and then more of him emerged. He was tall enough to reach the ground, of course. The water went up to his shoulders.

"Okay," he mumbled with a grimace as he brushed wet hair from his forehead. "That's very cold and wet…"

D shot a frantic look over to the hotel. Her first impulse had been to kick herself off the ladder and swim away from him as fast as she possibly could. But with her arms still feeling so weak, it would have been risky. She considered leaving on foot instead. But climbing up this ladder with his eyes on her, and then walking away in nothing but a wet bikini was no viable escape alternative either. (She could steal his bathrobe, of course, but she would still have to climb up there and bend down to pick it up…)

She glanced at him furiously.

"Are you stalking me now?" she fumed.

He huffed out a little humorless laugh. "To get you alone I actually *did* have to use my stalking skills, yes." It occurred to him that a stalker following his victims in bright daylight, barefoot and in a white bathrobe was somewhat absurd, but he refrained from pointing that out to her.

D glared back at him, her eyes sparkling angrily. "What do you want?"

"I need to talk to you," he said calmly.

She shook her head, dropping her gaze with an angry mocking laugh.

"Danny, I–" Joe started, then interrupted himself. "Oh, I forgot, we're probably back to *Danielle*, right?"

Her eyes flickered up to him and she drew in an angry breath through clenched teeth. "Just leave me alone!" she snarled. (And realized at the same moment that there was one sick part of her that was just so immensely glad to see him… She couldn't let this part get the upper hand here under any circumstances!)

Ignoring what she had just said, Joe kept a close eye on her, surprised that she hadn't made some sort of escape attempt so far. He could live with the scathing remarks and the furiously sparkling eyes. What really worried him was that she might try to get away and might do it faster than he could grab ahold of her. If that happened, and if it involved swimming, he didn't stand a chance. He was well aware of that and he had therefore considered grabbing her arm right here and now as a precaution. But he was almost certain that if he did that, she would kick herself free and take off for sure. So, as long as she remained hanging on to that ladder, glaring at him, it was okay.

"I want you to leave me alone!" she repeated with a snarl.

"I *will* leave you alone as soon as I've said what I have to say, okay?"

"I don't *want* to talk to you!" she hissed, her eyes flickering at him angrily. "I actually don't even want to *see* you!" She had hoped to sound a little more in command, but it had come out childishly angry.

"I know…" Joe said with some exasperation. "I'm *perfectly* aware of that!" With his good hand he reached up to the pier and held on to it. "That's *exactly* why I had to *stalk* you…"

D's look turned from cold to deadly. "If you think you can mock me here…"

"I'm not mocking you, *Jesus Christ!*"

"Go to hell!"

"Well, yeah... maybe I'll do that later," he said, realizing too late that now he was really mocking her.

Sucking in a sharp breath, she raised her free hand out of the water and for a moment there, he thought she was going to slap him in the face. But then she balled the hand to a fist and slammed it into the water right in front of him that it splattered in all directions.

Rubbing the water out of his eyes, Joe had to keep himself from laughing. This was just so her!

D glanced over to the hotel again, feeling desperate. Maybe she should just swim. Her arms were feeling a little better and she would make it somehow! And if not, drowning might be better than this. Or maybe not...

"I'm not going to talk to you. Period!" she hissed. "So..."

"Well, actually you don't *have* to talk," he interrupted her, realizing that he would actually even prefer it that she *didn't* talk because it was kind of demoralizing what she had to say. "Just listening would do just fine!"

Her eyes narrowed again and she was just catching her breath to shoot back, but he was faster.

"I *know* that you're mad, okay? And I know *exactly* how this looks–"

"Oh, really?" she cut him off with a sneer. "How does it look, what do you think?" Giving him a challenging look, she pulled herself closer against the ladder.

Joe couldn't help noticing that it was *her* mocking *him* now, but just as well. At least she was still here.

"Like I just run out on my *loving, pitiful and pregnant* girlfriend, turn off my phone and then lure *you* into I-don't-know-what..." he responded.

D raised her eyebrows and nodded, her lower lip sticking out as if she was very impressed with how he had hit the nail right on the head.

"It's not all that black and white, though, you know," Joe said darkly.

"Black or white, who cares?" she snapped. "Why don't you just–"

"Why don't I just *what?*" Joe inquired while leaning towards her a bit.

She gave him a stubborn look back but didn't supply him with the missing verb to her unfinished outburst.

"Why don't I just get lost, right?" he said.

She shrugged again, dropping her gaze.

"Okay," he ran his flat hand against the side of the pier boards. "So, you won't even listen, huh? Great." He shrugged. "But okay… You want me to leave then?"

Her eyes on the water, D swallowed. Something told her that a short *yes* or even just a nod would be sufficient and he would probably leave her alone for the rest of her life.

"Just say it!" Joe insisted. "Get it over with! Just say it and we can go straight back to Ice-age!"

Closing her eyes for a moment, she exhaled.

Joe knew he was pushing it. Even though she hadn't said it yet, he could already hear it ringing in his ears. Another *Go to hell!* or *Leave me alone!* or something of that sort. He was still trying to make up his mind if he would pursue it any further then or just grant her her wish and let it go. (Probably the latter.)

When after a few seconds she still hadn't said anything and just kept staring at the water, Joe realized that she might not be so determined to get rid of him after all.

"You can talk all you want," she said weakly, the anger and the testiness suddenly gone from her voice, "but it won't change anything!"

The sudden change of tone, along with her bleak evaluation of what he could possibly achieve here, threw Joe off a little. He was still scrambling for something to say that would prove her wrong, when she shot him an accusing look. "I just don't understand why you came back Wednesday night!" she said quietly. "*Why* in the world did you *do* that? It's just—"

Struggling to keep up with her just having jumped to an entirely different subject, Joe tilted his head. "What *part* don't you understand?" he asked and relocated his left hand to the handrail right above her hand.

She didn't answer and she didn't look at him either.

"I actually thought I had made that pretty clear," Joe said with some frustration. "Why I came back, I mean… But if you need some additional clarification, it's been the best thing I've done in ages. So there!"

He could see her swallow. Then she shook her head and finally raised her eyes to him. "Well, good for you," she said drily. "Couldn't you have found a different victim, though? I mean… what kind of stupid game are you—"

He let out a humorless laugh. "I'm not playing any game here, alright!? And as it happens, I didn't want some other '*victim*'." He raised his hands above water level to indicate the quotation marks. "Thanks a lot for that, by the way!"

D bit her lip, her gaze drifting to the side. Why did this have to be so screwed up! "What do you even *want* from me," she demanded, a tortured tone creeping into her voice. "You should go home to Liz, get married and take care of the baby…"

Joe drew in a deep breath and exhaled audibly. "Wow, Danny! What great advice! If you were trying to pack the three scariest words into one sentence, you really nailed it!" Leaning in a bit, he squinted at her. "Or are you serious???"

Her eyes darting back at him, D let out a bitter laugh. "Personally, I've always found the constellation of just *you* and *her* freaky enough – even without the marriage-part and the baby-part. But that's just me, you know…"

"Okay, I guess you were being serious then," Joe concluded flatly.

D shrugged. "Well, sorry, I'm just trying to be realistic here."

"Really?" his face had turned hard. "That's you being realistic, huh?" He gave a dismissive shake of his head.

Unable to hold his gaze any longer, D glanced to the side. Towards the water under the pier, where the light fell through the cracks between the boards.

"Nothing has changed, okay?" Joe told her sharply." What I told you Thursday hasn't changed… You hear me?" He leaned towards her again, his hand suddenly sliding down the handrail until it touched hers. "Danny!?!"

The touch lasted a fraction of a second and she moved her hand down further, a pained expression on her face.

Feeling increasingly frustrated, Joe sucked in a quick breath. "I'll spare you the details about all the things that are wrong between me and Liz," he finally said. "It's *really* not pretty and it's nothing you need to know or that I should discuss with you. Especially because it's got *absolutely* nothing to do with you. But you *may* remember that I told you that it's over with Liz. *More* than once. *Remember that?* I wasn't kidding about that and I was *not* playing games with you!"

He kept his eyes on her even though it distracted him immensely how she kept staring at some point under the pier, making it impossible for him to tell if she was even listening.

Rubbing his forehead with his braced hand, he decided to continue anyway. "And I'm not going back! Okay? No matter *what* she comes up with next..."

"I don't think you have much of a choice," she said, her voice choked up.

Joe was torn between relief that, obviously, she was still listening, and frustration at what she had just said. It was starting to dawn on him that he might not be able to avoid telling her at least the most basic facts regarding his issues with Liz. With the pregnancy thing out there, he pretty much had to.

"Okay, about that..." he said, trying to keep it as matter-of-factly as he could. "I don't know if she's really pregnant or not, okay? It could very well be, though, because things such as taking the pill are easily forgotten when you're too drunk or drugged to remember them." Despite all good intentions he couldn't help sounding bitter. "Even if she *is* pregnant, though, it *can't* be from me."

D's eyes flashed up to him. "Oh, don't give me that!" she blasted. "You lived with her for *how* long? Don't tell me you didn't sleep with her for months. Not that I even care, but..."

Joe bit his lip. God, did they really have to go there?

"Let's just say that *I*, for *my* part, have been pretty careful with protection, okay?" He paused for a moment. "And that I know as a fact that I wasn't the only one... sleeping with her." He saw D cringe, her hand clamping tighter around the handrail, but he really couldn't help her. She had pushed for it and he had told her. He could have, of course, skipped the last part, but it did kind of put a finishing touch on the disturbing picture.

D had felt her mouth go dry at his words and the images they provoked in her head. Reflexively she glanced up at him.

He gave an apologetic shrug and a half-smile.

Dropping her gaze again, she decided that at least he seemed to be honest – for what that was worth. And she hadn't left him much choice but to specify how exactly he could be so sure about the pregnancy.

"Listen Danny..." Stepping a little closer through the water now, Joe placed his hand onto the handrail right below hers, his thumb touching the side of her hand. "If you generally don't want to have anything to do with me, that's fine," he said. "I understand. Guess I gave you plenty of reasons. But if it's just because Liz called last night, that's just plain stupid!"

At the mention of *stupid* D looked up at him again. She was fighting with herself here. That look he gave her – along with his hand touching hers – made it hard to breathe. She should, of course, pull her hand away. She knew that! She should just switch hands and hold on to the other handrail. But somehow her hand refused to be moved. Apparently, the one disoriented part of her that had been so glad to see him had already started to infect other parts of her body (like the hand…) and deactivated defense and flight mechanisms.

"I *did* kind of like the experiments Thursday night," Joe suddenly said with a weak smile. "Even though, they *were* pretty cruel."

D tried to focus. The pure thought of Thursday night's experiments made her head spin, though. And to make it worse, he was gently running his thumb over the fingers she had wrapped around the metal bar. She bit her lip and did her best to appear unfazed. But this was one of those touches. If he knew what effect those had… Maybe Ice-age would be healthier!

Joe didn't seem to think so at all. He moved even closer and was standing right in front of her now. Caught in his gaze, D swallowed. If he came *any* closer… Then, she reluctantly admitted to herself, he would have her right back to where he had her Thursday night.

"Still listening?" There was a hint of a smile on his face, as he let go of the railing and softly brushed his thumb over jaw.

"Well, who could resist…" she mumbled grimly, trying to ignore the bolt of heat rushing through her.

"I didn't plan any of this, okay," he said softly and slid his palm against her cheek to where it was just lightly touching her skin. "My life's quite a mess as you may have noticed, and I'm afraid it may have screwed me up enough that I can't totally trust myself right now. So, I really can't guarantee how this is going to turn out – I mean, us…"

At the mention of *us*, D had turned her head to the side, away from the hand against her cheek. Hearing him say that kind of thing just stung. She looked over at the hotel. And felt his eyes on her. His hand back on the handrail now.

"Well, maybe this is stupid," she heard him say, "but I *do* think we've got *something*. Probably always have…"

As the words sank in, she turned her head and glanced back at him, her heart pounding heavily in her chest.

His eyes locked with hers, he blinked, chewed on his lower lip, obviously trying to decide how to proceed. Then his hand was back on her cheek and his thumb trailing over her lips. D tensed up. That thumb – she should probably just bite it off...

Maybe anticipating something like that, Joe slid his hand back, under her ear, to the back of her neck.

"Let me try something here, okay..." he whispered, already way too close.

Before D could even think about trying to escape, he had placed his braced hand against her back and took another step closer. Then, without waiting for any form of go-ahead or approval, he gently pulled her against himself.

D gasped for air. Well aware that she should put up at least some form of resistance. Like the gutsy environmentalists that jumped into the way of bulldozers.

"Don't..." she mumbled weakly, with a part of her praying that he didn't take her too seriously.

He didn't. He just leaned in and kissed her.

As she felt his lips on hers, she closed her eyes. First it was just this light, soft kiss. But when she didn't fight him, his mouth on hers started moving more intensely... And he pulled her away from the handrail to where she had to let go and put her arms around him for support instead.

As much as some inconvincible part of her wanted to, there was no fighting him because the rest of her was already disarmed and totally on his side by now. He was so close, closer than on the sofa and a lot less fabric between them. It made her head spin. His hand against her back, his mouth on hers, his chest against her top, his stomach, his legs... well yeah, and something else.

As she allowed herself to just go along with it, at least for now, she kissed him back. And pretty soon the kiss was starting to spiral off, into some kind of frenzy. His hand sliding against her lower back he pulled her even closer. Her head and her stomach were buzzing, her mouth and her tongue for that matter, in close exchange with his.

Then, in an inhumane effort, she reached back for the railing to pull herself out of his embrace.

Joe released her almost instantly. "Sorry." He raised his hands in a surrendering gesture and took a step back. "I guess I'm really losing it here! Sorry!" He seemed seriously troubled by his own unforgivable conduct. "I really didn't mean to—"

D stared at him, feeling strangely lost since he had taken his arms off her so promptly. "I can't go from standstill to a hundred in half a second," she grumbled.

Avoiding any form of eye contact, Joe nodded. "Yeah, I know."

D watched him stare at the water and felt this overwhelming pang of softness. Unable to resist, she reached out with her free hand and brushed a strand of hair from his forehead. She saw him briefly close his eyes as her fingertips touched his face.

"I guess you were right, though," she admitted quietly, as she dropped her gaze from his face to his shoulder, her fingertips tucking some of his hair behind his ear. "There's definitely *something*..."

Joe looked back up at her, first totally baffled, then, with a crooked smile slowly spreading across his face. "Well, as long as we agree on that..." he said with a little chuckle.

D nodded. Her eyes had just found the tiny scar on his shoulder that had always been there. And it felt so weird to stand half-naked in the water with someone whose body had once been so familiar. For a moment there, out of some crazy hazardous hunch, she tried to remember what it had been like to sleep with him. But she couldn't. Too long ago. Still, the idea of it made her stomach churn and her knees go weak.

"What?" his voice pulled her out of her sick contemplations.

"Nothing." Keeping her eyes on his shoulder, she shook her head – and suddenly noticed the little bruises there, next to the scar.

"What's that?" she asked with a frown.

"What?" his eyes flickered from her to what she was looking at and right back to her. "Oh, nothing..." he said lightly and shrugged, while running the thumb of his braced hand over the bruises as if to wipe them away. Then his hand slid back into the water and somehow landed on her hip. She glanced up at him, feeling slightly off-balance. A feeling that was only made worse by that look he gave her. Quickly she dropped her gaze again. And again, those bruises caught her eye. She squinted. There were four. And the way they were spaced and shaped, they almost looked like fingernail marks. Her throat suddenly feeling tight, she raised her eyes to his face. And the way he glanced to the side just as her eyes were about to meet his, somehow confirmed it.

Her hand was trembling a bit when she reached out and gingerly placed each of her fingers on one of the bruises, only her thumb being left out.

"Are those her claws?" she asked.

Joe huffed out a joking breath, his head turning to the side. "Just some minor war injuries!"

Shaking her head, D lifted her hand and gently ran her thumb over the little red marks, before lightly cupping his shoulder and the bruised area with her hand.

Joe exhaled. "Well, now that you're doing that, I think I'll survive..."

Her eyes darted up at him for a moment and then away again. Maybe it was that remark... the exact same one he had made in regard to the braced hand at the grill-party. Or maybe it was just intuition.

D slowly lifted her hand off his shoulder and placed it against the back of her own neck, giving herself a soft squeeze to loosen up.

"What about your *hand*?" she asked quietly.

"What *about* it?" he made it sound like he had no idea what she was talking about.

"Is that..." she swallowed, her gaze back on the bruises. "Is that a war injury too?"

He shook his head and huffed out a hollow laugh. "Why would you think *that*?"

"I don't know... Am I wrong?"

She met his eyes, and he looked away. Then, biting down on his lower lip, he shrugged. But remained silent.

"Joe?"

Blowing out some air through his nose, he slowly nodded. "Yep..." he finally said without looking up. "That's a war injury too."

"She broke your fingers?" D blasted.

Letting out a humorless laugh, he glanced back up at her. "Well, actually she was going for more, but then she only managed to get those two fingers."

D stared back at him – still in disbelief.

There was another little shrug from his side, but other than that, he just looked back at her with a relatively calm expression as if he were waiting for her to get over something he had tried to shield her from.

"But that's just…" D didn't even know that to say.

A crooked smile appeared on his face. "Yeah, well… That's kind of, why going back to there, getting married to her and taking care of a baby together didn't sound all that great when you mentioned it earlier."

"God!" she chewed on her lip. "How could you live with—"

"Hey," he interrupted her, giving her shoulder a gentle rub with his left hand. "Let it go, okay?"

With a helpless shake of her head she exhaled. And suddenly realized that he had gotten dangerously close again. But then he just gave her cheek a gentle brush of his thumb.

"I'd love to stick around," he whispered leaning in a bit, "but I'm getting kind of cold here. And it's not just the latest chilling topic. Your lips seem a bit bluish too…" His index finger trailed over her mouth.

All she could do was nod. She *was* getting cold, despite the heat waves he was causing.

"Are you going to be okay swimming back?" he asked.

She nodded again. (And hoped that she would actually be able to control her somewhat shaky limbs enough to where swimming *would* be possible.)

When Joe reached for the handrail, she swung to the side and got out of the way, so he could climb up. She avoided looking at him while he did. Even though part of her was dying to have a close look in bright daylight…

Up at the pier he picked up his bathrobe and slipped it on.

"There's one more thing, though," he said as he wrapped it around himself and tied the belt.

Surprised by the serious tone, and expecting maybe yet another disturbing revelation, D looked up at him. "What other thing?"

"Well… Do you think we could *please* save the status quo now? I mean, *this*…" With his hand he indicated himself and her. "*Us*. I don't want to get back to the hotel and have to start all over again, okay?" He paused. "I mean, can you *please* try not to let this evaporate between now and when we meet again?"

She swallowed and then nodded. "Would be pretty hard for this to evaporate…" she said with a weak smile up at him.

"Good!" he grinned.

She couldn't help chuckling at his delight.

He glanced at his watch. "We still got two hours until dinner," he said. "I think I'll use the hot tub back at the hotel. Might be good for you too, just to warm yourself up. So, if you want to meet me there..."

"Yeah, maybe." She didn't seem convinced.

He laughed. "Don't worry, I'll be good! *Top secret!*" He grinned down at her. "And there's absolutely nothing wrong with the two of us coincidently sitting in the same hot tub, just as long as we're far enough apart and you give me a mean look, which shouldn't be a problem..."

"I'll think about it," she said ignoring the side-kick. "Maybe." With that she pushed herself off the ladder and took her first stroke towards the hotel.

Swimming back turned out to be more strenuous than she had expected. Probably because she had already been so cold. She was glad when she reached the tip of the peninsula and could climb out of the water there. Barefoot and with her bikini dripping, she tiptoed on the gravel path around the spa lounge area. When she reached the sliding door and slipped inside, she was shivering. Quickly she grabbed her bathrobe from the rack next to the door and pulled it on over her wet bikini and her goose-bumps. With the goose-bumps there was, of course, the accompanying problem of her bikini top showing the small elevation of her nipples quite clearly. Thank God she had brought the bathrobe. There was *no* way she was taking that off again and getting into the hot tub now. She fished her slippers out from under a chair where they had landed somehow and slipped them on.

Finally she turned around and glanced towards the hot tub. She saw that Joe was already there. And that he wasn't alone. There was Sun, right next to him, sitting almost on his lap from the way it appeared, and there was Rick just getting in.

Suddenly Joe looked over and met her eyes through the room. one corner of his mouth turning up and his eyebrows rising briefly. She interpreted this to be his *Nothing-I-could-do* look.

She gave a little shrug and approached the hot tub, her eyes on Rick, who had just spotted her.

"Hey D," Rick said. "Have you been swimming out there till *now*?"

"Yep, got a little cold," she admitted, pulling the bathrobe tighter around herself. "I think I'll head upstairs, have a hot shower and dry my hair before it's dinner time..."

With that she headed for the corridor towards the elevator.

~~~

Sarah was sitting on her bed reading a book when D opened the door to their room.

"Oh, you're back," Sarah said without looking up from her book.

"Yeah. Hi…" D closed the door and stood there for a moment trying to decide what to do. "Are you're still mad?" she asked, slowly coming over to her bed.

"I've not *been* mad!" Sarah insisted in a tone that clearly indicated the contrary. "Why would I be?"

"Listen, Sarah," D perched on the back of the desk chair. "I know I've been… well, I know you just wanted to help. I'm sorry! Really!"

"It's okay!" Sarah grumbled with a little shrug, her gaze back on her book. "It's not my business what kind of messes you two get yourselves into. I should have kept out of it like I had planned."

Silence.

"I'm glad you didn't…" D finally brought herself to admit. "It *did* kind of help, I think."

Sarah glanced up from her book, her eyebrows raised.

With a helpless smile, D shrugged.

"So he found you then?" Sarah asked a little friendlier now.

Dropping her gaze to the floor, D nodded.

"Do you feel any better?"

"I guess," D said. "Against all odds and against any good judgment."

A sympathetic smile spread across Sarah's face. "Yeah, well – so it goes, I'm afraid."

"Seems like it," D said and got up. "I think I'll have a shower and get ready for tonight."

"I thought you weren't going to get your hair wet," Sarah said.

"I wasn't going to, but things didn't exactly go as planned…"

"I see," Sarah grinned. "Go ahead. I'm done in the bathroom. And you seem frozen."

"I kind of *am* frozen…"

# Italian Dinner with Friends

For dinner they took a nice twenty minute walk along the lake into one of the little towns. Rick had reserved a table in an Italian restaurant.

Joe's somewhat surprising return had been well-received by everyone and had boosted the mood of the entire group considerably. In the lobby as they were meeting to leave for dinner, Joe had delivered a brief statement along the lines of, '*As you can see, I'm back. Had to take care of some stuff at home. Don't want to go into detail of my personal mess with Liz, but it's definitely not the way she made it look last night. Sorry about that...*'

Everyone except for maybe Carrey, who was still eyeing him suspiciously, and D, who kept her expression as neutral as she possibly could, had reacted positively – with an encouraging smile (Rick, Sun, Gerry and Anja), a pat on the back (Jack) or a relieved nod (Sarah). After last night they were all only too happy to forget about the whole Liz-thing and enjoy some good food and a fun evening.

On the walk to town, D was walking at the very back between Anja and Carrey. Carrey was talking about her brother's girlfriend, a Thai girl, who had been unable to get a visa to come and visit him even though he would have vouched for her. Consequently, Carrey said, her brother had now decided to just go to Thailand and marry the girl because he loved her and he didn't want to deal with immigration issues anymore.

"My sister was going out with a guy from Pakistan once," Tony said, turning around from right in front of them. "He had a valid student visa and everything, but every time they went out to a bar or a disco or something and there were police controls, he was harassed one way or the other. Used to drive her so mad..."

Sun, Rick, Sarah and Jack finally got involved in the conversation as well, and very soon juicy stories about non-tourist foreigners and the problems and unfair treatment they had to deal with, were flying back and forth.

D couldn't help shooting a glance towards Joe and Gerry, who were walking in the very front, far ahead of everyone else, obviously immersed in a lively discussion about something.

She was somewhat glad Joe was so far away because functioning normally with him close-by and all the friends around was nerve-wrecking, to say the least. Of course, he didn't even have to be close-by to have an unbalancing effect. It was enough to just think of their encounter in the lake, and she was hit by a brief spell of breathlessness accompanied by slightly wobbly knees. The cover-up face worked fine so far, though. Thank God! No one would have ever guessed. Except for Sarah, of course. D knew that Sarah saw right through her, no matter what she said or did. Like twenty minutes ago in their room…

D had just stepped out of the bathroom and Sarah had looked up from her book.

"Your phone just beeped," Sarah had said. "You probably got a message. From Pete – or from my brother…"

D had taken the phone and checked the message, feeling Sarah watching her.

"Not Pete…" she had said innocently, her eyes on the phone.

"Good!" Sarah had said and turned back to her book.

The message had been from Joe,

> *Any way I can catch you alone this evening? If I come up with something top secret?*

D had quickly tapped in a short answer (*'Fine, Mr. 007'*) and then put the phone away. She had looked over at Sarah, who first pretended to be immersed in her book and then suddenly glanced up with an exaggeratedly innocent expression.

"I'm not saying anything," Sarah had said.

"But I can just see you *thinking*," D had laughed.

"I'm not thinking *anything*," Sarah had assured her. "I wouldn't even know *what* to think right now…"

"Good, that makes two of us then."

~~~

When they stepped into the Italian restaurant, D couldn't believe how hungry she was. The smell of pizza, garlic and oregano made her stomach growl. Not that it was a real surprise, though. She hadn't eaten much ever since the aborted dinner last night.

Joe didn't enjoy dinner very much. He tried hard not to appear too uninterested, but he just couldn't help it. While the others were babbling about all sorts of things, his mind was preoccupied producing a variety of ideas how a secret meeting with Danny could possibly be accomplished tonight. So far he had had to scrap every single one of those ideas right after they had popped up, however. It was annoyingly complicated.

He looked across the table where D was laughing about something Carrey had said. He glanced to his right and found Sarah watching him. Man, how he hated having her breathe down his neck all the time. What he would give for Sarah to instantaneously forget... (In fact, he wished he had Men in Black's little memory eraser wand to use on her.) He knew he was doing Sarah wrong, of course. She didn't mean any harm. She had even wanted to help him. He knew that perfectly well. But he didn't want her help. Under *no* circumstances. He needed to take care of some things with Danny himself and it might require some methods that Sarah surely wouldn't approve of. (A kiss as a means of persuasion, for example.)

"Anyone want the rest of my pizza," he heard D ask from across the table. On her plate she had a third of her pizza left that she pointed to now like an expert saleswoman at the vegetable market.

"I'll see what I can do..." That was Jack.

D handed him her plate and took his empty one in return.

Watching the scene, Joe felt a pang of fury. The way Jack had just taken that plate and touched her hand in the process... Joe suddenly remembered the conversation he had had with Jack. About the friendship Jack didn't want to ruin. Joe had almost forgotten about it, but there it was again! And it seemed even clearer now. Jack was in love with Danny! They came to parties together, she dished up his salad for him, he called her in the middle of the night, they traded leftover food like an old married couple...

Joe knew that she trusted Jack. Probably much more than she would ever trust *him* again. And if Jack was in love with her, it was probably just a question of time before he would throw all reservations about the wonderful friendship overboard and go for it.

Joe took another quick gulp from his glass trying to wash away the bitter taste that had suddenly appeared in his mouth.

Jack taking D's pizza led Gerry to comment on how he used to be slightly overweight as a kid because his two older sisters kept feeding him their leftovers.

"Poor Gerry," Anja said and rubbed her hand over his belly.

"Yeah, poor me! Thank God I have a wife now that eats most of her food herself."

"Oh, was that a requirement?" Anja teased.

"Of course!"

Gerry went on telling some other stories about growing up with his two older sisters. Kim held against it that her two older brothers had probably been far worse than those sisters. This triggered an avalanche of comments from everyone who had a sibling, and finally even Joe felt inclined to share with his friends that, as far as he was concerned, life with just one slightly older sister could be quite traumatizing. He was just in the middle of proving his point with some colorful anecdotes when Sarah kicked him under the table and started dishing up some stories about life with her younger, out of control Casanova brother...

It was almost nine when they paid and started discussing how to continue the evening.

D shot a look across the table where Joe was busy typing some message into his phone.

"I want to go to a place where I can dance..." Sun said dreamily.

"Yeah, music wouldn't be bad," Jack agreed with a quick look at Sarah, who nodded and shot a glance at D.

D shrugged. She didn't feel much like going out, and even less like dancing – especially since she definitely wouldn't be able to dance with the one she wanted. But it was too early to call it a night without raising some questions.

Rick asked the waiter for a good place to go to that had music. He promptly got the name of a pub just ten minutes away.

Tony suddenly remembered that he had seen another bar on the way over and decided that he and Kim might try that.

"I'll join you," Carrey said.

Jack looked over at Joe. "You're coming with us, Joe, right?" he asked.

Joe placed his phone on the table and looked up. "Oh," he blew out some air with his lower lip sticking out and shook his head. "Na, actually... call me boring, but I think I'm going back to the hotel. I'm just really tired. Didn't sleep a whole lot last night – for obvious reasons."

There was some understanding murmur around the table.

"I'll walk back with Joe then," Anja said to Gerry. "And you can still go out. It's really okay. I just want to still call Dad and then go to bed."

"I don't know," Gerry didn't seem convinced.

Across the table D was wracking her brain what to do. She glanced over at Joe, and for a very short moment he met her eyes. Then, saying something to Sarah beside him, he innocently tapped his hand on his phone on the table and let his eyes flicker over to her one more time.

Intuitively D reached for her own phone in her purse and pulled it out enough to see that there was a message. From him.

*Go w S and try to escape in 30 min or so. Let me know if it works.*

*Joe*

Letting the phone slide back into her purse she gave a short nod without looking up. Then she looked at Sarah, who was talking to Jack. "I'll come with you guys," D said.

"Yeah, me too," Gerry proclaimed.

So, they split up.

As she walked through the pedestrian area behind Jack and Sarah, D realized that, whichever excuse she would come up with to go back to the hotel early, Sarah would never buy it. But that was okay.

They reached the pub the waiter from the Italian restaurant had recommended. It turned out to be crowded and very loud. Determined, Rick and Jack pushed through anyway, with the others trailing behind. They headed for the bar since all the tables were taken.

Standing behind Jack, who was trying to get the attention of the guy behind the bar, D could feel people pushing and shoving from all sides, and there were still more people coming in. The band was incredibly loud and the air was stuffy. Jack had finally managed to get the barkeeper to look his way and was just turning around to ask her and the others what they wanted to drink. D realized that having to stay in this crowded insanely loud place for the duration of an entire drink seemed more like torture than like fun. On Jack's other side she spotted Sarah shaking her head vigorously and turning around to Sun.

"I don't want to stay here," she yelled in Jack's direction.

"Neither do I!" D shouted from her end.

Jack shrugged and looked at Rick and Gerry. Gerry pointed to the exit.

And a minute later they were all outside again.

"God, that was loud," Sarah sighed.

"Well, we can go and see what the place is like that Tony and the others went to," Jack suggested.

"I think I know where it is," Rick said.

"I think I'll pass." That was Gerry. "I'm kind of tired." And with a wink at Sarah he added, "And I'm a little worried to leave my wife alone in the hotel with your brother for too long after all the stuff you told us about him earlier."

"I'll go with Gerry," D quickly said, relieved about this excellent opportunity to get away. "You guys have fun!" she added.

In an attempt to avoid looking at Sarah, her gaze drifted to Jack, who looked back at her with a somewhat bewildered expression and then dropped his gaze.

"Oh, you two wimps," Sun teased.

"Yeah, really…" Jack agreed absent-mindedly.

# Boat Ride

On the way back to the hotel Gerry gave Anja a quick call to say he was coming back. While he was busy with that, D got out her own phone and quickly sent Joe a short message.

*Escaped.*

*D*

In the elevator she said goodbye to Gerry, who got out on the fourth floor, then checked her phone again on her way up to the sixth. There was a new message from Joe:

*Great! Let's meet at the rental boats.*

She sent a quick reply:

*OK. Just getting a jacket.*

She had to ask the receptionist where she needed to go.

The guy smiled. "Oh, you're looking for the young man that just picked up the key, right?" he said. "Because normally we don't rent them out this time of night…" He gave her a conspiring smile and told her to walk around the hotel on the outside to where the door from the spa area came out and then go down some stairs to the piers. She realized it must be somewhere around where she had started her swim in the afternoon.

Outside it was getting cooler and she was glad that she had brought the jacket with her. The path around the hotel was well-lit but once she reached the stairs that lead down to the piers, she had to watch her step because one of the lamps had a burned-out bulb.

She spotted Joe at the bottom of the stairs, sitting on a wooden box that probably held boat supplies.

"Hi there," he got up. "You got away…"

She walked down the stairs, feeling her heart pick up speed.

"Yeah, it worked out okay," she could hear her own voice cracking a bit. "Gerry left, too."

As she reached the bottom of the stairs, Joe was just stepping to the side, right into the unlit corner between the stairs and the wall behind the pier.

"Where are you going?" She followed him.

"I'm retreating into the dark," he whispered with a chuckle.

"Oh, why's that?" She tried to sound cool and maybe she even did, but her pulse was racing.

"So no one can see what I'm doing with my unsuspecting victims." He reached out, grabbed her arm and pulled her closer.

She couldn't help laughing as she stumbled forward and towards him, catching herself by placing her forearms and hands against his chest.

"Was that plural?" she asked. "Are you waiting for someone else?"

"No, just you..." he said softly and wrapped his arms around her.

"And why would you think I'm *unsuspecting*?" she challenged.

"Well, aren't you?" he gave her a disappointed look.

She huffed out a laugh and dropped her gaze. "Are you kidding? I'm actually expecting the worst."

"The worst being *what*?" He ran his palms up her back to her shoulder blades.

"Oh, I don't know..." she shrugged, suddenly feeling the dizzying effect of his touch.

"Tell me," Joe insisted with a grin while leaning in a bit, his face dangerously close to hers. "I need to know how high the expectations are."

Swallowing hard, she shook her head, suddenly unable to look at him. If he hadn't had his arms around her she would have pulled away.

Obviously sensing the sudden change in dynamic, Joe tightened his embrace and leaned the side of his head against hers. "Can we please *not* do that?" he pleaded, his nose pushing away her hair where it was covering her ear.

"Do what?" she asked quietly, even though she knew perfectly well what he meant.

"Take three steps back after we just managed to take one forward this afternoon," he said calmly.

"I'm not..." she claimed weakly.

"Sure about that?"

She closed her eyes and shrugged. Her mouth was too dry to even think of some kind of verbal response.

"Hey," Joe pulled away enough so he could look at her, both hands on her shoulders. "You said it's not going to evaporate..."

"It hasn't..."

"Well, good..."

He leaned closer again, the tip of his nose softly touching up against hers. He tilted his head.

She closed her eyes.

"Not going to fight it, huh?" he whispered and placed a first warm kiss on her lips.

"Against good judgment…" she moved her hands up, slid them against the back of his head and buried her fingers in his hair.

Once more he softly tipped his nose against hers and then his lips were back on hers. She kissed him back, pulling his face a little closer. Her head buzzing, her stomach tingling. She realized that this was *it*. The perfect kiss!

She had blocked out – for a long time – that kisses like this actually *did* exist. Because with Pete they didn't. They never had. And then Joe jumped back onto the scene, grabbed her and kissed her and it was still… perfect. It just worked. Warm, easy, playful, effortless. No awkward mishaps, clumsy touches, forced tongue work, embarrassed giggles. This was the kind of kiss that had the potential of a highly addictive drug. And there was a good chance he knew it.

Joe felt her lips move against his (and her tongue for that matter) and it made it inhumanly hard to focus on the actual agenda he had for this meeting. But he really needed to focus! Focus, focus, focus!!! He broke the kiss. Sucked in a quick breath. Felt her do the same. Leaning his forehead against hers, his arms still wrapped around her, he tried to catch his breath and recall the initial plan. It hadn't included making out on the pier the minute she came down the stairs – even if, right now, that seemed like a highly attractive alternative. Much more attractive, in fact, than getting on a paddle boat with seats so far apart that even holding hands would be a challenge.

Still, the boat ride was the perfect opportunity to be alone with her in a place where no one could suddenly barge in and where she couldn't just get up and leave if she didn't like what he told her. And there were still two things he really *needed* to tell her. Until that was done, he better not take this kissing-hugging-touching thing any further.

But then he couldn't resist. He leaned in and brushed his cheek against hers, placed a kiss against the side of her neck and thought he could hear her gasp for air. Good! He moved up and gently bit her earlobe.

"What's that?" she pulled away, giggling. "The alligator striking again?"

"Yep, very dangerous," he laughed and pulled her back into a close embrace. "You better be careful around these murky waters."

"I know," she said, glancing up at him, "I already encountered a really freaky and dangerous creature this afternoon when I went swimming."

"Oh, you did? Didn't hurt you though, did it?"

"Let's just say I got away just in time." She chuckled. "Or maybe I didn't seem tasty enough."

Joe laughed out loud. "Na, I would kind of doubt that!" He bit her ear lobe again. Then he let go of her and straightened up.

"Okay, let's go on a little boat ride," he said.

Looking a little dazed, she nodded.

Joe looked at the boats that were lined up along the pier he and D were standing on. There were four boats with a narrow wooden dock in-between. Each boat had a ring on the bow through which a metal chain was pulled and locked to the pier.

"I think it's the last one. Number four..." Joe said and pointed towards the end of the pier.

D followed him to the last boat.

Squatting in front of it, Joe grabbed the chain with his braced right hand and pulled it up until he found the lock. With his left hand he produced a little key from the inside pocket of his jacket.

Standing close-by, D watched him fiddled a bit clumsily with the lock and the key. That braced hand and the left hand didn't work well together on precision movements like this.

"Let me do it, okay?" she squatted next to him.

"Are you saying I'm too disabled?" he asked, pretending to be devastated.

"Well, if you drop the key, we'll probably have to spend the night diving for it," she said with a smile and took the key out of his hand.

"Yeah, we definitely don't want that," he casually ran his hand over her back as he straightened up.

D swallowed, struggling not to drop the key herself now. It was touches like that that got her every time.

She unlocked the chain and pulled it out of the ring on the boat.

She got up and handed him back the key. "Did you bribe them?" she asked.

"Not really," he motioned for her to get onto the boat first. "But they have a copy of my driver's license and my credit card number." He grinned. "If we sink this thing, I'm ruined…"

"Oh, wow. Then we better try not to sink it!" she laughed, settling in her seat. She took her sandals off and placed them in the middle console.

With his braced hand Joe pointed at the lever between them. "Why don't you steer."

"Great!" she shook her head with mock indignation. "Now I come down here thinking you're taking me out on a nice comfortable boat ride where all I've got to do is sit and enjoy the stars. And what happens? I get to sit on these hard plastic seats, I have to pedal, and now you even expect me to navigate this ship?!?"

"Yeah, now look what you've got yourself into!" He smiled triumphantly. "I wasn't looking for a pampered passenger, I needed an exploitable skipper!"

With a playful frown she grabbed the lever and adjusted it so they wouldn't hit the pier as they backed out of the parking position.

"Which way do you want to go?" she asked him as she turned the boat to face away from the pier.

"That's up to you," he said. "Just take us out there somewhere. Try to avoid any rocks and icebergs, though."

"Yeah, I'll be careful," she assured him with a quick glance over at him. "Because with a disabled passenger like you I have to be extra careful."

Joe pretended to frown.

She shrugged. "Well, if we capsize…– considering the shape you're in, I may end up having to save you!"

"Oh, come on, I'm not that…" he paused and raised his eyebrows in surprise. "Oh, you'd actually try to save me, huh?"

D laughed. "Just don't get too full of yourself here, okay. I've saved all kinds of creatures from drowning – a cat, two birds, several bees, one tiny lizard…"

"Oh, okay." Joe nodded. "Thanks for putting it into perspective!"

"No problem!" She gave him her best smile. Then she turned her head and looked out towards the water in front of them. "Let's go to the other side of this," she pointed up to the spa area and adjusted the lever while they were both pedaling.

"Back towards the pier where we were this afternoon?" he asked. Then he shrugged. "That's not very exciting, but I guess since we're on a top secret mission here…"

They pedaled for a while with no one saying anything.

As they passed the tip of the peninsula, the big flag flying softly in the bit of wind there was, Joe stopped pedaling.

"Giving up already?" D asked.

"Yeah, time to float and recover…" he proclaimed putting his arms behind his head and leaning back in his seat looking up at the sky.

"Nice night…" she said following his gaze up at the stars.

"Yeah, and pretty nice company…" he said with a quick glance over at her.

She pulled her feet up on her seat. "Do you know anything about the stars we have up there?" she asked, her eyes still turned upward.

He shook his head. "Nope. But if you want me to, I can quickly make something up."

She laughed, shooting him a look. "I bet!"

"Like…" He paused, still making up his mind as to what to tell her. "Like, see the seven stars that are kind of in an S-shape over there?" Joe made a grand gesture towards the sky to their left. "And the three kind of connected to those. That's the very famous *alligator*. It's rarely ever visible."

"And hardly ever correctly identified, I bet," D chuckled. "Only the most experienced astro–" she was momentarily scrambling for the right ending.

"Astronomer," Joe told her with a snobbish little nod. "That's right. It takes an experienced astronomer…"

"Only still waiting to be awarded a Nobel Prize, aren't you," D concluded.

"Exactly," he grinned at her. "And… Did you know that if you see a falling star, you can make a wish…?" He looked right at her, expecting her to shoot back something witty, and suddenly realized that he may have just said something horribly wrong. A shadow seemed to flash over her face and then her gaze flickered away from him and up to the stars.

"Yeah, so I've heard," she said dryly. "I remember trying that a few times. Didn't work…"

Even without her specifying the wish she was talking about, her tone and the way she had just fallen silent so abruptly, was enough for him to grasp that there was a good chance that one of these wishes had been about him.

Her eyes turned up to the sky, her expression was an unreadable mask now. And Joe could just see it: how every time it hit her how much he had really hurt her and that now she was sitting here with him, her mind rattled through all the reasons why this was sooo wrong.

"Hey, Danny…" He reached over and nudged her shoulder with his braced hand. "No evaporating, okay…"

She flinched. But then her mouth curved up in a weak half smile.

Feeling weirdly exposed, D struggled to chase away the memory of standing in the middle of Tower Bridge on one of the first evenings in London. She had been feeling miserable. Looking up into the clear night sky she had suddenly seen this falling star. And she had been stupid enough to see it as a sign (Hahaha!). She had made that one desperate wish – a wish that hadn't come true until unexpectedly three days ago.

In an attempt to ease the tension that seemed to have gotten ahold of them, Joe let out a theatrical sigh and shook his head. "When I decided on the boat ride I had *no* idea how far apart those seats would be…" he said.

D turned her head and looked at him. "Yeah, miles apart," she said, the weak smile starting to look more real now. "What were you thinking? Really didn't think that through well enough, huh?"

Joe nodded, laughing. "I was actually going for an electric boat with a narrow, cushioned shared bench, but those boats are put to sleep in the boathouse at eight and not even a platinum credit card and a big tip would have gained me access to one of them. So, I had to go with the paddle boat…"

She nodded, with an enlightened chuckle. "Oh, that's why…"

"Yeah, that's why…" He resumed pedaling.

She still had her feet on the seat. And he could feel her looking at him from the side.

"Joe…" he heard her say, her tone serious. "What *is* this?"

He gave her a short look and stopped pedaling again. "What do you mean?" he didn't dare look at her.

"Why are we here?" D specified. "What's the purpose of floating around in this boat?"

He shrugged, his gaze at the boathouse straight ahead. With his braced hand he traced the edge of the middle console between them.

Silence.

Joe knew that if he decided to do this, it would most likely destroy in a heartbeat any good vibes they may have just recovered. Did he really want to do it?

"There are two things I have to tell you," he finally said with a cautious look at her.

"Sounds dangerous," she said, her eyes fixed on her knees.

Silence again, except for the noise of some little waves splashing against the side of the boat.

"What?" she asked quietly. "*What* do you have to tell me?"

Joe let out a tense little breath through his nose. "Just hear me out and don't bite off my head before I'm done, okay?"

"Oh, is that why you took me on a boat ride?" she asked with a nervous chuckle. "So I have no way to run off and can't even reach over to kill you because the seats are so far apart?"

"That has never even crossed my mind," Joe said, trying for a joking tone. It sounded a little forced.

"Okay then," D said and drew in a deep breath as if to brace herself.

Joe took this as an encouragement to start. Glaring at the water beside him, he cleared his throat. "Sarah knows..." he then said without any further preparatory statement. "She... well, she knows that I was at your place those two nights. There wasn't much I could have done. Once she identified my sweater as the one she had seen under your sofa, she knew where I'd been." He exhaled. And waited for her to explode...

But then she didn't.

He glanced over at her. Just to make sure she was still there and showed vital functions.

She was still sitting with her legs pulled up and had put her hands over her feet as if to warm them.

"I already know," she said calmly. "She told me this afternoon."

It was unexpected. Joe had been prepared for her to rant and scream and possibly reach into the lake and shovel a load of cold water over his way. But instead she was telling him that?!?

For a moment there, he wasn't sure how to feel about it. Relieved that she hadn't jumped ship yet or furious that good old Sarah hadn't kept her mouth shut even though he had explicitly told her to.

"I'll kill her!" he said darkly.

"She was trying to help," D said. She had turned her head his way and looked at him, her cheek against her knee.

"Yeah, I bet…" He shook his head, definitely feeling more irritated than relieved.

"She only told me that you had left to go back to the house and not run back to Liz…" D informed him, obviously determined to defend Sarah.

Joe shrugged and turned away.

"Whatever," he grumbled.

"Well, you better thank her because before that, I thought that's exactly where you'd gone."

Chewing on his lip, he dipped his left hand into the water beside him and contemplated her remark. He was definitely *not* going to *thank* Sarah…

"Sarah just wanted to help you, okay," D insisted. "She even tried to make me… well… She said you weren't coming back."

He turned to look at her, his eyebrows raised. "She tried to make you do *what?*" he asked, genuinely interested in the one missing word.

"Nothing!" D claimed and looked away.

"No, *not* nothing," Joe pressed suddenly slightly amused. "Tell me!"

"Grrr, you're just…" she shook her head. "She… well, she wanted me to let you know if it meant anything to me that you came back."

Joe laughed out loud. Not a very happy laugh. "Like that would ever happen…" he scoffed.

Her eyes darted back to him. "What? That it *means* anything to me?"

"No, that you'd actually admit it."

For a moment she just stared back at him angrily, then she dropped her gaze. "That's not fair!" she said quietly.

"Maybe not," he admitted, caught off-guard by her reaction. "Yeah, I guess that really *wasn't* fair. Sorry…"

D nodded without looking up at him.

"I had told Sarah to keep out of it," Joe said, just to keep the conversation going. "And I wasn't really planning on coming back."

For a moment no one said anything. They were just floating, both following their own thoughts.

"But you changed your mind," D finally mumbled.

He nodded. "Yep, changed my mind… Don't ask me why."

"I won't," she said warily. "It's really none of my business." She turned to him and there was a little smile on her face.

He smiled back.

D straightened up in her seat, slid her feet off the seat and tilted her head from one side to the other a few times as if to loosen up. She placed her feet back onto the pedals and started pedaling again. "Come on!" she said.

With both of them pedaling, they made it almost all the way to the pier at the boathouse and then turned around.

As they started making their way back towards the hotel, Joe was debating if he should still try to bring up the shower issue. He had gotten off unexpectedly easy in regard to his first revelation. There was reason for concern, though, that the shower issue wouldn't go over half as well.

Maybe he should just let it go. Maybe it didn't even matter.

Only that it *did* matter! To him it mattered a great deal! It was like this dormant sliver that was always going to be in the way if it wasn't pulled out sooner rather than later.

"There's something else…" he said into the silence.

Even without looking at her, he could sense her tense up. She stopped pedaling and, from the corner of his eye, Joe could see her briefly turn his way and give him a questioning look from the side.

"*What?*" she asked, sounding a little breathless, maybe even scared.

Joe was scrambling for the right thing to say. Despite the fact that he had brooded over this a lot since yesterday morning, he still had no great concept how to handle it.

"It's about the time we broke up…" he finally said. The moment he heard himself say it, he knew that this had been a disastrous introduction. A glance at her confirmed it: she had jerked around, her feet sliding off the seat.

"Don't go there," she said with a freaked-out edge to her voice, her hands raised in a defiant gesture. "Just don't…!"

"Well, it's not my favorite piece of conversation either," Joe said a bit half-heartedly. "There's just something I think you really should know…"

"I do not want to hear it!" she retorted sharply.

"Danny, listen…"

"No, *you* listen," she pointed a finger at him, her hands shaky. "There was no *we* in that breakup, okay?"

Joe found himself looking back at her, his throat tight and his mind blank. He hadn't been sure how she would react. Now he knew.

"If I remember right," a scathing tone had crept into her voice. "There was just a *you* and a *her*. *You* screwing *her* or the other way round…"

412

Biting his lower lip, Joe exhaled audibly and nodded. Now that she had put it that way, he had no idea what else he could possibly still say.

D had stepped back into the pedals, and the way they were moving was a clear indication of how much agitation she felt. Well, he could contribute his own...

With both of them strongly pedaling now and no word being spoken, they made it back around the peninsula in no time.

They had only three hundred meters left to their parking position when D suddenly pulled her legs up on her seat again.

Surprised, Joe stopped pedaling too and shot her a glance.

Sitting in her seat like a limp doll, she was staring at the pier ahead.

He waited for her to say something. But she didn't. And even though he tried hard to come up with some icebreaker line himself, he just couldn't think of anything. Maybe now the lack of sleep was finally catching up with him. Thinking clearly suddenly was extremely hard and finding great solutions seemed impossible. He felt tired and empty and resigned. A bit like last night after his delightful phone conversation with Liz.

"Let's go back," he said and resumed pedaling. And as the boat slowly started moving again, he felt her join in.

D could see the pier come closer and closer. And even though she felt sick to her stomach and her hand was trembling on the lever, she steered the boat perfectly into the parking position, which suddenly seemed like a point of no return.

She knew she had overreacted. Totally. But it was too late to take it back now. Joe was absolutely *not* famous for his desire to talk things over, at least not while they had been together. So, if there was something he considered important enough to bring it up here and now, she should have let him say it, find out what it was! Why not hear him out? Why did the pure thought of him touching that time and those issues, bring on a feeling that resembled suffocation?

The answer, she realized, was highly complex: First of all she was a bit worried that he might produce some new evidence showing that she had made a mistake three years ago when she had refused to talk to him and just left for London. It was relatively unlikely, though, that such evidence existed.

What scared her much more was the fact that discussing the past would revive all kinds of horrible memories. And once that happened, it would be impossible for her to further ignore that this was the same guy who had already once left her world in shambles. And that glaring at the stars with him or rolling around half-naked on a sofa together, or making out in the lake was, therefore, not a good idea at all. If they discussed now what had happened three years ago, there was a very good chance that their little whatever-it-was here would evaporate faster than he could even blink.

Of course she realized that in the long run, if they kept seeing each other (if he even still felt like wanting to see her after what she had just thrown at him) they would have to tackle those issues from the past at some point. It was unavoidable. But she couldn't do it here and now.

The boat slid into its parking spot and Joe climbed out onto the pier. For a moment it looked like he was going to offer her his hand to get out, but then he pulled it back in mid-movement and just ran his fingers through his hair. Obviously he assumed that she would never take his hand now.

Stumbling onto the pier, her sandals in her hand, she realized that she so wished he had grabbed her hand – and her, for that matter – and ignored what she had just said on the boat.

Without giving her another look, Joe walked around to the front of the boat, snatched the chain from the floor and squatted to pull it through the ring on the bow.

Feeling somewhat paralyzed, D slipped her sandals on.

"You don't have to wait for me," he told her over his shoulder. "We can't walk up there together anyway. Just go ahead…"

His somber tone made her stomach cramp. So that was it then? At least for tonight…? The thought that it might not just be for tonight but that with her scathing remark she may have ruined it for years to come, made her throat tighten.

The lock clicked around the chain and Joe got up.

He gave her a weary look. "You're released," he told her a little impatiently and shoved his hands into the pockets of his jacket. "No need to stick around."

D felt her heartbeat up to her throat. They couldn't just part like this and go to bed. Or could they?

She drew in a deep breath, trying to pull herself together.

"I'm sorry," she finally said, trying to hold his gaze.

He raised his eyebrows in surprise. "For *what?*"

"I'm sorry about the *you-and-her* thing," she specified.

For a moment he just looked back at her with an unreadable expression. Then he shrugged. "Why? You're right. It was me and her..."

D reached for the handrail and grabbed ahold of it. "I–" she started.

Joe shook his head, his hands raised like in surrender.

"Let's just forget about it for now, okay," he said with audible exasperation. "You don't want to talk about it and neither do I if I'm honest. I'd much rather go to bed. And you should too."

"Maybe some other time?" she suggested weakly. "I mean... the talk."

Shrugging, he placed a hand against the stone wall where they had kissed earlier. "Maybe..." he said vaguely, his expression strained.

"Okay, well..." With a helpless shrug she took the first step up. "Good night then..."

"Good night," he said with a forced smile.

# Getting in the way of something?

Joe opened the door to his room and felt his heart drop. The room was lit and from the bathroom he heard running water. Shit! Jack was back already! How had that happened?

Feeling a little dumbstruck, he slipped out of his jacket and sat down on the bed. He was wracking his brain how he could possibly explain to Jack that he wasn't in bed yet...

The bathroom door opened and Jack appeared – his eyebrows raised.

"Oh, here you are..." he said.

"Yeah, I was..."

"In the park trying to figure things out?" Jack suggested dryly.

Joe squinted. What was that?

Jack unbuttoned his shirt and took it off, revealing some abs Joe hadn't realized he had. Not bad...

"Joe," Jack said with a firm look down on him and an unexpectedly stern voice. "What's going on?"

Joe blinked. "What do you mean?"

"I mean... What's going on with you and D?"

Joe huffed out a laugh that didn't quite sound real. "*What?*"

"Oh, come on now...," Jack said with some irritation. "I'm not dumb, okay? When you desperately need my swim shorts five minutes after *she* went swimming, and you both go home within half an hour of each other and then *you* don't show up in here until now... and Sarah and I run into D in the lobby..."

Joe bit down on his lower lip. Excellent! He let out a sharp breath through his nose and shrugged. "*Nothing's* going on," he claimed. "Just trying to straighten some things out, that's all..." He couldn't help wondering what story Danny had told them.

Jack shook his head, rolling his eyes. "Yeah, right."

Joe got up from the bed to at least be on eye-level with Jack, rather than having to stare at Jack's amazing abs while Jack looked down on him.

His eyes locked with Jack's now, Joe felt some of the fury resurface that he had felt during dinner when Jack had taken Danny's plate.

"What's it to you anyway, Jack?" he challenged, his tone a bit acidic.

"What's it to me?" Jack blasted, his eyebrows raised like he couldn't believe he would even be asked such a stupid question. "Well, to begin with, I'm pretty worried about a friend whom you have already messed with once."

Joe looked back at Jack with a frozen expression. That *teacher-lecturing-an-out-of-line-student* tone…

"You're my friend too, Joe," Jack continued more conciliatorily. "You know that, right? But in this case I'm *not* going to stand by again and let you do any more damage than you've already done."

"Oh, is that so?" Joe's eyes narrowed.

"Well, yeah…" Jack seemed a little confused by the confrontational approach. He had expected a little more insight and self-criticism.

"And that's really all you're worried about? Or is it more that I'm getting in the way of something here?"

"Huh?" Jack's eyes widened with bafflement.

"This is not just about me hurting your *friend*," Joe specified. "She's way more than a friend to you, isn't she? You said so yourself. Just still not sure, huh, if you want to ruin that *friendship* for – sex?"

Jack's eyes had gone from wide to squinting. He didn't get it. "What the hell are you talking about?" he shook his head. Then, just as Joe drew in an angry breath to lay it out in detail, it hit him. "*D?*" Jack looked bewildered. "You think I was talking about *D?*" He let out a little laugh. "I should have probably never even said anything," he said sounding almost amused now. "But since I have… No, Joe, I *wasn't* talking about D."

Now Joe frowned. Dropped his gaze. Let his mind review again all the information he had on the matter. It was clear, wasn't it?

"Yeah, go ahead," Jack said, throwing his hands in the air. "If you give it some thought, I'm sure you can figure it out. It's not that hard, really."

With that, he unzipped his pants, stepped out of them, hung them over a chair and went to sit down on his bed.

Joe shot him a puzzled look.

"Your sister…?" Jack suggested like it really was a no-brainer.

Within just two seconds, Joe's expression changed from puzzled to enlightened – and almost relieved. He leaned his head back, his eyes focused on the ceiling, and exhaled. "Yeah… Right… Why didn't I see that?"

"Because sometimes you're one freaking idiot," Jack retorted.

"I guess…" Joe admitted with a half-smile.

"Anyway," Jack said. "Now that we've got that sorted out, I'm going to go to sleep. Because I'm tired. And looking at you, I strongly recommend that you do the same. You look pretty wasted."

"I feel like it, too, thanks a lot," Joe mumbled. And, still processing the news, he slowly wandered into the bathroom.

When he came back, Jack was lying in bed, his arms behind his head, his eyes closed.

"I think you should go for it," Joe said quietly.

"What?" Jack opened one of his eyes.

"Sarah…"

"Oh…"

"I think you should go for it," Joe repeated. "Friendship sometimes just doesn't do it…"

His eye closed again, Jack nodded. "I'll see…" And after a little pause he added, "Be careful with D!!!"

Nodding gloomily, Joe went to turn off the ceiling light.

"I'm being careful," he mumbled.

# Drive Home from the Lake

On the drive home Sun was sleeping in the backseat.

D had the radio turned on, some music was playing and her brain was going in circles about last night. She was glad that Jack next to her didn't say much. In fact, he was unusually quiet. Almost as if he were brooding over something himself. D shot him a brief glance and found him staring out the side window, lost in thought. For a moment she considered, asking him what he was thinking about, but then she stayed quiet because she really didn't feel like talking. And he didn't look like he did either.

She was desperate to get to Deens. Drop Sun and Jack off and then go home, close the door and be alone. No cheered-up friends around her, no worried looks from Sarah and no glances from Joe that shifted away as soon as she tried to meet them. She needed to be by herself. And think. Make some sense of what was going on. Of what she was feeling. Of what in the world Joe was doing.

He had been evading her all day.

At breakfast, when they had happened to arrive almost at the same time, he had made sure he sat at the table with Rick and Sun (who had been about ready to leave), instead of just sitting at the big table with her and some other friends who were all just starting breakfast.

After breakfast they had decided to all go and play another round of mini golf. In the course of this, Joe had kept a five meters distance from her at all times and never even once met her eyes.

And then there had been this weird scene in the lobby just before they had left. She had checked out and was still waiting for Jack and Sun to appear, when Sarah and Joe had come down with the elevator. They had checked out, then Sarah had come towards her (with Joe trailing behind) and given her a message from Jack that he would be down in five minutes. Then Sarah had decided to still quickly use the restroom in the lobby and left her standing there, alone with Joe. For a moment there had been this tense silence with both of them glaring at the floor, then Joe had grabbed Sarah's bag from beside him and – carefully avoiding eye-contact – said something like *'Well, I think I'll load that into the car. Have a safe drive home.'* And he was off.

D tried to tell herself that all this had just been Joe being *top secret*. But an uneasy feeling that was residing in the pit of her stomach since breakfast, told her that it was way more than that.

~~~

Sarah stared out the window of the Volvo, pleasantly surprised that, for a change, her brother was driving in a perfectly civilized manner.

She glanced over at him. He had his eyes on the road and a somewhat strained expression on his face. She chewed on her lip, suppressing the urge to ask questions. As much as it had initially shocked and surprised her that he had hooked up with D again, the more she had gotten used to the thought since Friday morning, the more excited she actually felt that there might, after all, be some sort of happy ending. Only that Joe's face and somewhat strange behavior today gave reason for concern that the happy-end might not exactly be on track after all.

(She had even pretended that she needed to use the restroom in the hotel lobby, just to give D and him a moment alone. When she had returned, D was by herself, not exactly looking happy, and Joe had disappeared to the garage…)

"On Wednesday I'll meet Steve for lunch," Joe suddenly said. "You know, Liz's brother… He's got something to do around Deens and we still need to talk a few things over before he goes on vacation."

"You're covering for him?" Sarah asked.

"Mhmm" There was a short nod.

"When is that?"

"Two weeks from now," Joe said, "Sept 2$^{nd}$ to Sept 12$^{th}$. I'll be in Amsterdam from the 2$^{nd}$ to the 4$^{th}$ and then I'll cover for Steve at the office until that Friday. Then I'll probably come home over the weekend and go back there for the next week. There are some customers coming in and stuff, so I have to actually be there. Can't do it from here."

"Oh, okay…" Sarah muttered and shot him a cautious look from the side. "How is that going to work? I mean… Where are you going to stay? You're not going to stay with *her*, are you?"

The response was a quick violent shake of his head. "I'm just going to stay in the office," he said. "It's like a home to me by now…" He let out a bitter little laugh before he continued, "That office is fully equipped for overnight stays. Sleeper sofa, TV, shower in the hallway…"

"Oh," Sarah wasn't sure how to react. "Is that… how it worked?" she asked.

"Yep, sometimes." He shrugged.

"Oh, okay..." Sarah didn't quite know what else to say to this. Just another peek into what must have been the relationship from hell.

"Anyway," Joe said, "I just wanted to let you know that I'll be gone most of this coming Wednesday. First lunch with Steve and then I might actually try to go and see Mom afterwards."

"Have you talked to her yet?"

"No, I'll call her tonight and see if that would work for her. We could even go and see Grandma too, I guess."

"Well, if not this time, you definitely have to see Grandma sometime soon. She's been asking about you a lot lately."

"I know..." He sighed. "A lot of catching up to do while people still want to see me." He shot her a little smile. "Do you wanna come?" he asked.

"No, I've got to work until four," Sarah said. "And for a start, I think you should just go by yourself. Besides, Wednesday I'll meet with D after work. We'll go swimming or something and then for dinner and a maybe movie..."

She had considered adding something like *and since you're busy, I guess D will be still free...* 'but then she didn't, because at the mention of D, his face had turned hard. Sarah was still pondering that, when she suddenly saw his face brighten up. And then, with an almost devious look, he changed the topic.

"What's up with Jack?" he asked. "Got a girlfriend or something?"

"Ahm... not that I know of," Sarah muttered, slightly confused by the question. "Why?"

Joe was just winging it. Ever since finding out that Jack's secret love was Sarah, the idea of seeing those two together had grown on him – immensely. In a way it did feel a little weird, of course – probably comparable to Sarah's Teddy-and-Barbie issues, but the weirdness was outweighed by his conviction that Sarah and Jack would be a great match. An excellent match. The only problem was that he couldn't see how they would *ever* get together. They were so used to being good friends that it was going to take a real push to get out of that rut.

Jack usually was anything but shy, but in this particular constellation Joe was skeptical that Jack would ever work up the guts to make a move. It would probably require some form of encouragement or at least a little sign from Sarah. And Sarah (just like Danny) wasn't exactly carrying her heart on her sleeve – more like under one of those lead-plated aprons that you had to wear when getting an X-ray at the dentist.

So, even though Joe couldn't stand his sister meddling in his own love life, he didn't find anything wrong with his poking around in hers, as long as the meddling served a good cause. Which, he had decided, it definitely did!

This car ride seemed like the perfect chance to run some little general tests with her, figure out if her feelings for Jack were purely platonic…

"Why are you asking?" Sarah wanted to know, obviously not uninterested in the subject.

"Oh, no special reason," Joe lied. "Just seems like there might be someone… someone he likes. He's kind of dropped some hints but he didn't really come out with it…"

Maybe he was just imagining it, but he could have sworn Sarah had just straightened up in her seat and was tapping her foot (a sign of agitation?).

"Oh, really?" she said slowly. "What did he say?"

"Not much, really," Joe said lightly. "I thought *you* might know something."

"Never mentioned anyone to me," she responded, sounding a bit testy.

Silence.

Joe glanced over at her and found her staring gloomily out the window, obviously pondering the issue – and tapping her foot every once in a while.

"Just baffles me how Jack seems to always be single," Joe carried it further. "I would think as a woman I'd fly at him… but there's probably enough that do. We just don't know about them…" He grinned, hoping that Sarah would, at least deep inside, reject the idea that there might be anything about Jack she didn't know.

"Well, maybe he's just picky," Sarah suggested.

"Sure he's picky," Joe laughed. "But I guess whoever he's got a crush on now, meets the high standards. That's why I was wondering who it might be…"

"How do you know he's got a crush on someone if he didn't really tell you anything?" Sarah sounded irritated.

"Trust me, he's got a big crush on whoever it is. Maybe someone at work, or around where he lives, or… I don't know where else he meets women… But there's *someone*. I guarantee you that. Let's just hope it works out and she actually appreciates him."

Silence.

"I mean, not everyone knows him the way *we* do," Joe carried on. "He's smart, he's funny, he's got a real good heart and he's got some abs… wow! Even I stand in awe at that, and I'm not even the target-group. Gone swimming with him lately?"

"What?" Sarah looked at him. "No, I haven't… lately."

"Sauna?"

From the corner of his eye he could see her head turn his way even more. "I'm not going to the sauna with Jack!" she said like he was insane.

Joe had to keep himself from laughing. Good. He had her blood boiling and her imagination running wild with pictures of herself naked and sweating in a sauna with Jack and his perfect abs…

"Yeah, right. That would probably be weird," he admitted. "But you have for sure seen those *abs*?"

Beside him Sarah shrugged in a jerking fashion. He would have to turn and get a closer look but he would bet that she was blushing.

"To *you* he's just a friend, I know," Joe said saintly, "so you don't care about abs, I guess…" He paused for a moment to give her a chance to issue a statement, but she didn't.

"Anyway," he concluded cheerfully, "just wanted to pick your brains because I thought you might know something."

"Well, I don't…"

# I don't hate him...

D pulled the front door closed behind herself, parked her luggage under the coat rack in the entry way, dropped her purse on the dining table and hurried to the bathroom, the most important thing after a long drive like this.

A few minutes later she wandered from the bathroom to the living room a little aimlessly, shot a look out towards her tomato plants, straightened out the sofa cushions and then headed into the kitchen to get a glass of milk.

When she opened the fridge to take out the milk, the light didn't come on inside. She reached in and wiggled the light bulb a bit, but nothing happened. It stayed dark. She sniffled. Smelled kind of funny, too. Like spoilt food... She touched the milk package and it wasn't cold. Room temperature.

"Shit!" she hissed as soon as it dawned on her now that the fridge obviously wasn't working. A quick glance at the oven clock that was perfectly on time, confirmed that this wasn't a problem of a blown kitchen fuse or a temporary power outage but of a fridge that had obviously given up the ghost in her absence.

She pulled out the big garbage can from under the sink and started going through the entire contents of the refrigerator. She threw away what had surely not survived a weekend at room temperature and set aside all the things that would be fine.

Once the fridge was empty, she braced herself and opened the freezer door. Eeww! Determined to get this over with quickly, she reached in, grabbed a bag with frozen bread rolls and dumped it right into the garbage. When her hands pulled out the ice cream containers next, she paused, suddenly having this vision of Joe dishing up ice cream Thursday night. Exhaling sharply, she dropped the container into the garbage and continued, trying to stay focused on the fridge problem rather than Joe.

It was definitely time to get a new refrigerator. This one was ancient and there had been problems with it before. It had only been a matter of time until something like this happened. Both Robert and Jack had looked at it and told her that sooner or later she would need a new one. It seemed like the time had come...

Once she was done cleaning everything out, she sat down on a bar stool and opened her laptop. She spent the next hour on the internet, checking out new refrigerators and taking notes. She would swing by the electronics store Monday night after work, and if they had the model she wanted in stock, she would just order it and hope that it could be delivered soon or at least before she left for London a week from today.

She was still sitting in front of her computer when her phone rang from her purse. Her heart immediately kicking into racing speed and her stomach knotting, she slid off her chair and whisked around to the dining table from where she grabbed her purse. Part of her was hoping and praying that it was Joe, and part of her was scared to death that it might really be him. Well aware that she couldn't have it both ways, she pulled the phone out of her purse.

When the display showed her Dad's smiling face, D felt a sobering pang of disappointment mixed with a pinch of relief and realized that she might just be going crazy.

"Hi Dad," she tried for a cheerful tone.

"Hello," it was actually her Mom, calling on her Dad's phone. "Bad time?"

"No, it's fine!" D assured her. "How are you?"

"We're good," Mom said. "Just driving home from Robert's and Ann's, and Dad said we better check if our daughter is home yet or still out partying."

D laughed. "I'm back. Got back two hours ago. And it really wasn't a *party* weekend as you would imagine it…"

"You're a little old for that anyway," Mom teased.

"Thanks, Mom…"

Mom laughed. "Did you have a good time?"

"Yeah, it was nice." D said almost reflexively. "Just the getting-home-part wasn't so great…"

"Why? What's wrong?"

"Fridge is finally dead."

"Oh, no! – Her fridge is dead," Mom was informing Dad.

D could hear him say something, but she couldn't understand what.

"Tell Dad not to worry," she told Mom. "Jack has already checked that fridge a few times and Robert has too. It's just old – and now it's dead. I'll order a new one tomorrow. Already have one picked out. And in the meantime I can use the camping cooler that I have in the extra room."

"That's a good idea. I didn't realize you had one too."

"Yeah, I got that for the dorm, remember, and then used it a few times for camping…" Only in her mind she added, '… *with Joe.*'

"Well, good," Mom responded almost a little too lightly. "And I'm glad you had a good time."

"Yeah I did," D said, trying to copy her mother's light tone. "The hotel we went to is really neat. Pretty location, great food. There's a lot to do, too. We went up one of the mountains in a cable car, played mini golf, you can rent boats… You and Dad should go there sometime. For an anniversary or something like that."

"Sounds nice," Mom said, sounding a bit absent-minded.

"Yeah, it was nice." D said, trying to persuade herself that she was just imagining that her mother had something else on her mind.

"Well, good," Mom said. "Just wanted to check…"

"Robert told you, right?" D challenged.

"What?" Mom was such a bad actress.

"He told you about – Joe." (Wow. She hadn't used that name with her parents in ages.)

There was a short moment of silence.

"Yeah, well…" Mom was scrambling for the right response. "Robert said that… that Joe might be coming. And that you were kind of upset about it. But – I didn't want to ask you…"

"I *wasn't* upset," D corrected as if that was the most far-fetched thing in the world.

"Maybe that's not the word he used…" Mom backpedalled.

"Oh, I'm sure that's *exactly* the word he used!" D said darkly. "He's worse than Aunt Sauvie!"

On the other end, Mom laughed.

"He is!" D insisted while she scratched her left eyebrow and tried to decide what to do. She knew that Mom wouldn't press her on this topic unless she volunteered some more information. Did she want that?

"He was there," she finally said, like answering a question that she knew was floating around but hadn't even been said out loud yet. She had decided that she needed to talk about it to someone. And since there was no way she could discuss it with Sarah or Jack, and since she didn't want to admit it to Robert how much things had changed, confiding in Mom seemed like a good idea.

"Did you talk to him?" Mom asked cautiously.

"Yeah..." D slowly said. "I talked to him. Not that I had planned to but... yeah, I talked to him."

"Is he still together with that girl?"

"No." D responded quietly.

Silence.

"How do you feel about it?" Mom sounded concerned. "Are you okay?"

D was struggling with what felt like a lump in her throat.

"I don't know," she sighed, her voice unsteady. She was weighing if she should say any more.

There was silence on the other end. Her mother was obviously not sure if she could even ask what that meant.

D swallowed. "Mom..." she started.

"What?"

"We didn't just talk..."

"Oh..." One syllable uttered in total surprise.

"No, nothing really happened," D clarified quickly before Mom could imagine the wrong things such as activities that might result in grandchildren.

"Okay..." Mom said, her tone indicating that she wasn't sure what else to say.

"I was *so* sure I hated him," D said slowly. "And now... I don't hate him."

"You don't, huh?" Mom said, sounding more amused than surprised.

"You probably think I've totally lost my mind," D said unhappily.

Mom laughed out loud. "I don't think you've lost your mind. As far as I recall he's not a person that's very hateable. So, I don't blame you. I'm just surprised you admit it."

"Oh, God, not you too," D grumbled, suddenly reminded of Joe commenting that she would never admit that his coming back to the hotel meant anything to her.

On the other end she could hear her Dad's voice, obviously asking Mom what was going on.

"No, we're talking about *Joe*," Mom told him a little impatiently. "*Yes*, apparently he was there." And then, a little louder, now addressing her daughter again, she asked. "So, has he left again already?"

"No." D swallowed, as it occurred to her what his leaving Deens all out of a sudden would feel like. "He's still in Deens," she said into phone. "Seems like he's going to be staying with Sarah for a while."

"Oh, okay," D could imagine Mom nodding now. "But you're going to London for your conference thing next week, right?"

"Yeah. Coming back Thursday," D said, relieved that obviously Robert at least didn't seem to have told Mom about the job issue.

"Well, if he's staying with Sarah, that's at least something," Mom said, "gives you some time."

"Yeah, I guess. Just that – God, I really didn't want to…"

Mom laughed. "You got your principles and that's good. But when it comes to feelings, there's only so much even *you* can control. It's hard to give you advice, of course. But I think you shouldn't rule anything out just because of some principles. The main thing is, that twenty years from now you don't look back and regret things you didn't do or try."

"I know…" D exhaled audibly.

"Just take it slowly," Mom recommended. "And with your going to London, you'll have some distance and time to think. I think that's good."

"So, you don't think it's idiotic?"

"What? That you're talking to him again – or not just talking?" there was a trace of amusement in Mom's voice. "No, I don't think it's idiotic. People make mistakes, people change, people learn. That's life. And sometimes we just need to take detours to end up with the right person."

D thought about that for a moment.

"Thanks Mom, it's good to know you don't think I'm an idiot."

"I'd never think that."

"Yeah, because you're biased."

Mom chuckled. "Of course, I'm biased!"


After she had hung up, D sat down on the bar stool, her elbows on the bar counter and buried her face in her hands. Drawing in a few deep breaths, she tried to sort out the weird mix of emotions she felt. Talking to her Mom had been sort of a relief, as apparently her family would be just fine if she ever showed up on their doorstep with Joe again. But at the same time she felt shaky and edgy because she wasn't even sure Joe would want to cross her own threshold again – after what she had said to him on the boat. The memory of him on the pier after he had put the lock back on the boat made her stomach drop.

428

Glancing at her phone that was lying on the counter next to her, she felt this urge to try and make it right. Call him. Send him a message. But saying what? She couldn't put in words what she hadn't even sorted out properly herself. Plus, she really didn't want to seem desperate.

She got up from her chair and massaged the back of her neck to loosen up a little. Mom had said to take it slowly. And that was probably a good idea. She didn't have to call him right now. Some more time of reflection might serve them both well. And who knew, maybe *he* would call *her.* And if not, she could always call him tomorrow. Yeah, there was a plan: if she hadn't heard anything from him by tomorrow night and she still felt like wanting to see him, she would call him.

Having come to this decision, D walked to her bedroom and dragged part of the ironing pile to the living room. Time to iron…

# Are we still talking?

Monday turned out to be a busy and crazy day at work. D didn't get off until six, and when she did, she still had a list of errands to run on her way home.

First she stopped by the electronics store. The fridge she wanted was in stock. She paid for it and arranged for a delivery early Wednesday morning. She would just go to work a little later that day.

After the electronics store she drove to the supermarket and bought some milk, butter and other essentials that she had had to throw away the previous afternoon.

Finally she dropped by the post office to pick up a package she had ordered from Amazon.

She arrived at home around 7:20 pm, feeling tired, exhausted and with her stomach growling. She hadn't eaten much all day. And she didn't really have much appetite even now – thanks to the still unresolved situation with Joe. He hadn't called. He hadn't texted. And thinking about calling him herself, made her feel anxious and tense.

She realized that she needed to eat *something* to keep her going, however and, who knew, a full stomach might even improve her outlook on the situation. So, she pulled out the flyer from the Chinese restaurant she sometimes went to with Robert and called them for a delivery order of Eight Treasures. She was too tired to start cooking herself now. And just having a breakfast-style dinner with scrambled eggs and toast, something she sometimes had on evenings like this, wouldn't have worked since she had forgotten to buy eggs at the store.

After calling the restaurant she leaned against the bar counter, the phone still in her hand, and dared herself to just tap on the display and call Joe right here and now. Get it over with… But when the pure thought of it made her throat tighten and her heart race, she diagnosed that she definitely needed something solid in her stomach before doing anything of that magnitude.

The food came, she spooned some out on a plate, took the plate to the sofa with her and turned on the TV. Flipping through the channels, she got stuck on a movie with an actress she usually liked a lot. The film must have started already a while ago, though, and seemed to be in its end phase.

As D watched it while eating, she came to the conclusion that this was a brainless shallow motion picture with a totally unrealistic love story and a dialogue so sappy that it made her roll her eyes a few times. At the final exchange of the two protagonists, where the guy swore his love to the girl and she just melted into his arms, D let out a bitter laugh that almost got stuck in her throat.

Were there really people in real life that interacted in such uncomplicated patterns??? She didn't know anyone who did! *Joe* didn't, for sure! *She* didn't! *Pete*, well maybe Pete did it sometimes but usually with a somewhat manipulative element to it. Sarah definitely didn't. And neither did Jack – or Robert.

Of course, for these movie characters it was easy. The script was on the table and a happy ending was guaranteed. In real life, though, there was this constant tricky struggle where you never knew if you should actually let your guard down or not because there was just no way of predicting how the other side would react.

And that's exactly why it was so extremely hard to just pick up that phone and call Joe: she was scared to death of what he would say. And what she would say in response... And that the exchange might lead to the two of them sliding right back into – how had he called it? – Ice-age. With no way out.

Were they in a movie, it would be easy and straightforward as can be. It would go somewhat like this:

*She takes her phone and, without any hesitation, calls him.*

*He picks up at the second ring with a relieved sigh. "God, I'm so glad you called," he says with a dreamy smile. "I just didn't have the guts to..."*

*She whispers, "Yes, I know, I felt the same way, but I just couldn't stand it any longer, I really needed to hear your voice – and make sure that we're okay."*

*"Oh, it's so good to hear your voice too..." he assures her, "I missed you so much!"*

*She's too breathless for a moment to respond.*

*He asks her where she's at the moment.*

*She says smolderingly that she's at home.*

*And he tells her that he will be right over...*

*THE END*

Massaging her temples, D grimaced. No, that kind of thing wouldn't happen in real life. And because she was afraid of what *would* happen and not sure she was up to handling it at the moment, she decided that she couldn't call Joe tonight.

~~~

The next morning D woke up an hour before the alarm would issue its very first beep. (The first beep was the one that was slapped silent, just like the next three over the following half an hour until it was 6:15 am and time to get up...) It was 5:15 now. And despite the early hour, there was no way she would be able to go back to sleep. She was wide awake and the moment her brain had sprung to life, she had been hit with the edginess and the uneasily fluttering stomach that she had gone to bed with the previous night.

She suddenly remembered her grand plan from Sunday: to call Joe if she hadn't heard from him until Monday night. Well, she hadn't called him and he hadn't called her, and now it was Tuesday morning... And with every hour that passed it seemed to be becoming harder and harder to pick up the phone and make that call.

Before her inner eye she visualized this little rift that had been created Saturday on the lake and had since grown into this big gap that kept growing wider and deeper with every minute that passed and that would probably soon be impossible to step across.

Unable to deal with this disturbing theory right now, D threw back the sheets and rose from her bed. She should get ready for work. Because even if she wanted to keep the gap from growing wider, she could hardly call Joe right now, at 5:15 am. She would just have to wait until this afternoon after work.

The morning passed quickly, with lots to do at the office.

Then, for lunch D and June went to the company's cafeteria together, with June being obviously very, very down. She had spent the weekend with Jim, she had found it absolutely incredible, and then Jim hadn't called her as he had promised. And even though she swore she wasn't back in love with Jim, June was devastated.

Throwing in an understanding comment every once in a while, D listened to June's contemplations and worries while at the same time trying to gulp down her food and the lump in her throat caused by her own problems with someone who hadn't called (and who, from the looks of it, wasn't going to call).

D got home at 5:30 pm. She had spent the last two hours at work having the hardest time concentrating on anything.

Distraction number one had been this e-mail from Harry's assistant that June and she had received in the afternoon. It had contained their electronic flight tickets, hotel reservations and the itinerary for the trip to London. From the moment June had opened the message she had been babbling about that trip almost without interruption, while D had had a hard time looking at least half-way thrilled.

Distraction number two had been the ticking of the clock above the door that seemed to be getting louder with every hour that passed. A constant reminder that, as the work day came to an end, the looming question of what to do about that call to Sarah's brother would have to be tackled. And that (tick-tick-tick) the imaginary gap was still growing...

When D unlocked the door to her flat now, a nagging, hollow feeling in her stomach, she knew that there was no way around it anymore. Either she got Joe on the line and figured out what was going on, or she was going to go crazy!

She quickly drank a glass of milk since that was the only thing she could possible get down at the moment and then went to her bedroom to change into sweats and a T-shirt.

She needed to make this call, but she couldn't do it from here. She was going to take a little bike ride and find a place that felt right!

She got on her bike and rode for about fifteen minutes until she reached a gravel road through some fields. All the time her mind was buzzing with all kinds of call scenarios.

When she spotted a bench beside the road under a tree up ahead, she decided that this was the place to stop. It was a nice spot with a tiny creek flowing by. D put down the kick-stand of her bike, fished her phone out of the pouch on the back and climbed onto the bench. Sitting on the back of the bench, her feet on the seat, D drew in a deep breath. She leaned forward, her forearms resting on her thighs, and glared at the phone that she held cradled in her hands. Her heart was racing. Why on earth was this so hard?!?

Her gaze trailed off towards the creek. There was a little dam built of stones and pine cones, maybe the work of children. She remembered how

Robert and she used to just love to play along the creek behind their grandparents' house. Piling up rocks, letting paper ships float down...

She looked back on her phone. She needed to do this now or never! With shaky fingers, she scrolled down to Joe's name and, before she could lose courage again, she pressed call.

Holding her breath, she listened to the ringing. What if he didn't even pick up? She hadn't even considered that option yet. Was she going to leave a message? Or call again?

After the eighth ring, just as she was ready to hang up because the call would soon kick into voice mail, Joe picked up.

"Hello? Hi, Danny," he sounded out of breath but otherwise perfectly normal.

"Hi..." she tried to exhale without him getting the idea that she had been holding her breath. "Is this... Is this a bad time?"

"No, it's fine," he assured her. "I'm just out running. Almost didn't hear the phone."

On her end, D was scrambling for something to say. She had kind of counted on the first few seconds to reveal the general mood. But what he had said so far, and the absolutely normal way in which he had said it, didn't give her a lot of clues. He didn't seem mad or upset or nervous or anything – just out of breath for obvious reasons. But he also didn't sound relieved or even ecstatic to hear from her.

"What's up?" he asked lightly.

The casual question baffled D. Maybe she had overreacted. Maybe not talking in two days was just fine in his eyes.

"Nothing's up," she told him a little testily. "Nothing at all..."

What followed was total silence on his side. She suddenly couldn't even hear him breathe anymore. Then he cleared his throat. "I was going to call you," he finally said almost defensively. "But..." There was a short pause before he continued in a somber tone, "Quite honestly, I wasn't even sure *where* we stand."

D swallowed, taken aback by the unexpected admission. "I'm not sure either," she said quietly.

Again, there was silence.

"Guess we're still talking, though," he finally stated, his tone a little softer.

"Mhmm," D mumbled, unable to say anything more articulate with a mouth that had turned dry with his change in tone. Somehow it was just

434

sooo comforting to hear his voice… For a moment she wondered what the girl in the movie last night would have said in this situation. But everything that came to mind (e.g. *I think we should just skip the talking…*) was nothing that would ever pass her lips.

"I'm glad we're still talking," she said, her voice unsteady. This was as far as she could possibly go with admissions.

She heard Joe exhale on the other end. "Yeah, I guess" he said without any traceable emotion.

D felt her stomach cramp at his lukewarm reaction. "You're still angry," she diagnosed quietly.

"About *what*?" he made it sound like it was a ridiculous idea. "Oh, the *lake* thing?" he said then. "No, I'm *not* angry."

"Okay…" D said slowly. "Maybe not angry but… upset."

"I'm not upset either," Joe retorted stubbornly. "It's just… ahm," he fell silent for a moment. "I don't know…" He cleared his throat. "It just can't always be me, okay?"

D felt her throat tighten. What he had just said seemed to have something threateningly final. "What do you mean?" she croaked.

"It can't always be me keeping this going," Joe specified with audible exasperation. "I mean *you* and *me*. My trying to cheer you up, when at the same time I'd rather hide somewhere myself because everything's so fucked up!"

D felt panic creep up on her. Was this his announcing that he was giving up on it then? Or that he already had? She probably even deserved it. No wonder he was tired of it! She had successfully screwed it up.

"Sometimes I just…" Joe started again, "I mean – I've got enough problems on my plate with Liz, and I just can't–"

"…deal with me in addition," D concluded drily.

"I didn't say that…" he said defensively.

"But that's what you meant, right?" She was struggling to keep her voice steady when nothing about her felt steady anymore. She swallowed. "Well, why don't you just concentrate on Liz then!?!" she snarled. "Because I *really* don't need–"

"Danny, stop it!" He cut her off. "Please!" She heard him suck in a sharp breath. "Stop that, okay? I would *love* to concentrate on you, but it's kind of frustrating to have to kick-start this thing every time we meet. It just seems like, the second I turn around you're drowning in doubt and regrets…" He paused for a moment. "It feels a bit like fighting windmills, to be honest. And I'm not even saying I don't understand your reservations... But still, it's pretty frustrating!"

D wanted to say something, but her ability to speak seemed to have temporarily vanished. She felt like in a state of shock. And she expected him to end the call now, with some uncommitted *I-think-we-should- just-try- to-be-friends* line and hang up. She was just glad he wouldn't be able to see her face when he did that.

But then he didn't say anything at all for a while.

"I should have let you say what you wanted to tell me on the boat," D contemplated weakly. "I know, I was–"

"That's alright," he said flatly. "Really doesn't matter."

Silence again. Only that – to D – it didn't feel silent at all because she could hear her own heartbeat drumming in her ears. She wondered if something like this could be transmitted over the phone. It seemed unlikely... Fortunately!

"Can we–" her voice was cracking. "Can we meet, maybe? Sometime this week..."

"Sure," Joe sounded pleasantly surprised. "If you want... Might be a good idea." He paused for a moment as if to think about it. "I'm going to see Mom tomorrow night," he told her then. "And Sarah said she's doing something with you, so... But Thursday would work. Do you wanna meet Thursday?"

"Yeah, Thursday's good," she said reflexively and realized at the same time that what she really wanted was to see him right this moment. But obviously, to him, getting together had no urgency at all.

"Or Friday. That's fine too," Joe offered, making it sound even less urgent.

"Friday doesn't work," D said, barely keeping herself from snapping. "I've got this party–"

"Ah right, your party with *Peeete*," Joe said with a dry, irritated chuckle.

"And I'm leaving for a trip to London Sunday afternoon," D announced a little testily.

"Oh. I didn't know *that*." Joe seemed taken aback by this information. "What are you doing *there*?"

D swallowed. "Oh, just... Swan has an office there and we're... – well, three of my colleague and I are going there to attend this seminar/conference thing and meet with the people from the London office."

"When are you coming back?" he asked.

"Next Thursday."

"Oh, okay…" Joe said, sounding absent-minded.

"Anyway, if you want to meet Thursday," D said, steering back to the initial topic as the London issue was making her feel hot.

"Yeah…" he muttered, "Sure. I could pick you up like… – around six-thirty? We can go out to eat or something."

"Sounds good," D lied, suddenly painfully aware that not only did she not want to wait until Thursday, she also had no desire to sit in a restaurant with him. If she could make a wish she wanted him in her flat in ten minutes for another round of alligator experiments on the sofa. But since he obviously did not feel the urgency…

"Well, see you Thursday then," he said on the other end.

It was only then that it dawned on her that, what she had seen as a lack of urgency on his part, might simply be a lack of bad manners… He wasn't Pete, who just invited himself over no matter what.

If they were characters in a movie, she would tell him to forget about Thursday and come over right now. And he would do just that.

"Yeah, see you then!" she said instead. Because this was real life.

# Meeting with Steve

On Wednesday Joe left the house by foot and just walked the fifteen minutes to the restaurant where he was supposed to meet Steve. It was a foggy day. He arrived at the restaurant a few minutes early. To his surprise Steve was already there.

"Hi, Steve!"

"Hi, Joe! You look good."

"So do you." He slid into the bench across from Steve. "How's it going at the office?"

"Pretty good," Steve nodded. "Eric's taken over a lot since you're gone. He even called Jan yesterday. I didn't want to bother you with it and he was around – just a minor kind of thing. Sounds like they got along okay."

"Good. I told Jan that he might hear from a new guy."

"Yeah, that was nice. Thanks. But you're still going to do the trip next week?"

"Sure. I've already got the tickets, and the hotel is booked."

Steve nodded.

"Did you come over the highway?" Joe asked. "They mentioned some accident blocking the Deens exit on the radio..."

"Oh, I actually got off one exit before Deens. At Harrison," Steve said. "I had Liz with me."

Joe raised his eyebrows questioningly.

"Oh, she just wanted to catch a ride because she's got a few days off and wanted to visit a friend in Harrison. Caroline or something. Has invited her to stay for a few days and is apparently going to drive back with her. So, she didn't want to take her own car. Whatever... I guess it's good for her to do something... well, how should I say? – *normal* – to take her mind off you."

Joe nodded, feeling a little uncomfortable. "Yeah. I'm glad to hear she's actually doing something *normal*." He paused for a moment. "Funny though, I could have sworn that Caroline moved to some place down south. But maybe she's back... or I'm mixing something up. I only met her once. I didn't like her and she didn't like me. So that was that..."

"Which one was *she?*" Steve asked. "Or maybe I've never even met her."

"I'm sure you met her. She went to school with Liz as far as I know. Straight black hair…"

"Oh, *that* one," Steve grimaced at the memory. "Yeah. I can see how you didn't like her."

"Did Liz say anything else about…?"

"No, she didn't," Steve shook his head. "And if you hadn't told me about that call, I wouldn't even have a clue. She hasn't said a word to me. Not a word about possibly being pregnant. And not even really that you've split up for good."

"What?" Joe frowned. "I would have thought she's by now fed horror stories about me to every single member of your family and anyone else she comes across…"

"No, surprisingly, she hasn't," Steve said. "I think Mom and Dad don't have the slightest idea yet."

"Weird," Joe said darkly. "But whatever!"

"Well, to me it kind of looks like she keeps them uninformed because she still expects you to change your mind," Steve contemplated. "That's a lot less complicated if the parents haven't already crossed you off their list of favorite sons-in-law."

Pursing his lips, Joe raised his eyebrows. It did make sense what Steve said – in a somewhat unsettling way. But well, it was Liz's problem how she broke it to her parents.

"Anyway," Steve said, ready to move on to the topic they were here to discuss. "Let's see now. What did I want to tell you?" He opened his briefcase that was sitting next to him on the bench and pulled out a folder and a notepad. He opened the notepad and browsed through his notes. "First of all, Andrea from Italy is probably going to call about the update," he said with a quick glance up at Joe. "I haven't really had time to deal with that yet. Just tell him I'll get back to him after my vacation. There's no real urgency. He's said so himself." Steve looked at his notes again. "Yeah, and the two guys from Belgium are going to be there next Thursday. So…"

"Yeah, I'll just take them out to eat and have a chat with them," Joe said.

"Perfect."

439

They spent another half an hour going through business issues and things Steve wanted Joe to keep an eye on while he was on vacation. When they were through and Steve had packed away his notes and the folder, they paid and got ready to leave.

"How's your hand, by the way?" Steve said as he slid out behind the table.

"It's okay. Getting there. Should be fine once it's healed."

"Good. I'm glad to hear that."

"Yeah, me too. Really slows me down with anything I'm trying to do on the computer."

"I bet. You probably haven't been able to do anything regarding the program for Arlin yet, have you?"

"No, sorry. But I'll definitely have it done by the time they need it. I *do* have a concept in my head already."

Steve laughed. "Knowing you, that means the project is as good as finished," he said.

"Not quite..." Joe laughed.

They walked to the door together.

"How's the preparation for the wedding going?" Joe asked Steve, who was a few steps ahead.

"Oh, Susan is in charge of most of that. With the assistance of her Mom and her sister and her aunt..." He shot Joe a look over his shoulder, rolled his eyes and grinned.

"Sounds dangerous," Joe said.

"It is!" Steve laughed. "But so is the whole concept of getting married... Sometimes it scares me to death, I tell you. But then I remind myself that we've been living together for four years, I *do* really love her, we're a great team, we have fun together... So, why not?"

"Yeah, right," Joe said, scrambling to mask his surprise that even people like Steve obviously had cold-feet issues at times and even admitted it.

"You're still on as my best man, though, right?" Steve asked, pushing the door open to the parking lot.

"I guess," Joe had stopped just outside the door, "I'm not sure how this is going to work with your sister, but if you want me to, I'll do it, of course!"

"I do," Steve said in an exaggeratedly serious tone that indicated he was practicing for the wedding. "Yes, I do." Then he laughed and patted Joe on the back.

# Gone Car

"Where's your car?" Steve asked as they stepped out of the restaurant around 3:30 pm.

"I walked," Joe said.

"Do you want me to take you home?" Steve offered.

Joe checked his watch. "No, thanks. I'm just going to walk back. I only need to be at my aunt's around five, so I've got time."

On his way home, Joe got some flowers at a store along the way to bring to his Mom and Aunt Tess.

The flowers in hand, he got to the house and was just pulling out his key to unlock the door when he decided to put the flowers into the car right away. He turned around to the street again and suddenly came to a complete halt. He squinted. Hadn't he parked the car right next to the driveway yesterday? Right there. Where there was an empty spot now? He glanced up and down the street.

Shit! Where was his car? He may be mistaken about the exact spot he had left it in, but this was definitely the right street and there was no sand-colored Volvo here anywhere. It was one of these *I-think-I-must-be-dreaming* moments where you hope that, if you blink again and rub your eyes a bit, things will switch back to normal. He knew for sure that he had parked the car there last night. Sarah couldn't have taken it, right? Unlikely! Why would she? Her car had been in the driveway and it was gone now. So…

He pulled out his phone, not even sure who to call.

That's when he saw that there was a message.

From Liz.

A real bad feeling had crept up on him by the time he clicked to open the message:

> Got your car. We need to talk. Come to the viewpoint parking lot or I'll wreck it!

The message had been sent 30 minutes ago. Right after Sarah must have left.

Sitting down on the stairs outside the front door, Joe laid the flowers down next to him and rubbed his forehead, trying to manage some clear thoughts. This was just surreal!

What to do, though? Call the police?

He would have liked to but decided against it.

Go up to the viewpoint? Would be hard to avoid it...

Joe turned the phone around in his hand a few times. Then, clicking on a number, he put it against this ear and got up from the stairs. He walked down the street that he had just come up five minutes earlier. It was a fifteen minute walk to the viewpoint.

The phone rang a few times before Jack picked up.

"Hi, Joe," he sounded surprised. No wonder, it was in the middle of the afternoon and he was probably at the office in his Dad's car dealership.

"Hi, Jack... Sorry! I know you're at work," Joe said, "but it's kind of an emergency."

"What? Something wrong with D?"

"Na, has nothing to do with her... I've got a serious Liz problem..."

"What kind of Liz-problem?" Jack asked with audible concern.

"It's really crazy..." Joe let out a bitter little laugh. "But seems like she took my car and now she's up at the viewpoint and wants me to come there..."

"She did *what*???"

"Well, you know," despite his own shaken state of mind, Joe managed a light sarcastic tone. "She thinks we should talk. And since I've refused to do that, she decided to just take the car hostage, I guess."

"Oh boy..." Jack sighed. "So she had an extra key, huh?"

"She didn't *have* it, but yeah, there was one still somewhere in the flat..."

"Well, seems like she found it," Jack concluded dryly.

"Yep..."

"Do you want me to come with you?" Jack asked.

"I'm on my way up there right now," Joe said, "and I know you're at work, but..."

"I can come," Jack assured him. "Nothing going on here anyway."

"I would actually really appreciate it if you could come, yeah. Because honestly, I haven't got a *clue* what she's up to, and I would rather have a witness!"

"I *do* think you're well-advised," Jack said, "because from what it looks like to me, she's really lost her marbles..." He paused for a moment. "It's still going to take me 20 minutes to get over there, though. Are you sure, you don't want to wait and I'll pick you up?"

"No, that's fine," Joe said. "I can't sit and wait right now. And it's going to take me at least fifteen minutes to walk up there anyway…" He drew in a sharp breath. "I can't even tell you how angry I am!"

"Well, I don't blame you!" Jack said with a humorless little laugh. "But Joe… Don't do anything you'll regret, okay!"

"Yeah, yeah. Sure. Don't worry. I've gotten pretty good at holding back even when I want to strangle her."

"Yeah, don't do that! Please! I'll be there as soon as I can."

"Thanks Jack!"

Walking faster now, Joe dialed his mother's number.

"Joseph… Hi!" She sounded surprised that he would call her, when he was supposed to come by and pick her up in a little over an hour. "Is everything okay?"

"Hi Mom," he said, trying hard to sound calm. "I… I kind of got a problem with my car here…"

"Oh… Doesn't start, huh?" she asked.

"Yeah, something like that. Still trying to figure this out," he said. "The way it looks right now, though… I can't imagine how I'll be able to make it over to your place this afternoon. Can we maybe…"

"Sure. We can do it one of the next few days," she assured him lightly, "I hope you get the car running again."

"So do I," Joe said darkly. "I'll call you later, when I know more, okay? I'm really sorry!"

"Don't worry about it, okay? Good luck!"

"Thanks Mom. Sorry…" He hung up and swallowed, trying to choke down the lump in his throat.

When he reached the viewpoint parking lot, it was empty except for one single car that was parked at the opposite side from where the road came up. His car.

Even from 300 meters away he could see that the front was badly damaged on the driver's side. The headlight was smashed, the bumper was scraped and there was a big dent on the side.

He tried to stay calm. Swallow the anger. Breathe… The insurance would take care of it. He still had a free claim.

Still, even if there was no financial damage done, it made him feel sick to the stomach.

He could see Liz sitting in the car, her arm casually hanging out the open window. As he came closer across the parking lot, she looked at him expectantly. Or triumphantly?

When he opened the door on the passenger side she threw her head back, her blond hair falling over her shoulder. She gave him a victorious smile. "That was quick..." she beamed.

He held on to the door with his right hand and pressed his jaws together, feeling the overwhelming urge to scream at her or punch her with his left hand. He quickly shoved the hand into the pocket of his jeans as a precaution.

For a moment he just stood there, glaring at her and trying hard to control the anger. At the same time he was wondering what the hell had ever attracted him to her. He totally despised her now.

Liz patted the seat next to her and gave him an innocent smile. "Come on, Honey..." she tweeted pleadingly. "Let's make up..."

"Are you crazy or what?" he took a step back and shook his head. "Or drunk?"

"We need to talk..." she said in a tone that patient mothers use with stubborn little children who just won't listen.

"Sure Liz," Joe mocked, pulling his left hand out of his pocket and waving it in front of his forehead indicating that he thought she was crazy. "I personally think I should just call the police!"

She seemed confused. That was obviously not exactly the way she had planned it. "You can't do that," she said, shaking her head. "No one will believe you!"

Joe realized that she was probably right. No one would believe it. Or even if they did, part of the blame would fall on him. They would just be asking where she had gotten the key and – *Oh, she's the ex... Well, never leave your car key with an angry woman...*

He just hoped Jack was going to be here soon. Being alone with her was almost unbearable.

"Why don't you get in?" she was probably trying to sound friendly, but the way she said it, Joe felt strongly reminded of the freaky tone and behavior Snow White's evil stepmother-witch had used upon offering the poisoned apple.

"I'd rather stay out here, thank you very much!" he retorted.

Liz dropped her gaze, a disappointed pouting look on her face.

"What do you want, Liz?" he barked.

"I want you to come back!" she said like that was self-evident.

"Yeah, right!" he scoffed. "Looking at my car I can hardly stand the temptation... But guess what: That's not going to happen!"

"But I love you!" she yelled, her eyes filling with tears.

"Oh God, haven't we been through this often enough already?" He threw his hands up in exasperation. "However much you love me, Liz, I just can't deal with your weird way of showing it! Like that–" He pointed to the front of his car. "Or like that." He held up his braced hand.

"That's not fair", she choked. "It just happened!" And there was the first hiccup-sob.

"Liz, I was there," Joe said with forced patience. "And in contrast to you I was sober when it happened... And it didn't just *happen*. Besides, you know it's not just that!"

"I'm sooo sorry!" She was really crying now.

"Stop that, for God's sake!" he growled, rubbing his forehead.

"But I can't live without you," she sobbed.

"Oh God, Liz!" he had to keep himself from yelling. "You have to live without me because, as it turns out, I can't live *with* you. I think I've given it more than enough tries."

"Yeah, didn't you try hard?" she laughed – an evil laugh. (Again, Joe found himself reminded of Snow White's stepmother.)

"And when it was about fucking, things were just fine, weren't they?" she snarled.

Joe gasped for air. (Now that was a line that would probably not be dropped in the Snow White fairy-tale...)

"You pretty well know that it wasn't *me* who decided that every time something was wrong, we just patch it up by..." He threw his hands in the air and angrily shook his head.

Liz's eye's had narrowed and she leaned her head to the side.

"Oh, aren't you a saint!?!" she hissed. "I seem to remember that you didn't exactly need a whole lot of persuasion!"

"Yeah, right," he said dryly. "What do you expect when you focus all your persuasive arguments on the one part of me that functions largely autonomously and in total disregard of any good judgment?"

"Oh, is that *so?*"

"Yeah, that *is* so!"

"So, you didn't have anything to do with it then, huh?"

"I didn't say that," he retorted. "I'm just saying that it's no strategy to work things out. I didn't need that."

Liz glared back at him, obviously scrambling for a scathing response.

"And I sure didn't need that other crap we've been doing lately," Joe told her.

She let out a nasty little laugh. "Well, you were pretty useless there anyway."

His jaws clicking together, he resisted the urge to do something that, if Snow White had done it to her stepmother, it would have surely resulted in the mirror asking '*What happened to your nose?*' at their next encounter. Instead he sucked in a quick breath through clenched teeth. "Yeah, sorry about that!" he snarled. "I don't deny that that kind of stuff may have quite a bit of appeal on screen, but I don't really need it to happen in my own bed when I'm expected to still look the girl in the eyes the next morning during breakfast!"

"You asshole!" she screamed and slammed her fist into the seat beside her.

"Yeah, I know…" Joe shot a glance over his shoulder to look for Jack, when suddenly she started the car.

"Shit!" He flung himself into the car as it started rolling backwards. She had put it in reverse. And not too far behind them was the hill slope.

Joe tried to reach over and push the button for the hand brake. Liz blocked him with her arm. He tried to twist her hand off the key. She shoved him with her elbow. Somehow, after a little struggle, he managed to push her hand away far enough, so he could turn the ignition off and take out the key. And set the hand brake.

The car came to such an abrupt halt that he lost his balance and hit the side of his head against the windshield.

His head buzzing from the impact, he backed out of the car and took a step away from it. Rubbing his head, he looked around and then grabbed a thick broken branch from close-by that he shoved behind the back tire to keep the car from rolling back, no matter what Liz came up with next.

She stared at him from the car, an angry grimace on her face.

He shook his head and looked away. Towards the town below. This was why people came up here normally. To enjoy the view…

Suddenly he thought he heard the faint noise of a car coming up the street. Or was that just wishful thinking? When he glanced over his shoulder, he saw the headlights of Jack's Dad's Jeep appear across the parking lot. He let out a relieved breath.

"That's Jack," he said.

"What is *he* doing here?" Liz snapped.

Joe rubbed the side of his head where he had banged it against the windshield and turned around to her. "You think I want to be alone with you when you're like this?" he asked.

"Ahhh… I see!" Liz looked at him with a poisonous grin (again reminding him of Snow White's stepmother) and opened the driver's door. "Our good friend Jack!" With that remark she got out of the car, slammed the door shut and strolled over to where Jack was just parking the Jeep.


Jack had thought it best not to pull right up to the Volvo but keep his distance and just show some presence. Seeing Liz stroll towards him now, an ultra-sweet smile on her face like she was just absolutely thrilled to see him, seemed a bit eerie to say the least. Not quite sure what to expect, he got out of the car.

Joe was following a little ways behind Liz, rolling his eyes at Jack and waving his flat hand in front of his face indicating his diagnosis on Liz's mental condition.

Giving Joe a quick nod, Jack looked back at Liz, who was right in front of him now.

"Well, hello, Jack…" she chirped. "Remember me?"

"Hi Liz," Jack said dryly. Both her tone and her gaze seemed a little disconcerting. He remembered now that Joe had said that she wasn't always sober. This might be one of those times. That would explain the damage on the car too. She couldn't be *that* bad of a driver, unless she had done it on purpose, of course…

She was still pretty, there was no doubt about it. Her hair was longer than Jack remembered it, she was still wearing a little more make up than necessary, and she had definitely lost some weight, which made her look a little bony, except for her big chest.

"Liz, what's this supposed to be?" he asked with a reprehensive nod towards the Volvo. "Did you come all this way just to wreck his car?"

Joe had stepped up to them. "Thanks Jack, I really appreciate this!" he said.

Jack just nodded and suddenly saw Liz flying at Joe, screaming, "I bet you do, you..."

Jack got ahold of her before Joe could, and pulled her back.

"Slowly now," he said. "You need to calm down! Okay?"

First she was still struggling, trying to get away from him, pushing and shoving, but when she realized that it was futile, she changed her strategy: she threw her arms around Jack and sobbed, her face buried against his neck.

Reluctantly Jack put one arm around her and shot Joe a somewhat helpless look. "So, what do we do with her now?" he asked over her head.

Joe combed his fingers through his hair and shook his head. "I really don't know. And honestly, I can't say I even care."

"Well, we can't leave her here," Jack pointed out. "Who knows what she'll do next."

"Again, I don't really care," Joe growled stubbornly. "I can call the police, or I can call Rick's Dad and have her committed..."

Liz suddenly stopped sobbing, pulled away from Jack a bit and stared at Joe. "Are you insane?" she hissed. But a look at him obviously confirmed that he wasn't kidding. "You'd really do it, you ass..."

Stone-faced, Joe shrugged. "Well, I'd love to, but it would probably make things worse."

She gave him a look that made him wonder if locking her up somewhere wouldn't still be the safest choice.

"Okay, here's the deal," he finally said coldly. "Either you call Steve to come back and pick you up, or you take the train back... Today!"

For a moment Liz seemed to think about that. Amazingly her make-up still looked perfect despite all the tears. Waterproof must really be waterproof...

Jack watched the exchange in silence, feeling increasingly uncomfortable having Liz arms still wrapped around his neck and the left side of her body pressed against his.

"I'm *not* calling Steve!" Liz hissed at Joe, snuggling up to Jack some more as if she had suddenly chosen him to be her protector.

"Well, then *I'll* call him," Joe proclaimed. "I don't have a problem telling him that his crazy sister is not after all with Caroline, like he thought, but she's come all the way here to wreck my car and, unfortunately, *she* ended up having a nervous breakdown instead of me."

"I just wanted to talk to you," she screamed, "you wouldn't talk to me otherwise…"

Joe threw his hands up in the air, turned around and wandered a few steps away.

One arm still draped around Liz's waist, Jack got out his phone and checked on trains.

"There's a train at eight," he finally said. "She'd have to change once. I don't think it's a good idea…"

Joe looked at his watch. Still three hours. It was starting to rain. And as much as he would have loved to just leave her here or dump her at the train station, he knew that Jack was right. They couldn't leave her alone without risking that she did something really, really stupid. Not that taking his car wasn't stupid enough already, but he feared that there was still potential for worse.

He got out his own phone.

"What are you doing?" Liz yelled, trying to pull away from Jack. She knew exactly what Joe was doing. She tried to reach out and snatch his phone from him but he was faster, took a step away, and Jack grabbed her, pulling her back against himself so she couldn't go after Joe.

Crazy, Jack thought, just plain crazy! Something here reminded him of the taming of some wild, freaked-out animal.

Joe walked over towards his car. Perched on the hood, he waited for Steve to answer the phone.

"Hi, Steve."

Pause.

"Well… I'm doing not so great, actually. We've got a problem here…" He paused again, while Steve obviously said something on the other end.

"Liz is here," Joe said. There was another pause.

"Yeah, don't ask me how, but she's here. And she just took a little reckless drive with my car, so I get to have *that* fixed… Anyway, I'd rather not keep her here. And I don't dare to just put her on a train… and I definitely don't want to drive her back myself… Where are *you*?"

On the other end, Steve said something that made Joe nod.

"Yeah, I think that might be best. I know it's absurd, but…"

There was another pause, with Joe listening intently to what Steve was saying.

"We'll probably wait at my sister's house. Do you know where that is?"

Pause. Then Joe nodded.

"Yeah, okay. Thanks, Steve!"

He hung up and just sat there for a moment, holding his phone in his lap. Finally he looked over at Liz and Jack.

"He'll pick her up," he said. "In an hour or so. Needless to say that he's not exactly thrilled…"

Liz was fuming. "Great that you have to get him involved in this. And him," she nodded towards Jack, who had released her, but was keeping a close eye on her.

Joe shook his head. "Oh, now it's *me*?"

"So you really want to go to Sarah's in the meantime?" Jack asked skeptically.

"She's out anyway," Joe responded.

"Oh, okay." Jack nodded. Then he turned to Liz. "I think you better drive with me."

# Back off!

Joe motioned for Jack and Liz to sit at the kitchen table, then went over to the cabinet with the glasses.

"Anything to drink?" he asked. "Anything *non*-alcoholic, I mean?" He shot a dark side-glance at Liz.

"Man, aren't you sharp," she hissed.

"I'll have water," Jack said with an encouraging nod at Joe.

"Me too," Liz snapped.

Joe filled three glasses with water, sat one in front of Liz, who looked up at him narrow-eyed, and one in front of Jack, who had pulled the newspaper towards him.

"I didn't realize they finally caught that bastard," Jack said, pointing to the headline on the front page. A notorious bank robber had finally walked into a trap.

"Was about time," Joe said and went back to the sink to get his own glass. He took a sip and leaned against the counter behind him. He didn't really feel like sitting down with Liz here. He couldn't wait for Steve to take her away. It was hard to even be in the same room with her. He had known that she was irrational and crazy, but what she had done this afternoon went way beyond what he had expected her to be capable of.

Suddenly he thought he heard a car pull into the driveway. Steve couldn't have been that fast, could he?

"Maybe that's Steve," he said.

And then, instead of someone ringing the bell, he heard the key in the front door.

~~~

Sarah and D had met at the lake after work – each of them driving her own car. They had planned to spend some time swimming and chatting, before heading to their favorite Italian restaurant and later to the movies.

Things hadn't exactly gone as planned, though. It had already been cloudy by the time they met. They had gotten into their bikinis nevertheless and with stubborn determination had sat down on their towels despite the fact that the wind was picking up. Twenty minutes later it had started to rain. Finally accepting that this wasn't a good day to lie at the lake, they had quickly packed their stuff back up, changed into their clothes and driven back into town to the restaurant they wanted to go to. When then the restaurant had unexpectedly been closed due to a death in the family, Sarah had suggested taking out Indian food from the place across the street and bringing it home. They could have a cozy evening spread out on the sofa in her living room, eating their food and watching a DVD.

So, that's what they had decided to do...

After they had gotten the take-out food, Sarah had headed straight home to keep the food warm, set the table and make a salad, while D quickly went by a French patisserie to get some pastries for dessert.

~~~

As Sarah turned the corner into her street and got closer to her house, her eyes widened. Then she frowned and huffed out an irritated breath. There, along the street was Jack's Dad's Jeep parked right behind Joe's Volvo.

"What the hell?" she grumbled to herself. Joe was supposed to be gone, visiting Mom and not at the house with Jack!

This wasn't exactly convenient, as far as Sarah was concerned. When she had suggested to D that they could do dinner and a movie here, she had counted on Joe to be out. And now he was here? Sarah didn't feel really comfortable inviting D when Joe was around. Not when she didn't have the slightest idea what the current status was between these two, and when there was a good chance that bringing them together would cause a weird situation for everyone.

Well, too late now. Joe was here and D was coming...

Besides, maybe with Jack present as well, Joe and D would just strictly stick to the script of two people ignoring each other...

~~~

The moment he heard the key in the front door, Joe felt like someone had hit him with a baseball bat. It could only be Sarah. And, if worse came to worst, she wasn't alone.

"You're back already?" Sarah said from the hallway. It sounded a bit like a complaint. She walked right into the kitchen and, as soon as she realized who was sitting at her table apart from Jack, she came to a complete and sudden halt.

She shot Joe a look that reflected disbelief.

"What is this?" she slowly asked with another quick look at Liz, who had leaned back in her chair and was now inspecting her long pink fingernails like there was nothing more interesting in the world.

Sarah's eyes darted back at Joe, who still hadn't reacted to her question. He just stood there, a frozen look on his face.

"The short version?" Jack offered from behind her.

Sarah turned to Jack. "Yeah, the short version would be good…"

"She…" He nodded towards Liz. "She's come *all* the way here to steal Joe's car and threaten to wreck it unless he talks to her." He paused to give Sarah a chance to catch up with what he was saying. "Well, she wrecked the front of the car regardless… – you may not have noticed it outside… No? It's on the driver's side… Anyway, until her brother is coming to pick her up, we're kind of trapped here. Sorry!"

Biting her lower lip, Sarah turned back to look at Joe. "This is *not* a good idea…" she said darkly as she set the bag with the Indian food on the counter next to the sink.

Joe just nodded, a completely resigned look on his face. "I thought you were out…" he said almost inaudibly.

"I wish…" Sarah retorted.

For a moment there was absolute silence in the kitchen. Then the bell at the front door blasted through the silence.

Huffing out a sharp breath, Sarah took the step over to the automatic door opener on the wall next to the fridge. In passing she shot her brother a quick look. He looked back at her, his jawline hard, his arms crossed over his chest.

When the door opener buzzed and the front door was opened, Joe turned around to the kitchen cabinets. His hands against the edge of the countertop to the sides of him, he leaned on his stretched out arms and tilted his forehead against the cool wood of the cabinet door in front of him and briefly closed his eyes. He knew that was Danny coming up the hallway. And there was absolutely nothing he could do.

D appeared in the doorway, the paper-wrapped pastry in her hand, her expression already somewhat guarded after seeing Joe's and Jack's cars outside. She stepped into the kitchen and turned to ice the second she laid eyes on Liz.

"This gets better every minute," Jack said with dry sarcasm. "Hi, D. Welcome to our little party!"

Sucking in a quick breath, D reached out her free hand and got ahold of the doorframe. She needed to hold on to something or she was afraid her knees would give in. Her head was spinning. This couldn't be real. But Jack's comment had just confirmed, though, that she wasn't having some freaky hallucination but that it was, in fact, very real.

She glanced over at Sarah, who looked back at her with a strained expression and slowly shook her head. Next to Sarah, with his back to the kitchen, Joe had his head dropped against the door of one of the kitchen cabinets and didn't move. He was obviously not able or not willing to face the situation... Well, neither was she!

D wanted to turn on her heel and run away. She felt like she couldn't breathe here. She needed to get out!

But then a quick look at Liz changed her mind.

Liz was glaring towards Joe's back, eyebrows raised, an amused smirk on her face, one arm leisurely draped over the back of her chair, her long tanned legs that the tight short skirt didn't hide much of crossed under the table. Those high heeled sandals...

D struggled to pull herself together. She looked at Sarah again, who gave her a wide-eyed apologetic shrug now and folded her arms over her chest. "I can't believe you'd bring her here..." Sarah muttered with an accusing glance at her brother beside her.

Liz's eyes darted over to Sarah and her eyes narrowed. "Oh, it's so good to see you, too, Sarah..."

"Sorry, Liz," Sarah said without any trace of sorry in her voice, "but after that call you pulled off during the weekend – calling Anja to tell him you're pregnant..."

Liz expression lit up. "Oh, about that..." she said with the sweetest smile, "guess it was false alarm."

Sarah caught Joe's arm just as he whisked around and was about to lunge forward and maybe do something stupid such as strangle Liz. Huffing out a sharp breath, he shook his head and, Sarah's hand still clamped around his upper arm, let himself fall back against the counter, this time facing the kitchen table.

Liz shrugged, giving Joe a provocative look. "Must have just used the test the wrong way..." she said innocently.

D had watched the whole scene like through a haze. But then Liz's last comment somehow shook her back to life. Her heart was suddenly beating so hard against her chest that she felt like her body might be visibly jerking with every beat. This wicked, stuck-up bitch!

Not quite sure what was driving her, D quickly laid the pastry package on the microwave next to the doorway and took a step into the kitchen – towards Liz. "How is that possible?" she asked sharply, surprised that her voice didn't reflect any of the turmoil she felt.

Liz glanced over at her and squinted. "What?"

"How can you use a pregnancy test the wrong way?" D specified.

"Oh, I don't know…" Liz chirped lightly and shrugged. "Just screwed up somehow, I guess…"

"Well, I lack personal experience with that stuff," D snarled, her blood boiling now, "but don't you just have to *pee* on it? How can you screw *that* up?"

Liz shook her head in a mix of bafflement and irritation at the interrogation style.

"I don't know," she insisted with a provocative smirk.

"Well, did you maybe *suck* on it instead?" D inquired like she was dealing with a total imbecile.

From the other end of the table there was the muffled noise of Jack trying not to laugh out loud. When both Liz and D shot him an angry look, he raised his hands apologetically.

"That's actually an excellent question," Joe snarled from where he was standing, his face hard. "How *did* you do it? Or did you just make it *all* up?"

Liz gave him a stubborn look back and shrugged. "I just used it the wrong way, I guess…" she repeated innocently.

D shook her head. "Na, I don't think so! You can mess up and get a *negative* result even though you're really pregnant, but there's just *no* way you'd get a positive test where there really isn't anything. That's just ludicrous!"

For a moment Liz stared at D, a hateful expression on her face. Then, suddenly, her face seemed to light up again. Her eyes flickered over to Joe and then back to D. And then those eyes slowly and intently returned to Joe. Liz cocked her head at him and pursed her lips. "Oh, now I get it, Honey," she said in a toxically-sweet tone.

"Just shut it, Liz!" Joe cut her off.

Liz laughed. "Oh, *Honey*…" she said with a sneer. "You're already back screwing *her*, aren't you!?!"

D gasped for air, her mind momentarily blank. She couldn't have heard right, could she? She looked at Joe. He was staring back at Liz, looking totally shocked.

D straightened up and took another step closer to the kitchen table. "*What* was that?" she blasted.

Liz had been expectantly looking at Joe. Now she whisked around, seeming surprised to get a reaction from another side, when the punch had primarily been aimed at Joe. It wasn't like she even really believed or had thoroughly weighed what she had just thrown out there. She had just said it to wind him up.

"What was it you just said?" D repeated more threateningly.

"You heard me," Liz said with a shrug.

Giving Liz a piercing look back, D tapped her index finger against her lips as if she had some trouble recalling what Liz had said. "Right," she finally said, her enlightened expression showing that Liz's words had just come back to her. "I *did* hear you. Even though I still can't believe you really said that! But I guess that's just your style, huh?" She rubbed her forehead to chase away an oncoming dizzy spell and took another step up to the table. Placing one hand on the table right above Liz's knees, D leaned down a bit.

Staring back at her, Liz pressed herself against the back of her chair, obviously not quite comfortable with this stand-off.

"Let me tell you something, Liz," D made sure she dragged the name out in the most ill-sounding fashion. "Just between you and me, okay?"

Liz blinked back at her, an angry but confused spark in her eyes.

"He–" D nudged her head towards where Joe was standing. "He is *not* – how did you just put it so nicely? – back to *screwing me*. Okay? But if you really, really need to know, I wouldn't *at all* rule it out for the future."

Liz's face went blank for a moment. Then she huffed out a shrill-sounding little laugh and pushed her chair back a bit to get further away from D.

"Well, I hope it works better with you…" she hissed.

It took D a moment to process what she had just heard. One quick glimpse over at Joe confirmed, though, that this had really been a kick way below the belt line. Straightening up a bit she swallowed hard.

"Oh, did you have a problem there, Liz?" she asked sweetly, trying hard to keep her voice from trembling.

"Not me. *Him!*" Liz screamed.

D rolled her eyes so exaggeratedly that, for a second there, she was afraid of dislocating them. "Well, you know, Liz," she said in tone that doctor's use when they don't know how to break it to the patient. "I actually don't remember *ever* having any complaints in that regard – with him. Really don't." She gave Liz a casual shrug that did take all her strength, and then shot an obvious look at Joe. "Or do you, *Honey*?" She managed to perfectly copy Liz's way of saying it. It felt weird. She had never ever called him that. She saw Joe briefly close his eyes and bite down on his lower lip, as if he could hardly stand this. Trying to keep this image from getting to her, D quickly turned her attention back to Liz. "So, thanks so much for your concern, Liz," she said in a provocatively cheerful tone, "but unless you broke more than just his fingers, I'm pretty sure we'll be just fine once we get around to it… I mean, *screwing* as you like to call it."

With that evaluation, she lifted her hand off the table, took a step back and slowly turned around to the door, her whole body feeling unstable and shaky now. She kept her eyes on the floor. She didn't want to see their faces. And she surely couldn't look Joe in the eyes right now, if ever again.

She needed to get out of here! Before she fell apart!

She willed her feet out of the kitchen and down the corridor. She pulled the front door open. Staggered out. Out! She needed to get out! And breathe…

She could feel the cool soothing air flood her lungs. And like in a haze, she made it over to her car.

Joe caught up with her as she flung the driver's door open.

"Danny, wait!" He grabbed her arm.

She yanked it away.

"I really didn't know…" he started.

"That's pretty obvious," she blasted, avoiding looking at him.

"Danny–" He didn't try to touch her this time.

"Just let me go, okay?" she snapped and slid into the driver's seat.

"Not like that!" he grabbed the top of the door, preventing her from closing it, should she try to.

D leaned back in her seat. Her head against the headrest, she stared out the front window. She couldn't deal with him right now. She wished he hadn't followed her.

"I need to get out of here…" she croaked. "Let go of the door, Joe. Please."

"You were great," he said softly, his good hand tracing the rim of the car door.

She nodded darkly. "Yeah, thanks a lot. Only that it was all just show."

Silence.

She sucked in a sharp breath and looked up at him. "What I said in there doesn't mean a *thing*, okay? That was just between *her* and *me*. All for show… I would have said pretty much *anything* as long as it hurt her."

"Still, you were great," he said, his eyes firmly trained on her.

She shook her head and dropped her gaze to the pavement between them. "Let me go," she said and reached for the door handle to close the door.

"Only if I can I come by later," he said, still holding on to the door.

She shook her head. "I don't think that's a good idea…"

Her words had an effect on his expression as if she had slapped him.

"I really need to digest this. I need to think," she said, her tone softer.

He nodded, a dark look on his face. "That's exactly what I'm afraid of."

"Joe…" She pulled on the door again.

Even though she had dropped her gaze, Joe suddenly realized that she was fighting tears.

"Danny, listen…" he started again.

But the way she raised her hand, shaking her head, made him fall silent.

"Take your hands off that door… please," she pulled on the door. "I don't want to break your fingers…"

For a moment Joe hesitated. Then he lifted his hands in a surrendering gesture and gave the door a little push with his knee.

She pulled it shut with a bang.

And he opened the back door and slipped into the seat behind her.

She threw herself back into her seat and closed her eyes.

"Get out!" she growled.

"I'm not getting out before you tell me what the deal is here!" he said, scooting over further towards the center of the backseat, his left hand grabbing the right shoulder of her seat.

Scoffing, she opened her eyes, a distressed look on her face. "Just back off and leave me alone…"

Silence.

"I don't think it's going to work..." she finally said.

"What's not going to work?" he asked, his throat suddenly dry.

"You and me..." she said, her voice muffled. "Honey..."

He swallowed. "And you just realized that *why?*"

She chewed on her lip. "I just had a real eye-opening experience..." she finally said quietly.

"Meaning?"

"Meaning that–" She slammed her flat hands against the sides of her seat. "Crap Joe, I can pretend all I want that you're the same guy I used to know. It just isn't true!" She paused and ran both her hands over her face before she slapped them onto her thighs, digging her fingers into her pants.

"I mean, just now, in there... I look at *her,* and I look at *you* and I realize...– wow, you've been together for how long, *Honey...?*"

Joe huffed out an exasperated breath and let himself fall back into his own seat. "Just stop that Honey-crap, okay?"

Her eyes sparkling angrily she shot him a glance through the rear view mirror. "I'll stop that, don't worry," she said darkly. "But it *is* ironic, don't you think? You used to *hate* the Honey-Baby-Sweetie-crap. At least that's what you told *me.* And using the L-word, oh, we don't need *that.* You're just not that kind of guy..." She let out a bitter laugh and there suddenly was a tear rolling down her cheek that she wiped off quickly with the back of her hand. "And here she is, calling you *Honey,* and I don't even wanna start imagining *your* names for her." She sucked in a shaky breath and immediately huffed it back out through her nose. "I bet she helped your phobia regarding the L-word, too, didn't she?"

For a moment Joe sat motionless, his expression suddenly hard.

D kept an eye on him through the rear view mirror.

"Why on earth did you have to get involved with *her?*" Her voice was shaky and a bit shrill now. "I really don't blame you for getting tired of me. Happens all the time. If it doesn't feel right, you pretty much have to make a cut... But that you left with *her!?!* That's just ... Grrr... Couldn't you have found someone halfway sane?"

Staring down on the floor mat, Joe was scrambling for something to say. But what she was dishing up here was so complex that he didn't even know where to start with a possible response. That it hadn't been his being tired of her? That it had had nothing to do with it not being right?

Because it may have been perfect if he hadn't gotten cold feet? That he should have used the L-word with her, because there had never been more justification for it? That he knew pretty well himself that Liz had been a really bad choice?

"Danny, that's not…"

"Get out, Joe! Please… Now!"

His eyes darted up to the mirror. "Yeah, and then what?"

Instead of an answer she dropped her gaze.

"Explain to me, why what happened in there makes such a big difference to you," he demanded. "Because, quite honestly, I don't get it. You knew about me and Liz. It wasn't a secret, and it's not like you walked in there tonight and happened to discover the unthinkable just now. So what is it?" He leaned forward again, his hand back on her seat, his fingertips almost touching her shoulder. "It's not like you didn't know about me and Liz over the past few days while we were–" When he saw her face, he decided not to finish his sentence.

"Of course, I knew about you and Liz," she retorted darkly, her eyes trained on something outside. "Maybe I was in denial though, as to what this really meant – until I just saw her in there, larger than life…"

Shaking his head, Joe let out a bitter laugh. "Yeah, well, that's just her. And yeah, I don't know what I was thinking getting involved with her. You happy now? Had my learning curve, alright? Shit, Danny, what do you expect me to tell you?"

"I don't expect you to tell me *anything*. Because you can't solve the problem…"

"Which is?"

"That I'm just not sure anymore who you really are. I feel like… like maybe I don't know you at all."

For a moment he stared at her from the side, her words still eerily ringing in his ears. Then he exhaled. And nodded. "Okay," he said flatly, scooted over to the side and swung his legs out of the car.

"I'm sorry," she choked, "but that's what it is."

"I get it…" he scoffed and got up.

"I need to think…" she said, "…about everything."

"Well, yeah!" Joe nodded gloomily. "You should definitely think! I'll back off, don't worry! Take your time and think! I can't help you with that!" He slammed the car door shut and walked back to the house.

# Note from the author:

This is where we have to leave Joe and D - at least for the moment. There's still so much they have to work out – for themselves and between each other – that I couldn't have fit it all in this book. (It's longer than an average book anyway as it is…)

If you can't live with the ending, there is an alternate (happy) ending on my website. Read it and be done with CAN YOU MEND IT?...

If you're interested how the story really continues, check out part 2 and, if you're still interested after that, also part 3.

What is now the CAN YOU MEND IT? series started out simply as an experiment and to pass some time when I was bored at work. I had had a scene in my head forever and finally decided to see if I could put it into words that sounded (and felt) right.

I didn't plan to write an entire book, and I didn't consider how what I was writing would resonate with readers. Initially the whole thing was just meant for private use, and therefore it needed to be realistic, not sappy and it couldn't be told in the first person…- it needed to be something that I, personally, would like to read.

Somehow the writing got a bit out of hand, however. The story started to grow and grow in all possible directions, like something that just develops a life of its own. My little experiment turned into an obsession. Sometimes it was hard to find the time to write everything down that popped up in my head (at work during a meeting; in the middle of the night; while biking…).

The way I wrote the story is a bit chaotic, though… I just let the chapters 'happen' – piece by piece. Like a puzzle. It took a while before I had all the pieces and managed to make them all fit. (I had a lot of chapters of the third book before the first book was even halfway finished.)

Well, at the end I did publish the story after all. I had to split it up into three parts as I couldn't have handled it any other way.

And since in the course of my little obsession I ended up with a lot of unpublished, but relatively refined scenes of Joe's and D's past (the time when they first met), I might, if I feel like it, put those together in a prequel sometime.

Oh, and in case you're interested: the scene it all started with is 'It's still good music...'

Billy Wood-Smith

PS: Please take the time to review the book!